IT BEGAN AT THE AIRPORT . . .

"I'm going to say good-bye to you here," she said.

"But why?"

"Because I'm very much married."

"I'm completely harmless," he said.

No, she thought. You're not at all. You have no idea—of just how frightening you are.

His face turned dark. "I don't even know your name."

"No, you don't."

"Do you want to tell me why?"

"I'm married."

"My name is Aaron Carpenter." He picked up his briefcase. "And I want to thank you for one of the most enjoyable flights I've ever had."

He turned and walked out of the terminal. She followed slightly behind him, watching him get in a cab. "All your life," he said, "you'll wonder what would have happened if you had shared this cab with me."

Then the cab drove away. She watched it disappear into the night. And she thought, yes, I will. All my life . . .

Reluctant Goddess

Oleda Baker

A JOVE BOOK

Requests for permission to make copies of any part
of the work should be mailed to: Permissions,
Jove Publications, Inc., 200 Madison Avenue,
New York, NY 10016

Cover photographs of Oleda Baker by Barry Evans

First Jove edition published March 1981

First printing

Printed in the United States of America

Jove books are published by Jove Publications, Inc.,
200 Madison Avenue, New York, NY 10016

To my loving mother, Thelma Freeman.

To my loving father, Marvin Freeman.

To my dear friends Johnnie and Matthew who have always believed in me.

To my dear friend Vernice who will always be there.

With much love to my dear husband Steve.

To my loving son—my pride, my joy, my sunshine . . . David.

And with love to Carmen, Harry and Francey.

My special thanks to my very dear friend Gene Schwartz.

My special thanks to my editor Beverly Lewis for her continued guidance and valuable time spent on this book.

BOOK ONE

1.

Some girls run away from home at sixteen; it took Melissa Adams Johnson twenty-six years.

And the woman who finally broke Melissa's bonds, who took her away, forever, from all she had known and had thought she loved—was a woman Melissa met only once, for three minutes, and whom she never saw again.

By the time of this meeting, Melissa was married, had given birth to a beautiful son, and had been working as a floor-model in Sanger-Harris's department store in Houston for three years.

That morning, just before lunch, Melissa was modeling a sports outfit—tan skirt, tight-fitting yellow blouse—on the main floor. She noticed the woman come down the aisle toward her—a striking, elegant woman about forty years old; to Melissa she looked successful, independent, and quite pampered. The woman stopped in front of Melissa, who smiled her model's smile, spun and did a brief walk-away down the aisle, then spun again and walked back up the aisle toward the woman. She stopped three feet away from her, and said in her model's voice, "$59.95. Third floor. Better sportswear."

Melissa smiled again and the act was over. Now the woman should nod appreciatively, and go on her way. But she did not move. She took off her sunglasses and held them in her hand, then lifted them slowly to her mouth and began to nibble the tip of one stem. Her eyes never left Melissa's face.

"What are you doing here?" she asked Melissa.

"I beg your pardon?" Melissa said.

"What are you doing here?" the woman repeated in a matter-of-fact tone.

Melissa was completely flustered. "I'm a model in this store."

"You're not a model," the woman snapped. "You're a mannequin. A walking dummy." And then her eyes softened.

3

"But you could be a model. A real model." There was something in her face that Melissa had never seen in a woman's face before. "If you went where the real models are."

"I'm married." The words burst from Melissa's lips.

"How nice."

"I have a child."

"How marvelous." The woman unsnapped her purse, and put the sunglasses inside. Then she reached for something in the purse. "We're not talking about that," she said.

"I don't know what we are talking about," Melissa admitted.

"About where you belong." The woman had pulled a small notebook and a gold pencil from her purse. "About where your face belongs. In front of a camera. Or"—she was rapidly scrawling something in the notebook—"in front of my easel."

Melissa said nothing. The woman looked up. "Do you know what an easel is?"

There was silence for a second, and then Melissa said, "No."

"You're delicious," the woman smiled. "An easel is what a person paints on. I'm a painter—an illustrator, really, if that means anything to you. I make beautiful pictures for cosmetic companies, and they pay me a small fortune to do it."

The woman paused to stare again at Melissa's face. This time she held the gold pencil to her lips, and Melissa watched, paralyzed, as her tongue came out and touched the tip of the pencil. "I paint the most gorgeous women on earth," she said softly. "And they all come, sooner or later, to one place . . . New York."

"I'm very happy here," Melissa said carefully.

"You'll come," the woman replied. "You'll keep looking at yourself in the mirror, and then, someday, you'll know." Again she smiled. "And you'll come."

She tore a sheet out of the notebook and handed it to Melissa. "And when you do, you'll want friends. New York can be a cruel place if you don't have a little help."

The woman walked over to Melissa's side. She stood so close that Melissa could smell her harsh perfume, could feel the sleeve of her tailored jacket practically touch her bare arm. Melissa suddenly wondered if the floor supervisor would appear out of nowhere. A strange, creeping panic was moving up her arm into the rest of her body.

"This," the woman said, pointing to the first address on the paper, "is the top modeling agency in New York. It's got a one-word name, 'Victoria,' for Victoria Krane, one of my best friends. Call her and tell her I sent you; she'll see you in thirty seconds. And this," she said, lightly touching Melissa's arm, "is my name and address. Just pick up a phone."

Melissa started to react, but the woman had already moved away from her, and was putting the pencil and notebook away. "No need to do anything now," she said. "But just keep them . . . in case."

"Thank you," Melissa said automatically, knowing she didn't mean it.

The woman had her sunglasses out again. She paused before putting them on. "What are you, anyway?" she asked suddenly, sketching in her mind the extravagant, swelling curve of Melissa's cheekbones. "A cross between an Indian"—she stared for a full thirty seconds, trapped in the incredible blue of the younger woman's eyes—"and an angel?"

"I—"

"Never mind." The woman snapped on the sunglasses, and whirled away from Melissa. "It makes no difference." Then she swept down the aisle, out of the department, and out of the store, so rapidly that she almost knocked another woman out of her way.

Melissa stood there for a moment, still frightened, and then looked at the piece of notepaper in her hand, with its neat, strong writing. "Victoria Krane," she read. "Top modeling agency. So what? Who cares?" And she angrily crumpled up the piece of paper and threw it into the wastebasket behind the nearest counter.

She hadn't even bothered to read the name of the other woman. But she stared for a moment at the paper, as it lay in the bottom of the trash basket, and suddenly she understood why. A line from the Bible, that she had been read a hundred times in Sunday school, flashed into her mind:

"Get thee behind me, Satan."

She was safe again, secure again. The woman was out of the store, out of her life, for good. Melissa straightened her blouse and put her smile back on. She walked up the aisle to a browsing couple, spun around in front of them, and said, "$59.95. Third floor. Better sportswear."

They smiled, said, "Thank you," and walked toward the escalator.

Melissa watched them go. "Thank you," she said in return.

2.

That afternoon was one of the three days out of the week that she and Johnny did *not* make love at lunch time, so Melissa had the full hour to herself. Within minutes after she had stamped her time card, she was out of the store, across the shopping center, and into the supermarket opposite Sanger-Harris. There she spent twenty dollars in five minutes, buying things that she and Johnny had promised each other they wouldn't have on the table again for a month. Leaving the store, she saw that the bus was not at its stop, so she carried the heavy groceries to a taxi and spent another four dollars being driven home. She even had the cab driver wait while she packed the food into the refrigerator. She was back at the store and into another outfit, just in time.

By six Melissa was home again, this time to find Little John waiting for her. There were hugs, and tickles, and she would have given him "a thousand kisses," but her son was hungry and began to whine. Soon he was being stuffed with more coconut doughnuts than he had ever been allowed in his three-year-old life.

While he was happily eating, she was ecstatically presiding over her overloaded stove—frying not one, but two, full chickens, and making both a sweet potato pie and a banana delight for dessert. The tiny house that she and Johnny had built themselves—over two hard, wonderful years—began to fill with the odors of her cooking, and the babblings of her child; and her heart began to beat even faster than usual when she heard the car squeal to a stop outside, and the door slam, and the front door of their house crash open.

"My God," said the voice she loved, "it's Christmas in July."

She tore off the apron and grabbed a quick look at herself

in the mirror. Good Lord, she thought, I forgot to freshen up my face for him.

"Hey, Princess," he shouted, "where are you? Tell me the good news."

He rounded the corner and caught her just as she was turning toward him. His face was handsomer than ever, his smile so broad it filled the narrow hall. The strong arms flashed out and circled her waist. She was lifted up against him, and her mouth pressed against his. She caught her breath as always, felt her nipples swell as always, felt the sweet weakness and the burning want, opened her mouth and let her tongue greet his, knew that if she wanted to, the two of them would be in the bedroom in a second.

But he lowered her slowly, and then stepped back and looked at her, his eyes sparkling, his head cocked slightly to one side. "Tell me," he said. "What happened?"

"Nothing," she said half guiltily.

"Nothing, my nose," he laughed, and reached out and began to tickle her.

"Johnny," she giggled, and began to move away from him, toward the kitchen.

"You got a raise," he said. "How much?"

"No," she said and now the guilt was suddenly over-whelming her. "Really . . . nothing."

"They're going to use you in one of the shows up North." The two of them had now reached the kitchen. He reached out with the agility of a young tiger, scooped her up as though she were made of cotton candy, and spun her around in the air till her skirt whirled. "My Princess is going to be famous."

"No, Johnny. Let me down." Her hands slapped his shoulders. "Nothing happened."

He looked deeply into her face. Then a puzzled expression came over his, and he slowly lowered her to the floor. "Then why"—he turned and looked at the stove—"all this?"

"Because I love you," she said very softly. "And I'm so glad I'm your wife."

She watched him analyze the smells that were coming out of the stove, and tabulate quickly how much they cost. "That much?" he grinned dazedly.

"More."

The grin faded, and the tall blond man in front of her suddenly looked very young and very moved.

"Why?" he asked quietly.

"'Cause," she said.

"Twenty dollars' worth?"

"Twenty thousand dollars' worth."

He stared at her for a moment. He tried to form words, but none came. He looked at his child in the high chair, who was smiling back at him and waving sugarcoated hands. Then he turned and let his fingers run through his woman's hair. He threw back his head and roared laughter.

"yoooooowwwww! It *is* Christmas in July," he shouted.

Little John dropped one of the doughnuts in a white puff on the floor, and gaped open-mouthed at his father. "Shush," said Melissa, startled. "Everybody in the block'll hear."

"I want them to." And his head went back again, but her hand came up and lightly covered his mouth.

"No," she whispered. "It belongs to you and me—not to them. Besides which, if you do it again, you'll scare Little John right out of his wits. He'll think his mommy's beating up on his daddy."

He laughed, and took the hand over his mouth, and kissed it. And then licked the inside of that palm. And then—very slowly—bit that palm.

She felt a stab of desire, and her face flushed. Her voice deepened as she asked, "You're not angry at me for spending all that money on nothing?"

He turned their bodies slightly so that his movements were hidden from the child. Then he bit her palm again, and felt first her hand and then her body shudder. She looked down, and saw his trousers begin to bulge and swell, just as she herself was swelling and swelling by watching him.

"No," he said, "I'm not angry." His voice was a whispered growl now, and each word aroused her flesh even more. He began slowly to guide her backward out of the kitchen, till they rounded the corner where they could no longer be seen.

"Nothings are the best things in the world to celebrate," he murmured, as his hand reached up and unbuttoned her blouse. "Nothings make Christmas out of July. Don't you hear the snow falling outside?" he asked hoarsely. Her blouse was on the hallway floor now.

"Yes," she said submissively.

"And the sleigh bells?"

"Yes," she answered.

"And listen to the chimney. Can't you hear Santa sliding down it?"

Her brassiere was down around her waist now, and his hands were setting her breasts on fire.

"Yes," she said. "Anything you want."

"Merry Christmas," he said, as they reached the bedroom door.

"Merry Christmas," she whispered, and then gave out a gasp that she was afraid even the neighbors could hear.

3.

Later, when the big dinner was finished, and Little John put to bed, they sat at the table in their robes, having coffee. She knew she should get up and clear the table and do the dishes, but she was was too contented to move. And she kept wanting to tell him . . . and then knowing that she shouldn't tell him . . . and then just *having* to tell him.

"This woman came in the store today," she said finally.

"From around here?" he said, not really interested.

"No. From New York."

"Rich?"

"Umm. Must have had on a hundred-dollar suit."

He grinned. "Want to buy out the store?"

"No she didn't buy anything. Just came in, talked to me, and left."

"That is funny," he said, and began to scrape the side of his dessert dish. "What'd she say?"

"She said she wanted me to become a model, up North, in New York."

His fork stopped in midair. Then he lowered it to the plate. "Was she serious?" he asked intently.

"Maybe." Her tone was noncommittal.

"Did she have any connections? Did she give you her name?"

She looked down at her dish, began scraping a zigzag with her fork through the banana delight left in it. "I threw it away," she said quickly."

"What?"

"I threw her name away." She looked up at him, studying his face anxiously. "In the trash basket."

"Why? Was she a phony?"

"No . . . I don't think so."

He leaned over the table at her, and grabbed her arm as if she were a six-year-old. "Let me get this straight. This woman comes into the store, and you can see she's rich—right?"

"Right."

"And then she stops you, and tells you . . . what?"

She thought for a moment, looking down again at the plate. "That I'm not a real model down here."

"Goddamn right. Not on the salary they pay you. Then what?"

She couldn't look up. "Nothing," she said.

"Nothing what?" he almost screamed, frightening her.

"She said I was too pretty to stay down here," she answered quickly.

"Right too." His voice softened, and he settled back into his chair.

"She said that all the . . . prettiest women are in New York."

"That's for sure. You stick out here like a . . ." His voice trailed off.

"Like a what?"

He shook his head. "Like an angel who lost her wings," he said, looking away from her.

Her face was still buried in her chest. "Funny," she said.

He turned back to her; then reached out his hand and stroked her hair. "Funny what, beautiful Princess?"

Her hand reached up and touched his, but her eyes were still lowered. "This woman talked like no one I ever heard before. She said I looked like a cross between an Indian and an angel." Then she looked up, still clinging to his hand. "Isn't that funny?"

"Poor Princess," he said, moving both their hands across the table and kissing hers. "You still can't get used to it, can you?"

"Not really."

"Still the scrawny, thirteen-year-old kid inside, aren't you?"

"I guess so."

"You're beautiful," he said. "You see the store pictures,

the Christmas pictures. You're as good looking as any woman in New York.''

"She said I ought to be a photographer's model.''

His hand put hers down on the table. ''Was she a photographer?''

''No. Some kind of painter.''

"But did she have connections?'' he shot out.

She looked down again. ''She said she did.''

"With who?''

"With Victoria.''

"Who?''

"Victoria. There's just one word. No second name. She said it's the biggest modeling agency up North.''

He spun up from the table, did a slow circle around the kitchen, and ended up at the phone. ''Is it in New York?''

"That's what she said. What are you doing?''

"Calling up New York information, you ninny. I want to see if she was lying to you.''

He dialed information, got the phone number, and managed to persuade the operator to give him the address as well.

"It's on Madison Avenue,'' he said. ''It must be big.''

He stood by the phone, thinking for a minute. Then he began tearing off his robe and almost running into the bedroom.

"What are you doing now?'' she said, feeling the panic rising in her again.

"Getting dressed.'' His voice trailed out of the bedroom.

"For what?'' she called out.

"To go down and get that piece of paper out of that trash basket.''

"Johnny, stop it,'' she cried. ''Besides,'' she added more calmly, ''it won't do any good.''

He came slowly out of the bedroom. ''Why?'' he asked in a low voice.

"Because they empty the trash baskets every night right after the store closes. It's already in the garbage truck.''

"Damn!''

"Why don't you drive out to the garbage dump,'' she exploded. ''You could probably dig your way into it by morning.''

"Do you remember anything else from the paper?'' he demanded.

"Her last name.''

His face brightened. "Whose? The woman you met?"

"No. The agency owner. Her name is Victoria Krane."

"You are an angel," he laughed, and cupped her face in both hands to kiss her. He released her and was immediately back at the phone.

"She's unlisted," he said a moment later. He stood with the receiver dangling from the cord, not looking at her. "You know something," he said, "they're probably as lazy down at the store as they are at the plant. I bet they haven't even begun to load that garbage truck yet."

"But they empty the trash baskets into huge plastic bags first," she said. "It's one piece of paper out of ten thousand."

"What color was it?"

"White. White notepaper with lines on it, out of a little memo pad she carried. But you'll never find it."

"What the hell." He smiled—that gorgeous smile. "It's better than watching television."

He was out the back door before she could say another word. She heard the car door slam, the wheels screech, and he was gone into the night. She sat at the table for five minutes, staring at the used plates. She got up slowly and washed the dishes, then sat down at the table to wait for him. She waited one hour, and then two hours, and then two and a half.

At last his car screeched up the drive and its horn gave out six sharp bleats. The kitchen door slammed open and he was standing there, his arms black with dirt and printers' ink. A small piece of notepaper was clutched in his grimy hand.

"You're right," he said. "Her full name is Victoria Krane."

"Don't touch anything in this kitchen," she answered, "until you wash off every ounce of that filth."

"And the other woman's name," he said, throwing the crumpled piece of paper on the table and heading for the sink, "is Dorothy Howard." He turned on the water with his elbows, and began to chant as he washed himself. "Dorothy Howard . . . Dorothy Howard . . . Dorothy Howard."

She stared at the paper. Satan has been cast out, she thought, and Satan has returned.

"Dorothy Howard, baby," he said, this time directly to her. He wiped off his arms and folded the towel neatly before putting it back on the rack. "Our key to the world!"

She looked up. "I'm not going, Johnny."

"This is the answer to our dreams."

"We've had this conversation before. I don't want to go through it again."

"But this is a *way!*" He came across the kitchen, knelt down in front of her, and put his arms around her legs and thighs. She felt the strength of his flesh against the cotton robe surrounding her flesh, and she felt the weakness stir again inside her. But this time she stiffened at his touch, determined to fight it.

"This is a way, Princess," he whispered. "An opening. A connection. Everything we've dreamed about."

"Maybe she was lying," Melissa said.

"We could find out."

"How?"

"By your going." His hands began to rub now against her thighs. But she realized, with a shock, that there was nothing sexual about the rubbing; he was pleading. "By your going up there," he went on, "and calling that Victoria woman, and just letting her see you."

He looked up at her, and she saw again how young the face was, and how insecure. "All she has to do," he said, "is see you. Just let one person who knows—who *knows*—see you, and we'll have everything we need."

"It'll take months," she said.

"Three months," he replied, "or you come back."

"Johnny," she said, stroking his hair, "I don't want to be away from you that long. I don't want to be away from Little John either. I couldn't live."

"Mom will take care of him. She'll move right in." He grinned. "By the time you get back, he'll probably weigh ten pounds more than he weighs today."

Her hands traced his face; moved down his chin, neck, and shoulders. "Honey," she said, "I can't live without you."

"Sure you can." He began to pat her rump. "It's only a few weeks. I'll call every night. What does it matter if we spend a little money—think of the fortune we'll be making."

"But," and her face turned red, "I need you."

He looked puzzled for a moment, and then he smiled. "And I need you too. But we can stand it for a few weeks . . ." He pulled away from her and spun up, then threw his arms out and made a slow circle in the tiny kitchen. "If we can gain the whole world."

"What does it profit a man," she said quietly, not looking at him, "if he gain the whole world and lose his soul?"

He stopped and studied her for a moment, then dropped on his knees again, and this time folded his arms over her thighs and rested his chin on his arms. He looked up sadly at her, and the helplessness in his face was like a knife cutting through her.

"Princess," he said flatly, "I'm not going to make it this way. You know that."

"You're doing fine," she said, lying.

"Don't do that," he cried, and the pressure of his arms on her thighs made her feel as if he would break them. "You know it's going to take me eight years to finish night school. *Eight years.* And then what'll I have? A bachelor's of business administration. You know what that means? Three thousand more a year. And maybe they'll move me into Ryan's spot—when he dies."

She said nothing. He got up from his knees, and sat down in the chair opposite her. "You need a master's to do anything in this company," he said, "and you know it. It'll be fifteen years if I keep going on this way." He stopped, and the room seemed gray with misery. "Jesus Christ," he said bleakly, "Little John'll be in college by the time I get anywhere."

"You'll get somewhere," she said. "You've got what it takes."

"*You've* got what it takes," he shouted, and then calmed his voice when he saw her face. "Those models make thirty thousand dollars or more a year. That's more than Mr. Ferguson makes, and he runs the whole damn place. And there's not one of those women"—his finger shot back and forth at her like a piston—"not one of them who's prettier than you are."

She moved across the table and sat in his lap. Taking his head in her hands, she kissed his face and hair again and again. "It's all right," she said. "We'll talk about it tomorrow. We won't make up our minds about anything tonight."

"I could leave the company," he said. "I could go to college full time."

"I love you," she said, and started to kiss his neck.

"You don't love me."

"I love you," she went on, still stroking his hair, now

kissing the sensuous spot between his neck and shoulder. "I need you."

He tried to shrug her away. But then she put her hand onto his chest, and then began to stroke, and then scratch his nipples. His own hand began to move, automatically, against the back of her robe. And she knew it was all right again. It would go away. She wouldn't have to think about it until tomorrow.

"God, I need you," she whispered.

"I'm going nowhere," he said. And then grabbed her hair with his hand and kissed her so hard he bruised her lips.

4.

One moment she was sleeping the sleep of a woman who is completely satisfied, and the next moment she was lying in bed wide-awake.

Johnny was snoring quietly beside her. She turned gently and looked at the clock with its luminous dial. It was three in the morning. The house was pitch-black. She closed her eyes and told herself to go back to sleep. But that was impossible. And she had things to do.

She slipped out of bed, put on her robe, and felt her way out of the room. She closed the bedroom door, and shuddered a little as she heard its click. She froze for a moment, waited till she could hear the snores again through the door, and then felt her way to the light switch of the tiny dressing room.

She snapped it on, and was blinded by the light. Again she froze, then moved silently back to the door, and listened again. No change in his breathing. She smiled—I guess you could shoot off a cannon beside him tonight, she thought, and he wouldn't stir a muscle.

She walked barefooted out of the dressing room and into the kitchen, and snapped on that light too. She gathered up the tablecloth she had used at dinner, folded it and put it away, then tossed the napkins into the laundry basket. She tied up the garbage bag and carried it out into the hot Houston night, to dump it in the can. The stars were out, and she noticed there was a quarter moon.

She closed the kitchen door again and locked it, looked around to be sure that everything was neat and shiny, and smiled when she saw the kitchen was the way she liked it. Then she flicked off the light again, and tiptoed down to Little John's room.

He too was sound asleep, and she closed the door again and went back to the dressing room. There she opened the bottom drawer of the dresser Johnny had built for her, and pulled out a stack of six or seven copies of *Vogue*.

She stood there in the early morning silence, opening the magazines one by one. In each she found a few photographs she wanted. She folded down the corners of those pages, then placed the magazines on top of the dresser.

Then she turned to the full-length mirror that formed the back of the bedroom door, and looked at the image of the woman reflected there. She took off the robe and threw it over the dressing room chair. Turning back to the mirror, she said hostilely to the image in it, "Okay, hotshot, now let's see how pretty you really are."

She looked at the woman's figure first. "You're five feet eight," she said, "which is tall enough to be a model. Check one point there."

She turned sideways. "Good legs," she said. "They'll do for stocking ads." And then her eyes moved up. "But look at your body," she said angrily. "It's spindly." She touched the mirror. "Your ribs stick out. And here"—she traced a line in the mirror—"your back sways like an old horse.

"Come on," she said sharply, "pull in your belly." She studied the image, then shook her head. "No good. Your behind still plops out." She laughed silently in the tiny room. "And *you* want to go to New York?"

She turned to the *Vogue*s lying next to her on the dresser, thumbed through them rapidly, and found the bathing suit photos she had marked. She looked back and forth from them to the woman in the mirror. Then she cupped her breasts, squeezing them slightly to make them appear larger, and half-smiled. The women in the photographs were as skinny as she. It was just the way they held themselves. Someday, if she could just overcome her shyness . . .

Then she moved closer to the mirror, pulled back her hair

till it exposed every inch of bone structure, and studied the image she saw in front of her.

"Indian," she said. "You look like an Indian. Don't know where it came from, but it's there."

She looked down at the *Vogue*s again, this time checking the faces. "High cheekbones," she whispered gratefully. "They say a model has to have them . . . that the camera eats them up." She let the hair shake down around the face again. "Okay," she said, "you win there."

Then she looked at the eyes staring back at her in the mirror. Not until she was about eight years old had she realized how different those eyes were from other people's. All she had known before then was that if she tried, she could see both her shoulders at once while looking straight ahead. She had thought then that her eyes were ugly because they were so big. But her face had grown to fit them. And she looked at them now as though they were sapphires in a jeweler's display case. She knew far too well the effect they had on other people, especially men; the eyes required no analysis.

"But your nose isn't straight," she said. "It has a bump on the side. And your teeth are crooked. And . . ."

She threw back her hair again, and moved back a step. Now the light glanced directly off the cheekbones in the mirror, and the huge blue eyes, and the oval face that packaged them. She began to shiver in the heat of the house as she saw that face stare back at her . . . confront her . . . make its demands on her. And all her defenses were stripped away from her, she was forced to see her face the way the woman in the store had seen it that morning, and the way Johnny had seen it that night, and every night. And her eyes saw in the mirror the truth that she had run from since she had been an adolescent. Suddenly she felt overwhelmingly tired, and she noticed the bruise beginning to swell on her lip. She reached her hand and touched it, and felt its pain. And she loved the pain. She loved the fact that *he* had given it to her, when she wouldn't go where her face demanded she take it.

"It will go away tomorrow," she said to the mirror. "Or the next day. Or the next. It doesn't matter."

She turned away from the mirror and put on her robe. She put the magazines back in the dresser. After switching off the light, she stood still in the darkness till her eyes became used to it. And then she quietly opened the door into the room where her man was sleeping, and crawled into bed next to him.

It was five o'clock. She'd look like hell in the morning. She didn't care.

She rolled over and circled her arms around the man lying next to her. He grunted a little in his sleep. She felt the strength of his neck and his shoulders and his back. And she forgot about the mirror.

5.

The next morning, when Johnny finally got to the construction plant, he saw Murphy waiting for him in the parking lot, and knew he was in for trouble.

He checked his watch. Ten minutes late. Not that much. But if Murphy was wasting his time sitting outside, like a hunter in a shelter, there was going to be a big show. And Murphy wanted a ringside seat.

"You're up to your ass in shit, kid," Murphy said as soon as Johnny got out and locked the car. "Ryan wants to see you. Now."

"Why?" Johnny said. "I'm only five minutes late."

"Don't even bother to change. Just haul that pretty little ass of yours up to Ryan's office now."

Johnny instinctively started to move against the older man. But Murphy just stood there leaning against Ryan's car, arms folded, his face spread wide in a mask of hatred and glee.

"Now," he said. "Run."

Johnny drew in his breath deep, walked slowly to the plant door, and stepped inside. He looked through its window at Murphy, watching him, and then deliberately walked up the stairs, one by one.

Ryan's door was open. He was sitting with his feet on the desk, waiting.

"How many times is this, boy?" he asked when Johnny walked in.

"I'm not even ten minutes late," Johnny said.

"How many times this month?"

Johnny was silent for a moment, and then said, "Four."

"Five."

Johnny said nothing.

"Five." Ryan swung his legs down from the desk, and leaned across it toward Johnny. "Five times this month you've been late. Just like all the months before, except it's getting worse." And now Ryan began to shout. "Do you know that there's a crew of three men waiting for you to go out with them? And they're sitting around, picking their assholes, while you're doing what?"

Johnny's face began to redden. He felt every muscle in his body begin to tighten.

"While you're doing what?"

Johnny put his hands behind his back. He took his left hand and wrapped it hard around his right wrist, to keep his right arm from striking out at Ryan.

"I'll tell you what you're doing," Ryan screamed at the top of his lungs, with his finger pointing one inch from Johnny's nose, "you're fucking that high-strutting broad of yours."

"Shut up," Johnny said.

"Don't tell me to shut up, you pretty little bastard."

"You don't talk about my wife that way."

"Why not?" Ryan asked. "Too pretty to fuck? Too high and mighty to fuck? Won't even talk to the rest of us at the company picnic, will she? Just smile that . . . phony smile of hers, and nod like a queen, and sashay away till she meets someone that's fit for her to sit with."

"She can sit with whoever she wants."

"She can fuck whoever she wants. And you can fuck her as much as you want to, baby boy—five times a week at lunch if you want to—but you're not going to fuck that high-faluting face on my time."

Johnny's right hand came loose and his arm moved back. Ryan was as big as he was, but twenty years older. And Johnny was going to rip him to pieces.

"Go ahead, pretty boy," Ryan said. "Swing." He waited. "Swing. Hit me. One punch. Just one. And you're out of here for good. And the union can't save you."

Johnny's fist froze in the air. Ryan glared at him, both his arms hanging at his sides.

"Swing, pretty boy. Show me how much you love that fucking wife of yours."

Nothing happened. Johnny lowered his arm.

Ryan waited a minute, his breathing heavier than Johnny's. Then he looked down at the desk and grabbed some papers.

"You got five minutes to change and be on that truck," he said. "If you're late one more time, I'll fight it through the union and get you fired, if it takes the rest of my life."

He lunged out of the room. Johnny heard his laugh, and others, in the hall outside, then their feet clomping down the stairs.

Tears welled up in his eyes. It was the first time he'd cried since his father had died, when he was seven. You son of a bitch, he thought. You dirty bastard.

"I'll show you," Johnny screamed silently to the desk. "She's going to break out of here, and then I'm going to break out with her. And when I come back," he promised the man he saw walking across the parking lot, "I'm going to own you."

6.

That night, at dinner, his silence dominated the room. Even Little John hardly made a sound, but just sat in his high chair and dutifully stuffed everything he was given into his mouth.

There was no way she could draw him out, make conversation, get even a glimmer of a smile. And then when Little John was through eating, and dessert and coffee were on the table, he said, "Put the kid to bed."

"Now?" she said.

"Now."

"But he won't go to sleep yet."

"Then just let him lie there."

She started to object, and then saw into his eyes. She pushed back her chair hastily and picked up the child and carried him to his bed, putting three or four extra toys beside him and stroking him several times to make sure he was lying quietly. Then she turned on the night-light, closed the door, and walked slowly down the hall again, to the kitchen.

"Did the woman come back?" he asked, the moment she came into the room.

"Which woman?"

"The one from New York."

"No," she said, forcing a smile, "I never saw hide nor hair of her." She hovered beside her chair, wanting to go to him.

"It doesn't matter," he said. "You're going to New York."

"Honey, I can't."

He looked up. "You're going."

She felt her spine turn to ice as she saw his eyes. She wanted to wrap her body around him like a blanket, form a shield for him with her arms and legs, protect him somehow, with her flesh and her warmth, against himself.

"Johnny," she said slowly, "you're not slipping into another psychological storm, are you?"

"You're leaving."

"When?" she cried.

"Tomorrow . . . Tuesday . . . next week." He turned away from her again. "Whenever we can get Mom in to take care of the kid."

"But what am I going to *do* there?"

"You're going to see that Victoria woman. And she's going to make you a real model."

"Honey," she said, now daring to move closer to him, "it's a dream."

"Don't touch me," he said.

She stopped a foot away from him. It might as well have been a mile. "Johnny, I don't want to go."

"You go." He looked at her again, and his face was wild. "You go," he said. "You go . . . You go . . . You *go.*"

She was crying. She stood in front of him, her makeup smearing, and she was ashamed. "For Christ's sake, Johnny," she said, "please hold me."

He looked at her. His hand was dead white from squeezing the coffee mug. She thought he was going to break the mug and rip open his hand.

"Hold me or I'll die."

He got up from the table slowly and put his hands on her shoulders. She felt his thumbs sink into the flesh of her shoulders as he snapped her head back and looked at her face.

She could hardly see his own face through the tears. But she watched the blurred image of a smile grow across it as he leaned forward and kissed her aching mouth, and then began to lick up the tears.

"Princess," he said. "My Princess."

"Johnny," she begged, as she moved into his arms. "Don't leave me."

"I'm not going anywhere," he said.

"Don't leave me. Don't run away inside yourself again."

"We're not going anywhere," she heard. And then she felt his arm under her legs. "Except the bedroom."

He picked her up, and kicked the chair in front of him out of his way so hard that it fell and cracked on the kitchen floor. And then he carried her through the narrow hall, scraping his right shoulder against the plasterboard of the wall, and turned into the bedroom. He slammed the door shut with his foot, and threw her, face down, onto the bed.

"Johnny," she said, not daring to look up, "keep away from me."

She heard his pants zip down, and then the rustle of his shorts, and then his shoes being kicked across the room. She tried to push herself up on the bed, but his hand touched her back and pressed her down again. And then she felt her full skirt being thrown up around her shoulders, and her shoes and then her panties being pulled off. And then he turned her over on her back, pushed her flat down on the bed again, and spread her legs painfully till her ankles touched both sides of the bed.

She started to warn him off again, and then stopped, her eyes opening wide in amazement. He was standing in front of her dressed only in his black socks and his sweat-stained workshirt. He was leering down maniacally at her spread body, at her smeared face. But it was his penis that her gaze was riveted on. Never in the eight years that she had known him, had she dreamed that it could be that huge, and that erect. It was flaming red, engorged with blood, standing up so high that it almost touched the bottom of his flat belly.

He watched her staring at it, and then moved his left knee onto the bed, and then his right. Then he reached out his hands and grabbed each of her knees and slowly pushed her legs up on the bed to receive him.

"Don't Johnny," she pleaded. "You'll hurt me."

Now his hands left her knees, and took her shoulders, and

forced her head back against the pillow. She felt the outside of his thighs begin to scrape softly against the inside of hers. His right hand left her shoulder, and she felt his fingers reach down and spread her apart, and then there was a pause, and she felt the enormous head of his penis begin to ram itself into her.

"You're too big," she whispered, "it won't go . . ."

And then she felt him fill her as she had never been filled before. She felt pain, and stretching, and hidden flesh crying out against being invaded more deeply, more imperiously, than ever before. And then, in seconds, the pain gave way to the astonishment of enclosing, of capturing, of retaining an object that powerful. And then the man looking down at her began to move his pelvis against hers, his body inside hers; when he drew slowly back out of her again, her flesh contracted lustingly after his. Then he stopped, not quite half out of her, and began to thrust deeper inside her again; and the innermost part of her flesh reached out in joy as his flesh came back into it again, and completed her, and electrified her, and took away all the pain, and all the fear, and all the sorrow.

He looked down at her, and watched her turn her head away from him, flat onto the pillow, and her face flush and her mouth open and her breath deepen. He watched her right hand reach up and take the end of the pillow and stuff its border into her mouth. And he watched her shudder as his penis grew even harder at the sight of her biting the pillow.

At last her mouth flew open, releasing the pillow, and he heard her softly scream and scream and scream in orgasm, as the beautiful face, the exquisite face, the goddess face turned into that of a moaning, dominated animal underneath him.

This is what they'd like to do to you, he thought. But they can't. And I can.

I can. I can. I can.

Her sounds died out, and he moved slowly again, waiting until those incredible blue eyes opened, and she could see him. And then he began to rotate inside her—faster, and then faster, and then faster again.

"Johnny," she whispered. "Stop. I'll die if I do it again."

"Oh yes," he said.

"Please," she said. "Oh God!"

His hands were on her shoulders now. Her head was flat on the pillow again. "You're going," he said.

"Johnny!"

"You're going," he said. "Say yes."

She stuffed the corner of the pillow in her mouth again. He ripped it out. He seized her face and turned it harshly until she was looking at him. His pelvis never missed a stroke.

"Say yes," he said.

"Oh God, Johnny."

"You're going."

"Oh God."

"Say yes."

"Oh God," and then her entire body shuddered. And she threw up her hands and buried her nails deep in his arms.

"Yes," she said.

"Say it again."

"Yes," she moaned, beginning to cry again, crying as her body moved, by itself, against his.

"You're going to New York, aren't you? Say yes."

"Yes."

"You're going when I tell you, aren't you? Say yes."

"Yes. Oh God, yes."

"You're going to see that Victoria Krane woman, aren't you? And you're going to make her make you a real model."

"Oh yes. God, yes. God, yes. Yes." Her body had taken over. Her mind was gone. The room was dissolving in a blur of tears and joy. All she knew in the world was that his penis inside her was beginning to swell again, outside his control; that it was beginning to shiver and tremble against her all-enclosing flesh, outside his control; that it was beginning now to convulse, to erupt, to explode inside her—outside his control, outside her control, outside even God's control.

"Oh yes," she said. "Yes . . . yes . . . yes . . . yes."

7.

The buzzer on Victoria Krane's intercom sounded once a second for ten full seconds, paused two seconds, and then began relentlessly to beat out SOS in the Morse code.

"For Christ's sake, Arlene," Victoria yelled into the phone, "you know I'm trying to get this publicity piece done."

"It's Dorothy Howard again."

"Tell her I'm not in."

"It's the seventh time today."

"She'll give up."

"She never gives up and you know it. Look, Victoria," the crackling voice said, "Make up your mind right now. Either you hired me as a receptionist and typist, or you hired me to tell Dorothy Howard you're not in. Pick up the phone now, or forget about all your letters till next Wednesday."

"It's almost five-thirty," Victoria whined.

"She'll call you at the apartment tonight. She has the number."

"Tell her I'm sick."

"Look, do you really want her to wake you up at three o'clock in the morning?"

Victoria looked down at the piece of paper in her hand, then threw it on her desk, and slammed her finger down on the button. "Hello, Dorothy," she snapped.

"Victoria," the voice on the other end purred, "they finally caught you."

"You caught me, Dorothy. For what?"

"To do you a favor, love. Probably the biggest favor of your career."

"Dorothy, I've told you before and I'll tell you again—I don't want your favors."

"You'll want this one, love."

"Another girl."

"An angel."

"With you, Dorothy—"

"This one is different. She's dazzling. I've never seen anything as beautiful in my life. Not even you, darling, when you were young."

"Dorothy, I'm going to hang up."

"And cheat yourself out of a fortune?"

"I don't make money on your kind of girls."

There was a pause on the other end of the phone, and for the first time in the conversation Victoria winced. Why the hell had she allowed herself to say that? She had nothing against Dorothy's preference in sex. She didn't care what anybody did in bed, as long as they didn't mix it with business.

"You *have* sharpened a little lately, haven't you?" The voice on the other end was far more wary now.

"I'm sorry," Victoria said. "I had no right—"

"She's not my kind of girl," Dorothy said, "unfortunately. She has a husband and a child."

"Dorothy, again I'm sorry. But let me put it on the line with you. I sent you two of my girls. The first one you made a pass at, but she didn't tell me. The second one you actually wrestled with. And that, honey, is the end, as far as you and this agency are concerned."

"That's not quite true—"

"No one touches my girls. No photographer, no client, no ad agency, no man—and no woman."

"I'm not trying to rent a girl from you, Victoria. We've settled that. I'm here to give you one."

"Why?"

"Do you expect me to propose a trade, darling? I send you a model; you send me a bed partner in return? You are naive."

"I'm going to hang up."

"She's as beautiful as you were. Victoria, she's a younger you. Now hang up."

"It's easy."

"Do you remember ten years ago, before I left Don?"

The phone stood frozen in the air, halfway between Victoria's ear and its hook. Then her hand raised it again to her ear.

"Yes," she said simply.

"We were inseparable, the four of us, weren't we? You and Rory, me and Don."

"So?"

"I loved you then. Not physically—you know that." And then Victoria Krane heard a laugh from Dorothy Howard that she hadn't heard in a decade. "In fact," Dorothy said, "I think I was straighter than you were then. But I loved you, and you know it. I taught you. I helped you. I *shaped* you. And now you've been born again."

"This girl?"

"Yes."

"In New York?"

"No. She may never even come here. She's in Houston, working in a department store."

"And you called me—"

"Because I gave her your name."

"And what did she do?"

"Nothing. Simply told me she didn't want to leave Houston. Never even gave me her name. I had to get it the next day from her floor manager at the store."

"And that's all?"

"That's all. I don't even think I talked to her more than three minutes."

"Then why have you made all this fuss?"

"Just because she might come here someday. And if she does, I want you to see her."

A vision flashed through Victoria's mind, a scene from ten years before. She remembered a party the four of them had attended—she and Rory, Dorothy and Don. And she remembered the sudden, strange, animalistic look on Dorothy's face, a look she had never seen before. And then . . . and then her own shock, and fright, as she turned around and saw, not a man, but Helene Roberts, a flaunting lesbian, coming toward them for the first time.

A world crumpled in that meeting. A marriage dissolved. The Dorothy she had known and loved until that night was transformed into some alien creature. And now Dorothy's husband was dead, self-poisoned by sleeping pills and alcohol. And there was the continuous parade of new girls in and out of Dorothy's studio.

She knew that Dorothy was lying. Dorothy did no favors for any woman, not without at least a down payment. She wanted to slam down the phone. But there was one more step she had to take to protect herself.

"All right, Dorothy," she said. "What's the girl's name?"

"Melissa," the voice responded, genuinely pleased. "Melissa Adams is her maiden name. Melissa Johnson is her married name. She may use either one."

"I've written them down."

"You won't forget?"

"No. I promise you, I won't forget."

"You're divine, Victoria," the voice said. "We must have . . . tea together someday."

"Of course."

"She may never come. But thank you."

"It's a pleasure," Victoria said, and quietly put down the phone.

Her head was splitting. She'd waited all last night, till three o'clock in the morning, for Rory to call her from Chicago. She'd called his hotel room four times, but there'd been no answer. And then he'd called her this morning at eight and told her he'd changed rooms in the hotel because the bed was too small for him. He'd been locked in a conference till midnight, and hadn't wanted to call her after that, because he knew she always went to bed at eleven.

She'd spent the entire day knowing that she actually believed him. Because she had to believe him. There were fifteen years of marriage on the line. And besides, there was something in that sleepy voice from Chicago that made her believe him.

She buzzed the intercom and said, "Arlene, come in here a minute, please."

She picked up the notepaper with the two names written on it, Melissa Adams and Melissa Johnson, and she thought again of Dorothy's face ten years before. Dorothy, standing next to her own husband as Victoria was standing next to Rory, her face twisted with animal lust. And she remembered her own disgust when she'd turned, and seen the object of that outlaw desire.

What if the girl did come to New York, she thought, and was as beautiful as Dorothy said? And what if the agency hired her? How long would it take for Dorothy to know about it—one month, two months, three months at most. And how long would it take for Dorothy to collect on her favor?

She heard the door to her office open and then close. "Is the gorgon gone?" Arlene chirped.

"For good," Victoria said, "I hope."

"Really. What did you do?"

"I disappointed her. I took a bon-bon away from her."

"Oh?"

"It doesn't matter. I'm going home. It's been a rotten day."

Arlene smiled. "Rory called."

"When?"

"When you were on the phone."

"For God's sake!"

"He's coming home. On the 8:05, coming into LaGuardia."

"I can make it."

"Easy. You even have time for a bath. And a little repaint job."

"You're a doll. Cancel my appointment with Revlon tomorrow morning. Leave me free till lunch."

"Happy homecoming."

Victoria stopped at the door. "One thing," she said, walking back to her desk. "It's important. And I'm not kidding," She picked up the paper with the two names on it. "See these?" She handed the paper to Arlene.

"Melissa of the two names?"

"Melissa of the any names. She may come here someday. If she ever does, no matter when, and you let her see me, I'm going to fire you."

Arlene looked up, surprised. Then she saw Victoria's face and her perpetual smile vanished.

"I mean it, Arlene. Let me put it this way. I swear on my marriage to Rory, if you let that lady get to me, I'll not only fire you, I'll make sure you never get a job with any other agency in New York."

She leaned forward and kissed Arlene on the cheek. "And I'll do it," she said, "despite the fact that I love you. But I'll roast in hell before I let Dorothy use this agency to get that girl back in her bed. Or help Dorothy pay her for past favors."

She stood stock still for a moment, letting the younger woman read her eyes. And then, when she was sure that she'd been understood, she went out the door, and across the reception room, and into the elevator.

Arlene stared after her, and very carefully put the paper under the rubber band in the front of her appointment book.

Melissa of the two names, she thought, we won't forget you. And then she left the office, and locked the front door—tight.

8.

The day following the decision to go to New York, Melissa asked for and received permission to take a three-month leave of absence, without pay, from her job. And that evening she had the first of her three meetings with her mother-in-law.

She took along a yellow legal pad, and scratched down on its first page every fraction of every hour of Little John's schedule. Then she tore off the page, and wrote on the second each of the foods he could and could not have at each of his meals, and what his snacks consisted of. Johnny's mother sat watching her, bored and more than a little hostile, knowing perfectly well that she would run the child in her own way as soon as Melissa was ten blocks out of town. Melissa knew it too; and so, when Estelle Johnson had gone home that first night, Melissa made a copy of both lists, and tucked the copy in the bill file, where the other woman would be sure to find it at the end of the month; if she'd torn up the lists and developed trouble with the boy, she could refer to the new copy.

Next, Melissa started her clean-up campaign. If another woman was coming into her house, then every inch of it was going to be spotless. Each night after work she attacked a different room. The first night it was the kitchen, and every dish, plate, glass, and piece of silver was washed and polished till it gleamed, and then was put back onto an equally gleaming shelf. The floor was scrubbed and waxed, as were all the halls. The living room was triple-vacuumed, and the plastic slipcovers over the furniture were washed till they too shone. In cleaning Johnny's chair, Melissa detected a tiny crack in the back of the slipcover protecting it; by the next evening the flawed cover had been replaced by a new one.

The bedspread was washed and ironed and made perfect to be put on the morning she left. The bedposts themselves were waxed, as was the dresser and the chair and the furniture in the dressing room outside. The copies of *Vogue* were taken out of the dressing room drawer, and after she had removed the most important photographs and filed them in her suitcase, she threw away the magazines as part of a past she no longer needed. Every piece of clothing was taken out of the closet and inspected and cleaned. Those she was taking with her were put to one side; all the rest were rehung in precise order, like a file of soldiers on a parade ground.

Little John's clothes were ironed with creases so sharp his father could have shaved with them. The pantry shelves and the refrigerator were packed to bursting with food, every one of Johnny's and Little John's favorites repeated six times. The garbage cans were washed down with the hose, and then hand-scrubbed, and then washed down again until they looked like rather dull mirrors.

The house now sparkled, and she was ready to leave it. It was her house; she had helped build it, she had helped support it, and if she were now going to leave it—for three months, or forever—then she was going to show the next person who came into it that she had loved it. That she had been in love there, had been loved there, had given birth to love there. She was giving as much love to the house in leaving it as she had given in building it.

Now all the duties had been done, and all the problems had been solved. Except one—the most difficult. Her father.

9.

"No," Johnny said. "You tell him alone. It wouldn't be any good if I went with you."

"But it was your idea."

"Princess," he said, "it was the woman from New York's idea." He stroked his hands through her hair. "Why tell him at all? Just drop the old buzzard a letter when you get there."

"And what happens when I don't show up with you and Little John for Sunday dinner? No," she said firmly, "it wouldn't be fair. I never lied to my father, and I never ran from him. I'm going to tell him tonight. She reached up and touched his shoulders. "Come with me."

"No," he grinned. "He'd cut off my legs for letting you go. And I need them to walk."

She took back her arms, and then went into the bathroom and fixed her face and her hair. It was only three blocks from their house to her father's. At six-thirty it was still light out and still hot. Her father would be on the front porch now, finished with dinner, reading the evening paper. She'd phoned her mother, and she was waiting for Melissa, down the block.

"You going through with it, honey?" her mother asked.

"Day after tomorrow. Everything's ready."

"You going to tell him now?"

"Right now."

"He'll be mean as a hornet."

"Maybe," Melissa said, watching the house that her father had built with his own hands come closer and closer to her. "Maybe not." She stopped just out of hearing distance of the porch. "Maybe he won't be that mad."

"Honey," her mother said, "maybe you'll turn into a bird, and perch on top of that roof, and whistle us all a tune."

Melissa's legs felt as though they were going to melt into the sidewalk. She shook back her hair in the hot Southern evening, and looked at the porch.

"Does he know anything?" she asked.

"Might be. Sometimes I think he's got a second sight."

"You coming with me?"

"No, honey," her mother said. "You go North and you'll be free of him as long as you stay up there. But if I come with you now, and you go, then he'll take it out on me for months."

Melissa put up her hand to shield her eyes against the yellow glare of the sinking sun, and studied her mother's creased face, and lifeless eyes, and worked-out, babied-out body; Melissa was one of four children. God, Melissa thought, and she was so pretty when I was Little John's age.

"Your father's not a forgiving man," her mother added simply.

"I don't think you'd better be in the house," Melissa said. "Why don't you just walk down to the Armstrongs' and see how their garden's coming."

"I might just do that. Maybe I'll come back in half an hour."

"That'd be a good time."

"Take care now."

"Say hello to the Armstrongs."

She even walks old now, Melissa thought. She looked around the neighborhood—more than half the houses were self-built—and she thought how strong the men were, and how worn-out the women. And then she walked up to the porch and went inside, letting the screen door slam behind her.

It was as hot as an oven. No breeze anywhere. Her father didn't even rustle the paper. He knew.

"Daddy," she said.

"Evening."

"I want to talk to you."

"I figured," he said, turning the page of the paper. "I'm here."

She didn't know where to go with it. "You heard?" she asked.

"Something," he answered. "I didn't give it much credence."

She was going to ruin her blouse. The sweat was pouring down her, right through her shields. She couldn't keep standing there, talking to that newspaper.

"Would you please put down"—and then it burst out—"that goddamn paper."

"Don't use that word in my house." The paper dropped, and the axlike face, with its dark brown flintlike eyes, glared at her. "Don't ever use that word in my house again."

"Are you going to talk to me?"

"Are you going to take the name of our Lord in vain?"

"Yes. Unless you put away that paper and talk to me."

"So it's true."

"What's true?"

"The devil has got into you."

"What's true?"

"You're going North without Johnny?"

"Yes. With his permission."

"You're leaving Little John?"

"With his father. And his grandmother. Johnny's mom is moving in while I'm gone."

"You're going to become a model up North in New York City?"

"If I can. So we can have enough money to live decently. So Johnny can go to college full time. So—"

"Whore!" The paper flew across the porch and slammed into the screen door, making a huge dent in the screen. Melissa jumped from the impact, and hated herself for doing it.

"What do you think those fancy models do up there?" her father rasped, leaning across the heat of the space separating them, gripping the arm of his chair so hard that Melissa waited for it to break off and splinter. "They're whores. Paid-for women. Sell their bodies for money." And his voice turned into razor blades. "And you will too."

He's only a carpenter, Melissa pleaded with herself. He doesn't make more than a hundred dollars a week. He went busted—flat-busted—twice, when he tried to start his own business.

"Satan's whore," her father roared on. "The Bible said it all. A woman too beautiful is a trap for men and sucks them down into unremitting hell."

Don't panic, she warned herself. Don't move back an inch.

"Your man's going to let you go, is he?"

She started to say the trip was Johnny's idea. But she caught herself. No running. No blaming. Simple answers. Get it over with.

"Yes," she said. "He's letting me go."

"By yourself?"

"By myself."

"To New York. Sodom and Gomorrah."

"To New York. That's where the modeling agencies are."

"Where the whore agencies are." He spit through the porch screen. She'd never seen him do that before, never dreamed he would do that to his own house. Part of the spit hung from the screen. She could smell it across the porch. Her bowels had turned to butter. She wanted to vomit.

"You made him into a mass of spineless jelly, didn't you? Does he ask your permission to go to the bathroom?"

She said nothing. No defenses. No apologies. Just the facts. Just so he heard the truth, once, before she left.

"You're not going," he said quietly.

"I'm going the day after tomorrow," she answered.

"You're not going. We're praying for you. And the prayer will keep you here."

Melissa suddenly felt as though the porch had turned stone cold. She felt goose bumps rise on her arms.

"Who's praying?" she asked in dread and astonishment.

"We all are."

"Who's all?"

"The whole church."

"You didn't . . . you couldn't!"

"We had a special prayer meeting last night."

"*Who?*"

"The deacons. All of us."

"You didn't drag me out in front of all those people!" Melissa felt her face distort into a mirror image of her father's; heard her voice narrow and rasp into an echo of his. Words were clawing their way up her throat, words she had

never used with her father before. And she was choking on
them, fighting to keep them down.

"We all prayed for you," her father repeated.

"Prayed for what?" The words were breaking through
now. And for the first time there was no resistance inside her
to stop them.

"Your redemption."

"From what? Being a wife? Being a mother? Being in
love? . . . Being your daughter?"

"From losing sight of the Lord."

"And going to New York? And becoming a whore? And
selling my body for money?" She had never before known
that the voice talking now existed in her throat. "That's what
it was, wasn't it? You prayed for my body."

"For your soul."

"No. My body. You stripped my body bare in front of all
those men. And then you asked them to pray for it."

"Your tongue is the forked tongue of the—"

"Truth. And you're going to hear it, like it or not." She
stopped. Now she felt the heat of the porch again. And she
was on fire.

"Was my mother there?" she asked suddenly.

"What?"

"Was Deacon Charles's wife there?"

Now it was her father's face that was twisted in astonishment.

"Was Deacon Goldsmith's wife there? Or Deacon Barclay's
wife? Or Deacon Baker's wife there?"

Her father snorted, and looked away from her.

"Which of all your women were at the meeting? Which of
your women prayed for me?"

"Get out of here," he said.

"Were any of the women asked? Did you ask even one?
One of your beaten-down, used-up women to agree with you,
and pray for me?"

"You're lost," he said. "The devil has a thousand devious
devices."

"I could stay," she said quietly, and he turned around. "I
could stay, and become like them. I could be old at thirty-five
too. I could give you all so many babies that my body would
sag. I could give you so much work that my hands and my
face would turn into leather. And I could give you so many
broken dreams, and crying nights that I wouldn't open my

mouth for twenty years too. But I'll be damned—or I'll be blessed—if I'm going to do that.''

''Get out of here,'' he said, ''before I throw you out.''

''You don't worship God in that church,'' she said, ''you worship an idol. And the name of that idol is man.''

''You whore,'' he screamed. The chair shot back across the porch, and he was on his feet, towering above her. He was a full six feet four inches tall, and he could have crushed her face with a single movement of his hand.

She glared up at him, and their two faces were now one face. She could smell his breath, that had never been polluted by alcohol or tobacco, but had been polluted by the kisses of women other than his wife. She could feel his arms tremble across the inches separating them. And her own arms trembled with equal fury.

''Get out,'' he said.

''I'm going to New York for three months,'' she said.

''Get off this porch.''

''If it works, I'll bring Johnny and Little John up there.''

''Out of this house.''

''If it doesn't, I'll come back.'' She paused. ''No,'' she said, ''I'll never come back.''

''Get out of my life.''

''I will . . . gladly . . . now.''

As the screen door slammed, she spun around for a second and yelled, ''I'll send you the first cover from *Vogue*.'' And then she ran through the night, weeping, and praying that she'd have time to reach her bathroom.

''And never let me see you again,'' he muttered under his breath. Then he walked across the porch and picked up the paper. He looked at the dent in the screen, and he knew that he'd have to replace the panel tomorrow. Then he put the chair back in its place and turned on the porch light and sat down. As he opened the paper, he was surprised to find that his hands had not yet stopped trembling.

''I knew she'd leave me someday,'' he thought bitterly, and tried to read the paper.

10.

The last day at the store, some of the girls in her department took Melissa out to lunch at the Chinese restaurant in the shopping center. They had a gardenia corsage for her, and wrapped up a small travel clock as a going-away present.

When the lunch was over, Melissa went back to the store, finished her day's work, picked up her salary, and spent five dollars on flowers at the florist's in the shopping center.

She put the flowers in the living room, the bedroom and the kitchen. It was her last tribute to her house. Then she made special dinners for Johnny and Little John, and they ate them quietly, with little conversation.

At eight o'clock she put her son to bed. There were only a few good-night kisses. She had begun to numb herself for the trip, and all she could feel was the touch of her lips against his soft skin, and no emotion whatsoever.

She and Johnny went to bed at ten, and lay there, side by side, in the hot sticky Houston night. She wanted to reach out and touch him; she wanted him to hold her; but neither happened. As far as she knew, she never slept all night; and she never heard the heavy, even breathing of Johnny's sleeping either. Then gray crept in, and it was the next day, and at six-thirty the brand-new Oldsmobile drove up. Billy Anders, a friend of Johnny who made his living driving Northeners' cars back home, rang their bell. It was time to go.

Into the car she placed her six best dresses, which were hung in the back seat. Next came six hats, one for each dress, all carefully packed in hat boxes. Finally Johnny carried out a large suitcase, containing all the rest of the clothes and toiletries she needed, and the suitcase was wedged into the trunk, next to Billy's own luggage.

Johnny's mother had come over, and was holding Little John throughout the ritual. Melissa went up to her, and kissed her softly on the cheek. "Take care of them now, Mom."

"You bet," said the older woman, and kissed Melissa back. "Have a safe trip."

Melissa took Little John in her arms, and lifted him up once or twice high in the air, and spun him around. The child giggled, and when she pulled him close he wrapped his little arms around her neck, and she could feel their pudgy softness. Tears were begging to be released, but there was a smile on her face so she wouldn't frighten him, and she kissed him again and again. At last she held him out again at arm's length, to photograph his face in her memory, and said, "You be good." He said, "I do," and watched wide-eyed when she handed him back to Johnny's mother.

Then she reached out for Johnny, who had been standing by Billy, stiff and embarrassed. She put her arms around him so tight that her shoulders ached afterward, and pressed her face into his chest. She let it stay there for several moments. His hands came up and stroked her back and hair, and she smelled the smell of his body—the smell had to stay with her for weeks to come.

They let each other go. For a moment they stared at each other's faces in the bright sunlight, but they said nothing. Then she touched Little John again, and quietly got into the car. The door slammed shut next to her, and Billy shouted a gruff good-bye to Johnny, and climbed into the car beside her.

The engine turned over twice before it caught. She saw Billy's hand shift into first gear, and she turned to wave. Her son and her husband and her home—her entire past faded away from her as the car rolled down the sunlit Houston street.

She didn't cry until ten blocks later, when they made their first turn onto the expressway. Then she cried for two hours.

And she cried each day it took them to drive to New York. She said almost nothing to Billy. She never remembered, for the rest of her life, a single inch of the highway that took her away from her home, her husband, and her son. All she remembered was that she said to herself, over and over again, "It's going to be worth it. It's going to work. He's going to get what he wants. I'm going to get it for him."

BOOK TWO

NEW YORK—1961

1.

It all started, Arlene Connors thought, the wild second week in August, when the door to Victoria Krane's reception room swung open and every model in the room looked up from her magazine and then kept looking.

Arlene always watched the seated models first, and not the person who was entering the room. A roomful of models is the most critical audience on earth, and only two kinds of people could keep those heads away from those magazines for more than a glance. The first was a celebrity of the rank of a star—Sinatra, or Hepburn, or Presley. And the second was a woman so beautiful that even the most beautiful women in the world couldn't tear their eyes away from her.

When thirty seconds had passed and the models' gazes still hadn't returned to their magazines, Arlene looked over at the entrance to the room, not quite knowing what to expect.

What she saw was a minor miracle. Standing at the very brink of the room, unsure of how to cross the line of models to the desk, and wearing perhaps the most garish and misassembled outfit Arlene had ever seen, was a woman who possessed Victoria Krane's face as it had been twenty years before, but whose face was framed not in dark hair, but in dazzling blond waves that fell over her shoulders and almost to her waist.

She was an angel turned into a country bumpkin. And, as Arlene stared at her, she suddenly felt the ice-cold certainty that this beautiful creature was a deadly threat to her job.

The door finally swung shut, and the woman came awkwardly across the room to Arlene. How could anyone that radiant walk that badly, Arlene thought?

"Hello," the vision said.

"Good morning." Arlene tried to keep her voice neutral.

"I'd like to see Miss Victoria Krane, please . . . if she has the time."

"Do you have an appointment?" Just a little too crisp, Arlene, she thought. Try to cool it down.

"No. I'm afraid not."

Arlene looked down at her appointment pad. "Your name?"

"Melissa Johnson. From Houston, Texas." She hesitated. "I was referred to you by Miss Dorothy Howard."

Very deliberately, Arlene wrote the girl's name on a sheet of paper next to the appointment book. Half a million dollars in billings shot to hell, she thought. Melissa of the two names. Dorothy's girl friend arrives to collect her debt. Let her through Victoria's door, kid, and you end up selling pencils.

"I don't think you're going to have much luck," Arlene said quickly. "Victoria sees by appointment only. And I don't think we've heard of a lady by the name of Dorothy Howard." She looked up at the startled faces of the models seated behind Melissa Johnson. "Victoria seems to be booked up for the next"—she turned the pages of the appointment book gravely—"two or three weeks at least."

She watched bewilderment twist that incredible face. "I don't understand," Melissa said.

"Nothing much to understand," Arlene forced out. "You've simply come to the wrong place."

The bewilderment was mixed now with embarrassment at being treated so brusquely in front of all the other women. There was another pause. Run, Arlene thought. Save yourself the pain. Why don't you run, damn you?

"Could there . . . be the possibility of a cancellation in her appointments?"

This was going to be a bitch of a role, Arlene thought. "No one cancels Victoria," she said.

"But someone could get sick."

"Then there'd be three others who'd take her place, honey." She waved her hand at the line of sitting girls, who were watching her as though she'd suddenly developed rabies, but who lowered their eyes to their magazines the moment Melissa looked toward them. "Some of them have been waiting for a month."

"But I don't have a month," Melissa blurted out. She'd paid a week's rent in advance for her room. She couldn't last more than eight or nine days.

"Sorry," Arlene said, closing the book conclusively, and hating herself. "Come back when you have more time."

There was silence, and she reached out to a contact sheet and began checking off acceptable photographs. Then Melissa spoke, quietly but firmly. "I'll never have more time. I'll wait."

And so it began—what Arlene later labeled as "The Seige of Victoria Krane's Inner Sanctum." The young woman simply turned, walked to an empty chair, and sat. She didn't pick up a magazine, and she didn't look around the room at the other women. She just sat.

She stayed in the chair from nine to twelve, not moving. When Arlene knew that Victoria was scheduled to come out for her twelve-thirty lunch at Chauvron, she herself got up and, with a pretense of casualness, walked into Victoria's office.

"She's here," Arlene said, as soon as the door swung shut. "She's been here all morning."

Victoria looked up and studied Arlene's eyes; there was no need to ask who she meant.

"Why didn't you tell me this before?"

"Because I know your pattern perfectly," Arlene said too rapidly, too defensively. "You never come out into that reception room unless family's there."

"You thought she'd go away?"

"I was praying she'd go away."

"They never do." Victoria stuffed some photographs into her bag. "They never do. I'll take the private elevator down." The bag was snapped shut. "And I don't want you to go to lunch. Not today. Not tomorrow. Not as long as she's here."

"I'll send down." Then Arlene paused, calculated, and gambled. "But I still think you should look at her—even, if only through the door."

"I know she's pretty."

"Impossibly. But that's not the point."

"She's a young me," Victoria said slowly, and there was weariness in her voice.

"Dorothy told you."

"At once."

"But you can't believe—"

"You still don't understand!" Victoria exploded. And then she caught herself. "You don't understand," she repeated more calmly. "The fact that she looks like me just makes it worse. It makes the nonprofessionalism worse. And the self-disgust."

"You're right," Arlene said. "I don't understand."

Victoria stared down at her appointment calendar. "How

many beautiful young women will come through that outside door today?'' she asked.

''Maybe twenty. Maybe thirty,'' Arlene answered.

''And if we decide to represent them, how much money will each of them make?''

''Eight hundred dollars a week average. Over three thousand a week tops.''

''What percentage of them end up on Broadway or in Hollywood?''

Arlene calculated for a second. ''About one out of every three.''

''And how many of them marry millionaires?''

''That's easy. Two out of five. And I hate them all.''

''So we're a gateway,'' Victoria said. ''A gateway to paradise for those young creatures who come through the door out there. We make our living from the most exquisite, the most precious, the most fragile, and the most vulnerable commodity in the world—beautiful women. We make an honest living. We make a damn good living. And we manage to do both at the same time for one reason—we keep our own hands off those girls, and we keep other people's hands off those girls, unless those girls choose, after they come with us, to be touched.''

''After they come with us?'' Arlene asked.

''Exactly. Because we don't accept those girls on trade or barter. Do you know how many accounts I could have had— multimillion dollar accounts—if I had agreed to take a girl who *almost* had it, a girl with a 'friend' who was willing to swap a signed contract for nothing more, or less, than the reputation of this agency?

''One little swap,'' Victoria went on, ''and there goes our taste, our objectivity, our belief in ourselves, out the window.'' Her eyes blazed. ''But worst of all, there also goes our gateway, our help, our promise for those other girls who really deserve it, the girls who can make it on their own, and not by barter.''

Victoria ran her hand harshly through her hair. ''Dorothy Howard works only on barter. She can take the most beautiful thing in the world—perhaps that beautiful, already half-corrupted thing out there—and she can bleed the future right out of it, if she can bind it closely enough to herself, for long enough.''

She smiled, but the smile was old, and wounded. ''That's

why I don't want to to see that young woman out there. I'll never sell her to Dorothy, for any price. It's not latent lesbianism, honey, if that's what you're wondering about. It's latent morality." She grabbed her purse. "And, by God, I'm guilty of it as charged."

The encounter was over. The private elevator closed behind Victoria. And Arlene was left alone to go out into the reception room again.

At one Arlene had lunch. She sat awkwardly in the almost deserted room, stuffing into her mouth a sandwich that tasted like old bedsheets, while the beautiful blue eyes stared unblinkingly at her.

At two-thirty the models began to filter back in. At three Victoria's buzzer sounded, and the parade began in and out of the inner room. At four Arlene left the barricade just long enough for a trip to the bathroom, and when she came back she made the first attempt at real communication with the still-seated, never-moving figure in the last chair. She held up the bathroom key, and looked at Melissa. Melissa thought for a moment, and then walked to the desk and took it.

"It's three doors down, to the left," Arlene said. "And be sure the door locks behind you."

"Why?" the innocent voice asked.

"It doesn't matter." Arlene turned back to her photographs. "Just make sure it does."

Five minutes later the key was back, and Melissa was in her place. At five the room began thinning out. At five-forty-five the last girl left. And at six o'clock Arlene arranged the photographs in a neat stack on her desk, folded up the appointment book, and picked up her purse.

"We're closing now," she said.

"But I'm waiting to see Victoria."

"I'm sorry," Arlene said, "but I thought I told you that Victoria didn't have time to see you."

"But before she leaves . . ."

"She left." It was sad to see that even a face that gorgeous could look plain for a moment, with shock and puzzlement. "Hours ago."

"But when?"

"Oh, I'm afraid when you were down the hall." And then there was so much pain in the other woman's face, that she found herself instinctively throwing in, "She had an early appointment." And then again she hated herself because she had lied on a lie—and both lies were obvious, and only hurt more.

For a moment, it seemed as though the woman were about to react. And for that same moment, Arlene would have welcomed some trace of accusation or outrage. But none came. The face was still controlled, still accepting. The tall young woman turned and said, "Good night," and walked out the door.

It was a cheap victory, Arlene thought. Cheap and dirty.

2.

Melissa's room, the one she'd rented for three dollars a day at the "Y," was smaller than her dressing alcove had been at home. The dresser was packed under the tiny bed. There was a single creaky chair, a washbasin with rusty fixtures, and, above the basin, a chipped and distorted mirror hardly big enough for her to see her full face in.

The room was stiflingly hot, but once inside, she leaned back against the closed door and her body started shivering as though the walls were made of ice.

She put her hands up to protect her arms against the cold she was generating inside, and she stared helplessly at the blurred image of herself in the mirror.

"If you start crying now," she said to the mirror, "you won't stop all night. And then you'll have two walnuts for eyes when you go back there in the morning."

"I don't want to go back there," the mirror said. "They don't want me. I'm not good enough. They took one look at me, and they knew I wasn't good enough. But they don't tell you no in this town. They just kill you with polite smiles."

The woman in the mirror began to cry. "Stop," Melissa said. "If you've got any chance at all—if that Dorothy Howard woman wasn't lying—then you'll ruin it by crying."

But she went on crying, even when she turned away from the mirror. She was scared. They didn't want her. And tomorrow, when she went back again, they still wouldn't want her. And they had more words than she had, and more smiles. She didn't know enough to play their games. Tomorrow they'd just leave her sitting there again. Every day would be the same.

"Run," she heard the mirror say, even though she wouldn't look at it. "Go someplace else. Don't go back there again. They're too smart for you there. They're too good for you there. Go someplace else."

She turned slowly and looked at the mirror across the tiny room. "Where?" she asked.

The woman in the mirror looked back at her and said nothing. But the tears stopped rolling down her cheeks.

"Are you going to call him—right now—and tell him that you couldn't even get in to see Victoria? That she wouldn't even see you, so she could tell you to your face that you aren't good enough? Or are you going to lie to him, and tell him that you saw Victoria and that she turned you down—all because you're afraid to go back there tomorrow?"

The nails of her hands dug into her shoulders, making red welts. And she smiled into the mirror, proud of the fact that she could give more pain to herself than they could give her.

"You're going back there," she said. "There, and nowhere else. Because he wants you to go back there, and he won't accept anything else. And you're going to learn to play their games, even though they're smarter than you are. And if you're not good enough for them, that's all right."

And then she had to close her eyes, because the pain from her own fingers made her block out the mirror, and the room, and the city she was in.

"That's all right," she said. "But, by God, you're going to prove to them that you deserve to have them tell you the truth to your face. And then," she promised, through her own self-created blackness and her own self-created pain, "and then maybe I'll let you go home."

3.

The next morning at nine Victoria was in her office, and Melissa was in the reception room.

The models came and went. The hours came and went.

Noon arrived, and Victoria disappeared for lunch, though Melissa never knew it. At one o'clock Arlene's lunch arrived, and as she pulled the roast beef sandwich out of the brown bag, she saw Melissa open her purse and take out a peanut butter and jelly sandwich, an overripe banana, and a container of what, by now, must have been very cold coffee.

They sat there silently, chewing, and avoiding each other's eyes. At two-thirty the models came back, and the afternoon began. Sometime after that, Arlene journeyed down the hall to the bathroom, and when she returned, she again held up the key for Melissa. This time Melissa smiled, and slowly shook her head.

Four passed, and then five, and then six. At six-fifteen Victoria left in the private elevator, without having said a single word to Arlene about Melissa, without even having acknowledged her presence in the outer room. A few minutes later Arlene began to tidy up her desk and pack her bag.

"You're not going," Melissa said.

"Yes, ma'am. I'm afraid I am."

"But she couldn't have left."

"But she did." Arlene looked up, and thought how exquisite blond hair is when it reflects a slanting sun, just about to turn red. How does it feel to live with that hair, she wondered. And those eyes? "And she will leave, every day," she added.

"But how?"

"Figure it out. Think about it for a moment."

"There's no way."

"There is." She was moving into dangerous ground now. Sympathy. The first step toward humanity, and disaster.

Again, the dazzling face turned plain with bewilderment.

"They may not have them in Houston," Arlene said. "But they sure have them here."

The words exploded from Melissa's mouth. She half-rose from her chair. "A second elevator. In her office."

"You can't go in there." Arlene had no idea what she'd do if the woman actually tried to force her way through the door.

"I won't," Melissa said, not submissively, but proudly. She sat down in the chair again for a moment, and stared blankly at the wall in front of her. "Are there separate entrances to the elevators?" she asked.

"Yes."

"How far apart?"

"Too far. You can't cover both of them at once."

"So she can slip in and out anytime she wants."

"That's what they were built for—privacy." Arlene wrestled with herself for a moment, and then plunged on. "Melissa," she said, and it was a transgression even to use the name, "why don't you go home?"

"No."

"You're not going to see her. Really."

"Why?"

Arlene's emotions snapped shut. Her controls turned to "Lie." She knew her voice sounded too artificial when she said, "I don't know."

"You do. But why won't you tell me?"

"It's late," Arlene said. "I've got a date. I've got to get out of here."

"Why won't you tell me?"

"You've got to go."

"I'll be back tomorrow."

"That's tomorrow. Now will you get out of here . . . please?"

They looked at each other, and then Melissa's shoulders slumped, and her face broke into a faint smile. "On one condition," she said.

"What?"

"That you let me use the ladies' room key."

The smile was returned, and the tension evaporated. Arlene handed her the key. "I'll wait around for a while, till you come back," she said.

Arlene walked her to the subway—out of pity, Melissa supposed. They said nothing more than good night when they reached the entrance.

Melissa stopped for dinner at Horn & Hardart and stuffed $1.30 worth of food down her throat. When she reached her room at the "Y" there were no tears this time, just the heat and the feeling of worthlessness.

She sat on the bed and stared at the peeling wall for four hours. Nothing. She was nothing. And they were going to spend the rest of her time in New York proving to her that she was nothing.

And they were everything. Dorothy Howard had told the truth about one thing—they were the best. There was an article from *Fortune* magazine, framed on the wall of the reception room. She'd had plenty of time to read it yesterday and today. Its title was "Number-One Glamour Brings Number-One Billings." There was also a photograph of Victoria Krane—the Victoria Krane she couldn't even get to see—and her Arlene-bodyguard, and the fifteen or so other people who worked there, and then twenty dazzling models who had made it. Then there were a lot of figures—billings and profits—that meant nothing to her. But she'd studied the face of every one of those models till she'd memorized it. And now she couldn't even look at her own face in the mirror.

She stared at the blank wall for four hours, and her mind kept flashing one picture on that wall—the face of Victoria Krane.

"You have two elevators," Melissa said to that picture. "And you have to ride up one of them to get to your office." For the first time that night, she smiled. "I'm nothing," she said. "But nothings don't weigh anything, and they move awfully fast."

She got up from the bed, and began undressing for the long, hot, sticky night.

"You shouldn't keep your picture around," she said, "if you don't want to be bothered by nothings."

Then she lay down on the tiny bed, nude, closed her eyes, and erased the pictures at last. Funny, she thought. I would have sworn she looks something like me.

4.

The next morning at eight-thirty, when Arlene arrived in the building, Melissa was standing downstairs, waiting.

"It won't work," Arlene said.

"We'll see."

"You'll see." And the elevator door closed.

Today was check-in time, when Victoria called each one of her "children" back into the office, and reviewed the month's shootings with them, and pointed out the tiny mistakes and the hidden possibilities that only her eye could see. Yet, when the first model arrived half an hour later, there was no Victoria—the first time Arlene had ever known Victoria to be even five minutes late. By nine-thirty, the nine o'clock girl, and the nine-ten girl, and the nine-twenty girl were beginning to look quite annoyed.

Arlene realized that, in the perfectly comfortable, air-conditioned room, she was beginning to sweat. My God, she thought, how easy it would be for Melissa to get a man to help her cover both elevator entrances. What if she'd intercepted Victoria? What if . . .

But then the door opened, and Melissa's face appeared. She looked first at the line of models, now grown so long that some of the women were standing against the wall. Then she looked at the door to the inner room. Then she looked at Arlene. She closed the office door, and Arlene could hear her heels race down the hall again to the elevator.

By ten o'clock, after a call to Victoria's apartment proved fruitless, Arlene took matters in her own hands. Taking Victoria's place, she began to give the corrections to the models. She was amazed at how clearly and crisply the instructions came, how much the tones of her voice sounded like Victoria's and, especially, how readily the models obeyed her.

At ten-thirty the buzzer rang. Victoria was in her office. Arlene went inside, and saw a woman who had aged fifteen years overnight.

"How many girls are waiting?" she asked.

"Only your ten-thirty. I gave the other ones their little hints."

"Good," Victoria said quietly. "No trouble?"

"None."

"And what about the other one?"

"Still here."

"Get rid of her. I don't want her here anymore."

"How?"

"I don't care."

"But I can't throw her out."

"I don't care." Arlene had never seen such pain in the woman's eyes. "I can't deal with her now. Think of something . . . please."

How do you hold an empress in your arms, Arlene thought. How do you stroke her hair, and tell her it's going to be all right?

"I'll do it by lunchtime," Arlene said. "She'll be gone by then."

The smile broke through. "Thanks." And then she spun her chair so that its towering back faced Arlene. "Look," her voice came through the leather of the chair, "I'm a wreck. Can you handle the rest of the girls this afternoon?"

"It's a cinch, once you get your steam up."

"Then I'm leaving. I'll call in at five. If there's any trouble, I'll handle it then."

"There won't be. Why don't you run off to some undiscovered beach?" Arlene wanted to add "with Rory," but the words wouldn't come out of her mouth.

The older woman got up, still with her back to Arlene, and moved toward the elevator. "You're a doll," she said. "I'm sorry about the last few days."

She's ashamed, Arlene suddenly realized. Victoria Krane—ashamed! Of what? Of what in the entire world?

"It's all right," Arlene said. "It's all right." And then went out to the reception room again—and the job she had to do on Melissa.

5.

At one o'clock, when the room was empty except for the two of them, and Arlene began to eat her lunch, she was startled to see that, this time, Melissa pulled out of her bag only the peanut butter and jelly sandwich. The banana was missing, and Arlene had a strong feeling that it was because it represented a subway token home.

They ate in silence for ten minutes. Then Arlene opened the wrapper around her slice of chocolate cake, and studied it dramatically for a minute or two, her plastic fork hanging suspended in the air.

"I'm getting too fat," she said finally, as though to herself. She looked up at Melissa. "Would you like it?"

"No, thank you," was the immediate reply.

"It's a shame to throw it away. Look at it." And she tipped the plate toward Melissa.

"I really couldn't." But the words came out a little slower.

"Sure you could. It'll never show on you. And besides, as

my mother said, we've got to keep the poor children in China from starving.''

Melissa smiled. Her right hand wavered for a moment, then reached out and took the plate and fork. She began to devour the cake so rapidly that Arlene thought she'd cut right through the cardboard plate.

When she had finished, she gave back the plate, and Arlene threw it in the wastebasket. ''You know,'' Melissa said suddenly, ''when I was about ten, the boys in my neighborhood used to play a rotten game with me. It was called ''Monkey in the Middle,'' or something, and they'd get on both sides of you, and then one of them would steal your purse or a book, and they'd throw it to each other when you tried to get it back from them.''

''I know,'' Arlene said. ''They used to do it to me.''

''Did you like it?''

''I hated it.''

''Did you ever cry?''

Arlene paused a moment. ''Sometimes. If I thought I could get it back that way.''

Melissa looked at her, the sapphire eyes unblinking. ''Do you think I should start crying now?''

''No,'' Arlene answered without hesitation, and it was strange how the craziness of the situation made her smile. ''I don't think you can stop the game that way.''

''How can I stop it?''

''By facing the facts,'' she said. This time there was no shift in Arlene's voice as she slipped from honesty to deception. Because she'd solved the problem, and would rescue all three of them. What did a few more lies matter, when you were that close to salvation?

''That Victoria won't see me?''

''Not quite. That there's no reason for Victoria to see you. Because she can't use you now, and she has no time for the amenities.''

''For the what?''

''For courtesy. For etiquette. For making nice-nice. Not when you have to cover ten thousand dollars every week in overhead.'' Now Arlene leaned forward. ''Look, Melissa, I'll give it to you straight. You're very saleable. You could make a lot of money. But not here.''

''You mean you think I really could be a model?''

''Tomorrow. This afternoon, if I pick up that phone.''

"Then why doesn't she see me?"

"Because, my dear, you clash." She paused for a ten-count, to let the confusion of the unfamilar term sink in, to numb the other mind. "In the modeling world, you're a type. Blond, blue-eyed. High cheek bones, and therefore high fashion. Perfect for *Town and Country* and *Vogue;* lousy for catalogs. There are probably three photographers and ten accounts in town that would eat you up—the rest would simply let you go. You could earn maybe forty thousand dollars if you didn't clash with two other girls of ours that are exactly the same type as you are."

"And I'd take business away from them?"

"You sure as hell would. And they'd slit our throats if we let you set one foot on their territory."

Again, a ten-count. Then, the clincher. "That's the reason for the runaround. And—" and may the gods forgive her—"Victoria can't take you, but she won't give you to anyone else either."

Arlene waited to see the reaction. First, silence. The girl was piecing the story together in her mind, testing whether it fit. Would she swallow it? Was she really that naive?

The answer finally came. "But *you* would send me to one of these other agencies? Why?"

"For three reasons. First, because I like you." That at least was true. "Second, because Victoria would think that you had the intelligence to simply give up here and try another agency. And third—and I'm sticking my neck out now—because there'd be a little something for me at the other end if they took you." Arlene's lunch had suddenly turned to stone in her stomach.

"I see," Melissa said.

"Shall we get on with it?" Arlene persisted.

"With what?"

"With the phone call." She looked at her watch. "The person I want will be back from lunch now."

Again the sapphire eyes were like blue X-ray machines. "Why not?" Melissa said. "I'd like to hear what happens."

The situation had suddenly spun slightly out of control. Something was going on that Arlene hadn't planned—she knew that from Melissa's cool tone—but she couldn't figure out precisely what it was. Her hand trembled almost imperceptibly as she picked up the phone, and dialed Elegant.

"Sally," she said, watching Melissa carefully as she spoke,

"I've got a dream here for you." She held the phone close to her ear, so Melissa couldn't hear what the other woman was saying. She let the "You've got to be kidding" pass, and then went on with "Utterly beautiful."

She smiled at Melissa and nodded as Sally exploded, "Then why the hell are you sending her to us?" Then went on with, "I think you should see her at once. Why don't I send her over in a cab right now?"

There was a sputtering sound on the other end of the wire, and then Sally said, "She's sitting right next to you?"

"Absolutely, darling."

"It's a joke?" the phone crackled.

"You'll thank me for the rest of your life."

"The moment she sets foot in that elevator, you call me up, you bitch, and tell me what's really going on. You hear?"

"Then it's set. She's leaving right now." And she put down the phone before any more sounds could come out of it.

"Done," she said to Melissa. "As easy as that."

"Thank you," Melissa said flatly.

"Here's the lady." Arlene wrote Sally's name on a memo sheet. "And here's the agency. You can be there in ten minutes."

"Thank you," Melissa said again, still devoid of emotion. And then she turned and walked out the door.

Arlene waited a few breaths, now completely puzzled. When she heard the elevator door close, she went into the hall to see if Melissa was still there. Then she went back to her desk and filled Sally in with a psuedo-story, good enough to let Melissa's face speak for itself, but without the slightest mention of Dorothy. By then the girls began coming in, and the afternoon frenzy swept her along with it.

Victoria called, as promised, at five, sounding far away. She was told everything was fine, and was off the phone, without questions, in less than five minutes.

The last girl left at five-thirty. At five forty-five Arlene was so exhausted that she could hardly move, and was wearily gathering up her purse and newspaper when Melissa came back into the room. A glowing Melissa.

"Can I talk to you for a moment?" Melissa said quietly.

"It's late," Arlene replied automatically, numbly, warily. "I have a date tonight. I really have to—"

"It will only take a moment." She blushed. "I just have to say thank you."

Arlene hesitated for a second. But then she realized that there was one last scene left in the play. One last nicety before she could go home and forget that the travesty had ever happened. A discussion of contracts, salaries, assignments, advances, guarantees. And why not? Melissa had been put through enough hell. She deserved two minutes of crowing triumph.

"All right," Arlene finally said, smiling. "But only for two seconds."

"I want to thank you," Melissa said, "for giving me one of the greatest gifts of my life."

"I'm glad," Arlene said, playing her part.

"You made it possible," Melissa went on, "for me to be able to call home tonight, and talk to my husband without lying to him, or telling him that I couldn't make it in New York."

Arlene's face froze into a protective mask. "I don't understand," she said.

"I haven't been able to call them since I got here. I promised I'd call every night. But I couldn't. Because I'm no good at lying, and it would take Johnny three minutes to find out that up here I was a . . . a nothing." Now the blue eyes were wet, glistening, even more exquisite. "But I'm not. Am I?" Melissa said.

Arlene shook her head. "No."

"You're telling the truth now."

"Yes," Arlene said. "I'm telling the truth now."

"I'm pretty, aren't I?"

Arlene Conners blinked. In eight years of watching beautiful women, she might have seen two or three who could share a camera lens with Melissa Johnson's face. My God, she thought, we've robbed this child of her eyes.

"Yes," she said quite simply. "You're pretty."

"And . . . and even up here, I'm not a nothing, am I."

"Is that the word you invented for yourself?"

"That's the word you gave me."

Arlene sat down on the edge of the desk. She looked down at the appointment book—that magic book that made some women everything, and that made others disappear so that you couldn't even remember their names three days later.

"No," she said, glorying in the fact that her words didn't make her nearly choke on them, "if there's anyone in this room who's a nothing, you're looking at her."

"I found out the truth."

"Yes, you found out. At Elegant. When did they give you your first assignment?"

"Never. I walked out on them."

"You're out of your mind."

"No," Melissa said quietly, "I'm in my mind now. I finally figured it out. Dorothy Howard lied to me. She isn't a friend of Mrs. Krane's at all. The reason Mrs. Krane won't see me—and the reason you were lying to me all the time, when you're as bad at lying as I am—is because I was sent here by Dorothy Howard."

Again the shield sprang up in Arlene's mind. But this time she lowered it.

"I'm not saying you're right," she replied. "But do you want to tell me how you found out?"

"From the other agency, at the end of the interview. Your friend kept shaking her head. And then she asked me, 'Who sent you to Victoria, anyway?' And I said, 'Dorothy Howard.' And she smiled. She just smiled, and stopped shaking her head. And then she patted my hand and said, 'That's all right, honey, we're not as uppity here as the Queen Bird.' "

"That bitch. That mother-selling bitch."

"Now I've got another question to ask," Melissa said.

"I know."

"I don't know how to deal with you up here. You're so much smarter than I am."

"Not true," Arlene interrupted. "We've just been playing 'Monkey in the Middle' longer than you have."

"It doesn't matter," Melissa went on. "Because the only way I can deal with all of you is just to blurt out what I feel, and hope that . . . ." She stopped.

"I'm not lying anymore," Arlene said.

"Then what did Dorothy Howard do to—"

"But I'm not going to tell you."

"Why?"

"Because there's a big concrete city out there, and its streets are hard. And I walked those streets once for eleven months before I got this job. Now look," Arlene said, "if you don't like Elegant, we can find another agency tomorrow that—"

"I want this agency," Melissa said.

"I speak the truth," Arlene replied. "You're not going to get in here."

Melissa smiled. "Not at the cost of your job, that's for sure." She picked up her purse. "I won't be here to bother you tomorrow. Or the next day. You can count on that."

"Wait," Arlene said. "I have the names of places—"

"That I don't want to go to. Thanks for everything, though. Mostly for the truth." Again she smiled. "I think I have an idea what to do next, and it won't hurt you. Besides, I have a phone call to make, and it seems like I've been waiting forever."

And then she was gone, leaving an emptiness in the room that was like a desert. The battle was over. No one had won.

Hey, Arlene thought, I liked you. We could have been friends.

Hey, I even forgive you for being so goddamn gorgeous.

6.

Two days had passed since Dorothy's girl had gone back to whatever dark universe she had come from. Now Victoria Krane was able to fight a one-front war.

The taxi crawled along in the rush-hour traffic on Madison Avenue, a street that was really the world's most luxurious department store in disguise. Victoria stared out the window at the lighted store displays, listening to each one cry out to her as she passed by.

"Buy me," said the thousand-dollar gown in one window, "and forget what Rory did to you the other night."

"Buy me," said the ten-thousand-dollar sideboard in the antique shop, "and forget what Rory did to you the other night."

"Buy me," said the fifty-thousand-dollar painting in Hammer's, "and forget what Rory did to you the other night."

High-ticket tranquilizers, she thought. Wonder drugs for the ego. Who needs love when you have luxury?

Stop it! she thought. You sound like a soap opera. Rephrase! And this time be realistic. You have a husband who simply doesn't love you any longer, and is tired of pretending that he does. You've grown too old for a husband who's eight years older than you are. You make your living by surrounding yourself with beautiful young women; now he sees only their youth, and not you. The odds are that he hasn't done anything about it yet—he's still in the "building the excuse" stage—finding faults, picking fights, collecting injustices. The marriage hadn't crashed yet, in some twenty-five-year-old's bed. So she had options. There were recourses, if she didn't panic. If she didn't give way, as she had the other night. If she . . .

Her rationality gave out here, as it gave out every night. The last block on Madison Avenue passed by. The taxi moved faster now, toward Park Avenue, and the apartment, and tonight's confrontation with Rory.

The doorman helped her out of the cab, as always. She gave the driver a dollar tip, as always. She walked into the entrance hall of the building, as always. And then she stood stock still.

Standing before her, waiting in front of her elevator, was a woman with her own face, suddenly grown as young again as she had looked when Rory was courting her. It was as though she had entered a Coney Island fun house, but the mirrors were made, not of glass, but of time.

The woman who possessed the face was as startled as she, and for a second the two of them simply stood there, saying nothing. And then the younger woman said, "I'm sorry. I didn't mean to shock you."

"How did you find my address? No one knows it."

"The starter does," the woman said instantly.

"Who?"

"The starter in your office building."

"Nonsense."

"He gets cabs for you. He hears you give three addresses."

"Three?"

"I bought them all." Melissa smiled. "The first one was your exercise salon, on Sixtieth Street."

"I see."

"I went there two nights ago, and waited several hours, even after I knew the place had closed."

Victoria looked around, and saw the doorman staring at them. "There are some seats over there," she said, pointing to a small alcove. "Why don't we sit for a moment." Victoria was still too surprised to think decisively. So she'd listen—for a moment. "And then?" she asked.

"I went back yesterday and bought the second address. It was Elizabeth Arden's on Fifth Avenue."

"Every Monday night. Not Thursday."

"But I waited there till they closed too. I guess I would have gone back tomorrow if tonight hadn't worked."

"And how much did you pay for these three addresses?"

Melissa looked down at the carpeted floor.

"I'd really like to know," Victoria said.

"Ten dollars for the first two. Twenty dollars for this one."

"Forty dollars. The bastard."

"I don't want to get him in trouble."

"You won't, this time. But I will tell him tomorrow that if he does it again—ever—he'll be fired."

And then some instinct whispered in Victoria's mind, and she asked, "How much money do you have left after this research project?"

"Enough."

"Which is how many dollars?"

"Six."

"You spent forty dollars out of forty-six to track me down. You have got determination." She looked around at the doorman, and thought how simple it would be to have the girl ejected. But then said, "All right. Now you've got me. How do you feel?"

"Strange."

"In what way?"

"I didn't expect you to . . . look this way." She smiled again, and this time it was a child's smile. "I sort of feel like a stray cookie, that just met her cookie cutter."

Victoria laughed. "I like it." And then she became serious. "And I understand it."

"I have another feeling too. But I don't think it's funny."

"Which is?"

The girl was dead serious. "I feel as though God took out your rib, and made me."

Victoria thought for a moment. Weighed. Wrestled. "Let me ask you a question," she said. "What did you have to eat today?"

Melissa paused. "A peanut butter and jelly sandwich."

"No banana?"

"No. I wasn't hungry."

"Are you hungry now?"

"A little."

"Then why don't you come upstairs, and I'll have Mary make something quick for you. And you'll leave."

The girl looked startled at the last sentence. But she said, "Thank you," and rose.

They said nothing going up the elevator to the twentieth floor. And nothing in the hall. And nothing until the door was opened, and Melissa Johnson walked into Victoria Krane's apartment—and into another universe.

Only blurredly, in the pages of *Vogue*, had Melissa ever dreamed that interiors such as the one she was standing in now even existed. Her eyes could see the beauty before her—the color, the texture, the design, the coordination—but her mind had no way at all of deciphering the origin or meaning of the objects that bedazzled her. A hundred questions sprang at once to her lips, and every one of them was blocked. Where did the huge vase come from, that looked as though it had been made by fairies? Were the draperies in the living room made of cloth, or gold? How did anyone ever coax the legs of chairs to shine like that, and could you sit on them? She wanted to ask, touch, feel, learn. But all she could do was stare, enchanted.

"Mary," Victoria said, "is Mr. Krane home?"

"No, ma'am. He said he was held up at a meeting, and would be here at nine."

"Good." That set a time limit to the meeting. Feed her. Smile at her. Listen to her. And get her out.

"The young lady will have . . . eggs, bacon, toast, and jam." She looked again at Melissa. "Three eggs, Mary."

Victoria waited a moment, then said gently to Melissa, "Would you like to set there, in the living room?"

"Anywhere," Melissa said. "It's so . . ."

"What?"

"Regal." And then she blushed. "Isn't that funny," she said. "I never used that word before." She smiled. "I didn't even know I knew it."

They had now reached the sofa, and sat down. Melissa sat very gingerly, as though she were afraid that the weight of her body would bruise the velvet fabric.

Victoria glanced over the room, then at Melissa. "Is it very different," she asked brittlely, "from Dorothy's?"

"I beg your pardon?"

"Dorothy's apartment."

"Her apartment?"

"Of course." And Victoria felt the anger begin to rise again.

"I was never in Dorothy Howard's apartment. I have no idea what it looks like."

"But she gave you my name?"

"Yes."

"Where? How?"

"In the department store in Houston, where I worked as a model. She wrote it on a slip of paper for me."

Carefully rehearsed, Victoria thought. Perfect, down to the last detail.

"Why?" she asked.

"Because," and there was a brief pause, "she said I belonged up here, and not there."

"All this," Victoria asked, "in the store? The first time she met you?"

"Yes."

"In how many minutes?"

"Three or four."

"Really? What a beautiful fairy tale. She walks into the store. Looks at you. Is overcome with—what?—admiration. And right there, on the spot, gives you a passport to New York. To the place where you belong. To the fame and fortune you deserve. And all spontaneously, through sheer generosity."

Bewilderment distorted the girl's face. Rage distorted Victoria's.

"I'm not going to buy that," Victoria said.

"I'm sorry?"

"I don't believe a word you've said."

For one moment, blue eyes and brown eyes locked. And then Melissa gave a sigh of relief, and said, "Good. That's what I came here for. To find out why you don't believe me."

"Because it didn't happen in a store," Victoria replied instantly. "And because Dorothy Howard never did a favor for a women like you in her life, without getting a full and equally gratifying favor in return."

"I don't understand."

"Oh no, my dear, we both understand perfectly well. But what you don't understand, and what I intend to make perfectly clear to you right now, is that I don't take Dorothy Howard's girls.''

There was no meaning in the sentence for Melissa. She could only mutter, ''What?''

In fifteen years of business, in nearly a thousand rejections of aspiring models, Victoria Krane had never once needlessly inflicted hurt. But time was running out fast tonight, and her entire psyche was covered with welts, and this blond mirror-image of herself was sitting on the sofa, feigning innocence. She looked to see if Mary was still in the kitchen, and then she said, ''The front door of my office is not attached to Dorothy Howard's bed.''

It took a full thirty seconds for Melissa Johnson, wife of Johnny Johnson, mother of Little John, to realize what the other woman meant. And then she remembered Dorothy Howard's tongue licking the tip of her pencil, and her stomach wanted to force its way up through her throat, and spill out of her mouth.

''I'm married,'' she said automatically, as though that would answer everything.

''I know,'' Victoria answered. ''Dorothy told me.''

''I have a son.''

''I'm fully aware of that fact too.'' There was no softening, no understanding on the older woman's face. If anything, the look of disgust had deepened.

Yes, Melissa thought, that doesn't prove anything up here. And then the woman's anger infected her.

''Sometimes,'' she said, ''my husband makes love to me five times a night. And I still won't let him go to sleep,'' she said, her face crimson now with embarrassment, ''because I still haven't got enough.''

''Shut up,'' Victoria said instinctively. ''I don't want to hear about any fantasy sex life.''

''But it's not fantasy,'' Melissa said. ''It's the truth.'' And then she went on. ''Three times a week, he drives home from the plant and I come home from the store during our lunch hour. The moment he gets in the house, I'm there, with my clothes off, waiting for him in the bedroom.''

''It's a lie,'' Victoria cried. She thought of herself, lying in her own bedroom two nights ago, trembling . . . and begging. For the first time in her life, begging a man as he lay there, with his back turned toward her. ''Get out of here,'' Victoria said, ''you cheap . . . dike.''

Melissa's face broke into an angry, bitter smile. So this—*this*—was what all the suffering, all the torture of the past five days had been about. Her father, with all his Biblical prejudice and ignorance, had been right. New York was a city that expected whores. And she had come to New York—she had been announced to New York before she ever arrived there—as a bought-and-paid-for whore. And worst of all—and the smile grew deeper—as a whore who sold herself, not to men, but to women.

"Would it have made any difference," she asked quietly, "if it had been a man who met me in Houston and gave me your name? Then would you have treated me this way?"

"That has nothing to do with—"

"I'm sorry. But I think it has everything to do with it. I think you don't want me to work for you because you think I slept with a woman, and not a man, to get in to see you. Well, I didn't. I didn't sleep with Dorothy Howard, or any other woman, because I like to make love with men. One man. With the greatest face, and the greatest body you've ever seen—whose name is Johnny Johnson."

"I think you'd better go," Victoria said. "Now." She stood up. "I'll give you enough money to buy dinner outside." Her face was as hard and sharp as her voice.

Melissa, too, stood up. "You must be frightened," she said, "but I don't know what's scaring you. Is it the idea of wanting other women yourself?"

Victoria whirled around, and screamed out, "*Mary!*"

Melissa reached down and picked up her handbag. She was ready to be thrown out. And then she looked at Victoria's swollen eyes, and the creases that were etching their way down the sides of her mouth, and the worn-out skin under the cheekbones that came, not from age, but from misery. Then she said, very softly, so that Mary couldn't hear if she came out of the kitchen, "Or maybe there's a man hurting you so much that you want to run to women, just to get away from that hurt."

Victoria's hand slashed out, and turned Melissa's head sideways from its impact on her cheek. "Get out of here!"

The maid came out of the kitchen, carrying a silver tray. She froze as she saw Victoria pushing Melissa back to the apartment door, crying out at the top of her lungs, "You bitch! You blond bitch! Get the hell out of here!"

"I'm sorry," Melissa said.

"Mary," Victoria begged. "Mary . . . help me get her out of here."

7.

The overwhelming problem at that moment was simply not to cry.

You fool, she thought. You idiotic, childish fool. She leaned back, pushing her shoulders rigid against the unrelenting wall. She had to stay here in the hall until she could get some sort of grip on herself. If someone came out of the other two apartments, then she'd push the elevator bell. But until then . . .

Everything, she thought. You've done everything wrong. Why force your way into Victoria Krane's life when she didn't even want to see you? When she actually hated you?

And then she stopped, absorbing the silence of the empty hall, and then faint sounds of the dream-world lives that were lived behind those closed doors. And a one-word answer formed in her mind—Johnny.

Johnny had wanted her to see Victoria Krane. Johnny had sent her to New York to work for Victoria Krane. No one else. And she had tried to give him what he wanted, as she'd always given him what he wanted.

She suddenly realized that she was terribly tired, and desperately hungry. Her body was alive again. She'd shut it off for five days, because she'd had something to do that couldn't be accomplished if she'd allowed it to feel. But now it was all over and she'd failed. The gift she'd wanted to bring home for Johnny—acceptance by the best agency in New York—was gone. And there was a weekend to live through with only about three dollars for food. And then she'd finally be an adult, and go back to Elegant, and beg them to give her another chance.

She pushed the elevator call button. Horn & Hardart had huge sugar Danishes for fifteen cents. She would buy two of them, one for tonight, and one for tomorrow morning. Or maybe even both for tonight.

She nodded awkwardly to the elevator operator as she stepped inside. As they moved slowly, ponderously down, she leaned back against the wood paneling, watching the floor-number lights at the top of the elevator go down with them.

All I have to do now, she thought, is keep alive till Monday. Just till Monday.

As the elevator door opened, and she walked out through the foyer toward the street, the doorman stopped her.

"Are you the young lady who was just in Mrs. Krane's apartment?" he asked.

She nodded, expecting the worst.

"She wants you to go back up there again, please, as soon as possible. She's called down three times. I thought maybe I'd missed you when you left." He smiled. "And I knew that was impossible."

8.

When the maid opened the door, Victoria was standing in the foyer, holding a water glass full of vodka. The rim of the glass was covered with lipstick stains, the evidence of a dozen quick sips while she waited for Melissa.

Melissa walked toward her carefully, stopping about six feet away.

"I'm sorry," Victoria said bluntly.

"I'm so glad," Melissa replied. "I shouldn't have—"

"You most certainly should. I haven't had such stupid assumptions slapped so hard since I was in high school."

"I didn't mean to insult you."

"Of course not," Victoria said. "I know that. All you meant to do was enlighten me. Like the psychoanalyst, making the unexpected connection to snap the neurotic trance." Her face softened. "I don't think you quite know what I mean. Do you?"

"No," Melissa said. "I don't know your New York words."

"You don't really need them."

"But I'd like to learn them."

"I rather think you will."

"Someday," Melissa blurted out, "I'd like to learn your house, too."

Victoria Krane smiled at the echo of her own past longings. "Someday you will," she said. "Soon. Every object in it."

The maid interrupted. "Mrs. Krane," she said softly from the dining room.

"Of course," Victoria said. "Your food." She smiled at Melissa. "Can you eat after all this?"

"The plates, the tray, and the silverware," Melissa said.

"Wonderful." Victoria led her into the dining room, and watched in silence while Melissa finished every scrap of food. Then she began.

"I think we should set up a series of working rules," Victoria said, and the statement riveted Melissa's attention. "You have come to New York to be a model, and I can make you into the kind of model that you should become. Unfortunately, you were introduced to me by the wrong person, under the wrong circumstances. Because of those circumstances, I misjudged your relationship with that person, and reacted . . . irrationally and harshly to you when we first met."

Victoria smiled. "I don't like to think of myself as a harsh person. Therefore, I am prepared to make amends at this moment. But I can't work with you, and I can't train you, if we don't establish the proper business relationship at the very beginning. Do you understand?"

"Perfectly," Melissa said at once, despite the fact that she didn't understand the meaning of the word "amends."

"The plan is simplicity itself," Victoria went on. "We will simply assume that we have just met, at this very moment. And that anything—anything—that came before this moment, is completely forgotten. Is that agreeable?"

"Entirely," Melissa said, her heart beginning to pound so hard that she was sure it would drown out the conversation.

"All right," Victoria said, and her entire body relaxed. "We'll set up some test shootings and see how you do."

The napkin—the fine, lacy linen napkin was still on Melissa's lap. She reached down and picked it up, and began to place it on the table. Her hand was trembling so hard, however, as she raised it, that it fell onto the plate where the eggs had been. And as she saw the yellow stain of the eggs touch the napkin's edge, she began to cry. She sat there, not looking at the woman but instead at the napkin, and cried.

"Please don't," Victoria said.

"I don't want to," Melissa said.

The other woman's hand came out and touched hers, and she put her own hand on top of Victoria's and held on hard. Victoria waited till Melissa had regained control, and then she called out softly, "Mary."

The kitchen door opened. "Yes, Mrs. Krane?"

"Bring another napkin, please."

When it came, she handed it to Melissa. "Use it for your face," she said.

Melissa shook her head. "No," she said. "Let me have a Kleenex."

"Use it," Victoria repeated. "You might as well learn now that they're washable. And they were made to serve you."

And then she got up, and went over to her purse on the highboy in the foyer. "Here," she said, "is fifty dollars. It's an advance for the weekend, so you can rest up and look your best Monday."

Melissa looked at herself in the bronze-framed mirror. She watched the lace linen napkin as she used it to remove the smears from her makeup, so that she looked half-human again. And then Victoria appeared in the mirror too, and the two of them stood there for a second, studying the double image.

"This year," Victoria said, "they'll tell you that you look like me. Three years from now, they'll tell me that I look like you. And," she went on, turning sharply as she heard the key in the lock, "I'll be flattered as hell."

A man walked into the apartment. He was tall. He was tan. He had the kind of face that women followed across a room. And from the instant he entered, Melissa watched Victoria's entire body stiffen.

"This," said Victoria, holding up her cheek to be kissed, "is my husband, Rory. And this is Melissa Johnson, who I hope will be working with me."

"An excellent idea," he said. "A pleasure." He held out his hand.

Melissa took it, felt its strength and its confidence, and pulled her hand away as soon as she could.

"Melissa was just leaving, Rory," Victoria said, and then turned to the girl. "I'll see you Monday at one-thirty sharp. Not one-thirty-one, not one-thirty-two, but one-thirty. Do you understand?"

"Perfectly."

"Good. Come, let me walk you to the elevator."

"Good night," Melissa said.

"Come again," Rory said, and watched the two of them walk to the elevator. He gave his briefcase to Mary, and walked over to the bar to pour himself a drink.

As the ice clinked into the glass, he knew he had seen a miracle. He had seen his wife in time-present, and time-past. A younger incarnation of Victoria had stood beside her, and fifteen years had faded in the touch of a handshake. Amber scotch swirled over the ice, and he remembered the first freezing winter in Vermont, when they'd gotten drunk in front of the fireplace, and Victoria—the young, regal, untouchable Victoria—had first given herself to him in complete savage abandon.

Great God, he thought, touching the still-warm liquid to his lips, wouldn't it be glorious to have a body that young, that beautiful, that regal, surrender itself to his again.

Victoria returned to the room. Rory turned to her, and put the glass down on the bar behind him. He walked over to give her a second kiss. A real kiss. The first step, he thought, was to win back his wife—till she became as pliable as she was when they were first married.

9.

Victoria had told the elevator operator to have the doorman get Melissa a cab, and so Melissa Johnson took her first taxi ride through the sparkling night streets of New York.

She had never been as tired. And she had never been as happy. She could imagine Johnny's voice over the phone . . . the laugh so loud she wouldn't even need the phone to hear it . . . the glee, the questions, the demand for details . . . the love.

In the darkness, in the back of the taxi, she giggled. She

wished she could tell him, somehow, about the scrawny chickens. But he wouldn't want to hear that, not tonight.

The chickens, she thought. They'll never know—poor things—what I owe them.

When she was five and a half, her father had discovered health foods and vitamins. He decided at once that each member of the family should take a huge brown vitamin pill each night before dinner. Melissa couldn't swallow the pill but knew her father would not sympathize. She hated the fact that he had set himself up in control of her stomach. Besides, she already felt marvelous. She already had so much energy that she burned out her playmates, both boys and girls, when they all ran back after school to one front yard or another.

She decided, there and then, that it was his pill, not hers.

Every night, therefore, she repeated the same ritual, and repeated it for the next seven years. Before dinner was served, the family would line up in front of her father's chair. He would ceremoniously reach into the bottle and pull out one of the huge brown pills for each of them. First he would pop one into his own mouth, and then into the mouth of Melissa's mother, and then her older sister's and then her older brother's, and then Melissa's, and finally Melissa's younger sister.

All would then dutifully file to their chairs, and the meal would begin. Melissa would sit down with the pill feeling as big as a boulder under her tongue, and begin eating. She would eat a four-course meal every night on the top of her tongue, with the pill tucked away painfully underneath. It dissolved slightly, of course, and midway through the meal it began to taint all the food with its own bitter flavor.

Then, when her father rose from the table and went out to the front porch to read the evening paper, Melissa was allowed out in the back yard to play. She would walk over to the neighbor's chicken coop, and spit out the semi-dissolved pill into it. The chicken nearest to it would gobble it up in a second.

She learned then that giving-in tasted good only to chickens. And when she was twelve, her father's business failed, and money became tight, and the pills disappeared from the evening table.

The chickens grew up scrawny. She grew up, she suddenly thought, to be a model.

"A model," she said out loud. And the old man who was driving the cab turned around and said, "What, Miss?"

They were within two blocks of the YWCA. The Horn &
Hardart was still open.

"I said pull over here, please," she giggled. I owe myself
a present, she thought. A double present.

And besides, Victoria had said to look her best . . . for
Monday.

10.

At twenty-nine minutes past one on Monday afternoon,
when Melissa pushed open the door to the reception room, it
was obvious that Arlene had her hands full. She was trying to
pacify two annoyed clients, both of whom wanted Victoria's
immediate attention. Arlene was explaining that Victoria was
on an emergency phone call. Decorum should have ruled the
moment. But Arlene saw Melissa, she didn't give a damn.
She stood up from her desk, flung out her arms, and trumpet-
ed, "Peanut butter!"

Melissa turned flaming red, hesitated for a moment, and
then flung out her arms in return and said, "Chocolate cake!"

The two of them came together in the middle of the room,
clasped each other in their arms, squeezed cheeks, and patted
each other on the back. And then Arlene pulled back from
Melissa, with her hands still on Melissa's shoulders, and
announced, "Virtue is its own reward."

Melissa responded without a pause, "All the darkness in
the world cannot resist the light of a single candle."

"And what a candle," Arlene laughed. And they kissed
each other's cheeks.

Then Arlene turned to one the clients, a dignified gentleman who, she later told Melissa, sold more toilet tissue that
anyone else in the world. "My long-lost cousin," she said
demurely.

When he rose overeagerly for an introduction, she added,
"But we have years of family news to catch up on," and
pulled Melissa into the first booking room where the two of
them could be alone. She sent the girl from the booking room
out to tend the reception desk.

"You're going to be fired," Melissa said when the door closed.

"Honeysuckle," Arlene said, pointing to a chair, and seating herself on the empty desk, "nothing I do today could get me fired. You have not only resolved your own little problem with Victoria, but literally worked magic in the Krane home. And we are all on the honeymoon. And now," she leaned hungrily forward on the desk, "tell me exactly how you did it."

"I don't even know what you're talking about."

Disappointment inched its way across Arlene's face. "You didn't patch them up?"

"No. I hardly even said hello to him."

"No little homespun advice that made Rory see the light?"

"I couldn't have spent more than thirty seconds with him. He was just coming in as I went out."

"Damn," Arlene said. "It must have been you. You should see her. She's ten years younger. And just glowing with that we-didn't-get-out-of-bed-for-two-days glow."

"Oh, my good Lord," Melissa sputtered. "I can't sit here. I was supposed to see her at one-thirty sharp. She'll kill me."

Arlene's hand shot out, and pushed Melissa back on the chair as she started to rise. "No ma'am. Those two gentlemen out there come first. And two of the girls are sick—or drunk. So I am going to be your mentor for your first day."

She smiled, and Melissa realized it was quite a lovely smile. Then Arlene rubbed her hands greedily together, and chuckled, "You are, me proud beauty, in my power completely."

And the smile disappeared, and Melissa saw the business face of Arlene Conners. It was a serious face, of great intelligence, and she watched the eyes in it study her own face as though it were a sculpture that she was about to remodel.

"Your makeup," Arlene said, "hurts your face as much as it helps it." She opened a drawer in the desk and took out a large mirror. "No face is perfect," she said. "Each has its weak points and its strong points. Beauty is simply a balance in favor of the strong points."

"Here," she said, pointing into the mirror. "You have more than your share of strong points, but that doesn't mean you know how to bring them out. Your cheekbones," she went on, tracing the line of their reflection in the mirror, "are extremely exaggerated—the most pronounced I've ever seen —and therefore form the whole structure of what people see when they first look at your face.''

She made a smear on the mirror with her finger, under the cheekbones. ''On other models, we have to add the illusion of such cheekbones with highlighting, like this.'' And then she wiped off the smear with a Kleenex. ''But with you there's no need to do that. You have them, but you're hiding them—with rouge, like this.''

She took another Kleenex, and began rubbing it softly and precisely against Melissa's cheeks, erasing the rouge. Then she took a makeup kit out of another drawer, and repaired the erasures. Melissa involuntarily took in her breath, when she saw how her cheekbones now soared up from the bottom of her face, and how much brighter and larger her eyes had automatically become.

''This is not gilding the lily,'' Arlene said. ''It's giving nature's own genius its full chance to be seen. Now,'' she went on, ''your second strong point is, of course, your eyes. I'm not a real makeup artist and I don't pretend to be—we'll send you to one tomorrow or the next day—but I want you to get an idea right now of what your face really looks like—the face you've always had, but never seen.''

She worked for a few precise minutes on Melissa's eyes, and again they seemed to have grown till it was almost impossible to focus on anything else in the mirror.

''Now you're beginning to look like a professional,'' Arlene said, feeling the old pain beginning to seep back again, as she made the beautiful more beautiful, and had, at the same time, to watch her own face in the mirror with it. But her voice never lost its crispness as she went on. ''Your third strong point is your hair, but that will be taken care of in a few days. Your skin is good too, but you have no idea now of how to make it look like porcelain—so smooth that people will want to rub their fingers against the magazine page when they see your photo on it.''

She put both hands on Melissa's shoulders, and squeezed, and sighed. This was always the critical moment for the girls, the watershed that separated the winners from the losers. ''But now nature takes her revenge, and she's played a few tricks on you.'' Her finger touched the mirror. ''See this?'' she said. ''The upper part of your nose has a wide bridge—

right here. The camera won't like that. So we're going to do a little plastic surgery''—she reached back down into the makeup kit—''with a glorious little invention you've probably never even heard of, called shading. And we apply it here . . and here . . . and the camera will never even see that bump. Right?''

Melissa's heart was beginning to pound with excitement. ''I can't believe it,'' she said. ''You're a miracle worker.''

So far, so good, Arlene thought. ''Nonsense,'' she said. ''Wait till you see what a real professional can do for you. But,'' she smiled, ''it isn't bad. Cost you a thousand dollars in Hollywood. We do it for half a penny.''

''I want some of that.''

''You'll have all you need. When you go on a trip, honey, you'll pack it before you put in the pill.''

Melissa turned pink from her shoulders to her hair. Arlene made a mental note that the woman was truly naïve, and that this was going to cause discomfort when she started going out into the model's world. She had to be shielded a little. And, Arlene thought, I guess I'm nominated.

''Now smile,'' Arlene said.

Melissa pulled back her lips self-consciously.

''Your teeth are not terribly good,'' she said bluntly, and then waited. No reaction—the girl had already seen it and admitted it. ''So you have to do one of two things. You can have them fixed,'' and she saw Melissa wince, ''or you can learn how to hold your face for the camera, so that your smile is so overwhelming, your teeth don't matter.''

Melissa looked up bewildered. ''There are certain angles,'' Arlene added, ''camera angles, that you're just not going to be able to allow. And you have to learn those angles now, and never let the camera trap you in them. All right?''

''All right,'' Melissa said at once. ''Show me.''

''No. Not now. Later, when you get in front of the camera, where it counts.'' Arlene relaxed. It was all systems go. No ego-blindness at all. The rest was sheer detail, and hard work.

''Your hip bones are a little wide,'' she said almost absentmindedly, ''but we can compensate for that easily. However, honey-child,'' she smiled, and the business face vanished, ''on the whole, you are a real package. And now let's put the wrapping on it.'' She looked at her watch. ''You have your first shooting in exactly one hour. But first we've got to get you on our charts. Come, my leetle butterfly.''

Now Arlene took her into the working heart of the agency. This was the chart room, the booking room, the assignment room. Here Melissa was plopped down in a hard wooden chair, and all her vital data squeezed out of her in a half hour's inquisition—every measurement, from her foot to her hat size, every sport she had every played, every hobby, every "activity," from looking real with a martini to looking real with a cigarette to looking real with a sunburned man.

Melissa had never dreamed she had so many qualitites to be analyzed, and recorded, and sold. Good legs, good hair, good hands, good skin, good nails, good smile, good shoulders . . .

Then she had the enormous joy of seeing her name hand-lettered in the "daily" chart. This, she was carefully and forcefully told, was the way the agency kept track of her, every single hour of every single working day. Here were entered her "tests," her "interviews," her "go-sees," her "bookings." Here was the control-center of her life, from this moment on. Here was the source of all contact, all fame, all money—the umbilical cord that she had to hook up to in order to learn what adventures, what opportunities, what drudgeries, and what performances were expected of her the next day.

Forty-five minutes later, she was back in Arlene's room—now a documented product. "You're on your way, honey," Arlene said, "to your first clandestine assignation with a photographer. We're going to let his camera lap you up, and then we're going to sell that beautiful face to a million magazines."

"Will you go with me?" Melissa asked at once.

"No, ma'am." The answer was immediate. "You have to get used to running around town by yourself. And to dealing with that strange breed of animal called photographers—all by yourself."

She scribbled an address on the back of one of the agency cards. "Have you got any money?" she asked.

"Plenty."

"Okay. His name is Henry Jackson. He's good. He'll work with you for about an hour. Then come back here."

"Right, boss," Melissa said, practically skipping to the door.

"One small point," Arlene said nonchalantly.

"What?"

"He . . . uh . . . talks dirty."

"Oh?"

"That's the way he gets his jollies. He's a verbal flasher . . . do you know what I mean?"

"No. Not really."

"Then look," and Arlene's face broke into an enormous leer, "just forget everything he suggests. Don't listen to a word of it. Because, baby, even if you said yes, he couldn't find it. And even if he found it, you couldn't feel it."

Melissa turned beet-red again, sputtered for a moment, and then fumbled her way out the door.

Arlene leaned against the desk, and laughed. It's going to be hard, she thought, to keep from pushing that blush-button every so often, just to see if it's still there.

11.

The room was huge and bare. Against the back wall was a sheet of pure white paper, about twelve feet wide, that stretched down to the floor, and then across the floor to the camera. It was anchored at both ends and in the middle by bricks. And then there were lights everwhere, strange looking lights she had never seen before, and pure white silk screens and umbrellas to reflect those lights.

A young girl, about eighteen, had opened the door. She was wearing a black sweater and a tight skirt. Her hair was cut only an inch long and was pasted down in black wisps over her forehead. She had no shoes on, just stockings.

"You're the new one from Victoria," she said. "You're early."

"I'm sorry. I don't know how to judge . . ."

"Come in. Sit down. Henry'll be with you in a minute." She padded away, leaving Melissa to close the metal door.

A middle-aged man who looked as though he'd been glued together out of marshmallows, was bending over the camera. He was shooting a tall, thin, dark-haired girl wearing a bikini bathing suit. Melissa stood enchanted, watching the girl flow from one elegant, then sexy, then naive, then athletic pose to another. Each pose was held for less than five seconds before she would melt into a completely different one for the next *pop* of the lights and the next *click* of the camera.

And then the posing-dance was done. The marshmallow man straightened up, and the glaring lights went off. The huge studio seemed dull and dark, and the girl seemed nothing more nor less than tired.

"You're a winner, baby," Jackson said. "They'll come all over the contacts."

"Is that it?" the girl asked.

"Unless you'd like to play after."

"Sure," she said, and walked off the paper, stepped into slippers, and then disappeared into the dressing room.

"Felicia," Jackson said, "get me some coffee." He turned and looked at Melissa. He had rather pink eyes and a tired face—not threatening, almost gentle. "You're pretty," he said.

"Thank you." Melissa somehow knew it was a huge compliment.

He sat down in the chair next to her. His smile was also gentle. "Have you ever done a shooting before?"

"'Fraid not."

"Are you Southern?"

"Houston."

"I like Texas. It's always summer there." He took a sip of his coffee. "There's nothing to this," he said. "It's just like having your picture taken by your boyfriend, except we don't get the sun in your eyes."

She laughed.

"And we teach you how to be smarter about posing for those pictures."

"How?"

"By helping you find your proper faces."

"I don't understand."

"You will. Do you want to try it? Nothing much will count here today, so you can relax and kind of enjoy it. Okay?"

"Fine."

"Just walk over there and sit down on the chair my young friend has prepared for you. All we're going to do is take head shots today, so don't worry about your clothes. Okay?"

"Fine," she said again.

"Felicia," Jackson said, "take off her jacket, please." He began adjusting lights and umbrellas. "Good. And unbutton the top two buttons on her blouse."

"You *are* pretty," he said, looking down into the top of his camera. "You're prettier in glass than you are in flesh, and that's what makes a model."

For the first time in her life, Melissa felt the hot lights of a studio reflect off the surface of her face. She could feel the glow move back and forth, up and down her cheeks, as he adjusted the screens, the umbrellas, the huge tin lights. It was as though he were a makeup artist, and was using light as his cosmetic. She held her head rather stiffly, not quite knowing where to put her face, feeling intense self-consciousness, and then the warm glow of vanity, as this skilled man began to study and refine the image he was creating out of her face.

"Turn slowly left, please," he said. "Slowly." There was still no movement of his finger on the camera. So far the images were all in his eyes. He was seeing the dozens of photographs, perhaps even the hundreds and thousands of photographs soon to come.

"Now turn your body around in the chair, and face the other side." He adjusted the camera slightly. She could almost feel its motion as he tilted it up slightly.

"Good," he said. "Now we can shoot."

"What do I do?" she asked, still not knowing where to look.

"You make faces," he answered softly, "just like you did when you were a kid. But this time you learn what feeling makes what face. And every time you want to show that face, you just pull out that feeling."

"I don't know how to do that."

"I'm going to teach you," he said. "There are only a few commercial faces, maybe eight or ten. And I bet I can get you to show every one of them before you leave here today."

"Can you really?"

"Sure. But if I do . . . what'll you give me?"

She froze. Her entire body went rigid. And he smiled.

"A stick of chewing gum?" he asked.

She looked at the girl leaning against the far wall with her arms crossed. Her expression was one of sheer boredom. Nothing was going on. Nothing but New York kidding.

"Is that all?" Melissa asked.

"Sure," he said.

"Even two sticks if you teach me well," she replied.

The lights went *pop*, and her eyes were blinded for five seconds, and then he asked, "Are you okay?"

"Yes," she said. "Just surprised."

"That's the first thing you've got to get used to. Pretty soon you won't even see it. Here we go again." And there was another *pop*. "Once more," he said. And another *pop*. This time her eyes recovered almost immediately, and there was no jolt in her body at all.

"Good," he said. "You were born for the camera. Now you're going to start making feelings. And the feelings are going to start making faces."

She waited stiffly, not quite knowing how to make a feeling.

"Let's start with sweet," he said. "What's the sweetest thing you know?"

She thought a moment, flashed past food, and then realized that she'd been away from home for almost two weeks now. "My son," she said.

"That's nice. He must be pretty young."

"Two and a half."

"I said sweet, not sad," he said coaxingly. "Tell me, do you like to bite him . . . every so often, when nobody's looking?"

"Yes," she admitted.

"Where?"

She smiled. "On the neck."

The lights went *pop*, and she heard the click of the camera. "That's your sweet face," he said. "That's what you think about when you want to look sweet."

She turned her face slightly, and stared in astonishment at him. She could see the pudgy body crouched over the camera, and the little fuzzy bald spot at the top of his head. She knew he was smiling at her through the lens, and she knew that he was proud of himself.

"Now let's do it over and over again, till it becomes automatic. I want you to think about that little pink shoulder meeting that little pink neck. Think about leaning over, ever so gently, and . . ."

The lights *popped* again. The camera clicked. And she froze her muscles in place the way they were when the click came, and she memorized the feeling of those muscles.

"Perfect," he said, his voice sharpened slightly with surprise. "Now turn your head around, and see if you can give me the same look on the other side."

She turned slowly, purposely thinking of Little John's sweet chubby neck, and then she felt the muscles of her face snap into place again, and she heard the camera click.

He straightened up, and took a slow lingering sip of coffee. "You're smart," he said, his voice not quite so gentle now. "Most girls take ten or fifteen run-throughs at *least*, to get a new face down pat." He put down the coffee mug and adjusted the lights slightly. "It's almost frightening to see someone that pretty and that smart." His hand touched the side of the camera, and his fingers began to run up and down over its dimpled black surface. "What face will we do now? Any suggestions?"

"Not a one," she said immediately, eager to get on with the next lesson. "Anything you choose."

"Good. We've done sweet." He bent down again over the camera. "Now why don't we do sexy?"

Her body turned rigid again.

"Half of all the things you sell," he said, "will be sold sexy."

"I guess so," she replied.

"Even refrigerators."

"All right," she said, blinking her eyes just once. "Let's try."

"Good," he said. "That's good. Now—again—you've got to make the feeling before you can make the face. So you'd better tell me what makes you feel sexy, so I can tell it back to you."

"I don't know," she said.

"C'mon now. Sure you do. What makes you feel sexy?"

The lights were beginning to feel hot. "Nothing."

The gentle voice became harsher now. "Something has to turn you on. You're married, aren't you?"

"I suppose so."

The question came exploding out of him. "Is it when he takes off his pants?"

She felt the instant rush of anger. "I don't . . ." she started to object, and then caught herself, still unsure of the rules. "No," she said.

"No," he repeated, "It's certainly not that. You don't look sexy at all. So maybe it's when he puts his hands inside your blouse?"

"No," she said, turning away from the camera.

"You can't do that," he snapped, the voice now strained and coarse. "I can't take pictures of the back of your head.

You can't make any money from pictures of the back of your head.''

She stared for a moment at the white sheet of paper at the rear of the studio. Then, slowly and painfully, she turned her face around again, but she was still not quite able to look at the camera.

"That's a good little girl," the voice said. "You just do exactly what I tell you to do. Now," he went on, "is it when he pulls down your brassiere? Is it when he begins to finger your nipples?"

"Henry!" the girl's voice interrupted suddenly.

"Shut up," he practically screamed.

Melissa's eyes flashed to the girl. Her eyes were wide circles, and her face was dead white. "Henry," she said again, pleadingly, "How about another little sip of coffee?"

"Shut up," the voice behind the camera said, "Or get out."

The girl started to speak again, and then stopped. She looked at Melissa in panic, and Melissa knew that something had gone wrong, something even worse than what Arlene had expected.

"Do you have anything else to say?" the voice behind camera demanded.

"No," the girl said meekly.

"Then we go on with the shooting." His hand was caressing the head of the camera now, perched on top of the tall, gleaming white tripod. Melissa looked at the hand moving up and down on the camera, and she felt a little sick. He was a runaway, she thought. All her life, she'd been dealing with runaways. Men who couldn't control themselves when they got around her. Teachers, starting when she was ten, who kept her after school, and then tried to convince her that she was bad and had to be spanked. Bosses, who couldn't keep their hands off her, even when other people, including their own bosses, were around. Men at parties who wouldn't go away, who kept trying to squeeze her to death on dance floors, who kept trying to press their knees against hers on couches, who kept begging to take her home, to meet her for lunch, to agree on a time when they could call her, even though Johnny was watching them across the floor.

This man is a runaway, she thought. Out of control, and the girl knows it. Going so far that . . . what?

His voice began droning again from the camera. "How

about when he slides his hand down your belly?'' it said. ''Does that turn you on?''

''No,'' she replied calmly, suddenly gaining the answer. He was attacking one of Victoria's girls. He'd just been cute-dirty before, but now he was being savage-dirty, and the girl was afraid that Melissa would go back and tell Victoria, and that Victoria would cut him off from ever photographing any more of her girls. He was going to cut his own throat, Melissa thought, and the girl knew it. And all Melissa would bring back from her first shooting was—not photos, but trouble. And she knew that she couldn't let that happen. She had to stop this man. She had to get this man out of trouble, if only because he had shown her how to find her own sweet face. And she wanted her other faces out of that camera. Even her sexy face.

''When he does that,'' the voice said, ''do you reach out and—''

''You're way off track,'' she blurted out. ''All that man-stuff doesn't make me feel sexy at all.'' And she felt her lips curl into a strange smile. ''You're just turning me off.''

She watched his face come up from the camera. ''Really?'' he said.

The smile on her face spread. It turned as wicked as Arlene's smile. ''Do you want to know what really makes me sexy?'' she whispered.

He looked at his assistant. Then he smiled, and put his hand on the camera again, and bent down. ''Tell me,'' he whined.

''If I do,'' she said, ''then will you take all the pictures of me that I want?''

''Dozens of them.''

''Really?''

''Anything you want . . . tell me.''

''What really makes me sexy,'' she said, and she could feel the muscles of her face flowing into sensuous new shapes and patterns, ''is pecan pie.''

There was dead silence in the studio for a moment. Then she went on. ''Pecan pie,'' she purred, ''half an inch high. With the crust so thick that it cracks when you press the fork into it. And with the pecans shining on the raisins and the fork, when you lift it up and start to slide it into your mouth.''

The lights *popped*, and the camera clicked. She felt the first imaginary bite of the pie touch her tongue, and the camera clicked again. And then she turned the imaginary pie around, and began cutting into the back end of it first, and the camera kept clicking . . . and clicking . . . and clicking.

From behind the camera there came a man's giggle. And then his voice—the gentle voice—saying, "You bitch." And she let her mind go from the pie to Johnny, and pulled down his pants like the man said, and reached out her hand . . . and the clicking got faster, and faster, and faster.

"Wait," Henry's voice pleaded from the galaxy of popping lights. "We're out of film. Freeze. Get another piece of pie."

The girl rushed in with another camera. The world had righted itself again. And Henry's voice came floating to her from behind the lights: "For Christ's sake . . . don't lose that face!"

12.

But the skyrocket really took off three days after Melissa went to work for the agency.

Once the contact sheets came in from Henry Jackson, Victoria realized that, though she'd recognized gold in the flesh, what she actually had in the glossies was diamonds. Henry was a magician, and the girl had poses, and looks, and emotions that translated themselves through camera to paper, and that would sell millions of dollars worth of goods. The only remaining problem was to polish her, to remove even the slightest hint of a flaw from her face, her hair, her body, and her hands. She had to be made photo-perfect, and this required the efforts of a group of specialists.

"Where do we start?" Victoria asked Arlene, as they studied the contact sheets together.

"By getting her out of church," was the instant answer.

"You're right," and Victoria's nail tapped one of the most incongruous prints. "That hair style has to go."

"She could melt steel with that look," Arlene quipped, "but the hair makes you feel like she's screwing in the front pew."

"Reginald?"

"The best. Reginald. Tomorrow."

"Set it up."

"Melissa, my precious," Arlene chanted when she'd reached her on the phone. "Prepare thyself. You are about to be sheared."

And so at nine-thirty the next morning Melissa was sitting in New York fashion's holy of holies, the perfumed private styling room of Reginald himself. For the first half hour nothing touched her hair but his genius hands—judging, measuring, shaping, suggesting, correcting, reshaping. Melissa sat hypnotized as she watched the procession of styles parade across the top and sides of her head—and the different faces that each new style, in its turn, produced in the mirror in front of them. Several times she wanted to cry out, "Stop there," or, "That one's perfect," but the long, womanlike hands moved on, and an even more dazzling shape, and an even more exquisite face emerged within the precise circle of those wizard fingers.

Finally he paused, his eyes glowing at the ring of gold that now surrounded her cheeks, her chin, and her shoulders. Their eyes met in the mirror. He questioned her without a word, and she nodded wonderingly. They were conspirators in beauty, accessories in a divine illusion. He smiled—an androgynous smile that adores itself in its own creation, and bent her head forward into the basin, and began to play the hose into her hair, to wash away the mediocre and the provincial from it forever.

An hour and a half later, the final shape was glowing back at her from the mirror, a pure, simple flow of hair that looked completely natural. She had no way of knowing it, but he had spent more time with her that morning than he had ever spent with Mrs. Whitney or Mrs. Rockefeller. Reginald was twice a genius; his merchandising mind was as talented as his artist's hands. And he saw in this new face, in this exquisite natural bouquet of hair, a new image for his salons that would capture the desire of hundreds upon hundreds of the country's best-kept women. And so, when he sent her out into the street again, after a genuinely affectionate kiss on the cheek, and one final, lingering look at his own creation, he picked up the phone and called Victoria.

"Is everything all right?" she asked. "Did she get there on time?"

"Yes. She just left," he said.

"Really." Victoria glanced at her desk clock, measured the amount of priceless extra time he had spent with Melissa, and waited breathlessly for the payoff.

"I think you'll be delighted," he said.

"I have no doubt I will be."

His voice hardened. There was no trace of the homosexual now, only the businessman.

"I want her. Tomorrow. For a whole new series."

"Local or national?"

"*Vogue*. *Harper's Bazaar*. The works."

Incredible, Victoria thought. Impossible. It just doesn't happen. Not in this business. "On what terms?" she asked.

"Exclusive. A year's contract."

"No."

"For hair."

She held her breath. Thought of the twenty new Reginald salons that were about to open throughout the country. Estimated one hundred and fifty thousand dollars apiece. Threw in half a million to a million dollars more for advertising. And then decided to ask for the moon.

"Fifty dollars an hour," she said.

She heard him take in his breath. "You're insane."

"Seven hours maximum," she went on, her tone as flat as the top of a steel table. "Three hundred and fifty dollars a day tops if she goes on location." She paused, and listened to the silence. "The extra hours you can have as a token of our appreciation."

"This is ridiculous. She's never even worked before."

"Exclusive only for hair. And only for six months, not a year."

"No!" the voice boomed over the phone.

"Fine," she replied, "It's your choice. Send us a bill for this morning. Put in the extra time you worked on her."

She put down the phone gently, and counted. She sat at her desk and studied the small Degas drawing on the wall, and counted past fifty. When she reached one hundred and twenty, the phone rang again.

"Only Wilhelmena gets that much," he pleaded.

"And she's worth every penny of it. So is this girl. And you know it."

"Forty," he said. "No new girl has ever got that much before."

"Reggie," she said, "I don't negotiate. Shall I put down the phone again?"

Again, silence. Again she studied the Degas, and counted. When she reached eleven, he said, "You're a brigand."

She smiled. "You'll get most of it back from us on the other girls. You'll just take an hour longer with each one of them."

"Two hours," he chuckled. "And their hair will come out purple. When do we start shooting?"

"Tomorrow, as you wished."

"Nine-thirty. At Cleon's."

Now it was her turn to catch her breath. At Cleon's, no less. A thousand dollars a photograph. She should have asked for sixty dollars an hour. She put the phone down slowly, and looked again at the Degas. There was a mate to it at Hammer that she'd admired for months.

"Arlene," she said into the intercom, "get me Victor Hammer on the phone. And when I get through with him, come on in. I've got a fairy tale for you that you just won't believe."

13.

Ever since she was a teenager, Melissa Johnson had peered through a tiny peephole, called *Vogue* magazine, into a gold and silver and diamond world that she never quite believed existed. In this heaven-world, all the women were young and beautiful, all the men were handsome and rich, and all their clothes, and their houses, and their jewelry, and their cars, had been made by angels.

And now, at the scratch of a pen across the bottom of a contract, she herself was transported into that world, and set at its center. Just one day after Reginald had shaped her into his alter ego, she walked into a photographer's studio that made Henry Jackson's brick-lined working space look like a hovel. It was a dream-factory so vast that an entire dining room could be contained in just one of its corners. It was peopled by over thirty men and women, who had no other goal except the creation of the perfect illusion. And when she arrived there the first morning and found Victoria herself waiting, she realized immediately the supreme importance of the occasion.

The first hour was occupied by Reginald's working again, tirelessly, on her hair. Victoria sat watching, as fiercely focused as he, never letting her gaze move an inch from Melissa's head.

Then it was done, and he snapped his fingers, and a short dark swarthy man, dressed in a brown cashmere sweater, came over. He studied Melissa intensely, dispassionately, his face seemingly all eyes, his mouth closed tightly in a mass of wrinkles. He circled her slowly, five or six times. And then the small dark face broke into a radiant smile, and he turned to Victoria and Reginald, and said simply, "Superb."

"We'll start with the tea shot," Reginald said.

"Of course. Let me show you what I've done."

They walked away, and a girl in her twenties came and took off Melissa's skirt and blouse. "Your shoes too," she said.

Behind her, another girl was wheeling in a portable clothes rack, and Victoria and the first girl thumbed through a line of sports outfits, till Victoria found exactly the one she wanted. It was a beige tailored skirt, and a V-shaped sweater—extremely simple, extremely chic. Melissa couldn't believe for a moment that wool could be that soft, or feel—yes, feel—so expensive against her skin, or be given color so much like that of a just-opened flower.

"How much does it cost?" she asked Victoria.

"Two hundred dollars."

As much as five complete outfits at home—just for a sweater. It was a foreign world.

Victoria studied the expression on her face, and then asked, "Is it worth it?"

Melissa stared back at her for an instant—the feel of the sweater struggling with twenty-six years of being a carpenter's daughter. And then she said, without guilt or remorse, "Yes."

"Good," Victoria replied.

"Does everything in this city cost this much?"

"No," Victoria said, "only the best. For some people, only the best will do."

Melissa instinctively moved her shoulders, so she could

feel the sweater against them. "Will I be one of them?"

"Possibly. If you work hard, and learn," she said, as the next person approached them. Melissa quickly put on the skirt and shoes.

The man who joined them was small and pudgy, exquisitely dressed, and carried a large velvet case. He placed it on the table before them, opened it, and started taking out small velvet bags.

The first bag contained a diamond ring. The man took Melissa's hand, removed her gold wedding band, and slipped the diamond ring on her finger. It fit perfectly.

"It's a four-carat ring from Harry Winston," Victoria said before Melissa could ask the question. "Winston is the best jeweler in New York." She brought the light on the table closer to Melissa's hand. "It's a pear-shaped cut, just coming into style. A flawless blue-white diamond like this sells for fifty thousand dollars."

"My good Lord," Melissa said. "Aren't they afraid I'll lose it?"

"No, not in the slightest."

The man opened the second velvet bag, and took out a green wedding band.

"This is jade," Victoria said, "carved in China about two centuries ago. We could have used a diamond wedding band, but it would have been too ostentatious—flashy—with the other ring. The woman you'll be today, the woman who's going to sit in front of that camera and stare out at millions of other women all over America, would never wear a diamond band with a diamond ring that large. You've got to learn how she feels, so you can make other women want to feel that way too."

The third bag was opened, and a bracelet of midnight blue enamel, and tiny gold stars set in that field of blue, was slipped on the wrist of Melissa's right arm.

"Czarist Russia. Made about 1910, and probably worn by a duchess till 1917. The name of the man who did it was Fabergé. It took almost a year to make, and it's possible that someone either risked, or lost, his life getting it out of Russia. By the time your son is as tall as you are, there will be no more in the world to buy."

"And women wear things like these . . . with sweaters?"

"In this world, yes. But remember, they do it with infinite grace. So the jewelry belongs with those sweaters."

"Are you ready?" Reginald called out impatiently.

"Of course," Victoria answered, and lead Melissa into the first setup.

It was the corner of a Georgian dining room, perfect in every detail. The walnut paneling had been shined and polished. A single chair was drawn up to a dark brown table, and on the table was a silver tea set, along with two delicate china cups. Behind the table, in front of the paneling, was a large breakfront, crowned by a vase filled with flowers.

As soon as Melissa sat down on the chair, person after person began fussing around her. The wardrobe girls corrected every crease and line in her sweater and skirt. The makeup man retouched her face four separate times in response to the new, subtle lightings that Cleon was arranging on every side of her. Reginald shot in and out every five minutes, not quite satisfied with her hair. And Cleon spent as much time fussing with the flowers and her jewelry as he did behind the camera.

Melissa looked at Victoria though the haze of studio lights. "Is everything here real?" she asked.

"Even the paneling."

"But doesn't it cost a fortune to rent?"

"Of course."

"But why? Couldn't they have used something . . . newer?"

Cleon stopped his efforts for a moment and looked down at her, his brown eyes bright when he smiled. "And therefore—less expensive?" he asked in his French accent.

"Yes," she said, slightly flustered.

"But this world, here," and he waved his hand to embrace the entire set, "does not know the meaning of price. Only quality. And we want to bring you, and all the women you stand for, into that world of quality."

"But would they ever know if it wasn't real?"

He laughed, and there was a strange music, and a strange wisdom in his laughter. "My dear beautiful youngster," he said. "Do you know who Sarah Bernhardt was?"

"Not really," she admitted, rigid with self-consciousness, knowing that the entire production had stopped, and every man and woman in the studio was staring at them.

"Sarah Bernhardt was the greatest actress of her age, at the beginning of this century. And she had the genius to find a producer for her plays, who was as great in his way as she was in hers."

He removed one of the flowers from the vase, and handed

it to an assistant. "One year, in 1906," he said, "the producer cast her in a new role, as the Czarina of Russia. But the
play didn't go well in rehearsal, and Bernhardt refused to catch
fire in the role. So do you know what he did? The night of the
final dress rehearsal, he went out and bought the finest ermine
cape in the world. It cost, in 1906, mind you, twenty-five
thousand dollars. And when Bernhardt stepped on the stage
that evening, he wrapped her in the cape. And then he went
back to the first row of the theater, and sat next to the
director. And the director asked him the same question you've
just asked me. Why, when it cost twenty-five thousand
dollars, did the cape have to be real?"

Cleon moved back to the camera, and again studied the set
through its single, universal eye. "And," he went on, "the
producer said, without hesitation, 'Because the moment I put
it on her shoulders, she knew that the cape was real, and
therefore that the role was real. And tomorrow the audience
will know that both of them are real. And soon the world will
know that they are real.' "

He began to move the people around him into position for
the shooting. Melissa watched Reginald and Victoria fade
silently behind the lights as a new vision began to give wings
to their dream. She heard the first test *poppings* of the lights.

"Now, beautiful one," he said, "I have put my cape on
your shoulders. It is real. Now, become for me, and for the
world, equally as real."

Melissa looked into the camera, and reached for the first
cup and the teapot, and felt the muscles of her body and her
face flow into an attitude and an expression that matched the
new world that surrounded her. She heard the click of the
camera, and the reaction of the audience behind that camera,
welcome her into that world, as their young, but equal peer.

14.

The first full week of shooting had been heavenly. They
had proceded from one magnificent set to another. There was
the ballroom scene, with its gown that was hand-embroidered

in pure gold. The riding scene, where for the the first time she felt the excitement of leather boots, and the power and strength of a thoroughbred horse, even though it was made to stand still underneath her. The afternoon shopping scene, and the white silk suit that had been made to order for her. The beach scene, and the delicious feeling of getting slowly drunk on Dom Perignon, as Cleon had bottle after bottle opened to get the right iced effect, and she sipped glass after glass until he was finally satisfied that not a single detail was wrong.

Every little girl had played this most glorious game in the world with dolls. For one full week in August 1961, Melissa Johnson played it with reality. And, when it was all over, the most amazing part of all was that she was paid—actually paid, simply for loving every minute of it.

The day after the shooting had ended, the first day for a week that she had been allowed to sleep late, she was paged on the hall phone at the YWCA by Arlene, and told to report to the agency at one o'clock.

When she arrived, there was no one there, except a leering Arlene, and a fat brown envelope.

Arlene picked up one edge of the envelope and wriggled it back and forth, so that it crinkled.

"Hear that sound?" she asked. "It's the prettiest sound in the world. Better than opera or symphonies. It's called money."

"Money?" Melissa repeated blankly.

"Uh . . . you get paid. The fifty dollars a week we've been advancing you—that's not what you earn. That's a token of good faith."

She crinkled the envelope again, slightly faster. "This is what you earned, my love. Last week. Nine hundred and fifty dollars. You are in miracle city. You are the genie's beloved." She handed the envelope to Melissa.

Melissa looked at it, felt the weight of it in her hand. She could say nothing.

"Open it," Arlene chirped. "Go ahead. Ordinarily, we pay by check. But just this once, the first time, I kind of felt that you'd like to see it as cash . . . and touch how much you're really worth. Besides," and she herself was getting a little embarrassed now, "the bank's right downstairs, and it's open."

Melissa's hands trembled as she pulled out the thick cluster of new bills, as she tried to separate one crisp twenty from another, as she saw, for the first time in her life, what a one hundred dollar bill actually looked like.

''I thought you'd like one of those,'' Arlene said. ''Why don't you carry it with you, as mad money.''

''Does anybody . . . take it?''

''Try it on people. You'll find out awfully quick.''

Melissa held the money in her hand, unwilling to put it away again. ''I don't know what to do with it,'' she said. ''Well, first I'll pay Johnny back—that's two hundred dollars. And then I'll send two hundred dollars down to run the house this month.'' Her face suddenly glowed. ''And then I'll open a bank account for Little John for a hundred dollars—for college. And then I'll put another hundred dollars in a different account—for a rainy day.''

Arlene shook her head and smiled. ''That's only six hundred.''

''That means I've got three-fifty left.''

''Yes, my love, you have three-fifty left.''

''Goodness.''

''Gracious.''

''I don't know what to do. Should I put the rest of it in the bank too?''

''It's one week's income.''

''But that was a special week.''

''You should see the list of clients we have waiting. You'd better do nothing Saturday and Sunday but sleep.''

There was a pregnant pause. Then Melissa stuffed the money into the handbag, spun around, and practically sprinted to the door.

''What did you decide?'' Arlene shouted after her.

''Saks,'' echoed back the answer from the hall. ''Bergdorf's.'' And, as the the elevator door opened, ''Tiffany's.''

Four hours later, weighted down, drunk with happiness, Melissa arrived at her closetlike room at the ''Y'' and dumped the five packages on her little bed.

Three sixty dollar silk blouses from Saks. A calf's leather bag from Bergdor's. And a silver bracelet from Tiffany's. She'd run out of money before she'd even thought of getting a skirt good enough to wear with the blouses.

She sat down on the single, rickety chair. Oh well, she thought, next week I'll get the skirt. And then . . .

But then was next week. Right now, she had a call to

make. A call to Johnny, and Little John, to let them know that it was Christmas in August.

She had called collect every other night since she had joined the agency. But she'd never had news like this. And she certainly couldn't talk about it in the hall, where she had made the other calls. So she slipped on her shoes again, carefully locked her door, and went down the street to the pay phones at Horn & Hardart.

God, she thought, as her finger began dialing for the operator, she could hardly wait to tell him. It was the end of their worries, forever.

Johnny was home. And Little John, too, of course. First she spent several minutes cooing at her son, trying to decipher what he was burbling at her, hurting a little inside—even now, even with all the excitement—because all she could touch was the phone.

Then Johnny took the phone away from the child, and his voice boomed at her again. "Hi."

"Hi."

"Love me?"

"Sure do."

"Been a good girl?"

There was a split-second pause in her voice as she thought of the shopping spree, but she didn't dare feel guilty, and she didn't dare let her voice change as she shot back, "Sure have."

"Still on that big fancy job?"

"Nope. It's over for a while."

"So what'd you do today?"

She smiled. "Something," she said teasingly.

"Good?" he asked, and she knew he was smiling.

"Real good," she said.

"New client?"

"Nope. Better than that."

He laughed. "New hat?"

"No, silly," she said. "Lots better than that. I got paid."

"Good," he said like a shot. "Glad to hear they pay you up there." His voice was still grinning. "Send it all down. We sure as hell need it."

"It was a lot of money," she said. Now she was beginning to quiver in anticipation.

"Really? More than you got in the store?"

"Stop kidding," she whined. "Lots more."

"Two hundred?" he asked. "Cash?"

"Nine hundred and fifty," she said. "Cash."

She waited. But nothing happened. No sound at all. She thought maybe the phone had been cut off, but there was no click. "Johnny?" she asked.

"Yeah." His voice sounded suddenly far away.

"Did you hear what I said?"

"Yeah," he said. "I heard you."

"Well, what do you . . . think?" she pleaded.

"That's nice," he said. "That's . . . real nice."

"I sent you back your two hundred dollars," she said hurriedly. "Then I sent two hundred dollars for the house this month—"

"Thank you," he said.

"And then I opened a bank account for Little John." Somehow she couldn't bring herself to say how much money she'd put in it.

"Nine hundred and fifty dollars?" he asked.

"That's right," she answered. Maybe it hadn't sunk in.

"In a week?"

She thought for a moment. "I guess."

"That's more than I make in two months," he said.

She stared at the phone. She felt trapped in the narrow, hot booth. She looked around her to see if anyone was watching. No one was. "Things are kind of funny up here," she said.

"They sure are," he said, but then he caught himself. "That's good," he said. "That's real good."

"We can do all kinds of new things."

"That's right."

"You and Little John can come up real soon, just as soon as I know that I'll be making this kind of money regular."

"Do you think you'll be making that much money next week?"

"No," she said instantly, and apologetically. "Arlene says it was a once-in-a-lifetime week. I probably won't make half that much next week. But still . . . it's pretty good . . . isn't it?"

"Yeah," he said. "It's pretty damn good."

"Johnny," she said plaintively. "You love me, don't you?" There was a pause. "Sure," he said.

"Say you do."

"I do."

"Say it . . . Please, say it."

"I love you," he said. "I gotta go now. Gotta feed the kid, and get down to the bowling alley. We. . ." He stopped for a moment, then went on. "We're bowling for the league championship tonight. The prize money's forty dollars."

"Good luck," she said. "Go out and kill 'em, champ."

"Yeah. Well, I'll talk to you in a couple of days."

"Johnny," she cried out into the click on the other end. "Johnny," she said again into the silence. And then stood there for a moment, holding the dead phone in her hand, not quite understanding what she had done wrong.

The day had turned into ashes. She stood there with the phone in her hand and began to cry. Across the room, just in front of the men's lavatory, an old unshaven bum was standing against the marble wall, with an unlit cigarette in his mouth.

She stood there in the phone booth, and let him watch her cry.

15.

Johnny Johnson walked away from the phone and opened the refrigerator door. He pulled out a bottle of beer and tore off the cap so hard it soared across the kitchen. He emptied the bottle without stopping, and hurled it into the garbage can. Then he pulled out another one.

He got dinner out of the stove, put Little John on a chair in front of the table, and placed the dinner plate in front of him. Woman's work. He'd been turned into a woman. He poured some milk in Little John's glass. The poor little bastard was scared stiff and Johnny ran his hand roughly through the kid's hair. The old lady would be over in twenty minutes to sit for him. He wasn't going to wait for her. He wanted to get out of there fast.

He went into the bedroom and got the bowling ball. On his bureau was a photograph of Melissa that she'd sent him from New York. He could hardly recognize her. The face still belonged to him, but everything else about her—the makeup, the hair, the clothes, the way she held her head—belonged to New York City.

He picked up the bowling ball in its bag and swung it over his head—once, twice, three times. Then he turned and swung it at her mirror, letting it go for a second and then catching it just before it escaped his fingers. He knew he wanted to continue the game till he couldn't stop the ball anymore. He knew he wanted to hear the crash of the mirror. But the old lady was coming over. So he carried it out the front door and threw it in the back seat of the car.

But he didn't start the engine, not yet. Hell, he thought, the damn car was worth less than nine hundred and fifty dollars, and he still had to work his ass off another year to pay for it. He kicked the dashboard, knocking the glove compartment door open. Then he kicked it closed again, hoping it would fall off.

He was afraid to start the car. He was afraid to put the car in gear, and take off feeling this way. He was beginning to sweat. And he sat there, sweating cold sweat in the steaming hot car.

He stank, he thought. And then he thought of the black-haired one—the one who bowled in the next alley when the men didn't take all the lanes. The one who began to smell after the second game. The one who looked at him all the time. She was a waitress downtown. She'd been married once, and she still wore her wedding band on her right hand. He smiled to himself. She stank and he stank. She was black-haired, and dumb, and she'd been looking at him now for three months.

He rolled down the window of the car, and spit out the window toward the house; then he started the car and screeched off in the direction of the bowling alley.

16.

The rest of the weekend was torment for Melissa. There was no sleep for her in her little prison cell at the ''Y,'' and on Monday morning, when she washed her face and began to apply her makeup, she realized that she looked ten years older. Today was her first shooting for a catalog house, and she thanked heaven that meant full-length photographs of bathrobes and nightgowns.

She ate no breakfast, and no lunch. An hour seemed to pass between each camera click. Finally the afternoon ended. Melissa wanted to flee back to the ''Y,'' but Arlene had said that she wanted to discuss the next day's assignment, and so she went to the office instead. It was so late that only Arlene was still there.

''My God,'' Arlene said immediately, ''what happened to you?''

''Can I use your phone, in the booking room?''

The questioning stopped immediately. ''Of course. Or use the phone in Victoria's office. It's more private.''

''No,'' Melissa said. ''I can't do that. I'll use the booking room.''

She closed the door after her, and walked slowly over to the desk. She put down her bag and stared at the phone for a minute. She had no idea what she was going to say, only that she couldn't live another hour bearing this pain.

She picked up the phone and dialed for the operator.

The conversation lasted only three or four minutes. It was as confusing to her as the one the night before, but absolutely its reverse. He couldn't have been happier to hear from her. Yes, they had won the league championship, by only five pins. Then they had all gone out and got a little swacked, and his head had felt like a basketball all day. He loved her. He was already thinking of ways they could spend the new money. He was proud of her. He couldn't wait to see her again. To get her in bed again. Did she love him? Was she angry because he'd been rushed the night before? Did she really love him? He couldn't wait to get his hands on her again.

His voice was sparkling, and happy, and seductive. Its tone was low, and he fairly growled when he talked about making love to her again. For the first time since she'd been in New York, her body began to come alive at the excitement in his voice. She had to fight that aliveness, because it did her no good at all where she was. And she didn't know what to say to prolong the conversation, to keep that electricity and that happiness pouring through the phone and into her.

Everything was all right again. She had her man. She was whole.

"Hey," he said. "I gotta go now. I gotta get dinner for the kid."

"Kiss him again for me."

"Kiss me, and I'll give it to him for you."

She kissed into the speaker. "I love you," she said slowly, tasting each delicious word as it came out of her mouth.

"I love you," he replied. "When are you going to call again?"

"After the weekend?"

"Too long. Tomorrow. I can't wait that long."

"Tomorrow," she said.

"Tomorrow," he said. And she heard the slow click on the other end.

She sat down. Her legs were weak. She wished she smoked. Or really drank. Or did something to celebrate. She should have known. She shouldn't have been such a little dummy. He was always like a bear before a big game. She always had to handle him with kid gloves then. She'd had so much to say that she hadn't let him talk first.

What kind of wife was she?

And then she began to smile and cry at the same time. When the crying was over, she dabbed at her eyes with her handkerchief. She had to fix her face, and think about what little lies to tell Arlene.

17.

A week later Victoria flew up to Boston to be with her mother during an operation. That same afternoon, a call was left for Melissa, while she was being photographed for a fashion series, that she was to report to the agency after the shooting session was over, no matter how late, to discuss "urgent business" with Arlene.

It was just past seven when she arrived. She pressed the bell; no one answered. She tried the door; it was unlocked.

The reception room was empty, Arlene's desk deserted. The only lights were in Victoria's office.

"Arlene?" she called out.

A man's voice answered. "Come in," he said. "Lock the front door behind you."

Even though she had heard the voice only once before, she recognized it at once. She walked slowly into Victoria's office.

"Would you like a drink?" Victoria's husband said, standing at the bar, his back turned to her.

"No. I don't drink. And I'm not thirsty. Where's Arlene?"

He turned around. Very tall. Very attractive. Very deadly.
"Gone," he said simply.

"And the urgent business that I was brought here for?"

He took a sip from his glass and smiled. "Us."

There was no change of emotion in her face. No shock. No disappointment. She had known it from the evening she met him at his apartment. "Do you do this often?" she asked.

"Never," he replied.

"Of course." Some things were exactly the same in New York as in Houston. "Is there anything else?"

"We could—"

"No. I mean before I walk out?"

"I don't understand. What, for instance?"

"A penalty," she said. "Do I get fired, for instance?"

He slammed the glass down on the bar. He was very big. Very strong. She mentally measured the time it would take her to reach the front door.

"Who the hell do you think you are?" he said.

"A friend of your wife's," she answered immediately.

"And I'm a bastard?"

"Yes."

"Ripping her guts open in public?"

"When you do this with the girls she works with—yes." She turned to leave. The only weapons this one needed to beat up his women were words. There were tears in her eyes now, but she didn't care. She turned around and faced him just once more. "What in the world did she do to you?"

He stared at her for a moment. Then he picked up the glass. "You wouldn't understand."

"I might."

He poured more scotch into the glass. Then he held it up to

one of the ceiling lights and looked at it. A shadow covered his face. "She grew old," he said.

Melissa moved back a step in shock. "You're lying," she said. "You must be lying."

"You see her here in the office," he said, "where the light is precisely controlled. Have you ever seen her in the daytime, in the sun? No. But I do, all the time. And I see her in the morning, without her makeup, when the sun comes streaming through the windows and she wants to make love."

He began dropping ice cubes into the glass. "When I first met her, she had skin like yours. And to make love to her then was to be God in His heaven, and watch spring spread slowly across the earth." He raised the glass, and saluted Melissa. "But she drinks. And she smokes. And she loves the sun. And she got old."

"But everybody does."

"And so will you."

There was no answer. But Melissa heard her own death sentence spoken, for the first time in her life.

He leaned back against the bar. "She was as beautiful as you are," he went on. "And I loved her insatiably. I couldn't get enough of her. Day and night, to make love to that face. To see it become even more beautiful in bed. To—"

"I don't want to hear about that," she said.

He shrugged his shoulders. "To walk down the street with her, and watch the look in other men's eyes, and know that—somehow, impossibly, illogically—she belonged to you. That this incredible face was yours, forever."

He started to reach again for the glass, but stopped his hand. "But forever is a long time. And for beautiful women like that," and he looked at her, "forever hurts. It's not so bad for plain women. You can watch a plain woman grow old, and fat, without much pain. But when an orchid begins to die—"

"Then you begin to die," she said.

Surprise crossed his face. "Yes."

"I don't think the problem is that she's growing old," Melissa said. "It's that her growing old means that you're growing old too."

"Touché."

"You don't feel the pain for her. You feel it for yourself." Her voice became surer now. "You look in the mirror every hour, right?"

"So you're not a child," he said.

"But you are. And Victoria acts as the mirror you can't run away from, doesn't she? You can't be married to an older woman, no matter how beautiful, and still stay young and pretty yourself. Can you?"

"I was wrong," he said quietly. "I don't want to fuck you. I just want to hit you. Till you start bleeding from the mouth."

"You will never," she said, "have the courage to hit anyone, even a woman." She turned and walked toward the door. "But if it's any consolation, I'd like to do the same to you."

With the door to the office closed behind her, and her finger pressing the elevator button, she tried to come to terms with what had happened, and especially with what it said about Victoria's face was true. That magnificent face was growing old far too fast.

And she now realized that every time she had looked at Victoria, it was as though she had looked into a trick mirror, and watched—far too soon—age destroy her own face. And she felt the knife thrust of that realization, and the chill it sent through every cell in her body.

She was only twenty-six, but now she knew that time was like a roller coaster that never went uphill, only down, and only faster and faster.

She stood in the marble hall, insulated as though she were in some strange church, and she made a silent prayer.

I am going to find a way, she thought fervently to herself, to stop old age. I am going to declare war on old age. I am going to beat old age—somehow—some way—not only for myself, but for every woman.

I am. I am.

18.

The next week, Melissa began to buy one medical book after another. Volume after volume on anatomy, physiology, diagnosis, biochemistry, and especially one huge twenty-year-old text on dermatology made their way to her room. Night after night, she would fly home from her modeling assignment, stop off at Horn & Hardart to pick up a quick dinner, and spend three, four, even five hours pondering over the massive pages, studying their colored illustrations, trying desperately to decipher the giant, foreign words that blocked her in every sentence, in every book. She bought a three-pound dictionary, but the definitions of the words she looked up only led to other words that were equally foreign, and equally difficult. By the end of the first week she knew that she couldn't do it alone. She needed expert help, and she had no way of finding and enlisting that help . . . yet.

And so she had lost one battle, for the moment. But at the same time she knew she was losing a far more important battle, one in which she could never afford to surrender. The shield was beginning to crack. The insulation was beginning to wear thin. And her body, the body she had put on ice from the moment she left Houston, was beginning to need again. And want again. And demand again.

For years, ever since she was a teenager, she had built a shield—an invisible wall—around her body and her emotions. She had realized that this was the only way to survive in a world where so many men wanted to take her to bed. And where, if she spoke a single inviting word, or if she gave off the slightest sexual vibration, she might have to wrestle her way out of another catastrophe of misunderstandings. And so she became an expert at turning off her body. And this skill, developed over ten years, had protected her for this entire first month in New York. But now it was crumbling. And she was beginning to lose more and more sleep.

That Friday during a coffee break at a catalog shooting, she was chatting with a stunning red-haired model named Pamela Haas. As they were sipping coffee, Pam suddenly looked up and asked, "Are you doing anything tonight?"

Melissa thought wistfully about the medical books for a moment, and then said, "No. Not really."

"Good," Pam said. "I've got a friend who's taking me out. And he's got a buddy—honey, you wouldn't believe him. Six feet four inches tall, before he steps on his wallet. And ten feet tall after."

Melissa became strangely flustered. She didn't quite know how to reply. Finally, she just stuck out her left hand and said, "I'm sorry. I'm married."

Pan took a bite out of a doughnut. "I know. But he's down South, isn't he?"

"Yes." Melissa knew that she should simply cut the conversation off—dead. Normally, she would have done just that. But the girl was so open, and Melissa was so lonely, that she couldn't block one tiny revelation. "He certainly is," she added.

"How long have you been up here?"

"A month. Thirty-five days."

Pam leaned across the table, then looked around to see if the photographer could hear them. "Good God, honey, aren't you horny?" she whispered.

"No," Melissa answered instantly.

Pam sat back in the chair and looked at her. She put the sandwich down on the plastic plate. "Very," she corrected. "Isn't there anything you can do about it?"

Run, Melissa's mind said. "No," she replied hesitantly.

"If I go a week without it," Pam said sympathetically, "I start climbing walls."

"You're not married?"

"Once. A long time ago. It was a hell of a lot worse than what I'm doing now."

"I'm very much married," Melissa said.

"Nobody cares up here."

"I care up here."

"But it hurts," Pam said.

Melissa shrugged.

"You could go out with us and talk," Pam said. "There's no contract. Nobody's going to try to wrestle you into anything."

"No," Melissa said. "It wouldn't work."

"Why?" Pam leaned forward and touched Melissa's hand. "I don't want to pry," she said. "But I don't really understand. And I would like to know."

It was so hard, Melissa thought. If only she weren't so bad at words.

"Because I belong to someone," she said.

"For how long?"

"For as long, I guess, as there is."

"That's a pretty long time," Pam said.

And then the log jam broke. And the feelings became words. And she told this stranger truths that she had never even dared tell herself.

"My body could do it, but I couldn't," she said. "And the worst thing about it is that it would feel good. I know that it would feel good. But I just couldn't do it."

"But why?"

"Because there's no love, and just body." She looked down at the table. "I'm spoiled," she said. "I've never made love without love. I've only known one man . . . I've only been in bed with one man . . . and I love him, and he loves me. And I don't want to lose that."

"You are spoiled," Pam said, "magnificently. Don't ever lose it—ever—if you can help it."

"I believed what the preacher said. Till death do you part. Nothing else could separate us."

"Then why do you stay up here?"

Melissa blinked in surprise. "To make money, so I can help bring him and my son up here."

"I mean on weekends. Surely you could go down there at least once a month."

"I don't understand."

Pam smiled. "You must make five hundred dollars a week now."

Melissa hesitated. "I guess I have, for the last couple of weeks."

"A round-trip plane ticket to Houston couldn't cost more than a hundred and fifty dollars. You could leave this afternoon, after the shooting. We'll be through early. You could be home by ten"—the smile grew broader—"in bed by eleven. And you could be back here Sunday evening."

Melissa sat there with her mouth open. She had never realized . . . people flew to Houston. *She could be with Johnny tonight.* And she could hold Little John in her arms. She could be home tonight. She could be home.

"I've never flown in a plane," she said.

"You'll like it."

"I don't even know . . . how you get on them."

Pam laughed again. "Honey, don't ever change. Just walk down that hall. See? There's a phone. You call information, and get the number of Delta Airlines. You make your reservation now, and they'll take a check when you get to the airport. Don't even bother to go home and pack—you probably have plenty of clothes down there."

"What'll Johnny say?"

"I think he'll say, thank God."

Melissa reached out and grabbed the woman's hand. "I really can be home tonight?"

"Sure. If you hurry."

Melissa scraped back the chair, and then stopped for a minute. "I love you," she blurted out, and then ran down the hall to the phone.

19.

And at ten o'clock that night he was there at the gate, towering over everyone else in the crowd, glowing like the lights of Houston had glowed when she'd flown into it, jumping up and down like a little boy when she first saw her, waving his arm at her as though she couldn't pick him out of ten million people, and then pushing his way awkwardly to the front of the crowd. He held out his long arms to her as she walked up the ramp, picked her up as though she were made of cotton candy, and just held her there, a foot and a half above the ground, while they squeezed each other, and touched each other's hair, and ran their fingers over each other's faces.

Then he lowered her gently to the ground again, and stood back a little, and just stared at her.

"You haven't kissed me yet," she said, sensing his awkwardness about her New York face. "It's not hard. It's as easy as this." She reached up and kissed him. And they were Johnny's lips. And she was safe again.

Then he bent down quickly and kissed her a second time—his kiss. And then he looked around, a little proud and a little embarrassed, and said, "Do you have any luggage?"

"No, silly," she said. "I just came."

"Good," he said. "Then we can get out of here."

They took each other's hand and walked through the terminal, across the parking lot to the dumpy old car that looked beautiful to her. He slid into the front seat beside her, looked at her for a second in the dark glow of the parking lot lights, and then lunged across the seat to her, and she was in his arms and his tongue was in her mouth and they were touching, and kissing, and caring not at all about the people walking by.

It was when he began to slip his hand beneath her silk blouse that she pushed it away, and reluctantly slid across the seat to the door. "Johnny, there are people all over here," she said.

"I know," he said, leaning back against the seat, pushing with both hands against the steering wheel. And then he laughed—a boyish laugh—and said, "Look at me, would ya. I can't believe it."

And she looked down at his crotch, and saw that his dungarees were almost splitting. And she flushed. She began to feel what she hadn't felt since the last time she'd been home. The swelling. The dampness. The readiness. She looked around the parking lot, to see if anyone was near them. And then she reached out her left hand, very slowly, and let it fit itself over that bulge in those dungarees, and let it squeeze that bulge and feel the strength of its pushing back, and feel the electricity pouring up through that rough fabric. And then his own hand came down desperately on hers, first to squeeze, then to lift her hand against his chest where she could feel the beating of his heart against the hair and bone and hard masculine flesh of that chest.

"We gotta stop," he said. "I'll never make it home."

"God, you feel good," she said.

"It's like you were never gone."

Oh, she thought, it was like I was gone for a million years. But all she said was, "Johnny, get me home. Please."

She threw her left arm around him, and he turned onto the highway. They drove with the wind blowing her hair against his cheek, her hand caressing his left shoulder, and his big right arm rubbing itself up and down between her thighs. They were home in twenty minutes, and within a few seconds more she had thrown open the car door, torn through the kitchen and past Johnny's mother, and was in Little John's room.

He was lying on his stomach, sleeping. In the yellow and pink light of the night lamp, her son's face was turned to one side, his thumb was in his mouth, and his right arm was stretched out, holding a fur bunny. He had new cotton pajamas on, but they were unbuttoned in the back, so that a couple of inches of skin showed between their top and bottom. She stood there, looking at that skin, and she remembered the photographer Henry Jackson asking her what was the sweetest thing in the world. And she said again, silently, into the sleeping quiet of that room, "My son." And she bent forward very gently, and kissed that little island of exposed flesh.

All she wanted to do was cry. Because all the lostness and loneliness that had been locked up inside her in New York was now exposed again in Houston. She had missed one full month of her child's life. There were a thousand smiles that had passed those little lips, that she had never seen. And she wanted to cry for those lost smiles. But she knew that Johnny would want her face intact later on. So she simply bent down again, and kissed the sleeping face, and pulled up the sheet, and then kissed the face again. Tomorrow, my love, she thought.

When she got back to the kitchen, Johnny's mother was gone. He had opened a bottle of beer and was leaning against the refrigerator, drinking from the bottle. He'd been drinking before he came to meet her at the airport—she'd smelled it on his breath, tasted it on his tongue, and it had excited her. The men she'd met in New York didn't drink beer. She didn't think of them as having bodies. Johnny did. And all she could think about now was his body.

"I didn't say hello to your mother," she apologized.

"She understood. I told her I'd want her to leave quick." He looked at her in the kitchen light now, a little shyly. "Does the kid look good?"

"Great," she replied. "Must have grown an inch. You took great care of him."

"Mostly the old lady."

"Gimme a sip." She took the bottle out of his hand, then tipped the top of it slowly into her mouth, and let the beer run down over her tongue and into her throat.

"Tastes good," she whispered, handing him back the bottle, and then leaned over as he took it, and licked the center of his chest. "You taste good," she said.

"You look gorgeous," he said.

She stepped back from him. God, she thought, so does he. She put her hand on her blouse, and undid the first button. "Would you like to see all of me?"

His hand came out and stopped hers. "Not here," he said. "And I'll do it."

"I wasn't thinking of here," she said. "And you can do anything you want."

He motioned to the hall. She walked into the bedroom and turned on the lights. She stopped in the center and turned around, watching Johnny closing the door behind them.

"Do you like what they've done to my face?" she asked.

"I can't believe you," he said.

"This blouse," she went on, "is silk. They only have it in New York. I bought it at Saks Fifth Avenue. Go ahead and touch it."

He reached out and touched the blouse. Then his hand glided down, and she could feel the pressure of his thumb on her nipple.

"I took the bra off in the plane. All you have to do is unbutton it."

"Not yet," he said. "Just stand there. Just let me touch you."

Both hands were touching the blouse now. She felt his fingers trace her shoulder lines through the blouse. Then they came down the arms of the blouse, and stopped, and then ran slowly up the blouse again. Then with his forefingers only, he traced the inside curves of her breasts. And then his whole hands followed them, and he was stroking her breasts from outside the blouse.

Her nipples swelled so tight that she thought they were going to break through the silk. She wanted to throw her arms around him, wanted to drag him down on top of her, onto the bed. But he didn't want that yet. And she wanted him to want her, his way. And so she stood there, and let him swell her breasts, harden her breasts, mold his huge hands to the silk for as long as he wanted to.

"You're prettier than your pictures," he said.

"I'm glad you think so."

He opened one of the buttons at last. He pulled the blouse slightly open, and she could feel the silk slide slowly toward her nipple.

"I'm not going to take it off," he said. "I'm just going to unbutton it and leave it on."

"And then you're going to . . . make love to me in it. Is that what you want?"

"That's right." And the next button came undone. And her left nipple escaped into the air. And then the right nipple. And he pulled the blouse out of the skirt, and opened it completely, and she watched his eyes as he saw both breasts, and as he moved his hands up again and held both breasts.

"I can't believe you," he said.

"I'm real," she said. "And I'm yours."

"Say I can do anything I want with you."

"You can do anything you want with me . . . anything in the world you want."

He unclasped the skirt and let it fall down. It was as though he had never seen her before, as though the slim lines of her legs were a complete surprise to him.

"Kick the skirt away," he said.

She did. She was standing there now in an open silk blouse, and panties. Panties that were already damp.

He put out his hands and touched her thighs. As he came close to her, she could smell his manliness again. She wanted to reach out and bite, or lick, or kiss. But she stood stock still instead, feeling his hands on her thighs, and then his thumbs slipping under the bottoms of her panties. His thumbs began slowly moving toward each other under the panties. She felt them go from skin to hair, and then move slowly across the hair till they met, and then push the panties down beneath them, and spread apart her swelling lips, and begin to slide up and down slowly, along the full length of those lips.

She felt her breath suck in sharply and her vagina contract from the very first second he moved inside her. Her thighs trembled as she opened them further, as she tried to make the thumbs move up deeper from the lips, probe into the emptiness, begin to fill her up again, give her the first hard shock of man she needed so desperately again.

But then he reached down and unbuttoned his shirt, and threw it on the floor behind him. His shoulders were massive, and they were covered by a fine blond down.

"Take the panties off," he said.

"You don't want to do it yourself?"

"No. You do it. Slowly."

She put her hands in the elastic, and pushed down two inches, till the hairline showed. Then she paused, and smiled, and he undid his belt. Then she pushed them down to the middle of her thighs, and she felt them clinging to her, and his gaze clinging to her, and she saw his fly come open, and the white shorts bulge out of the blue denim at her. She let the panties slip to the floor, and lifted them up with the toes of her left leg, and took them in her hand, and tossed them onto the bed in back of her. All she had on now was the open silk blouse. And she felt a hundred times more naked in it than she had ever felt before in her life.

"Come here," he said. "Take down my shorts. Slowly."

His hands were on her shoulders. She could feel the strength of his fingers through the silk. She reached down and took the shorts and pulled them slowly away from the mammoth flesh they were concealing. She saw his own hair come into view under the ridges of muscles, and then she saw his penis being bent down by the shorts as she pushed them down farther and farther, and then she saw the edge of the shorts finally scrape over the very head of the penis, and then snap away from it, and she saw it rise up again free and hard and frightening and magnificent, and she felt Johnny's hands begin to push down on her shoulders, and she felt her own body begin to bend down along with the shorts till she was on one knee in front of him, and her face was only an inch away from it.

"Tell me you'll do anything I want," he said.

"Johnny," she pleaded, suddenly frightened.

"Say you'll do anything I want," he repeated.

"I'll do anything you want."

His hands left her shoulders, and came up to her hair. At first they began stroking the hair, moving through it slowly, feeling its new shape and its new texture. Then they came around to the back of her head, and began slowly drawing that head toward him.

"Johnny." Instinctively, she fought the strength of those demanding hands. "I'm afraid."

"Taste it," his voice whispered down from above her.

She felt his hands on the back of her head grow stronger. She put up her own hand against his thigh, and pushed back. The pressure at the back of her head stopped.

She looked up at him. "If I want to," she said, "I'll do it. And if I do it, I'll do it my own way."

She looked down again, and a lifetime of Biblical teaching flashed before her eyes. She was on her knees, as she'd been on her knees a thousand times in church, as she'd been on her knees the day she and Johnny were married. But now she was at a new altar, and she was being called upon to perform a new sacrament. "Do you take this man," she heard, "to love, honor, and obey." To love—yes. To honor—yes. To obey—yes . . . yes . . . yes.

Her head moved forward—slowly, tenderly. She heard a

gasp of surprise from him. His hands trembled through her hair, then dropped to his sides, and his voice was transformed into a continuous moan, and then the moan became a great masculine scream of surrender, and his entire body shook as though she were holding onto a sapling in a hurricane, and then his hands came up to her hair again, far more gently this time, and he sank down to his knees on the floor beside her and covered her face with kisses and ended up with his tongue inside her mouth, exploring the taste of the two of them mixed up so miraculously together.

They leaned back against the bed, still clasping each other. She put her head on his shoulder and stroked his pounding chest. After a few minutes she said quietly, "Anything you want."

"Including more? Feel," he said, taking her hand and kissing it and then sliding it slowly down his chest and stomach till it reached the warm, wet hardness below. "I can't believe you," he said.

He began kissing her breasts, with the open silk blouse scraping against his cheek. He rolled her back onto the bedroom rug, and moved his body gently over hers. She felt her body take him in, and she felt her flesh contain his strength, and she felt the great circular hidden muscles of her inner body expand to give love for love, and joy for joy, and wildness for wildness. And she knew that her body held wonders that she had never dreamed of, and that one full month of loss and pain was more than made up for by every single stroke of the man who was now beginning to dominate her flesh.

20.

When Melissa awoke the next morning, with the harsh Southern sun streaming in around the shade, and the huge bulk of Johnny breathing noisily next to her, she couldn't help noticing how crude and coarse the bedroom looked.

Thirty-six days before—could it have been that short a time?—she had left this room cleaned and polished. And she had pictured it—and longed for it, and longed for the man who slept with her in it—with almost a child's eyes. With naive eyes. But now she came back to it, only thirty-six days later, with a woman's eyes. Educated eyes.

Now it was no longer Melissa Johnson alone looking at this room. It was Arlene Conners looking at this room, and Victoria Krane looking at this room, and—above all—Cleon looking at this room. And they saw, not the lack of money that had been spent here, but the lack of taste. They saw a room done with love, but not beauty. They saw a room whose walls were lined with imitations of imitations. They saw a room that had been wasted. And, Melissa thought, with a chill as though ice water had been poured into her veins, the room was a symbol of a life—her life—that could have been equally wasted.

She moved silently out of the bed, and out of the room. She fled from the past to the future. Her son was awake, and his arms shot up automatically into an eager circle that her body filled, and she scooped him off the floor, and spun him round and round and round, pressing him gently to her, and then sat down on the floor with him standing in her lap, and the two of them kissing each other, and his hands exploring her face, and words—words that she had never heard from him before—coming out of that sweet small mouth.

They played for an hour before his father woke up. Then the three of them had breakfast together, and got in the car and went for a drive. She sat next to the little one, and she held his hand, or touched his head, and looked outside the car at nothing, and was incredibly happy.

That afternoon Johnny called her father's house, hoping her mother would pick up the phone. She did, and Melissa took the receiver. She could hear the fright in her mother's voice at once. They talked less than a minute, so Melissa's father wouldn't take notice, and they agreed to meet in the street, a few blocks from the house, at five.

There was no outward change in her mother, but when the two of them came close to each other, and Melissa started to lean forward to kiss her, her mother pulled back, and Melissa felt as though she'd been slapped by an invisible hand a hundred times more powerful than her father's.

"You look good," her mother said.

"Thank you," Melissa said.

"I can hardly tell it's you."

"This is the way they make up in New York." Somehow Melissa felt that she was apologizing.

"Dress good, too." Her mother touched the blouse. Melissa watched the worn hand touch the smooth silk. "You make a lot of money?"

"Yes. A lot."

"It's gonna last? The job?"

"I think so."

"Then you're staying up there?"

"Yes, I'm staying up there. For good."

"And Johnny's going up too? And little John?"

"Next month, I guess."

Her mother looked at her. All emotion had been washed from her eyes except tiredness, like a shirt that had been through the laundry too many times. "That's good," she said. "That's real good."

"How's dad?"

"Same. Health's all right. Business is bad. He's not very happy."

"Does he ever . . ."

"No, honey. We don't even mention your name. If he saw me here, he'd break my back." She swayed slightly on the broiling street. Words fought to come out, and she fought to hold them back. But the girl had to know, especially if she were going to come down again.

"He pretends you're dead," she said. "For the first couple of weeks after you left, he had them say prayers for you in church. But then he heard you were making money. Someone told him how much. And he just decided you were dead."

When she heard the words, Melissa expected to feel something. She waited a second for the feeling to come. But she felt nothing. No feeling at all. He was right. She was dead—to him.

"And you?" Melissa asked.

"No change. I guess I'll always be the same." Her mother paused a few seconds, then she said, "You look good, honey. I gotta go. He'll start asking questions if I stay away too long. You take care."

She turned. But before she could begin to walk away, Melissa reached out and touched her shoulder. "Mama," she said to the woman's back, "It's me. Melissa."

The woman stopped in the street. Melissa moved closer, and slipped both her arms around her mother's shoulders.

"Mama," she repeated quietly, "It's still me. Melissa. Don't lose me. I love you."

"I haven't lost you," the woman said to the street.

"Then turn around and look at me. Touch me. I'm not dead. I'm here. Mama, I belong to you. Don't lose me. Don't ever lose me."

The woman Melissa was holding turned around, and her eyes had come back to life, and she was crying. Her arms folded themselves around Melissa's waist, and she held onto her daughter as tight as she could.

"I missed you, honey," she said. "God, how I missed you."

"I missed you, Mama, too. Every day." Neither one of them cared now who walked down the street and saw them.

"But I'm glad you're gone," her mother said. And when she pulled back, Melissa saw an unknown strength in her face. The strength of endurance. The strength of a woman who could only serve as a shield for other people's escapes. Who could only stand, and suffer, and protect.

"Don't you ever come back again," she said. "Maybe to visit, if you have to. But never to stay. You got out, honey. You stay out." Her hands came up and traced the outlines of Melissa's face. "You hear?" And then she pulled back. "You hear?"

"I hear, Mama."

"When do you go back?"

"Tomorrow afternoon."

"Good. You get there safe, now." And then she turned away abruptly, and walked down the street.

There was no place to go after that, except back to Johnny, and home. She had thought she'd see some girl friends, but she knew it would be no good. They'd treat her like a stranger. They'd be afraid of her. And she'd hurt their lives. So she went home.

They had dinner, and then watched television, just as they'd always done. The shows were the same. Johnny laughed the same. The beer tasted the same. But she knew now she was different. And when Little John had been put to sleep, and they went to bed, she began to realize how different she was. And how much pain the difference made.

This time, her body was no longer hungry for his. Last night had been perfect. But tonight there was a coarseness in his hands, and a roughness in his body, that she'd never sensed before. He almost jerked the clothes off her. He almost hurt her when they touched. His body pounded hers, as though he were trying to beat her, and not love her.

She reached up and put her hands on his head, and whispered, ''Gently.'' But he pulled the hands down again, and held them above her on the pillow, and pounded harder. And then, after a while, he stopped, and made her do what she had done the night before. But this time there was no love in it, and she gagged, and had to pull back from him, choking, on the mattress. Then he rolled over on top of her again, and finished himself off. She felt nothing. Even the weight of his body no longer registered on her flesh. There was no final touch, no final kiss. Only his body rolling off her, and the snoring.

They'd made love with the light on, and she looked across the bedroom to the dressing room, and she saw one of the photos that Cleon had taken—the beach shot when she'd been slightly drunk—stapled to the dressing room wall. She felt as though she'd been that photograph come to life. And that Johnny had used it, and her, to masturbate with.

And she felt that now she should go back up on that wall, and wait . . . until the next time he wanted to pull her down, and repeat the same lonely act.

21.

She spent all the next morning with Little John. After lunch Johnny became restless, and drove away for an hour. When he came back he sat on the bed and watched her make up for the trip back to New York.

''Do you have to go?'' he asked suddenly.

''The plane leaves in two hours,'' she said.

''I mean, go at all,'' he said.

She stopped looking at him in the mirror, and turned around to look at him in the flesh. ''I have to be at work tomorrow,'' she said, the fright beginning to grow like a worm in her stomach. ''We have a shooting at eight.''

''We could make do.''

"No," she said.

"We don't need that kind of money. You could get your job back at Sanger-Harris. They'd pay you more now, 'cause of what you did up there."

"I can't live down here now," she said.

"Sure you can." He looked at her, and his eyes were the blue of the water nearby—flecked with green. They had tides in them. You could drown in them. Drown in them forever.

"I want you back," he said. "I love you. I miss you." He stood up. He was beautiful. He was her husband. She felt the thinking part of her brain go numb at the mood he was creating. She felt like a dog that was being whistled back from a pasture, to be put on a leash.

"I love you," she said, fighting to keep her brain awake, fighting to keep her will intact. "You have no idea how much I've missed you."

"Not enough," he said. He walked across the room and took her by the shoulders. She felt small next to him. Frail next to him. She felt that he could bend her back, and snap her, with his kind of love, like a twig.

"I've missed you too much," he said. "I want you back."

"No," she said, wondering what the sweet poison was— some drug in the blood, born into them all when they were made women—that shut off their brains, and commanded their bodies to obey. "No," she said again, begging him to believe her.

"Yes," he said, revolving the two of them around, so that they faced the bed. "I'm going to smear that makeup. I'm going to break that New York face. I'm going to turn you back into my Melissa."

He bent down and kissed her. There was no way she could keep her body from reacting. She felt the programmed weakness surge through her veins. She felt the fatal strength of surrender, of being totally loved and totally servile, of being nothing more than wife and mother and body.

But then he stopped kissing her, and deliberately began to scrape his face across hers. He hadn't shaved that morning, and she felt as though his beard was ripping through the makeup into the skin. A hundred tiny pieces of steel wool were trying to tear the skin off her face, were trying to tear the cover off her soul, and she fought her body free of those imprisoning arms, and lurched away from him against the dressing room wall, looking at her own bruised face in the mirror of that wall, and the tall young man behind her, with half his face streaked with red and brown.

"What happened to you?" she gasped. "What happened to you since I've been gone?"

"Nothing," he said. "I just want you back."

"Where did you go? You're not you anymore."

"I need you back."

"I can't come down here any longer." She sat down at the dressing room table, forcing herself to make up. "I can't breathe down here any longer."

"Don't leave me. Don't leave me alone. Please."

"I'll bring you up," she said. "You and Little John. As soon as I can. Up there. Where there's not all this—poison." She turned back to him. There were tears in his eyes, and in hers. "Johnny," she said, "where did you go?"

For the first ten minutes in the car they said nothing. Then, as they turned onto the airport road, she reached out and touched his arm. "Johnny," she said, "I've got to tell you something."

He said nothing. He refused to take his eyes off the traffic to look at her for even a moment.

"You've got to know," she said quietly, "that I can't live without a tender love. I'm fragile, Johnny. You've got to protect me, even when I look strong." She looked out the window at the dozens of cars crawling along the rush-hour road nearby them. At the dozens of lives contained in those cars, people trying to make sense out of their worlds. "I'm a woman," she said. "I need gentleness. The only thing you have to bring with you to New York is that."

He said nothing. She wasn't even sure that he heard her. She wasn't even sure that he knew what the words meant anymore.

22.

She was given a window seat on the plane. The seat next to hers was empty. In the aisle seat was a man.

When he got up to let her past, his head almost touched the roof of the plane. He was taller than Johnny by at least three inches. He was also at least ten years older than Johnny. He had the most sensitive and intelligent face she had ever seen.

They said absolutely nothing to each other for an hour. He took papers out of a briefcase, put them on the pull-down table in front of him, and began to write on a large yellow legal pad.

She looked out the window. Tried to forget Houston. Tried to love Johnny again. Tried not to see the reflection of the man in the window.

When the stewardess came with the drinks, he took a martini. She had nothing. She almost expected him to offer to buy her a drink. But he simply continued to write on the pad.

When dinner came, he put the pad and papers back in his briefcase. The stewardess slipped a tray on Melissa's table, then on his. Melissa looked at the tray, and then pushed it away from her. He too ignored his food. Then, after a few minutes, he turned to her. "I'm sorry," he said. "I don't mean to intrude. But I do have a problem."

She turned to him, looking directly at him for the first time, across the empty seat. "I don't understand," she said.

"I'm European," he said. "And I'd like to have my dinner now. But I can't, unless you do."

"I'm afraid that I . . ."

"Don't know European customs. Of course. May I explain?" He smiled, and the smile startled her. His face, when it had been serious, was strong and intelligent, but there was no emotional appeal in it at all. But when he smiled, he was devastating.

"You see," he went on, "because you're sitting there, and I'm sitting here, we are, in a sense, having dinner together. For example," and he lifted his plastic fork, "there's simply no way that I could raise this rather cheap utensil to my mouth, without noticing that you are not raising your rather cheap utensil to your mouth.''

Despite herself, despite the day she had just lived through, she was forced to smile.

''Good,'' he said. ''You're beginning to understand the delicacy of the situation. Now, think deeply about it for a moment. Are you really prepared to let me starve? Are you, shall we say, prepared to take the responsibility for having the airline carry this oversized body off the plane, when, just as easily, you could allow it to propel itself off under its own power?''

Her smile grew broader. ''What in the world do you do?'' she asked.

''If it's a noble profession, will you feed me?''

''Yes. All right. I give in.'' He made her want to bubble.

''Then I'm afraid I really will starve,'' he said, and the smile became a touch more serious. ''I own an advertising agency. I confess freely to being a professional seducer—of the millions, through words. Right now, for example, I'm engaged in turning hotels—the hotels we passed over when we took off—into just such words.''

''Which ones?'' she asked.

''Can I answer you while we eat?''

Again she laughed. Outside the sun was going down. Inside it was coming up. She picked up her plastic knife and fork, and began to cut her plastic-looking veal piccata. He did the same.

''Good Lord,'' he said after the first bite, ''perhaps you weren't sad after all.'' And suddenly she was looking into the deepest and gentlest eyes she had ever known. ''Perhaps,'' he said, putting down the knife and fork, and picking up the martini, ''perhaps you weren't eating, simply because you're innately wise.''

She picked at her food silently for a moment. He spoke like a book, and in that beautiful European accent. She knew she could listen to the voice for hours . . . or for years.

''Well,'' he said, ''shall we starve together? Or shall we have indigestion together?''

She looked at him again, and decided to trust him. ''Is it really that bad?''

''Yes,'' he answered at once. ''It tries to be something quite wonderful. But it fails to do it quite badly. It would be far better if they served some simple American food that they could do well.''

She extended the trust one step further. ''The word, innately. What does it mean?''

''Born into you. Given to you at birth. When I said that you were innately wise, I meant that you were born wise—and haven't quite found out yet how to tap all that wisdom.''

She had forgotten completely about dinner. She was ready to grow again. Ready to learn.

''Do all Europeans know that many . . . beautiful English words?''

Again, that potent smile. ''No. But words are my tools. I use them to build beautiful things.''

She hesitated a moment, struggling between politeness and need. The proper thing to do now would be to ask about his work. Instead she said bluntly, ''If I do have this—innate wisdom, then how can I tap it?''

The smile was put aside. His face became intense and focused again. His eyes seemed to stare through her eyes, directly into her mind. ''By feeding it the ideas it needs to grow,'' he said. ''Ideas that are packaged in words like the one you've just learned. And by feeding that neophyte wisdom a full, rich diet of words like these every day—just as you feed your body the right diet of food.''

''Neophyte,'' she said.

''Yes.''

''How is it spelled?''

He spelled it for her.

''It's a strange spelling.''

''It's a Greek word. We've simply borrowed it because it works so well.''

''And what does it mean?''

''Actually,'' he said, ''it means young—neo—and plant—phyte. Young plant. Something just bursting into life, just beginning to grow.''

''It's very beautiful,'' she said.

''It's a volume of poetry in a single word.''

''Neophyte,'' she said slowly, tasting the word. ''Isn't it strange,'' she went on. ''That's exactly what I've felt like for the past month.''

''In New York?'' he asked.

''Yes.''

''When you moved there from Houston?''

She felt shutters begin to close behind her eyes. "When I came there from Houston."

He looked down at his plate. "But we don't talk about that."

"No," she said flatly. "I don't think we should."

"Words are safe." He looked at her. "Feelings are dangerous?"

"Please."

"It can't be that bad," he said. And then his voice shifted tones. "Tell me, would you like to learn how to break new words apart, so you can learn four or five of them every day?"

She knew exactly what he was doing, and she was filled with gratitude. "I'd love to," she said. "How?"

During the remaining hour and a half of the flight, he taught her more about language and words than she had learned in all four years of high school, and all the haphazard reading she had done on her own. Five minutes after he had begun to speak, she borrowed the legal pad from him, and by the time they had touched down at Idlewild, she had filled fifteen pages of it. Now she had her key—the key to unlock the doors of the new world that she had felt barred from before. And she had no idea at all of how to repay the man who had given it to her.

They walked together off the plane, and she felt her body begin to stiffen.

"Do you have luggage?" he asked.

"No," she said.

"Neither do I. That's marvelous. We can simply leave right away."

Twenty-six years, she thought. Twenty-six years in Houston. Six years of marriage. Her father, Johnny, Little John. Especially Little John.

"I'm going to say good-bye to you here," she said.

"But why?"

"Because I'm very much married."

"I'm simply asking you to share a cab into the city."

"No. I think it would be better if we said good-bye here."

"I'm completely harmless."

No, she thought. You're not at all. You have no idea of just how dangerous you are.

"I want to thank you," she said, extending her hand. "You've taught me so much." She began memorizing the face. She didn't want to lose the memory of the face. "You've been so kind."

"You really are serious," he said. "And I don't even know your name."

"No, you don't."

"Do you want to tell me why?"

"I'm married."

"But—"

"I'm married."

His face turned dark. "Yes. You are." He picked up his briefcase. "My name is Aaron Carpenter. My agency has the same name. I want to thank you for one of the most enjoyable flights I've ever known." He had become so formal that she almost expected him to bow. "Good-bye."

He turned and walked out of the terminal. She followed slightly behind him, watching him get in a cab, and then looking at her as the cab drove away. She started to hail another cab, and then watched in astonishment as his taxi suddenly backed up, and then screeched to a halt next to her. He had rolled down the window. Now he leaned out of it, and smiled the magnificent smile at her.

"All your life," he said, "you'll wonder what would have happened if you had shared this cab with me."

Then the cab drove away. And she watched it disappear into the night. And she thought, Yes, I will. All my life.

23.

On September 17 the first advertisement for the Reginald Salons appeared on page 11 of *Vogue*. In the advertisement was a beautiful young woman, immaculately groomed, stunningly coiffed, sitting in an exquisite room, pouring tea. She was in complete control of herself, her life, and her world. All over America, women thumbed through the magazine to that page, and then stopped, and studied it, and dreamed.

In San Francisco, Mrs. Ronald Handler III spent five minutes of her busy morning with the page. She propped the magazine open next to the breakfast tray, and studied the look of the young woman. There was a carefully bred elegance there that came from finishing schools in the East—that much was evident at once. She looked for the testimonial and the name; there was none. She studied the jewelry, especially the brace-let, and realized that she would have to take a buying trip to New York before Christmas. Then she rose from the table and appraised her own hair in the mirror. Thursday was the opening of the Opera House. There was no time to spare. She made a note to have her secretary call the Reginald Salon that had just opened in Maiden Lane.

In Cincinnati, eighteen-year-old June Nevelson tore out the page before her mother had even opened the magazine. She hid it in her drawer, and that night, after everyone else had gone to sleep, she taped it to the mirror in her bedroom. Then, for an hour, she worked on her face and her hair to see if she could get that look. Despairing, she wanted to cry. But then she looked at the face of the woman in the photo again, and she saw something there that was more than cheekbones and hair. She saw strength in that face. An infectious strength. And she said to herself, "I'm going to lose twenty pounds. I'm going to lose twenty pounds in the next two months."

In Akron, Helen Canaday was in a rage. She too tore the page out of the magazine, and then crumpled it up and threw it on the floor. Two months ago, she had turned down the chance to buy a Reginald franchise for thirty thousand dol-lars. An aging fag, she had thought; she could do better on her own. Now it was going to cost her fifty thousand. She picked up the phone, and began to dial New York.

In Carmel, California, Dorothy Howard opened the magazine, stopped at the page, and laughed. So the Texas angel had gone to New York after all, she thought. And Victoria and she had met. God, she was exquisite. A young Victoria indeed. A new birth for all of them. Too bad, she thought, and then she laughed again. Even something as appetizing as that, she thought, wasn't worth the trip back to New York. "Estelle, darling," she called out to the sixteen-year-old in the bedroom, "Come see the present Mama gave a friend."

In New York, after Rory had left, Victoria Krane opened the magazine to the page, and laid it on her dressing table in front of the mirror. Then she stood, forcing herself to look at the mirror and the page. She had refused even to allow herself the mercy of make up. She wanted the full revelation, and the full pain. She stared at the picture, and at herself, for five minutes. Then she picked up the pack of cigarettes that lay on the dresser, and took the cigarettes out one by one, and squeezed the tobacco out of them and into the wastebasket.

In New York, Melissa Johnson bought twelve copies of the magazine from the newsstand at 49th Street and Madison Avenue, and stood there, holding them in her arms for twenty minutes, while she watched five women come over to the stand and buy the magazine. She wished that one of the women would open it as she began to walk away from the stand, and would pass Melissa as she reached the page, and would ask Melissa, "Is that you?" But none of them did, of course. And after twenty minutes she began feeling like an idiot, and took the magazines up to the agency to park them there while she went on her morning assignment. There were fifteen or twenty prospective girls waiting in the reception room for an interview when she walked in. Arlene stood up from her desk, pointed at Melissa, and announced loudly to the girls, "This is what all of you want to be when you grow up. Meet page 11 of *Vogue*." And then she ran across the room and threw her arms around Melissa, twelve copies and all.

And in Houston, when Johnny Johnson arrived at the plant the next day, a copy of the advertisement was taped to the door of his locker. The men waited till he saw it, and then burst out laughing. "Is that all your fancy wife gets paid to do in New York?" yelled one of them. "Does she lift up her little pinky-poo when she drinks her tea?" roared another. And then, as Johnny spun around, trying to figure out which one of them to go after first, he saw his boss walk out of the crowd and step up to him. "Hey, Johnny-boy," he said, "what do we call you now, Mr. Melissa Johnson?" Since he never expected Johnny to hit him and lose his job, his arms were hanging at his sides. It was easy, that way, for Johnny to break his jaw in three places, and then walk out of the plant for good.

And, at the same time, in New York, Aaron Carpenter sat in his office for half an hour, with the phones cut off and the door shut, staring at the advertisement, and at the married young woman staring out of it at him. Four times he closed the magazine and tried to put it away. Four times he opened it again and continued to stare at it, and heard again that exquisite, questioning voice. Finally, he picked up the phone, and he called the advertising director of *Vogue*.

BOOK THREE

1961—1962

1.

The 1960s were a decade of parties. In art galleries, there were parties. In museums, there were parties. In couturier salons, there were parties. And in photographers' studios, when a great visual concept had triumphed, and had seized the public's imagination, there were, of course, great parties.

And so it was inevitable that, two weeks after the *Vogue* ad had swept across the nation, Cleon and Reginald would have declared a joint celebration. And that New York's most dazzling men and women, those who had won fame and fortune with their faces, or their minds, or their birth, would have gathered together in the vast studio now turned banquet hall. And that the guest of honor, the new-crowned queen of this miracle of the imagination, should be the twenty-six-year-old woman who, only two short months before, had not even dreamed that a party such as this could be assembled anywhere on the face of the earth.

It took Melissa Johnson six hours to prepare for her entrance. First, she was sent to Elizabeth Arden's, and for two hours massaged and bathed and exercised and pampered, till her entire face and body glowed with the feel of skin made into satin. Then, with her hair carefully wrapped in a towel, she joined Arlene in a cab, and ten minutes later she was in Reginald's salon. An hour later, the face had its regal crown.

"Something's happened to you," Reginald said when he was finished.

"Nothing that I know," she replied.

"Something very good."

"Well, I went home."

He thought for a moment. "Perhaps. If you wish." And then he smiled. "Whoever he was, see him again."

Melissa blushed, and the blush lasted till she reached the cab outside again, and found Victoria herself waiting for her.

"Let me see the front," Victoria said as Melissa slid into the seat beside her. "Now the back."

For a full ten blocks, Victoria was silent. Melissa waited breathlessly for the judgment.

"In high school once," Victoria said, "I had an English teacher by the name of Miss McCullough. I thought she was the most beautiful creature who ever walked on the face of the earth. She was your age, and madly in love with a . . . a twerp of a physics teacher, who mistreated her horribly.

"Miss McCullough invited me to her room two or three evenings, for tea. I sat there and talked Shelley and Keats, and never even told her that she was beautiful, or that she deserved far more than a man who would brutalize her for the rest of her life. She taught me how to sit, and stand, and walk across a room with pride and dignity. She gave me a heritage—of dignity—that was far more important in my life than Keats and Shelley."

Victoria opened her purse, took out her mirror, and checked her make up. "Then, on the last day of school, when I was about to leave for Smith, we shook hands good-bye in front of the gymnasium. And she told me that she thought I was the most beautiful young woman she'd ever known, and that she hoped that she'd given me—the 'tools,' she said—that would help me gain the most from that beauty in a world that was not quite as beautiful as the books we'd discussed."

The cab cut across the flow of traffic, and pulled up before a white granite building with a small bronze plaque on its front, engraved "Trigère." "All I could say then was 'Thank you,' and walk dumbly away." She put the mirror in her purse, and looked at Melissa. "But now I want to say the same words to you. You are the most beautiful young woman I've ever known, and I may be more experienced in this field than Miss McCullough. And I hope that I can give you at least some of the tools you'll need to get the most from that beauty—and give the most from that beauty—in this not very beautiful world. Your makeup is superb. Your hair is divine. That's what I wanted to tell you. And I don't want you to tell me a single word back." She paid the driver, and added her dollar tip. Then she stepped out across the sidewalk into the white building.

Melissa followed her, stunned, unable to utter a sound. All she wanted to do was throw her arms around the woman. And she knew that never in her lifetime would she have the courage, or the permission, to do it.

2.

The dress that Pauline Trigère had selected for Melissa was full-length black velvet, bare-shouldered. It was severely simple—there was no visible pattern or design to it. All it did was follow every line of Melissa's body, and turn those lines into rippling black electricity when she walked.

The car that came an hour later to pick Melissa up—with Victoria in the back seat, majestic in a violet gown—was a huge black limousine, as long as some of the boats that Melissa and Johnny had gone fishing in.

The party they were going to was already filled with three hundred people, though Melissa did not know that. All those guests were restlessly milling about Cleon's studio, waiting for the entrance of one young woman, to see if she could possibly be as beautiful, or as regal, in person, as she was in the series of advertisements that had brought them all here. For the second advertisement had now appeared in *Vogue,* the one with the horseback riding theme, and it was an even more spectacular success than the first. Reginald's salons were booked for three months in advance; he had sold seven new franchises in two weeks, at whatever price he named. *Harper's* and *Vogue* were battling for cover shootings with Melissa. She could now work eighty hours a week, at sixty dollars an hour, if Victoria had allowed it.

Cleon and Reginald, of course, did not greet Melissa at the door. As mentor and discoverer, they were waiting for her inside, in the center of the vast, flower-bedecked room, in the very middle of the enormous crowd. Instead, when the chauffeur clicked open the door and Melissa stepped out into the street in front of the studio, there was Arlene. Her arms shot out and she kissed the air a thousandth of an inch away from Melissa's pristine cheek. And then she held Melissa back the length of her arms, and took one quick look at her in the light that came streaming through the open door.

"Oh, honey," she said, "what you're going to do to all those poor defenseless people."

"You like it?" Melissa asked, begging for even more reassurance.

"Of course she likes it," Victoria said, taking Melissa by the arm. "Come. They're waiting for us."

They walked through the door, into the long narrow hall that led into the studio itself. Melissa began to stiffen as soon as she looked down the hall, and saw the first fraction of the huge audience ahead. She slowed her pace against the steady pressure of Victoria's arm. "What—"

"There are three hundred people inside," Victoria interrupted. "They're waiting for you. They expect the same woman that they saw in the advertisement. Every detail of her. And you're going to give her to them—you're going to be her for them—right now."

Cleon saw them coming, touched Reginald on the shoulder, and they both turned toward them. Melissa froze. Stopped dead in the hall. Stared helplessly at Victoria with her mouth wide open.

The older woman looked at her, and her face softened, and her eyes were suddenly the same eyes that Melissa had seen for the first time in the taxi that afternoon. "You're going to be that woman for those people," Victoria said quietly, "because you are that woman. You've always been that woman. You've just never known it until now." She reached up and took Melissa by the arm again. "Come. Come with me now, and introduce that woman to all of us."

Somehow Melissa's feet began to move again. She saw now that the studio had been transformed into a mammoth ballroom, ablaze with hundreds of flowers. A tremendous, lace-covered table had been set up at the back of the room, and it was weighed down with seventy different varieties of glazed, cut, and sculptured foods.

Face after face . . . dozens of faces . . . and then hundreds of faces were turning to the two of them now. The conversation in the vast room dwindled and then hushed. They were now stepping out of the shadow into the light. Melissa felt Victoria's hand give her arm a final squeeze, and then let go. But the power of that hand on her arm remained. The confidence and trust and strength of that woman who was now leaving her to go on by herself—remained. She knows me, Melissa thought. She recognizes me. She believes in me. There's no way in the world that I'm not going to be what she wants me to be.

Victoria blended into the crowd. Cleon, in the center of all the light and all the people, held out his hand to her. Melissa walked toward him as she knew Victoria would walk. She held her head and shoulders as she knew Victoria would hold her head and shoulders. She put out her hand, and she took his.

Cleon was shorter than she, but he carried himself like a king. He took her hand in the hushed room, and he bent slowly over it, and kissed it.

From somewhere in the crowd around her, someone began to applaud. At first, just a single pair of hands. It was a breach of good taste. Models were not applauded at such parties. Only artists, actors, movie stars, writers. Models were only tools for photographers to work with, and not an equal breed of artist themselves. But the single pair of hands kept applauding, and then a second pair of hands took up the beat. And then a third. And then a dozen. And then, spreading through the vast ring of people surrounding them, a hundred. And then, suddenly, every person in the room, in this most sophisticated audience in the world, was applauding.

Cleon looked up from her hand. Only she saw the look of astonishment on his face. Then, still holding her by the hand, he ceremoniously presented her to one part of the applauding audience after another, turning her from one corner of the room to another. Everywhere there were smiling faces. Everywhere there were applauding hands. Everywhere, love and approval. Melissa began to feel tears well up in her eyes. She knew that in half a minute she would begin to cry, and that the facade would break, and the act would be over.

And then, without warning, Arlene was behind her. And Arlene's whisper filled her ears. "If you start to water up right now, sugar child, you'll smear your makeup. And then I'm going to rip off that two-thousand-dollar gown, and show three hundred apoplectic people your beautiful boobs."

The tears turned to laughter. And the laughter was interpreted by the crowd around her as an even more radiant smile. And she and Cleon, hand in hand, stood there, and squeezed each other's fingers, and waited out the applause.

3.

Reginald finally came over to her, took both her hands in his, and kissed them. He took her by the arm, and for the next thirty minutes presented her, one by one, to the people who shaped the future of an entire country. A stream of faces, names, accomplishments flowed by her. Arlene walked behind her, and commented on the reputation of one person, the eligibility of another. But splendid as they were, Melissa realized hollowly, they were not enough. She saw them, reacted to them, was overwhelmed for a second by the sheer power of their presence, and then automatically caught herself looking beyond them, scanning the packed room as though it would be completely empty if, somewhere within it, there was not one particular, longed-for face.

Then the introductions began to dwindle, and the one face she had waited for had not emerged. She began to feel suddenly drained, unbearably weary. Reginald looked at her. "I think you need a drink."

"Please. Wine."

He left her alone to get it. And as she continued to scan the room, she suddenly saw Pam Haas standing about twenty feet away from her, just looking at her, not coming forward to say hello.

"Pam," Melissa said. "Oh, Pam."

They moved across the room toward each other, and Melissa threw her arms around the redhead's shoulders. "I'm so happy to see you," Melissa said. Then she stood back and asked, "Why didn't you come over before?"

"There were so many people."

"But that had nothing to do with it. They weren't anywhere near as important as you."

Pam smiled, a little bitterly. "I wasn't quite sure you'd remember me."

Melissa shook her head, and kissed Pam's cheek. "I could never forget you. You gave me my wings."

"Was the trip what you expected?" Pam asked.

"It was—" Melissa said, and then stopped. From one corner of the room, where the crowd had thinned, he was coming. He stood head and shoulders above the people he was slipping past. He had on a tuxedo, he carried no glass or food in his hand, and he moved with electrifying grace. She could feel the space close, step by step, between them. "It was the most marvelous trip I've ever had," she said to Pam.

He came up to them, and said to Melissa, "Congratulations."

"Thank you," she said. "But I've really done nothing. The credit is entirely Cleon's." Then she turned to Pam and said, "Pamela Haas, this is Aaron Carpenter."

"I'm most pleased to meet you," he said, and she watched Pam react to the smile, melt at the smile, and knew that she was right.

"And I," she said, "am Melissa Johnson."

"Oh," he answered. "I can't tell you how delighted I am to meet you."

"And I can't tell you," she replied, "how delighted I am to have you meet me."

"I'm sorry," Pam said, "but I don't get it."

"It's quite simple," Aaron said to Pam. "I've never had the privilege of meeting the lady. But we have spent several"—he looked quizzically at Melissa—"unmet hours together."

"Fascinating unmet hours together." And then Melissa could hold it all in no longer, and she took Pam by the shoulder and burst out laughing. "On the plane back home from Houston."

Pam looked at Melissa, and then at Aaron, and then again at Melissa. She smiled. "I did give you wings," she said, and then turned to Aaron. "Lovely to have met you. Have fun." And then she kissed Melissa, and disappeared into the crowd.

He turned. "Hello, Melissa Johnson," he said.

"You say it very well."

"I knew a week ago."

She smiled. "I rather hoped you read *Vogue*."

"You're not angry?"

"That you did what I hoped you'd do? No."

"And you're still—"

"Very married? Yes. But very much in need of a friend."

He blinked, and the mood in his eyes changed almost imperceptibly. "Then you have one. Whenever, and for as long as you want."

She watched Reginald coming up behind him with the drinks. The music had begun. Couples were moving out onto the center of the floor. She saw several men from the crowd begin to move toward her. She wanted to grab Aaron's arm and run . . . run away somewhere into the night . . . run away from the crowd and the camera and the fact that she was Melissa Johnson and that this party was for her. But she knew that was impossible, at least for now. Victoria was still here. And obligation was still here.

"How good a friend?" she asked quickly.

"Name it," he answered.

"Stay here, until I leave."

"How easy." he said.

4.

Four times in the next two hours, she managed to disentangle herself long enough to see or speak to him. Once, for three minutes, close to midnight, they danced. The music was slow, and he was incredibly tall. She fit, perfectly, against his chest. His chin rested lightly against the top of her head. His arm came around her waist, and held it gently. He led, she followed. His body was tall enough to shield her from the crowd for those three blissful minutes. She closed her eyes, and listened to the music, and just felt the manliness, and the tenderness, that guided her across the floor.

Then, of course, someone else cut in. And she had to listen politely to a recitation of how much money that nameless face made. Until the music stopped, and she could pull herself away, and flee to the safety of Arlene.

"Who were you dancing with before?" Arlene asked.

"I don't know."

"No. Not the pudgy idiot. The tall oak, that you nestled up against like a little squirrel."

"His name is Aaron Carpenter."

"Oh," Arlene whistled. "Heavy. Heavy. Good for you, honey. He's so bright, they call him supernova."

"What?"

"Brilliant star. He manufactures money with his fingers. They say that if he grows any faster, he'll own Madison Avenue."

But by then the time of trial was past. The crowd was now beginning to thin out. Victoria came up to Melissa, and asked, "How are you?"

"Fine."

"You're remarkable," Victoria said. "I would have thought, when we were driving here, that there was no way in the world that you could look more beautiful. But you do—you actually do—now."

"It's been the most incredible evening of my life. Thank you."

"I'm proud of you. Cleon will never forget tonight. Nor will I." She looked around the room for a moment. "Would you like me to drop you off at home?"

"No, thank you." Melissa, in spite of herself, blushed. "I think I may have a ride."

"Strange," Victoria said, smiling. "I rather expected that." She leaned over and kissed Melissa on the cheek. "Have a good ride home. And I am proud of you. Immensely."

Arlene looked at Melissa, leered, and winked. Then she followed Victoria into the narrow hall. Melissa watched the two of them until they disappeared from sight. And then she felt a chill run down her back. For the first time, she realized that Victoria was here alone. Despite the importance of the party, Rory had not come.

"They seem to have left you," Aaron's voice said from behind her.

She whirled to face him. "Yes, I seem to have been abandoned."

"To what dire fate?"

"I'm afraid . . . to you."

He smiled. I must learn to resist that smile, she thought. If I'm going to keep seeing this man—and I am going to keep seeing this man—I must learn to build a shield against that smile.

"But are you ready to accept your fate?" he went on.

"Partially," she said.

"Enough to come with me for a drink?"

"Yes."

"In the most easily escapable apartment in New York?"

"Positively yes," she said. "But I have to tell a few people good-bye first."

"I'll wait here, anxiously."

"I won't be a second."

Ten minutes later they walked through the narrow hall, away from the public light, and into the silence of the dark street. He hailed an approaching cab, gave a Sutton Place address, and they began to race through the almost-empty city.

After fifteen blocks, she took her right hand off her bag, and placed it on the seat beside her. Three blocks later, he took it in his. Again, there was the feeling of her own wonderful smallness, of his tender warmth, of complete protection. They said nothing, simply watched the city pass by in silent procession. When they reached the apartment house, they walked through the empty lobby, hardly noticed by the half-asleep desk clerk. In the elevator, Aaron pressed a button marked "PH." They glided up twenty-five floors, still holding hands, still not talking.

There was only one door outside the elevator. He opened it with his key, turned on the lights, and asked her to step in.

The room was even more dazzling than the studio had been. It was a three-story living room, whose ceiling reached thirty-five feet high. Ten-foot windows overlooked the East River. Airplanes were landing in a string of red and green dots, at LaGuardia. But in the room itself, on every one of the ten- or twenty-foot walls, was a massive painting. The one hanging over the couch was on raw canvas, and on that canvas some artist unknown to her had taken swirls of paint, and whipped them in red, yellow, blue, violet, black, and amber strings of color, spirals of color, slashes of color, five to eight to ten feet long. She felt that she was looking at the universe, trapped in a single frame.

She was speechless, and he made no attempt to break the spell. Another painting was made of nothing but great tangled beams of black and white paint that seemed to have exploded on the wall, and then somehow been frozen there. In a corner was a bronze statue of a man, ten feet tall. The air of the room seemed to have pressed in on the man, and squeezed and flattened him almost to the point of extinction. Yet he radiated dignity, and, once seen, would never be forgotten.

A dozen other objects of art were spread across the room, but her eye was already exhausted. The intensity of the room, its magnificence, its sheer richness simply overwhelmed her. She looked at the tall man standing beside her, studying her reactions. "My God," she said, "what do you think when you come into a room like this?"

His response was not at all what she had expected. A hardness which she had never dreamed could exist in his face, began to dominate it. And it was accompanied by a sadness, as deep as the intolerable sadness she had seen in the statue in the corner.

"Do you really want to know?" he asked. "It's not pleasant. And it doesn't fit the end of an evening such as this."

"I don't care," she said. "I really want to know. Any truth about you."

He turned away from her. His European accent was thick now, and his voice was slow and somber. "I think what I think when I see any room, anywhere, anytime." His eyes met hers, and he studied her face to gauge what his words would do to her. "I wonder how many partisans—how many disguised soldiers—I could sleep on this floor. And then I think of how quickly I could get those soldiers out of this house, and into the woods, if someone signaled that the Germans were coming." He closed the door behind him, and leaned against it. "That way of thought kept me alive for five years," he said, "And I simply can't lose it now."

5.

Fifteen hundred miles away, in Houston, shortly after midnight, Johnny Johnson and the black-haired woman came out of a bar on the south edge of town. They were both half-drunk. They piled into the car, and he reached out and grabbed her, and forced her head to his, and plowed his tongue into her mouth. Then he pushed her over to the other side of the seat, she giggled, and the car screeched off into the hot Houston night.

She lived in a cheap tract-home. They stumbled out of the car, through the banging screen door, into the kitchen. Neither bothered to turn on the light. He opened the refrigerator, pulled out a bottle of beer, flipped the cap off, then put his arm around her and half-led, half-dragged her into the bedroom, spilling the foam from the beer behind them as they went.

When they got into the bedroom, with its unmade bed from the morning, he pushed her over to the wall by the window, and pulled up her sweater with his free left hand. She had no bra on, and he began to suck the sagging right breast. Then, holding her pinned back against the wall with his left hand and his mouth, he put the bottle of beer down under her skirt, and lifted it up, till its top touched the crack in her panties.

She giggled, and tried to push him away. He slammed her back against the wall, and kept trying to get the top of the bottle under her panties. She stared at him, wide-eyed in the moonlit room, realizing that he was drunker than she'd thought. She pushed against his shoulders now with both her hands.

"No, honey," she said. "Stop it."

"Leave me alone," he said. "I want to."

"We can't tonight, honey," she said, bringing one hand up from his shoulder and running it through his hair. "Not tonight. Next time, I promise. But not tonight."

"Why?" he asked, pulling slightly away from her.

Her smile was crooked, ashamed. "I've got the curse," she whispered. "But it's okay. You just lie down here on the bed and I'll blow you. Like we've done before, honey. It's okay. It'll be even better."

"Damn!" he said.

"Don't get mad."

"Damn! I don't want your lousy blow job. You don't know how to blow a man."

He grabbed her away from the wall, spun her around, walked her back to the bed, and threw her down. The springs groaned.

"Honey, we can't."

"Shut up. We'll do what I want. I'm not afraid of your curse."

She started to rise and he shoved her down again. When she tried to get up on her elbows again, he drew back his arm. She looked at the size of his hand in the moonlight, and she looked at his eyes, and she sank down on the bed again.

"Honey, please."

"Shut up. Don't say anything more."

He flipped up her skirt. Then he grabbed the sides of her

panties with both hands and ripped them off. She was wearing a Kotex belt. He laughed, and ripped that off too.

He shoved her thighs apart. "Don't move," he said. "Don't talk." Then he unbuckled his belt and unzipped his pants, and tucked his shirt up under his chest. He pulled down his shorts. He was ready, and he rammed himself into her as hard as he could.

She screamed softly when he entered her, and then became perfectly still. He reared up and down on her for five minutes, wrapping her legs around him, beating her body and the bed beneath it, crying out in some strange pain of his own when he came inside her.

For thirty seconds after, he remained completely rigid, still supporting his head and shoulders half a foot above her, but now with no sound. Then he pushed himself away, rolled over, sprang up off the bed, and disappeared into the bathroom. She heard the splashing of the sink water, and his cursing, and the flushing of the toilet. Then the bathroom door slammed open, and he lurched out toward her on the bed again.

"You made me filthy," he said, towering over her.

"I told you we shouldn't do it," she said.

"I do what I want, bitch. I do what I want."

She started to cry.

"Stop crying," he said. She went on, uncontrollably, lying helplessly on the bed.

"Stop crying," he said. He reached down and grabbed her hair in his hand, and said, "Stop crying."

He lifted her head, by the hair, off the pillow. When she still couldn't stop crying, he pulled back his right hand and struck her, full-force, across the face. He watched her head spin sideways as far as the hair in his hand would let it. And then—dazedly, wonderingly—he pulled back his hand a second time, and struck her again across the other side of her face.

Again, her head spun as far as the hair he was holding would let it. He laughed. A little boy's laugh. And then he threw her head back on the pillow.

"You do what I want," he said, weaving above her, "or I ruin your face." No sound came from the pillow. "Do you hear?" he shouted.

"I hear," she whispered, not moving, not looking at him.

"Then remember that," he said. "They all do what I want, or I ruin their faces."

Then he turned, and walked out of the bedroom and out of the house. Nothing had moved in the darkened bedroom by the time he started his car and pulled out into the street again.

He drove five blocks, to the underside of a railroad bridge, just before the main highway. Then he pulled the car off the road, underneath the bridge. And he began to sob, quietly, like a child who has been lost at the circus.

A million miles away, in a different universe, the same moon was beginning to descend outside Aaron Carpenter's terrace windows. "Would you like a drink?" he asked Melissa.

"No, thank you." She knew she didn't dare.

"Would you mind if I had one?"

"Not at all."

He walked over to the foyer and took out a large brandy glass, and poured a quarter of an inch of forty-year-old Remy Martin V.S.O.P. "Shall we sit?" he asked.

"I'd love to. Can I have the armchair, so I can see the painting over the couch?"

"Of course."

When she was seated, she asked, "Who did it?"

"A man by the name of Jackson Pollack. He's dead now."

"I've never seen anything as powerful."

"You have marvelous taste. It's the best thing in the room." He took a sip from the glass. "Do you want to talk about the art?"

"No. I want to sit here and look at it. But I don't really want to learn anything about it yet. I don't want words to block what I feel about it now. Does that make sense?"

"Eminent sense. What would you like to talk about?"

"Anything I want?"

"Yes."

"You."

"A trivial subject," he said. "Hardly worth the time."

"You shocked me at the door."

"Perhaps I shouldn't have—"

"Told me the truth? But I asked you to."

"It's a harsh truth. Why would you want it?"

She stared at him, seeing him leaning toward her across the magnificent room, under the great painting, incredibly elegant in his tuxedo. Why would I want it, she thought. Because I want every part of you. Because I want to know every day you've lived. Because I want to stop this act that I'm forcing both of us to play, but I can't. Because the only way I can touch you now is with words.

She felt her face begin to flush. She threw back her hair in defense, and realized that she had nothing to do with her hands. "Perhaps I will have a drink after all," she said.

"Of course. White wine again?"

"You're very observant."

"I was trained to be. But I'm afraid that nothing in the world you could do—or want—could ever escape my memory." He had opened the bottle, and brought it back in a cooler, with a tall thin glass.

"It's a Puligny Montrachet," he said. "A very good white wine." He watched her as she tasted it, felt in his spine the red outline of her lip on the glass. "I think you'll enjoy learning wines," he went on, trying to make some sort of acceptable conversation. "Like art, they take years to master. But they're equally gratifying at the end."

"I want to talk about you," she said. She looked up at him. "I'm dead serious."

"Then you'll need much more wine."

"I have it here," she said. "I can serve myself."

"All right," he said. "If you wish. But I'm going to take off my jacket." He stood up from the couch, enormously tall. He unbuttoned the tuxedo jacket and tossed it on the couch beside him. She had never seen him without a jacket. His shoulders in the white shirt were even broader than Johnny's. He undid the black bow tie, and let both ends dangle down on the white shirt. He opened his collar and the first button on the shirt.

"Where do we begin?" he asked, sitting down on the couch again.

"Are you married?" she said spontaneously.

He smiled. "That isn't the question I expected. But no. Not now. I was, sometime ago. But . . . not now."

"Divorced?"

"Yes. Completely."

"Do you have any children?"

"No." And his face darkened again. "Somehow I never thought I could."

"Why?"

"I don't really know. Perhaps it has to do with the war. Something that happens to you in the war."

Suddenly the room turned cold. "Were you wounded?" she asked.

He smiled again, not quite looking at her. "Yes," he said. "But not there. I'm perfectly capable of having children, physically."

"But?"

"I don't know. Perhaps—again—the war."

"Tell me about it. Please."

He looked around the room—at the paintings by Kline and DeKooning and Gorky and Picasso. At Giacometti's sculpture of existential man. He looked at the bookcases—an entire shelf devoted to Shakespeare, another shelf devoted to Camus and Sartre. He thought of the renaissance that had sprung up all over the Western world after the war. Of Sartre, almost killed in the resistance in France. And then he thought of himself, and the horror if he had not lived to know these men's work. And he thought of his war, and the terrors he hadn't let creep into his mind for a dozen years.

"Please," she said again.

He raised his glass and saluted her. "I was born," he said, "one-quarter Jewish. Three-quarters Lutheran. But to the Nazis I was all Jew, and therefore all animal, to be hunted down and killed."

"Where?"

"Born? In Austria, in a small town called Graz. I was in my third year of high school, fifteen years old, when the Nazis came. We fled—my father, my uncle, and ten children —into Hungary and then Rumania. Then the Nazis came again, and we ran south toward Yugoslavia. They jumped ahead of us. We were on foot, they rode in tanks. I remember—I'll never forget—spending day after day in the stinking cellar of some farmhouse, not daring to make a sound, hardly even allowing ourselves to breathe, wondering whether the farmer would honor the piece of silver my father had given him, or turn us over to the Germans anyway."

His glass was empty. He refilled it. She picked the wine bottle out of the cooler and filled her own glass.

"It's strange," he said. "The city people would have betrayed us. The farmers never did."

"How old were you then?" she asked.

"Eighteen. I was as tall as I am now. Very difficult to hide. Always standing out in the moonlight when we ran from farmhouse to farmhouse. Always a danger to the others, as well as to myself."

And, she thought, were you as magnificent? Was your face as strong as it is now? Had you ever kissed a woman? Was there a farm girl somewhere, young and unafraid, who eased that pain for a moment?

It's blurring, she thought. Then and now. Too much wine, and too much moonlight. I should stop drinking, she thought. I should stop listening and feeling.

Instead, she asked, "And where did you go?"

"Nowhere. To Yugoslavia, of course, but the Germans were already there. Then south to the mountains, where the partisans were. Two of us—" He stopped.

"Go on. Please."

"Two of us—the youngest ones—never made it." He looked away from her and spread his hands out, palms upward, as if to show that they were clean. Then he went on. "We met a partisan group, and fought with them for a year."

She wanted to ask about the two children. But there was something in his face, something in the gesture of his hands, that kept her silent. Instead, she refilled her glass.

"Then, after a year, five of us were captured. We expected to be shot at once, of course, but we weren't. They were building roads, and they brought us into a camp and used us as labor. Every morning," he said, "we were marched out into the woods to build the road. The guards were vicious, and if a man stopped work, or looked sick, he was simply shot on the spot." He put down the brandy glass. It was empty. He did not pick it up again.

"There was one guard," he said, "who was the worst of them all. One night, in December, he came into the shed, and chose four of us, all about the same age. He gave each of us a shovel, and told us to get outside." He looked out the window. "There was a full moon—much like tonight. It was freezing. We had scarves over our mouths, and by the time we were out of sight of the camp, frost had formed on the scarves. When we reached the point where the road began, he told us to stop and dig separate graves.''

He was staring at her. Staring into her. ''I don't think you should drink anymore.''

''I know. I won't.'' She turned the glass upside down and put it in the cooler. ''Go on,'' she said.

''When we were through, he collected the shovels from us. Then he shot the other three boys in the chest, one by one. He did it systematically, from left to right. I just happened to be the one on the far right—the last one. The other three fell back into their graves, and he pointed the rifle at me. I felt nothing. I didn't even feel the cold any longer.''

He smiled sadly. ''His rifle jammed,'' he said. ''The cold had finally penetrated even the rifle. He stood there in front of me and started swearing at it, pounding it with his glove, trying to force back the bolt. Nothing worked, and so he just took the rifle and bayoneted me.''

''He what?'' she asked in astonishment.

''He bayoneted me,'' he replied quite calmly. ''He drove his bayonet through the front of my coat, and my body, and the back of my coat, as hard as he could. It knocked me back into the grave, and he left.''

''But why didn't it kill you?''

Again, the sad smile. ''I thought it had. I lay there in the grave, the wind knocked out of me, for a few minutes, waiting to die. But I didn't die. The bayonet had hit nothing vital, and because of the cold I didn't even bleed. Finally I realized that if I kept waiting there, I would die—from the cold. So I climbed up to the road again, and I checked the other three boys and made sure they were dead. And then I walked. I walked up and down all night long, slapping my arms to keep alive in the cold. There was nowhere else to go. All farms had been cleared out for tens of miles, and I would have starved or frozen to death had I gone anywhere else.''

''You couldn't escape? You couldn't run?''

''No. Only to death. They knew that. They'd planned that. So I waited for the sun to come up, for the camp gates to open. And when they did, I saw the work party come out, and march to the spot where we'd been the night before. He had some of the prisoners fill in the graves. He never went near them. No one told him that one of them was empty. And, while he was watching that, I joined some of the other men carrying fallen trees. That night, when we were herded back to camp, as we came in under the gate light, I saw him examine my face. I lowered my eyes like any other prisoner, and he shrugged his shoulders and walked away. He never noticed me again. He never bothered me again.''

His voice trailed off. The sky outside was changing color. The black was beginning to melt to gray. The paintings surrounding them began to take on a new light, a new vibrancy. Everywhere she looked was beauty. Everything she heard was horror.

''That poor boy,'' she said.

''No,'' he answered slowly. ''He was the lucky one.''

''To live,'' she went on, ''when all those others died.''

He stared at her in surprise. She stared back at him, wanting to reach inside that man in the dress shirt, and touch the boy who had waited to die with the others. She had drunk half a bottle of wine, but the haze it had created in her mind now seemed to be totally gone. If anything, it had only intensified and sharpened her feelings. She wanted to reach out beyond the man, and take the boy, the eighteen-year-old boy, and hold him in her arms, and heal the wound. And she wanted to smooth away the hurt, and the guilt, to smooth them into nothingness—with love.

''I can't believe that the person in that story was you,'' she said quietly. ''I can't believe that anyone could go through all that, and then build something like this.''

''Many of us have. These—''

''No,'' she said, glancing at the paintings, and the sculpture, and the books. ''I don't want to talk about them. I want to talk about you. It's imperative—is that the right word?''

''Yes,'' he said, smiling. ''That's the right word.'' It was the same smile she had first known. The smile that made the paintings look dim.

Were you, she suddenly thought, as beautiful then? Was that smile there when you were eighteen? And those eyes? And that jaw? Did some fool with a gun almost cut off forever that strength, and that intelligence, and that power to give joy and life? And you think that you can't have children. Why? Is it because you think that somewhere inside, a part of you is dead? Let me take that part of you, she thought, and let me bring it back to life.

''Prove it to me,'' she said. ''Prove you were the boy in the story.''

His eyes narrowed. ''How?''

"Show me the scar. Where the bayonet went in. Take off your shirt and show me."

"No," he said.

"I want to believe you. I know it hurts to show it to me. But I want to see it."

"No," he repeated.

"Are you my friend?"

"Yes. Of course."

"You said earlier this evening—"

"I had no idea—"

She stood up. "Are you more than my friend?" she said.

He sat in front of her, hands on his thighs, palms upward. His face was dark, and stern, and beautiful. Then he shook his head, once, quickly, and stood up, towering over her. He pulled off the black bow tie and threw it behind him on the couch. His eyes never left hers. Then he took the white shirt and opened its buttons, one by one. The hair on his chest was black, but not thick. Under his rib cage, his stomach curved in. There were horizontal waves of tight muscles, running down it, into his belt.

He opened the shirt all the way. On the left side of his body, two inches in toward the stomach, was a white-rimmed, ragged scar. It was almost two inches long, vertical, and the suntan of the rest of his body had not touched the whiteness of its rim.

While she stared at it, he pulled the shirt out of his trousers completely, and pulled it off his shoulders and back. He let it drop, and stood in front of her, with the tremendous shoulders, the long, muscled arms, the tight flat stomach, and the vertical scar.

"You poor thing," she said.

"No," he said. "I lived."

She reached out and touched the scar. His skin burned her fingers. She could feel the ragged edge, where death had almost crept in.

"Oh God," she said. She might never have met him.

"I lived," he repeated. "It's over."

"No," she said. "It's not over." Without thinking, she suddenly fell on her knees in front of him. Lowered herself to her knees in the magnificent Trigère gown. Reached up and held the sides of his body, just above his belt. And then slowly moved her lips toward him, and kissed—slowly kissed—the scar.

With her lips, she felt his body tremble. She kissed the scar again, trying to drain the pain and horror from it. She moved her hand around to the back of his body, and felt with her fingers the smaller vertical scar that was there also. Then she turned his body carefully around to the side, and kissed the back scar as well.

He turned again to face her. "Melissa," he said softly. And she suddenly knew that she had to erase the scar. That she had to use her tongue to make it disappear forever.

"Be still," she said. "Don't move. Let me help you."

Again her face moved closer to his body. But this time her lips opened, and her teeth parted, and she felt her tongue come out of her mouth. It touched the top of the scar lightly, and she heard him moan. She ran her tongue down to the bottom of the scar. And then up again. And then down. His flesh was delicious. She was in ecstacy.

Her hands had slipped down now from the sides of his body to his belt. She was holding on now to the belt of the velvet-striped trousers, pulling down on them. More of the flat stomach was coming into view. The hair at its bottom had begun to thicken.

She moved her head back a few inches. The scar had not faded. She had not expected it to. Now her fingers slid inside the top of his trousers. They moved together till they joined at the buckle. Her thumbs touched the hard silver metal of that buckle. Her tongue was tingling with the taste of his flesh. She knew that all she wanted to do was open that buckle.

She leaned forward, and pulled the loop out of the far side of the buckle, and against the center tong that was binding it. He made no move to stop her or help her. His hands hung powerlessly at his side. He watched as the tong came out of its hole—as the belt snapped open.

Redemption, she thought. The ultimate healing. The move now against the deeper scar, against the inner wound that could be cleansed and banished. The gift of life, to a man who thought he had no life to give. She looked up at him, at the beautiful, gentle face. And then she threw her arms around his hips, and buried the side of her face in his thighs, and cried out, "No. I can't. I want to, but I can't."

His hands now came alive, and began stroking her—one hand against her hair, the other against her face. "It's all right," he said. "It's all right."

"I'm not naked enough for you now," she said. "I can't make myself naked enough for you now."

He reached around behind his back, and gently separated her hands. Then he sank down on his knees beside her, and put his arm around her, and held her close, and safe.

"I don't understand," he said. "But it doesn't matter."

"Are you more than my friend?" she asked.

"Yes."

"How much more?"

"Infinitely more."

She pulled away from him. Knelt, looking straight at him. Exposed. Vulnerable. Begging. For the first time in her adult life, begging. "There's another way to say it."

"You know it already. You knew it when we left the plane."

"There's a better way to say it. You have so many words. I want only one."

"You have it. You've had it from the moment we met."

"Then say it. Say it."

"I love you. By the God that kept me alive for this moment, I love you. And I swear that I've been able to do nothing, since we left each other at the plane, but love you."

"Then shall I stay married? Shall I wear that shield against you?"

In the darkness that came over his face, she saw a despair that she swore to eliminate forever. "I'll be with you under any terms," he said, "or any conditions."

"I love you," she replied. "I have only one word for it. But it fills the universe."

"I've asked you a dozen times if you were still married."

"And the answer now, if you want it, is no."

"But out of all those people who adored you tonight, why me?"

"Because I love you."

He laughed. "She loved me for the dangers I had passed. And I loved her that she did pity them."

"What's that?" she asked.

"A line from Shakespeare. In a play called *Othello*."

"But I loved you on the plane, long before I knew that there were any dangers."

"Why?" he asked softly.

"Because your eyes were so gentle. And I needed gentleness so much then . . . and now. And you helped me grow, even on the plane, in an hour. I was a new me when I was with you. A me that was more than a face, that was a mind, and a heart.''

They were sitting now on the rug, in front of the couch. The sky outside was streaked with red. The room glowed. His hand held hers. There was no place in the world but this room.

"Then why did you leave me?" he asked.

"Because I was still in Houston, even when we reached New York. And, most of all, because of my son."

"And what will you do with him?"

"Go get him," she said instantly. "And bring him up here, where he belongs. Where he's always belonged."

"And his father?"

"Am I still married?"

He looked at the exquisite face, and then reached out and touched it. The blond hair, equally touchable. He put his hand on her shoulder, and then ran his fingers down her arm. He was making her availability real to himself. He was making tactile the fact that she was giving herself to him. The feeling of destiny, of fate, of the interlock of past and future, overwhelmed him. He knew that he had waited for this moment all his life. He knew that there was some purpose here that he could not comprehend. He knew that she had been sent, and that, by some miracle, she loved him as he loved her.

"No," he said. "You're not married."

"Then I'll tell him tomorrow. And I'll go down and end it."

"And what will he do?"

"Nothing. He doesn't want me anymore—he just doesn't know it. I threaten him. I drive him into an anger he can't control. He's never lived in a world where women were equal to men. He'd only be hurt up here, and he'd only hurt in return. It would have ended in a few weeks anyway."

"Then?"

"I belong to you. Do you want me to give myself to you now?"

"If you have to ask—"

"I'll do anything you say."

"If you have to ask," he went on, "something is wrong with now."

"Yes," she said. "Something is wrong with now. I've

only made love to one man. I was married to him, and I believe in the sanctity of marriage.'' She stared at the massiveness of his shoulders, and shivers ran through her body. ''There's nothing in the world I'd rather do right now than go to bed with you. Every inch of my body is begging for you. But I'm not naked enough for you. I have to take off my husband, or I won't be able to give myself to you fully.''

''I agree,'' he said.

''And there's one thing more, maybe even more important.''

He waited.

''It's hard to say,'' she went on. She looked away from him. ''I take the pill. I want to stop taking it before we make love.''

His face turned dark again. ''Why?''

''Because of the look on your face. Because you don't believe you can have children. And I know you can. And I love you. And I can't love you without wanting to have your baby.''

He turned away from her. ''And if I can't?''

''You can. I know it. I feel it. Let me prove it to you. Let me stop taking the pill.''

''No,'' he said.

''Let me make myself completely naked for you,'' she said. ''Please.''

So there was a purpose, he thought, far beyond his ken. And this was the first new step, out into danger. ''It won't work,'' he said.

''Let me try.''

He touched her hair again. ''You do love me.''

''I adore you.''

He got up from the rug and reached for his shirt. ''I think I should take you home now.''

He helped her to her feet, and took her face in his hands. He kissed her lips for the first time, and felt his body react to the absolute assurance of love behind those lips. Then, as he moved his head back, she put her hands out and kissed him again, this time deeper, this time with her body trembling as she felt his tongue inside his mouth, as she drank in the source of those words.

She belonged to him now, she thought. But he belonged equally to her. The seal was formed. She was home, at last.

She was safe.

7.

The phone call the next morning to Johnny was a disaster. There was no way to soften her message, no way to explain it. It was over, had been over even before the last time they'd made love. They lived in different worlds now. There was no use bringing him into her world, and prolonging the agony.

Everything they owned together, she told him, was his—the house, the car, the savings account. She wanted nothing back from the six years during which she'd worked and contributed—not a penny.

"You've been fucking someone up there, haven't you," he said.

"No."

"Was he a good fuck?"

"Johnny, it's none of your business. But the answer is still no."

"He must have been a good fuck. Well, let me tell you something, big shot, I've been fucking someone down here too. And she's a hell of a lot better fuck than you are."

There was no shock, no surprise, no feeling at all. Only the recognition that it had to happen. And even if she had known, she still would have stayed out of Aaron's bed until she had left Johnny.

"It doesn't matter," she said. "Congratulations. I'm coming down on the four o'clock plane."

"If you try to take my son away from me," he said, "I'll kill you."

"Then be ready to kill me at four-thirty, because I'll be at the house then. And I'll have a taxi waiting while I pick up Little John." There was no sound on the other end. "And, Johnny," she went on, "if you try to hide the baby from me, I'll hire every lawyer in Houston, and have you thrown in jail for kidnapping."

She put down the phone. The panic that she'd held down while she was talking, now spread out over her entire body. She wanted to call Aaron, and ask him to come with her. She knew he would be there in minutes. She needed his strength, his protection. But she knew she couldn't ask for it. This was the end of an old life that she'd made of her own free choice; she would now have to leave—alone.

She boarded the plane. Made the flight. Hired the taxi at the airport for the round trip. When they pulled up in front of the house, she said to the driver, "If I'm not out in ten minutes, call the police."

She entered the house through the kitchen. Johnny was sitting at the table, drinking beer; eight empty bottles were lined up neatly in a straight row in front of him. He looked up at her. They said nothing to each other.

In her bedroom drawer, she had a high school sorority pin. It was the only thing she wanted from the house. She walked past him into the dressing room and bedroom to get it. When she reached the dressing room she stopped, and froze in horror.

On the mirrors he had taped up thirty or forty photographs of her—both the *Vogue* ads, almost two dozen contact sheets, blow-ups from shooting after shooting. And from every one of them the face had been torn out, or cut out, or picked out, or slashed in the middle with an X.

She heard the kitchen chair scrape back, and the kitchen table being pushed away, and she knew that he was rising. She heard his footsteps across the kitchen floor, and she raced into the bedroom, and opened the drawer, and took out the sorority pin, and ran out into the hall. She met him there, between the bedroom and Little John's room. He was standing with both arms spread out, like some giant bird, blocking her way. He was grinning.

"Do you like your face?" he said.

"Let me through, Johnny," she said, her heart pounding so hard that she could hear it throbbing in her ears.

"That's the way your face should look," he said. "Your father was right. It's the instrument of the devil."

"Let me through, Johnny. Give me my baby."

"Your face is evil," he said. "It spreads evil."

"No!" she screamed, and then quieted her voice. "No. You make it evil, by the way you see it, by the way you want to use it. Look at it, Johnny. Look at it. Is it evil?" She pushed her hair back and raised her face toward his. "Is it really evil, Johnny? You know it better than anyone else in the world. If it's really evil, Johnny . . . smash it. Smash it now."

She waited. His hands slowly came down from the sides of the walls. She watched, numbly, as he looked down at his right hand, and then balled that right hand into a huge fist. He looked at her, and there were tears in his eyes—and he drew back that arm and rammed it as hard as he could into the wall, three inches away from her face.

The wall was made of plasterboard, and it simply smashed into splinters as his fist went through it. She saw the splinters fly out and hit the other wall. He drew his fist out of the gaping hole he had made. In his bedroom, Little John began to cry.

"Go 'way," Johnny said. "Go 'way, please."

"Not without the baby." She waited. "There's nothing you could do with him anyway. There's no way you could give him what he needs."

Johnny screamed in pain, and threw back his fist, and smashed it into the wall on the other side of her, this time only an inch away from her face. This time she felt the rush of air as his fist went by, and the cracking of the wall behind her. And then she felt something sharp cut into her cheek, and a trickle of blood began to run down toward her chin.

"Oh, my God," he said, reaching up and touching the blood, trying to stop the blood with his finger. "Oh, my God," he said.

She reached up and took his hand in hers, and kissed the blood off his finger. Then she kissed the bruises that were beginning to form all over the knuckles of the hand. "Johnny," she said to the hand, "I have to go. It's over."

"I know," he said. "I knew the day Billy's car drove away with you."

"It was good," she said.

"Was it?"

"It was very good. It just ended. Some things . . . just end."

He wiped away a little more of the blood. It had begun to stop. "Will I ever see you again?"

"Yes. Certainly."

"And the kid?"

"Anytime you want. Just ask, and I'll send him down."

He turned away from her. "Get out of here."

She started to say something else, and then stopped. She ran to Little John's room and threw open the door. He was on the bed, crying. She scooped him up in both arms and fled out of the room—looking once more at Johnny's back—and then out of the house and into the taxi.

She was trembling. She couldn't stop her body from trembling until they were safely locked into a hotel room near the airport for the night.

8.

When they arrived back at Idlewild the next afternoon, she asked one of the stewardesses to sit with Little John for a few minutes, while she made some calls. There was no way she could take him with her to the "Y," or move in with Aaron yet. So she needed a place to stay for the night, or even for a few days.

She dialed Arlene. The phone rang five times, and then Arlene answered, quite out of breath.

"Am I disturbing you?" Melissa asked.

"Absolutely," Arlene answered. "But I needed the break, or I'd be dead in an hour. Just don't ask me what I was doing."

"I left Johnny. I brought my son up here with me."

"Already? Here?"

"At the airport. I need a place to stay tonight."

There was a long pause, and then Arlene said, "Melissa, I love you. I'd do anything in the world for you, except let you come here tonight."

"I understand," Melissa said too quickly.

"You don't. You can't. In your entire life, you never will. Melissa . . . Melissa, honey, I found him. I found him. He's here right now. He's been here ever since the party." She laughed. "He's in the bathroom now, trying to prove that he can use it for something besides screwing. He's not gorgeous and he's not rich. He even comes from Cincinnati. But he likes me. He even says he loves me. No one said that since my mother. And, honey, I just can't let you come over tonight, not when he's going to leave tomorrow."

"I'm so happy for you," Melissa said. "I'm so incredibly happy for you."

"The one man in the universe for me. And he was standing

there at the bar, drinking Jack Daniels and ginger ale.''

"Me too," Melissa said.

"Really?"

"Yes, at the party."

"So that's why you've got the kid up here already. Hey!"

"What?"

"We made it together. The big payoff."

"Yes," Melissa said. "The big payoff."

"We were lucky for each other. I knew when you walked in the door."

"Me too. I'm so happy for you. I'm so happy for me."

"Hey, gorgeous, he's coming back now. Wish me luck."

"I do. See you tomorrow." She put the phone back on the hook, and stood there a moment, glowing. And then she thought, where now? At first nothing came into her mind. And then she knew that she had at least one more chance.

She looked up the name P. Haas in the phone book. Pam picked up after the second ring.

"Pam, this is Melissa."

"Hi."

"I left my husband in Houston. I have a three-year-old son. I went down and got him and brought him back. I have no place to stay."

Pam laughed. "I've got milk, and vodka, and slightly stale hors d'oeuvres. Does he like hors d'oeuvres?"

"No," Melissa smiled. "But I guess I can stop at a deli on the way."

"God," Pam said, and her voice was singing, "I haven't had a kid in the house in five years. Get here as fast as you can . . . will you?"

9.

They were outside the farmhouse. You could hear their trucks drive up, hear them climb down and walk across the field, see their boots and their uniforms through the slits in the cellar walls.

No talk inside. No motion. They could hardly breathe.

Outside the soldiers sat now on the grass, put down their black rifles. They were SS. They killed slowly. Some of them were laughing. One of them, lying back on the grass, lit a cigarette.

The smell of the cigarette, drifting in through the slit in the cellar wall, woke up Aaron. He switched on the light immediately. Looked around the bedroom. Saw that the painting by Mark Rothko was still in its place opposite the bed. He put out his hand and touched the reality of the clock, saw that it was four in the morning. He extended the hand and touched the reality of the phone—the phone that connected him with Melissa, that had told him, tonight, that she was back in New York, safe, and the child now safe with her.

He sat up on the side of the bed. He had to fight falling back to sleep. He had to stay out of that dream. He had to stay in the present to be with her, to believe in her.

But he hadn't really slept for three nights. His mind was fogged. His body was drained. Coffee, he thought, coffee was the solution. He rolled over, and his body fell back on the bed, as his eyes closed.

One of the soldiers outside had taken out a pot and was making coffee. The smell of the coffee drifted into the cellar. They hadn't had coffee in weeks. They had hardly eaten. Their stomachs were twisted in agony.

They sat there, waiting, watching the soldiers pour coffee. They heard the boots of the soldiers upstairs in the farmhouse, heard bags of potatoes being dragged out of the kitchen. They heard the trapdoor from the kitchen to the cellar creak open. They heard a single pair of boots clump halfway down the stairs. They saw glints of a flashlight shine through cracks in the wood partition they were hiding behind. Then they heard the footsteps climb up again, and the trapdoor slam shut.

The bags were being hauled up on the trucks. The soldiers were finishing their cigarettes. The coffee pot was being put away. Then suddenly one of the men stood up, pointed across the field, and yelled at the others.

"Deer," he shouted in German. "A deer."

Aaron shifted his body slightly, noiselessly. Now, through the slit, he could see the young deer, standing frozen at the edge of the field, staring at the men in uniform who were shouting at him, and for some ungodly reason not bounding into the forest and out of sight. Then Aaron saw the reason why. The deer's left forepaw had been cut wide open, was bleeding onto the grass. He could not support his weight on it. It was held up, several inches from the ground. The deer could hardly move.

Rifles had already been scooped up. The first shot echoed through the field and crashed into the trees behind the deer. A second shot exploded, and then a third. And then suddenly there was the deafening roar of a submachine gun, and the deer was literally torn apart by a stream of bullets.

The soldiers rushed across the field to seize trophies from the deer. They were shouting, laughing, slapping each other on the back. But inside the cellar, at the same moment, one of the children, a two-year-old boy, began to cry.

His mother had her back turned to Aaron. She was holding the child in her arms. Aaron could not see the child, but he could hear him. The cry was not loud because the child was weak from lack of food. But it was loud enough for the soldiers to hear when they came back. They would look for the source of that cry. And find them all.

The mother tried to shush the child. It did no good. The soldiers were coming back. She tried to rock the child. It did no good. The soldiers were getting closer. She put her hand over the child's mouth. It did no good. The soldiers had almost reached them now.

The child was still moaning and still crying. In a moment the soldiers would hear the cry, and they would all die.

The mother was wearing a scarf around her neck. It was a silk scarf, that had come from Hungary. She ripped the scarf off her neck, folded it into a ball, and stuffed it into the child's mouth. The cry stopped. The sounds stopped. The soldiers came back and picked up the rest of their rifles, their knapsacks, the pot of coffee, and all the rest. Then they walked across the field, still laughing, and got into their trucks, and drove off.

The mother pulled the scarf out of the child's mouth. No sound came out of his mouth. No sound, no breath, ever again came out of his mouth.

The mother sat there, not moving, still holding her child, and rocked and wept. No one in the cellar moved . . . but Aaron.

He slowly raised himself to his feet, and began to move across the cellar toward the dark-haired woman who had killed her child to keep him from crying out. In the dream he moved very slowly, as though the air between them were a wall that he had to wedge his way through to get to her. Each step took an hour. And as he came closer he realized with surprise that her hair was very blond, and very long, and very, very beautiful. She was wearing black, and her hair was perfectly cut and set, as though she had been in the beauty parlor only an hour before. He began to slow his pace, and he began to feel the cold of the cellar sink through his skin, and fill the bones of his body.

But there was no way he could keep from coming toward her. Closer . . . and closer . . . and closer. And as he came close enough to touch her—as he saw his hands begin to lift and reach out toward her—she slowly turned her face toward him. And he saw the first outline of her cheek emerge behind the blond hair. And he recognized that cheek. And he knew that it was impossible for him to bear to see any more of that face, and that he had to—

Wake up! Into the cold dawn of the fall morning. His body was wet with sweat. The sheets of the bed were soaked. Terror pinned him to the bed as he tried to catch his breath, to force in huge gulps of air, as though it were he who was being smothered. Trying to think again in English. Trying to prove that he was alive, in New York . . . now.

He forced himself up on his elbows. Thank God it was light. The dream was fading. His breath was returning to normal. This was New York. There was a new life—a new woman and a new child—waiting.

The dream flashed back into his mind. He blocked it out completely. It was a devil's dream. There was no truth to its ending. No truth. No meaning.

He had found the woman he loved. He had found the woman he was destined for. He was going to marry her. And she was going to give him the child he had lost in that dream.

10.

The next week Melissa and Aaron made a pact. They would see each other every day for a long lunch and then a quick dinner. Then she would rush to Pam's and be with

Little John for his dinner, and then stay with the little boy and Pam for the rest of the evening—in case the child woke in the middle of the night, in case there was any anxiety at being alone, in case there was any fear whatsoever of the new city, or his new life.

His baby-sitter during the day cost fifty dollars an hour—but didn't charge a penny. From the moment Little John came through her door, Pam fell hopelessly in love with him. Five years before, flat broke, and after a scarring legal battle, she had been forced to give up her own son to his father. But now a new incarnation had miraculously appeared in her life, to be tucked into his own bed in the spare room, to be picked up just before he went to sleep, and hugged and squeezed and kissed, and to actually be kissed and hugged and squeezed in return. All night long, games that had lain dormant in her mind for five years suddenly came alive.

The next morning Pam went to the phone, and cancelled every shooting appointment she had for the next week. She had three dinner dates for that week; she broke them in less than a minute apiece. For one glorious week, before Melissa moved in with Aaron, Pamela Haas had a small boy to love again. And she wasn't going to waste a single second of that time on anything as trivial as making money, or playing the dating game.

For the first four nights, Monday through Thursday, Melissa would be with Pam and Little John. Then, on Friday afternoon, she and Aaron would drive away to a friend's house he had borrowed in Connecticut. There, they would be truly alone—together for the first time.

In just four nights, Melissa thought, as she went into the bathroom during Little John's nap, and took her birth control pills out of their case, one by one, and flushed them down the toilet.

She was destroying her last shield, her last protection against Aaron. She was rendering herself completely naked. Open. Fertile again. She was also, she realized, in the process of transferring her love from one man to another.

Until now, she had given herself to one man only. She had been owned by one love only. Now she was about to be owned, just as thoroughly, by another. It was, for her, cere-monial. That was why she had insisted that she and Aaron not make love yet. She looked at her face in the bathroom mirror. In the sharp September sun, she could still see the imprint of

Johnny's skin upon hers. She could still see the small, slowly healing cut that Johnny's rage had slashed into her face two days before.

Purification, she thought. A ritual cleansing. In five days, the cut would be gone. Her face would have forgotten Johnny's skin. She would be new again for her new man.

The body heals itself, she thought. The body purifies itself. When I come to him, no longer will I have been touched by another man. I have loved before, and I will honor that love, but I will not bring it to bed with my new man. I will give myself, free and clear, to him. A baptism by time, she thought. A rebirth. And then she smiled bitterly. If my father knew, he might even be proud.

11.

During their lunches and dinners together, she made sure that they spent most of the time exploring Aaron's life, and Aaron's mind. Her self-assigned task was to grow into his world. And his, in response, was to feed her the love, and the knowledge she needed to grow into that world.

The first great step, of course, was art. And so their first two lunches, on Monday and Tuesday, were held at the Museum of Modern Art and the Metropolitan Museum of Art. To reach the art that he owned, and that she would soon own, they had to start at the beginning of the modern period. And so he took her to the great Impressionist and Postimpressionist rooms. Slowly and tenderly, he began filling in the gaps in her knowledge with dates and biographies and histories, showing her the hidden relationships between Monet and Renoir, between Gauguin and Cézanne and Picasso, between the Fauves and the first Cubist paintings.

Each day, as they walked, she noticed three or four people trailing behind them, listening discreetly from a distance. For Aaron loved art, and his words were a wire that conducted the electricity of that love from his eyes to the eyes of his listener. Painting after painting that had become dusty with time, was cleaned and set sparkling by the caress of his words. It was as though he had cast a spell over the entire museum, and suddenly the brush had been applied to the canvas only yesterday, and the footstep echoing through the museums might very easily belong to Degas, or Van Gogh, or Matisse.

The second wedding gift to her was great food, and great wine. Her introduction to this vast realm of sensual delight, on Wednesday, came with a prolonged lunch in the sun-drenched first room at Pavillon, and then an early dinner in a quiet corner upstairs at Lutèce. These were, he told her, not only two of the finest restaurants in New York, but in the entire world. Both had master chefs. Both had wine cellars stocked with treasures that could be obtained almost nowhere else. The food she reveled in. But it was the complexity and subtlety and sheer myth and ritual of the wine that made her glow.

At lunch he ordered a modest Corton Charlemagne. But at dinner she tasted her first bottle of Château Lafite-Rothschild, 1947. She asked a hundred questions. She learned why 1947 was a true vintage year, and why 1948 was only mediocre. She learned how many years it took a superb wine to reach its peak, and for how many years thereafter it stayed at that stage of perfection, before it began to go downhill. She participated in the age-old drama of the first pouring of the wine. She watched the amber fluid trickle into the bottom of Aaron's huge glass. She watched the wine steward and the captain hover above him as he reached out and picked up the glass, holding its bottom in his palm. Then he gently held the glass beneath his face, and judged the quality of its bouquet. When he finally tasted the wine, neither the captain, nor the steward, nor she herself breathed for that one moment of judgment. And then Aaron's face broke into a beaming smile. All was well with the world.

The third wedding gift came Thursday. It was, she often thought, the best of all. It started in Central Park, at the Children's Zoo. He was waiting for her at one o'clock, at the gate, when she had finished her shooting. He kissed her, and then led her by the hand to the cafeteria, where he bought them two hot dogs apiece, and a Coke. They sat outside on the terrace of the cafeteria, eating their lunch, watching the seals play in the pond in front of them, saying little. When they had done, he took her again by the hand, and walked back past the caged tigers, and the monkeys, and the bears, out into the expanse of the park itself.

It was a lovely autumn day, quite warm, and the park was filled with all kinds and colors of people, strolling among the grass and trees, as they themselves were strolling. When they reached the boat basin, he rented a rowboat, helped her in, and then climbed in after her. He rowed to the middle of the lake, and she let her hand trail behind her in the water, cool and surprisingly clear. Once they almost crashed into another boat, but she leaned over quickly and pushed the boat away from the impact, almost fell into the water, and got her right sleeve wet up to the shoulder. For the next ten minutes she lay in the boat, laughing and running her bare foot up and down his calf, underneath his pants leg.

After the boat ride they each had to hurry to return to work, but at the 60th Street exit from the park, he paused to take her lightly by the shoulders, and kissed her, first on the forehead, and then on the cheek, and then lightly on the mouth. "I happen to love you," he said. "I think it's incurable."

"I intend to reinfect you," she said, "every day, for the rest of our lives."

When he left, she stood there for a moment, and watched the way he walked. So, she thought, the third gift was intimacy. Comfort. The ability to be alone together, and do or say nothing in particular, and adore every instant of it.

Funny, she thought, how much more precious that is to me, than even wine or art.

12.

The fourth wedding gift came Friday, just before they left on their trip.

She had packed a bag, and kissed Little John, and come down to meet him on the street, where his convertible was parked. He came out and kissed her, put the bag in the trunk, helped her into the car, and then sat behind the wheel. He made no move to start the car.

"It's a lovely day," she said.

'The loveliest day of my life."

"Aren't we going to leave?"

"In a moment," he said. "I'd like to give you something first. I didn't want to wait till we got there. This may not be exactly the right place, but I think it's precisely the right time." He opened the glove compartment, and took out a small box, wrapped in white paper, with a delicate red ribbon tied in a French bow around it. "It has no card," he said. "I . . . for once in my life, I have no words."

She sat there with the box resting lightly in her left hand. The street was lined with cars and trees and people, and she was afraid to open the box in front of them all, though no one was looking, and no one really cared.

"You pull the end of the ribbon," he whispered.

"I know," she said.

"Please," he said. "I want you to have it now."

Her hand trembled as she untied the ribbon. It trembled as she snapped open her purse, and dropped the ribbon into it. She didn't want to lose a single part of this moment. She pulled away the paper and felt the velvet surface of the box beneath. She looked up at him.

For him there was no outside, no street, no people. The world was inside this car. She had never seen so much love, and so much concern, in a man's face. She had never known that a man's face could be that strong, and yet at the same time filled with that much love.

She slipped out the velvet box and opened it.

In the box there were two rings. She had seen both rings before. She had worn both rings before. She knew both of them, intimately. She wanted both of them, limitlessly. But she had never dreamed that someday she would own them.

They were the two rings that she had worn in the tea-pouring photograph. One of them was the perfect four-carat diamond from Harry Winston. The other was the Chinese jade wedding band, that had been carved two centuries before. Now they were hers—not just for a day, but forever.

"How did you know?" she asked. "How in the world could you know?"

"The first ad. I saw them on your finger. I knew they belonged there. But then, I didn't have the right." He touched her hand. "I do now."

His eyes were still riveted to her face. She had made up for an hour for the trip, and now the makeup was being spoiled by the tears that were running down it, and dropping onto her skirt.

"I can't put them on," she said.

"Just reach out," he said. "They're yours now."

"I don't want to. I don't want to do it myself. I want you to do it for me."

"Of course," he said. "I should have known." He took the diamond ring out of the box, and held it up into the gleaming light. Then he took her left hand and slipped the diamond on her third finger.

"The other one too," she said.

The jade band came out of the box. It had taken a craftsman a full year to carve its almost-invisible pattern. He took the diamond ring off her finger for a moment, and laid it on her skirt. Then he put the jade band on, and then the diamond again in front of it.

"We'll do this again, formally," he said. "But I wanted you to have both of them now."

She stared at her hand with the two rings. Doubly claimed. Doubly joined.

"God, I love you," she said.

"I have a strange way to say it," he replied. "But it's important to me. I want to say it to you from my past as well as my present. From the boy you love, as well as from the man you love." He took her hands in both his hands, and bent down to kiss them.

"*Ich liebe dich*," he said, and lifted up his face and kissed away her tears.

13.

It was one o'clock when they arrived at the house in Connecticut, and they were thirsty and hungry. The day was exceptionally hot for September. The engine stilled, and then there was silence, and then the sound of the wind in the trees, and the birds. They were alone. And she was suddenly awkward and nervous.

"It's a marvelous house," she said.

"It's entirely ours," he said. "There's no one in it. Even the servants are gone."

She looked at him, knowing the moment had come for him to dictate the order of the ritual.

"It's completely isolated," he went on. "The trees shield it like a living wall. There's no one around for acres."

"Then we can do—"

"Whatever we want." He touched her hair. "Whenever we want to do it."

She took his hand in both of hers, and kissed its palm. "And what will that be?" she whispered.

"I want to make love to you right now," he said, "on this lawn, under these trees and this sky, more than anything else in the world. I don't want to go in the house, I don't want to unpack, I don't want to eat or talk, or do anything right or civilized. I simply want to make love to you—now."

She opened the door and began to climb out of the car onto the lawn. But he grabbed hold of her hand and held it. When she turned around, he was smiling, and the smile was not gentle now, but strong. Immensely self-confident. Immensely seductive.

"You've kept me waiting five days," he said. "I understood, and I agreed. But now," and the smile broadened, "I shall keep you waiting an hour."

She felt the surge of disappointment flow up her body and show on her face, and she was half-proud and half-ashamed that it showed. She had given him command, and he had taken it.

"I have a very good light lunch in the cooler," he said. "I suggest we change into our bathing suits, take a swim, have lunch, and talk about our other plans later."

He got out of the car, unpacked the trunk, and waited for her to follow him into the house. She opened the car door slowly. She suddenly realized that this marriage was not going to be at all like the one she had known with Johnny.

14.

There was a bottle of Chablis in the cooler, still chilled, and they drank every drop. By the time they had finished the chicken and cheese, the sun had dried their bathing suits and her hair, and she was feeling more than a little tipsy. They were sitting on a thick purple beach blanket by the pool, and she had not heard the sound of a car or of another human being for over an hour.

He drained the last drop from the long thin glass, and then turned it upside down, and slipped it into the crushed ice of the cooler. He was completely relaxed. And massive in his white trunks. He had muscles, rippling muscles, everywhere. And she had done nothing, for over an hour, but watch the muscles—and wait.

She could never remember, afterward, what they had talked about during that lunch, though she knew that they had talked throughout it. Words had passed between them, but the words meant nothing. She thought, over and over again, that his hour was worth fifty times more, in sheer wanting, than her five days.

He reached out across the blanket and touched her calf. His fingernails scraped their way slowly down her calf. She felt the scraping all the way up to her shoulder blades.

"It's still quite hot in the house," he said.

"I noticed," she replied.

"I doubt if it will cool off till night."

The nails moved up her calf again, slowly. Past her knee. Then onto her thigh. She moved her legs slightly open, to welcome them up, as far as they wished to go.

"There's no doubt that the house would be too . . . stuffy," he said.

"I agree." Her thigh, with the nails moving slowly up it, began to tremble, almost invisibly.

"The water was quite delicious, though, wasn't it," he went on.

The nails had reached the white fabric of her swimsuit. They slid off the skin of her thigh, and onto the white fabric. His great hand was now centered between, the middle finger barely touching the fabric. She watched in fascination as the nails came together and suddenly scraped their way down the full length of the white fabric.

She almost cried out in shock and joy from the sensation. She was wet and open in an instant. Her mouth had opened automatically and taken in a huge burst of air. She knew that if the nails scraped again, there would be nothing she could do. She would give way to orgasm, on the beach blanket, by the pool.

His hand, however, slowly moved away. She wanted to grab it with both of her hands and pull it back, but she could only sit and watch it move slowly away. He was in command. He had already showed her the first taste of what that command could accomplish. All she could do, in response, was follow.

"The water was delicious," he said again. "Wasn't it?"

"Very," she replied, trying to keep her mind thinking.

He rose to his feet. He was a bronze giant above her. "Shall we try the pool?"

"Anything you say."

He took her by the hand, and walked with her to the shallow end of the pool. They carefully lowered themselves, hand in hand, step by step, into the pristine, pure-green water. She shivered slightly as the water came up to her ankles, and then her knees, and then her thighs, and then past her already wet bikini bottoms, and then up to her rib cage as they waded to the four-foot marker at the shallow end of the pool.

They turned and faced each other. He put wet, cool hands on her shoulders, and then slowly slid the wet hands toward each other along her back, till they met, and she felt the cool water trickle down her spine till it touched the water of the pool. The skin of her back and shoulders was tingling, as he slowly drew her toward him. Her mouth came open automatically as it neared his, as his head came down to join hers, as his lips—still tart and cool with wine—flowed over hers, and his tongue came out and laid claim to every moist inch of her mouth, and her tongue, and her teeth.

Next she felt his hands slide from her back once more to her shoulders, and he gently pushed her away from him so that her back rested against the edge of the pool. His thumbs slipped inside the straps of her top, eased the straps off her shoulders, and then lowered the straps till they came down around the elbows. She felt the swimsuit top catch for a second on both hard nipples, and then the nipples sprung free into the glowing sun, and she was naked from the waist up.

She searched his face as he looked at her naked breasts. It bore the same expression she had seen when he stood in front of a Monet, or Van Gogh, or Gauguin. It was a strange mixture of the aesthete and the animal. Of the urge to adore, and the absolute need to possess.

He moved her slightly now, so that her body came deeper

into the water, and the cool water inched up till it touched the very bottom of her nipples. Then he stopped, and bent forward, and surrounded her left breast with his mouth. She felt the warmth of his tongue mixed with the coolness of the water from the pool. He rotated his tongue around her nipple, mixing warm and cool, alternately chilling and heating, hardening the already firm nipple till she thought it would burst.

His hands had left her arms, and the top of her swimsuit was now floating away from them, sinking slowly into the blue-green water. His hands scraped down against her ribs and then her sides, and she felt the sudden rush of cool water that filled her pelvis as her bikini bottom was slowly lowered beneath her knees, and then slipped off though the clear, shimmering water to the bottom of the pool.

Her head turned against his chest, and she watched in hypnotic attention as he opened his trunks, and dropped them alongside hers at the bottom of the pool. Through the rippling water he was huge and beautiful, and she watched her hand float out to take him, and she felt the thrill of his flesh surrounded by her hand, and she closed her eyes and shut off all her senses but the feel of her hand, and the tremendous power and safety and ownership that that hand, and the object in that hand, gave her.

Her eyes were still closed when she felt his hands on her back again—wet hands against the exposed, hot back. And then those hands sliding down again along her flesh into the water. And then slowly curving themselves around her buttocks. And then slowly picking up her body, lifting her partially out of the cool water, as though she were a feather.

Her eyes came open, into the sparkling blue and green afternoon. She saw the purple beach robe by the side of the pool, and the wine bottle turned upside down into the ice of the cooler. She felt her thighs being spread wide apart by his hands, felt her wet legs begin their long journey around the sides of his thighs and then buttocks, felt her ankles lock together behind him, felt her body being lifted up and forward toward his pelvis, felt the hard contact of male flesh against female flesh, felt herself spreading and widening to accommodate the width and strength of him, felt first the water rush in, and then the water being forced out as he slid inch by inch inside her. Then her eyes again closed, and she concentrated on nothing but the overwhelming entrance of her new man inside her—slowly, smoothly, triumphantly—inch after inch after inch till she wondered if he would ever stop. And then, the end, the soft, intimate grinding of pelvis against pelvis, and the almost fantastic accomplishment of being able to contain, within herself, every tiny fraction of this man.

She looked down at his bronze body, cradling her white body. They were now locked together in the cool clear water, immersed in it almost up to their shoulders. He was beginning to move her lower body smoothly and deliberately back and forth against himself. Her arms had reached up and encircled his neck, and their mouths had met again, and their tongues were exploring a wetness different from the wetness of the pool around them.

Now he began moving her in a wide rotating motion—carefully, and not too rapidly. She leaned her head back a little, and rested her shoulders gently against the tile of the pool. Her hands clutched his arms, and she could feel each of the smooth flowing efforts his arms made in pulling her back and forth, to and fro, up and down around his groin.

Suddenly she discovered that she was quite buoyant in the water, and that there was no need for her to continue circling his body. With a sense of wonderment, she unlocked her ankles, and saw her toes float by themselves in the water just above the surface of the pool.

He felt the movement, and looked behind him, and smiled. Then he took one step to the right, and then another—never breaking the rhythm of his arms or the movement of her body. Now her waist and breasts were above the water as well, and her knees were floating out of the water, and her toes were straight up, with their gleaming red polish sparkling out of the blue-green pool.

He began moving her faster now—breathing deeper, harder, louder. His hands were beginning to dig gently into the flesh of her buttocks. She was astounded to find that his penis inside her had again begun to swell, that it was becoming wider and wider, that it was beginning to push up slightly against the very back of her vagina, against the cervix itself. At first it felt uncomfortable, then incredibly exciting. She could feel it now with exactly the same sensitivity, the same intensity that he could. She knew that the man inside her was swelling and swelling to the very point of explosion.

His face was exquisitely flushed. His brown hair was tossing and gleaming in the sun. His deep brown eyes had turned jet black. The planes of his face had tightened and lifted. He looked years younger, a thousand times stronger than the day she had first met him on the plane. And, in the brilliant sun, in the hundred spotlight reflections dancing across his face from the pool, Melissa knew that he had to be, at that instant, the handsomest man she had ever seen.

Now, as he moved her more and more quickly, more and more powerfully, waves began to form between their two bodies, and ripple up to the surface. The entire pool was now churning, from end to end. Her knees were moving through the water like pistons. She suddenly caught her breath, as she became aware that each time he moved her back and forth now, with all the frenzied power of those immense arms, great bursts of water were being sprayed against her exposed clitoris, and that these repeated spurts of water were maddening, and that she herself was moving, uncontrollably, ecstatically, as rapidly as he, toward the first double orgasm of her life.

"Are you ready?" he gasped.

"Yes," she screamed. "For God's sake, yes!"

Suddenly, the waves between their two bodies grew, and shot to the surface, and exploded there in huge crystalline bubbles, spraying both their shoulders and faces with cool, stinging water.

She felt her vagina contract around his penis, and then spasm against his flesh as rapidly as the bubbles had exploded on the pool's surface between them. At the same moment, he lifted back his godlike head, and gave out an animal cry so loud that it seemed to echo back to them in all directions from the trees surrounding them.

They must have stood there clinging to each other, her body still cradled in his arms, for ten minutes, as the waves in the pool, and the waves in their bodies, slowly diminished, and allowed them to climb up out of the water again.

15.

That same Friday night, after the office had closed, and she had come home and read the note, Victoria Krane began slowly to kill herself.

She had been wrong. It wasn't a twenty-five-year old. It was a twenty-one-year old. And it had been one of her own models, a girl who had been with the agency six months, who had had a brilliant future, and who was now on a plane with a man two and a half times as old as she, heading ecstatically toward disaster.

Victoria went to the bar and began pouring bourbon into a glass. Straight bourbon, no ice, into a water glass. Halfway full. The most subtle poison. The least painful. The most prolonged. The least blameful. You simply killed yourself and the other person lived on, to kill himself later in his own way.

Mary had been sent home. The apartment was hollow, the weekend was empty, and free. No one to bother her for the first experiment. No need to reappear until Monday. No visible signs, at least for the first month or two.

The nerves went first. They took away the pain.

The face went next. That took away the source of the pain.

After a while, the eyes went numb. They no longer felt what they saw.

She saluted the image—the image that had dominated her life—in the mirror. Then she threw the glass at the mirror. It shattered, and her image became nothing but a gaping hole. Growing old gracefully, she thought, reaching for another glass, is the greatest lie. There is always someone standing nearby, to slash your grace to slivers.

Sunday afternoon they were lying together on the lawn, without the blanket, naked bodies touching the grass and the earth. It was late afternoon, slightly overcast. They were holding hands, dozing. From outside the trees, along the dirt road, they heard the harsh, grinding sound of a truck—the first sound they had heard from the outside world for two days. She felt his hand tighten on hers, to the point of pain. Before she could open her eyes, he was sitting up, his entire body tensed, ready to spring to his feet, his eyes searching wildly for the nearest patch of trees.

"It's an old truck," she said quietly.

His body eased. She watched his arms relax, his shoulders slacken. She heard the breath come rushing out of his lungs. He turned the other way, his back toward her, sitting up on the grass, his arms wrapped around his knees, listening as the sound of the truck faded in the distance.

She rolled over, rose to her feet, and threw her arms around his back and shoulders. She kissed the side of his neck, and placed her cheek against his. "Are you all right?" she whispered.

"Yes," he said. "I'm sorry."

"What happened?"

"A memory. The truck. It must have been very old."

"Do you want to tell me about it?"

He turned to look at her. He reached up and touched her hair. "No," he said. "No. I don't want to talk about it. Ever."

Oh God, she thought, the sadness in his eyes.

17.

They had made love twice a day since they had been there—marvelous love. But that night, when they went to bed, when he drew down the sheet and looked at her face and body, all he could see was the color of her hair. In the light of the single bed lamp, what he suddenly saw lying in front of him, waiting for him to enter her, was an Aryan woman. Not quite German, perhaps, but nevertheless Aryan. And therefore, *verboten*, on pain of death.

He stood on his knees in front of her, slowly moving his body from side to side, desperately in love with her, and absolutely impotent.

She looked up, first at his body and then his face. She rose to her elbows. "What's wrong?" she asked.

"I can't," he said. "I can't."

She had no history to deal with this. She had never known Johnny, even when he was so drunk he couldn't drive, not to have an immediate erection the second he took her to bed. One surprise—one revelation—crowded all others from her mind. It was thrilling to know that there were men in the world so sensitive that they could not always be instantly animal.

She smiled. She let her delight show on her face. "You have," she said, "a year to repeat this afternoon's superb performance. I'm not good at figures," and she began to count on her fingers, "but I think that leaves eleven months, twenty-nine days, sixteen hours, and nine minutes."

He looked down at her, startled.

"But there is one condition," she said.

"And that is?" he asked.

"That I can still touch it." Her face took on an innocent, little girl's look. "Or even, if I want to, kiss it."

"Do you want to?"

The little girl's look never faded. "Very much."

"Even now?"

"Especially now."

She knelt, and moved slowly toward him. "Please," she whispered.

"Yes," he said. "Yes . . . yes . . . yes."

Three minutes later, she looked up at his face, and then down at the human miracle she held again in her hand. "I want him inside of me," she said.

"Of course," he said, taking her face, and her beautiful hair, in his hands. And then laying her gently down beneath him, he entered her, and felt the power of her body, and her love, liberate and unchain his own.

She awoke at four in the morning. There was a light patter of rain on the roof above them. He was lying rigidly on his back beside her, soaked in sweat. His face was twisted in agony. He was mumbling words—words in German—words she could not understand.

"Aaron," she called out.

"*Stille*," he replied. "*Das kreiger . . .*"

"Aaron," she called again, and leaned over and touched his shoulder. As she did, her hair fell softly over his face. His face changed the instant he felt her hair. His hand shot up and pressed her hair against his face. His fingers clutched her hair so desperately that it was all she could do not to cry out in pain.

"Your hair is long," he said, his eyes still closed.

"Yes," she said. "Very long."

"It's blond," he said. The eyes were fluttering now.

"Yes," she replied.

His eyes had not yet quite opened. His mind was not yet

quite clear. "Her hair is black," he said. "It's short, isn't it?"

"Yes, very short," she answered, not knowing, not caring what he was saying, as long as it was in English.

His eyes opened. They studied the outlines of her face in the dark room, as though that face was about to disappear from his life forever. His hand relaxed its grip on her hair, and then began to stroke it gently.

"I'm sorry," he said.

"There's nothing to be sorry for."

"I have this dream. Sometimes it comes back. Most of the time it's gone."

She knew better than to ask him what it was.

"Stay with me," he said, "and the dream won't come back."

"Then it's gone forever," she whispered, kissing his cheek, wiping away the sweat from his face and forehead.

He fell asleep again with his hand still stroking her hair. She waited ten minutes, but heard no more words, and felt no more rigidity in his body. Then she moved softly out of bed, and walked barefooted to the window.

Outside, there were the clouds, and the trees and the rain. She stood leaning against the side of the window, first thinking about Aaron, and then simply listening to her body. She had always listened to her body, ever since she was a child. Her body told her secrets that ordinary people never seemed to know. Now her body was sending up strange signals, signals she had heard only once before. Women who could not listen would take weeks to know, and would have to be told by someone else. She knew tonight.

She turned and stared at the figure in the bed, now sleeping peacefully. You have given me so many gifts, she thought. Now I have a gift for you. The greatest gift of all. Part you. Part me.

It must be a blessing from God, she thought. My redemption, for leaving home. For breaking with my father and my husband. For daring to be all that I am. And your redemption, she thought, for some past I shall never know. For some fear, that made you believe that you could never share this gift with me.

She shook back her hair in the darkness. We have made that fear a lie. I have you now, inside me as well as outside. I have searched for you all my life. And I have you now. You have me. And no force on earth can ever separate us now.

BOOK FOUR

1975

1.

It all exploded like a bomb, when Victoria died.

August 10, 1975. In a hospital room with three other women. The face was unrecognizable—puffed round with edema, yellow, withered. The hair gray. The hands yellow. The eyes never opening. The breathing hoarse. Only Melissa and a short stocky Burmese intern were with the woman who had been dying for years, from self-administered poison.

For five days Melissa had sat there, waiting for the eyes to open, waiting for her hand to be felt on Victoria's hand, waiting for some sign of recognition. It never came. She was beyond medical help; she was beyond human reach. On the fifth day, at five minutes past four, the hoarse breathing simply stopped. There was no change in the color of the face, in the temperature of the already cold hand. Nothing happened, except the breathing stopped.

The intern reached for the other hand, sought for a pulse. Then he looked up at Melissa—they had developed some sort of silent bond during the five days—and pulled the intravenous needle out of the vein in Victoria's arm. Melissa held the other hand even more tightly. As though, somehow, if she held it tightly enough, Victoria wouldn't feel the pain of the needle being drawn out.

The intern pushed the inverted glucose jar away from the bed, so it bulged out against the white curtain. He reached for the phone, then looked up at Melissa. "You should go home now," he said.

"When will they come for her?" she answered.

"In five minutes."

"I'll stay here till then."

"It isn't pleasant."

"I'll stay here."

He called the nurses' desk. Then he put down the phone. "You should go home," he said again. "The orderlies—they have no soul. They're very rough with them when they die." He had dark brown eyes in a dark brown face. The eyes were very deep. "It will hurt you," he said, "very much."

"I don't care," she said, both her hands now shielding Victoria's hand. "Would you," and it was all she could say to him after five days, "leave us alone now?"

"Of course," he said, and walked silently through the part in the white curtain.

Melissa watched the curtain billow back slowly, and then again surround the bed. Then she lowered her cheek to Victoria's cold, cold hand, and began silently to weep.

2.

Three days later, at the graveside service, there wasn't a cloud in the sky; the sun sparkled, and Melissa wore dark glasses to protect her eyes against the light, and other people's eyes.

They had taken the wrong turn, and were ten minutes late. There were only twenty people gathered around the open grave when they got there. A man in a dark suit was reading from a small black book, and when Aaron helped her out—and then the two children behind her—she could hear what he was reading:

> —yet, do not grieve;
> She cannot fade, though thou hast not thy bliss
> For ever wilt thou love, and she be fair!

Of course, Melissa thought, Keats. Across the open grave, across the mahogany casket suspended above it, Melissa saw Arlene Conners for the first time in years. There had been letters passed between them, of course—Christmas cards every winter, and a few phone calls. But no photos. It took nearly a minute before Melissa could link the face with her memory of Arlene—who had gained twenty, or perhaps even thirty pounds, and whose face had sagged, had grown thick and coarse with the years. She stood bareheaded in the harsh sun, clusters of wrinkles etched across her skin, and she saw Melissa's involuntary expression, as Melissa reacted to the damage on Arlene's face.

The man's voice droned on:

> More happy love! more happy, happy love!
>   For ever warm and still to be enjoy'd,
>   For ever panting and for ever young.

There were seven or eight models from the agency—none from the last few years, of course. All were from the fifties or early sixties. All had grown too old now to earn a living in front of the camera. Of them all, only Melissa was still sought out, still commanded eighty dollars an hour, was still featured in advertisements, covers, and billboards all over America. The others had faded. They had married, well or badly. Or they were divorced, or were living with whomever they could. They too shuddered in the sun. They too were living ghosts around a grave.

The poetry went on, burning stronger than the heat:

> When old age shall this generation waste,
>   Thou shalt remain, in midst of other woe
> Than ours, a friend to man, to whom thou say'st,
>   'Beauty is truth, truth beauty,—that is all
> Ye know on earth, and all ye need to know.'

There was a pause, and then the snap of the black book being shut. "I'm sorry," the man said, "but those are the only words she wanted spoken." He looked around. There was no movement, no response. "We shall now lower her into her final resting place."

The cords under the casket began to give way, and the huge mahogany box began to sink slowly into the cavity beneath it. Melissa clutched Aaron's strong hand, and watched the box descend. Then her lips began to move of their own accord, and she whispered quietly to the woman who could not say the words herself, "Our Father which art in heaven, Hallowed be Thy name . . ."

When the prayer was over, she halted for a moment. There were no tears in her eyes now, but it was only Aaron's hand that kept her standing straight.

"Father," her lips went on, as the casket jolted into the solid ground beneath it, "Take this beautiful soul into your breast. And give her peace."

There should have been tears, but no tears would come. Only pain.

"Since no member of the immediate family is here," the gray man said, "I shall place earth on the casket."

He bent down stiffly, and reached his hand into the pile of fresh brown soil next to the gravesite. He took a small handful of the soil, and it rattled down on top of the casket. Then he rubbed his fingers together, and walked away, toward the waiting line of cars.

Melissa looked across the grave at Arlene. They both nodded at the same instant. Melissa took off her glasses, and handed them to Aaron. Then she and Arlene stepped forward, to the huge pyramid of brown soil. They bent down together and picked up a handful of the rich moist earth. Then they rose and poured the earth on top of the casket—to cover it, to seal it, to honor it. They moved back to their families, and Melissa replaced her dark glasses.

Again there was a pause. And then, one after the other, each of the models moved out of the line, and offered her contribution of earth. When the last of them had finished, the line broke, and they all began walking toward the cars.

As soon as they had crossed the green grass, and reached the stone path again, Arlene ran over to Melissa, and they threw their arms around each other. Aaron and the two children stayed to the side, and Arlene's husband came over and shook his hand. But the two women simply took each other's hands, and walked in silence ahead of the men and the children, up the path, till they reached the cars.

"Can I see you for a moment" Arlene said, "away from the men?"

"Of course," Melissa said, glancing at Aaron, and then leading Arlene away from the cars, onto the other side of the gray cemetery street.

"I need help, badly," Arlene went on. "If I don't get it"—she looked back at the gravesite—"I think I'm going to end up like her. And I think you're the only person in the world who can give it to me."

"Stanley?" Melissa asked.

"Me," Arlene answered. "Do me a favor. Take off your glasses again."

They were standing directly in the sun—far too bright for Melissa's eyes. But she reached up and removed the glasses.

She watched Arlene's professional eyes study her face. "Then it's true," Arlene said. "I thought they'd airbrushed your photos. I've been cutting out your ads for months now.

Actually studying them with a magnifying glass. I knew that I would detect any kind of retouching. But I couldn't believe it. I couldn't sit and look at my own mirror and believe it.''

She reached up her hand and gently touched the skin around Melissa's eyes. ''You haven't aged over a year,'' she said. ''Not a month over a year. Your face is stronger now. The lines are more defined. You look . . . a mature twenty-seven. And I hate you for it.''

''But you—''

''Nobody has to tell me how I look. I wake up to it every morning. I go to sleep with it every night. I see it in Stanley's eyes every time he comes to bed with me.'' She held up her hand, blocking Melissa's question. ''No. Nothing's happened yet. At least nothing I know of. But I'm drowning, honey. I'm drowning in fat and wrinkles. And I can watch him beginning to swim away. I even talked plastic surgery with him. But he says he doesn't believe in it. He says this is the way it's supposed to be with women as old as I am.''

''No,'' Melissa said, ''this isn't the way it's supposed to be with women as old as you''—and then she caught herself—''as we are.''

Arlene's hands shot up and grabbed Melissa's shoulders. ''I'm dying, like she died. I'm where she was, fifteen years ago.'' The hands tightened on Melissa's shoulders. ''But I don't want to drown myself like she did, honey. I've got two kids. So for Christ's sake . . . please . . . please . . . teach me how to be young again.''

3.

Pamela Hass stood outside the cemetery, a block away from its entrance, with the taxi waiting a few yards behind her. She saw the cars go in, she waited, and then she saw the cars come out again. She was partially hidden under a tree, and so no one recognized her as they came out. She saw Arlene. She saw two or three of the models she had known. She saw Melissa, wearing dark glasses. Behind Melissa, in the back seat of the car, she saw Little John, now a tall teenager, and her heart turned over. Sitting next to him was Melissa's girl—what was her name? Lacey—and the girl looked out of the car window, and her face came into the light, and Pam caught her breath.

Then the car turned, and they were gone. Pam waited a minute, to see if any other cars were coming out. When none did, she walked along the wall to the entrance and looked in. There was nothing but green grass, and gray roads and paths, and here and there the glint of a tiny bronze plaque. No headstones. No visual clue at all that this was a cemetery. No way to find Victoria. So Pam stood at the entrance, and bowed her head and said a tiny prayer that she had learned as a child.

Then she walked back to the cab, and was driven home to her apartment. It cost thirty dollars—half the money she had in her savings account.

Inside, she went straight to the mirror and started putting on makeup. The face was still good, she thought. You couldn't photograph it, but men still bought it in person. But the body was gone. Too much booze. Too many men paying off with fancy dinners. Had to make love now with the lights dim.

All these years, she thought. All these years in the same town, and she hadn't seen Melissa. And Melissa's girl, Lacey. Incredible! Had Melissa been that gorgeous at thirteen? What did people say when they saw the mother and daughter together? She scanned her memory. No photos of the two of them. And it would have been a natural. Great publicity, or a fabulous ad campaign. Good, she thought. Melissa's still Melissa. Keeping the girl out of the papers. Letting her stay a child for a while. So easy the other way. This goddamn town had so many tricks to seduce you.

I want a drink, she thought. But not here. Not alone. I want to call Melissa, she thought. I want to say hello, do you remember me, I took care of your son once for a week. I fell in love with your son once. Do you remember?

She smiled. Oh, the smile stayed. After a while, it came automatically, tailor-made for the camera. Even when it hurt. Even when you remembered that Melissa didn't break with you, that you broke off with her. That there were five phone calls, over two weeks, that you didn't return. And then the phone just stopped ringing.

She finished her makeup. The makeup would work, at least for tonight. I want a drink, she thought. I want a man. It's seven o'clock. It'll be dark in an hour. I don't want it to be dark, alone. I'll go to Charlie's, she thought. They get the Irish crowd. The young ones. The big ones. They're easy.

She shook her hair fluffy and loose. She smiled the camera-smile at the mirror. She opened the door. She couldn't spend this night alone.

4.

Suddenly Arlene's hand stopped flashing across the legal pad. She dropped her pencil, and looked up at Melissa across the black shining cocktail table that separated them. Then she quickly counted the five pages of stenographic notes she'd just taken. "No wonder you haven't aged. How much of this material do you have?"

"I don't know," Melissa answered. "Probably tons of it."

"When did you start putting it together?"

"The first month I was with the agency."

"Why? You were only twenty-six then."

Melissa looked back across the cocktail table at Arlene. Looked across the fourteen years to that excruciating evening with Rory, when he'd stood there and told her, in a matter-of-fact way, that his wife's face had grown too old for him.

"I met a woman," she said, "who showed me how painful it was to grow old too soon." She saw Arlene wince, but there was no other road but the truth. "So I began studying. You know the medical books I bought?"

"Of course."

"I couldn't read them until I met Aaron. He taught me how to break them down into Greek and Latin words, and then build them up again until they made sense. He opened the door for me to that world of words." She smiled, at herself, at the wonderful intensity of those years. "When I made up every morning, before I went out for a shooting, I used to tape a list of four or five of them on the mirror." She lowered her head, still smiling. "I still think of collagen and colloidals as being a lipstick color—flaming red."

Arlene turned to the bartender for the fourth time. "Another martini. Double. And another wine." Then she turned back to Melissa. "And don't tell me we shouldn't. Not tonight. Just go ahead."

"After a while, I was able to talk to doctors at parties in their own language. I was able to use what they said." She looked straight at Arlene. "Thank God, I was pretty. I bribed doctors with my face—and low-cut gowns—the same way most women bribe rich men."

The bartender came with new drinks. He tried to keep from staring too hard at Melissa.

"There's more," Melissa said. "Hundreds of tricks and techniques like the twelve I just gave you."

"Why don't you write a book?"

Melissa had known the question was coming. She'd talked as much as she had in order to provoke Arlene into asking that very question.

"I can't. The words won't form. I make notes. They're no good. I file them away. I have a drawerful of them by now."

"And what does Aaron say?"

Melissa lifted her glass. It was bad wine—cheap California. She took a deep drink of it, and twisted her mouth in distaste. "He doesn't know," she said bluntly.

There wasn't the slightest sign of surprise on Arlene's face. Melissa felt somehow as though she'd been caught masturbating. "Do you want to talk about it?" Arlene asked.

"No. Not really."

"Yes. Really."

"I don't actually know," Melissa said. "I have a . . . beautiful life. Two marvelous children. I love my huband, he loves me. We live well. There have been financial problems lately, but we still live well. We have exciting friends . . . close friends. I still have my career, years after I have any right to." She looked down at the glass again, took another drink. "I don't know. It's a beautiful life."

"The all-American dream," Arlene said. She finished the drink. "You're what all of us wanted to grow up to be. So what went wrong? No Rory-trouble with Aaron?"

"None. I'm sure of it. It just doesn't fit."

"Then what? Because it has to do with Aaron."

Melissa looked down at the glass in her hand, and was surprised to find it empty. She pushed it aside.

"What?" Arlene asked.

"There's already one writer in the family," Melissa blurted out.

"Okay. You're the face. He's the brain." Arlene turned toward the bar. "We need another drink."

"No."

"Yes. This is Walpurgis Night, baby. All the witches are coming out on their brooms. Time to get drunk." She turned back to Melissa. "You get the waiter. He doesn't know I exist."

Melissa held up her hand, and the waiter came over quickly with fresh drinks. Arlene intercepted her martini in midair, had it half-finished before the man could exchange the glasses and turn back toward the bar. "So," she said. "You've got a book inside you—growing all over the place. And your husband doesn't know about it. And you don't even know where to go"—she smiled, a little crookedly—"to get an abortion."

"It's not as simple as that," she said quietly.

"Go on."

"Aaron has a book, that he can't write."

"That doesn't make sense. He's a ballet dancer on paper."

Melissa felt the tears fight to penetrate the surface of her eyes. Fourteen years, and she'd told no one. Would she tell Arlene, even now, if she weren't leaving on a plane for Cincinnati tomorrow morning?

"It writes itself," she said. "At night."

"I have no idea what you're talking about."

"He dreams—the same dream. Over and over again. It keeps pounding against his brain, begging to come out."

"Do you talk about it?"

"After I wake him up. Until he can go back to sleep. But only once in the daytime. Only once. Nine years ago."

"Nine years ago! What in hell happened?"

Walpurgis Night. Graves open. Witches mount their brooms. Wine flows. "I took German lessons," she said. "Because he talks in German when he has the dream. Five years after we were married, when we were at Saint Martin's on a vacation, he had a particularily bad night. I should have woken him up at the very beginning. I knew that. But for the first time I could understand most of what he was saying. For the first time, it made sense." She drained the glass. "So I let it go wherever it wanted to. I let all of it out."

She looked at the waiter, and then at Arlene.

"Of course," Arlene said. "Fast."

She gave the order. Waited till the glasses came. And then began talking again. "Somebody died in the dream. I think it was a child." She looked up from the glass at Arlene. "I think the child's mother killed him, to keep him from crying out, when the Nazis were chasing Aaron and whoever else was with him. And I think the dream is true. I don't think it's made up. I don't think it's symbolic. Except . . ."

Arlene's hand was on hers. "Hey, honey, I'm sorry. You don't have to go on. We're just two old friends, getting a little . . ."

"Except," Melissa said, "this night, when I didn't wake him up, he turned around in the dream and looked for me. He called out for me in the dream. Called out for me three or four times. And I still didn't wake him up. And then, the mother put down the baby, and took the scarf she'd used to smother it, and came after Aaron. Then I woke him up.

"He couldn't sleep the rest of the night," Melissa went on. "We both stayed up till the next morning, till we saw the dawn come up over the beach. Then I told him what I'd heard. I told him it wasn't a dream at all, but a memory. A memory that he was trying to bury, but that wouldn't stay dead. I told him that I couldn't protect him against it anymore; that the only way he could get rid of it was to put it into words—English words—and let it live again. Then it would be outside of him, not inside. Then it would be a book, and not a dream. It would go away."

She drained the sixth glass of wine. She had never drunk as much in her life. She had never needed to.

"He . . . changed into something else," she said when Arlene remained silent. "Became someone I never met. Never dreamed could live inside Aaron. Even his face changed. We argued for hours . . . until the management rang up and told us the other guests were complaining. Then we just packed up and left. We'd only been there two days."

"And you never brought up the subject again?"

"Never."

"And if you told Aaron about your book?"

"I don't know."

"If you told Aaron?"

"He'd probably help me. But he'd know, damn you. He'd know that I was doing what he should be doing. And it would be nine years ago all over again."

Arlene shook her head. "We've got a great way of celebrating," she said. "You know, all those fourteen years—it's like you turned around, and it was a day. A long day, with kind of blurred memories. Nothing's changed except my face. Not your face, but mine. And the kids have grown up."

"We think we've come so far," Melissa said, "and then you look over your shoulder—"

"And you're still at square one. Let's get out of here, beautiful, or we're going to end up crying on each other's shoulders." She started to slide out from the seat. "Melissa—" For a moment the drunkenness vanished in Arlene's face. "If Victoria had had your book fourteen years ago—"

"I know."

"If I had had your book fourteen years ago—"

"I know."

"If five million women I know had had your book—"

"I know. Honestly, I know."

"If you ever do the book," Arlene said, "I'd like to have a copy of it."

"You'll have it," Melissa said quietly, "one year from now."

"And Aaron?"

"It will be dedicated to him. I wrote the dedication just now, in my head, when I thought of what would happen if I didn't write it. If I went back into the lie and buried myself all over again. Would you like to hear that dedication?"

"Of course."

"To the man I love," Melissa said. "To the man who gave me the tools I needed to build this book. To the man without whose support and encouragement this book would never have been written."

5.

How could six glasses of wine numb you this much, Melissa thought. And then she realized that she'd had no lunch, and no dinner. And that it was twelve-fifteen. And that she was confronted by a massive problem: how to get up the stairs in her apartment, and—thank God—into bed.

By some divine miracle, the key had slipped immediately into the lock of the front door. The door had opened soundlessly. The first floor was dark, and quiet—and turning slowly. Now she had reached the stairs. There were fourteen steps to the bedroom floor. All you had to do was count from one to fourteen and you were home free. She raised her left leg and counted one. Then she raised her right leg and counted two.

She made six easily enough, but there was no seven. There was just six, and then nothing. The stairs were carpeted, and she thought it was funny how nice they felt—like a bed with square bumps in it—as she rolled down them and onto the disagreeably hard floor below. She rested there for a minute, out of breath, and decided that the whole problem was her shoes. There's a way to do everything, she thought. The proper tools make the good craftsman, her father had said. And it was her shoes that were causing all the trouble. It didn't matter that there was light coming from the bedroom floor. If at first, she thought, and began propping herself up on her elbow, and bringing her left shoe up where she could see it.

Hands—very strong and very gentle hands—slipped around her back. She saw a pajama knee bend close to her upraised foot. A huge male face—not quite focused but still very lovely—came into view. The face looked at her face and then began to smile. And then began to silently laugh.

"Are you there?" Aaron's voice whispered.

"I think so," she whispered back.

"Are you all right?"

"I'm fine," she said. "Perfectly fine."

He moved his head closer. "I think you fell down the stairs."

"I think I did," she nodded. "It was the shoes."

"You're absolutely right," he said. "We've got to take those off."

One of his hands came out, and gathered both the shoes inside its vastness.

"Don't leave them down here," she said. "The kids'll see them."

"I'll take them with us," he said. "Don't worry."

"Are they asleep?"

"Sound asleep. You couldn't wake them up with a cannon."

"I almost did," she began to laugh. "I was almost a cannon."

"You certainly were." And he was laughing with her. "Do you think we can get you up now? You really ought to be in bed."

"What a lovely idea," she purred.

"It's as simple as this," he said, slipping one arm under her back, and the other arm beneath her knees. "We just go up—like a feather."

She felt herself rise in the air. She put her arm around his neck. She kissed his neck. It was bristly, and sweet.

"You're light," he said. "You're so light." He kissed her back. "You'll have to get tipsy more often."

"First time in my life," she whispered proudly, as they began to climb the stairs.

"Honestly?"

"Swear to God."

"Do you like it?"

"No. But I like you liking it."

"I like anything you do," he said, kissing her again. "My beautiful Valkyrie."

"Really? Anything?"

"Anything at all." He silently pushed open the bedroom door with his bare foot.

"Anything?"

"Yes. Shush. Here we go, down to the bed."

"That's nice," she said. "That's so nice."

He had her clothes off and her nightgown on in a minute. Then she was under the covers, tucked in, and he was sitting beside her, stroking her hair.

"Go to sleep now," he said. "Just give in to it. And you'll feel fine in the morning."

"Do you love me?" she asked.

"God, yes."

"You won't tell the kids?"

He laughed, and kissed her forehead. "No," he whispered. "I won't tell anyone." She felt his hand, gently, slowly stroking her hair. "You don't tell anyone," he whispered. "I don't tell."

"That's nice," she said. "That's real nice." Maybe it won't be so horrible, she thought, as the room began to whirl again . . . after all.

6.

When the light finally went out in her mother and father's room, Lacey stared at the luminous dial on her clock till five full minutes had rolled by, and then snapped on her own light.

The light always blinded her a little when it went on in the middle of the night. She stood stock still, pretending she was a Central Park statue, until her eyes could see again. And then she didn't move for another minute, until she was sure that there were no other sounds anywhere else on the bedroom floor.

There weren't, and she now ruled the apartment. Everyone else was asleep—prisoners in Sleeping Beauty's kingdom—and only she was awake, and alive, and able to grow older, and control time. Everyone else had to sleep—eight hours a night. She only had to sleep four. She would live twice as much. Twice as long.

She walked soundlessly across her carpet, and soundlessly closed her door. She had heard every word of their conversation, every tiny whisper. Her mother had got drunk because she was so sad that Victoria had died. Getting drunk was dying a little. Her mother had died a little because Victoria had died so much.

She moved across the carpet again, and began transforming the room. She took the photographs out of the drawers, and carefully laid them out across the desk. She looked at herself in the mirror and then took off her nightgown. She was now naked, and sacred. Tonight was a sad night, and there was much to do.

Should she be twenty-six tonight, she wondered, and be her mother, and look in the mirror and compare herself to the photographs in *Vogue*, and decide whether she was beautiful enough to leave Houston? She'd heard the story a dozen times—she'd begged for it over and over again. She'd acted it a hundred times. Compared her face, and her body, not only to the magazines, but to her mother's photographs. But now she was thirteen—half twenty-six—and tonight was a more important night than leaving the sheepherder's home. Tonight it wasn't her mother she had to prove in the mirror. Tonight it was Victoria.

There were ten photographs of her mother, and three of Victoria. She took the three pictures out of the line, and pushed them forward on the desk. The pictures of Victoria were taken when she was twenty-five, and twenty-seven, and twenty-nine, when Victoria was as successful as her mother had been.

We live in the mirror, she thought, all three of us. The camera is just a mirror with two sides to it; anyone can look through and see us at the other end. We live in the mirror. The mirror proves us. The mirror is our judge.

She began the ritual of proving herself in the mirror. "My hair is brown," she whispered, "like Victoria's." And her eyes were Victoria's eyes, made slightly dark. The rest of the face was also Victoria's face, with almost no change at all. Oh, the nose was slightly longer, but the rest of her face would grow faster, and erase that. She was Victoria's grandchild—the mirror said what nobody else admitted. The mirror had its own truth.

She thought of the sheepherder's house, in Houston. How had her mother got there? Gypsies? Kidnapped as a child? Sold, for what? She thought of the old woman who lived in that house, posing as Melissa's mother. She had met that sheepherder's wife once, when she was eight years old. She had been told that that wrinkled old woman was her grandmother. She'd been expected to kiss that old woman. She did. She felt the leather of that old woman's skin. Her lips had told her it was a lie, even more than her eyes. She had said nothing, and then gone outside, ten minutes later, and spit.

The old woman was still living, in Texas. There was no way Melissa could bring her up North, because of the old man. But it was a lie. Melissa had escaped the sheepherder's home, and come to New York, and found her real mother. Victoria. Queen. The queen who bred queens. Now dead. Why didn't Melissa cry? Why didn't she herself cry, if her mother couldn't?—Why didn't she cry now, when the truth came out at night.

She felt a pain in her groin. She looked down at her naked belly, at her naked lips in the mirror. Still waiting for hair, still waiting for blood. Sarah in her class was the same age, but two months younger. She'd gotten it three weeks ago. When she went home and told her mother, she said, her mother had slapped her in the face, and then kissed her, because she was Jewish. What would Melissa do to her when she got hers too? Not slap her. Never any slaps.

She wished she was Jewish. She wished her father was more Jewish. She wished she could have her period. She looked at the dresser. What would happen if she opened a safety pin, and pushed it up there, to start it?

She looked at the three photographs again. She felt cold and naked, and she put on her nightgown again. She knew that she wanted to hurt herself so she could feel, and then cry. It was so hard to feel if you lived in a mirror. The mirror was cold, and glass. Photographs were cold, and paper. But the mirror didn't feel anything, and you never got old on the paper. Victoria never died on paper. Nobody ever died on paper.

She walked over to the bed, and she sat and cried.

"I'm afraid of dying," she whispered, talking to the night, talking to Victoria. "I don't want to sleep in a casket, even for a little while."

She looked up at the photographs. "They don't slap you," she said. And then she thought of school, and the boys there, and even Little John's friends. "Nobody slaps you," she said to Victoria. "Did anyone ever slap you?

"I need someone to slap me," she pleaded to the night. "I need someone to slap me, and crack the mirror, and let me feel."

7.

Aaron woke quickly, passing from sleep to full awareness in a second. There was not the slightest lingering in a dream. He was fully on guard. Everything that had happened the day, and night, before was instantly in his mind. He kept quite still, turned his head slightly, and checked to see that Melissa was still sleeping peacefully.

He rolled back the sheet, slipped out of the bed so carefully that the mattress never moved, picked up his slippers and glided out of the room. Outside, next to the door, he'd placed an old slacks and sweater set. He took them, and the tennis shoes, into LJ's bathroom, dressed, and went downstairs.

It was ten o'clock. He hadn't slept that late in years. Lacey was somewhere playing. LJ was waiting for him at the dining room table. His summer in Houston with Johnny Johnson had been interrupted by this brief trip home for the funeral.

"Is she okay?" Little John asked.

"Fine," Aaron replied. "I guess she's just worn out from yesterday."

Little John looked up at his New York father, remembered the whispered scene at the bottom of the stairs last night, and smiled in loving conspiracy at the huge man who had come downstairs in slacks and sweater, unshaven, on a Wednesday morning, when he had forty-four people waiting for him in the office.

"I'll have a second breakfast with you," LJ said.

"Second? Or third?"

"Fourth." Again, the smile. "But who's counting?" He spun around to the kitchen door. "Alice," he called out, "The old bear's here—starving."

"For Christ's sake, LJ," Aaron said.

"She likes it."

"But your mother doesn't. She's trying to sleep."

"Oh," Little John shifted to a stage whisper. "Then we'll tipie-toe the conversation till the beautiful one gets up." There was a slight pause, then: "You're not going to the office looking like that, are you?"

The eggs, bacon, toast, and potatoes arrived. "You're not going back to Houston till tonight, are you?"

"Eight o'clock," Little John said.

"I thought we might throw the ball around a little in Central Park. My arm needs practice."

Little John broke into the smile again. He couldn't help himself with Aaron. "That's for sure," he said.

The toast paused halfway to Aaron's mouth. "What's for sure?" he asked menacingly.

In an instant, the smile turned innocent. "That we could throw the ball around in Central Park." The innocence became angelic. "It's big enough to throw a ball around in."

"Maybe I should ship you off to Houston at once."

"Maybe you should finish breakfast, so we get to the park before flight time."

"A nickle a catch?"

"A dime. I won five dollars last time."

"But you got flabby in Houston. I saw it the instant I looked at you."

"All right," Little John said, scraping back the chair, "You've gone too far now. Get on your feet, big shot. Today is going to be a ten dollar day. And I'm going back to the South rich."

"I want to see how much money you brought with you," Aaron said, "before I take a step outside this house. We don't take IOU's up here, Southern boy."

They were both on their feet now, heading for the ball and the gloves in the foyer. Little John loved the fact that, even though he was now six foot two, he still felt like a kid alongside Aaron's six foot six. He reached out and threw an arm around Aaron. "Only a Southern boy," he said, "for two months every summer."

"That's true," his second father said. "Thank God for the fall."

8.

It was still slightly before the lunch hour when they reached the park, and it was a rather cool, overcast day for New York in the summer. The park was fairly empty. They walked to one of the small, open, grassy areas, surrounded by a few benches where elderly people sat, and Little John shot away from Aaron like a greyhound. He took up his station under some giant brown trees about a hundred feet away.

"Okay, big shot," he called out, "start lobbing them in."

"Steaming them in, you mean," Aaron retorted, and fired the first ball across the green, half a foot away from Little John's right shoulder.

"Not bad for a creaky hinge," Little John laughed, snapping the ball out of the air. "Especially for one that old."

"Wait till I get warmed up, Sonny Boy. Better run out and buy an extra mitt."

The ball started sailing back and forth between the man and boy. There was a natural, beautiful rhythm to the flow of it. Little John was throwing at the limit of his strength, and Aaron easily handled the ball by the time it reached him. Then, when he moved the ball from his glove to his right hand, he placed it in the air again as carefully as he would fit a word into a sentence. The ball always arrived just a foot or two away from the boy on either side of him, and with just enough strength to keep it at shoulder height. The men and women on the benches watched the first four or five throws. Then, when they had witnessed the control, when they realized there was no danger, they turned back to their talking, or their newspapers, or their memories.

"Hey," Little John's voice came across the green field, "throw one a little harder this time, huh?"

Aaron smiled, and nodded, and this time the ball was placed two feet away from Little John's shoulder.

"No," Little John called out, tossing the ball in his hand once or twice before he threw it back. "Really harder. C'mon."

Again Aaron nodded, and again the ball sailed through the air—this time three feet to the right of Little John's shoulder, still precisely five feet off the ground.

Little John twisted, caught it in the webbing, and suddenly began to feel a little desperate. In the five weeks he'd been gone, he'd forgotten how carefully Aaron threw. But he was part of a team down South that wasn't careful or gentle. And Big John was the coach. This year, for the first time, they had a chance of winning. But he was dropping half of the balls hit to him. Last Sunday, he'd dropped two runs. And Big John was no Aaron. After the second drop, when the game had been lost, Big John had come on the field and cursed out his own son, in front of both teams. There was no way that Little John could let them know that, up here. But the next game couldn't happen that way again. And he needed fast balls now, to practice. Not baby balls. Not throwaway balls. His face twisted. Sure, he loved being with Aaron, kidding around with Aaron, basking in Aaron's gentleness. But Aaron was going to stay up here in New York tonight. And he was going to have to fly back to Houston, and face Big John and the rest of the team next Sunday.

"Hey, I'm not kidding," he yelled, when the ball arrived

at the same spot, with the same speed, the next time. "I'm serious. Throw me some real fast ones."

"We're warmed up now," Aaron said. "How about our dime a catch?"

"I don't care about the money," Little John said. "Honest to God. Throw me some fast ones." He felt something build in him that he had never felt before with Aaron. Something that came from the South. Dark humid nights. Big John. Something that was born in your blood. "Stop treating me like an infant," he shouted across the green field.

Aaron paused for a moment. For a moment his eyes were troubled. Then the arm circled out again, and the ball came back with the same speed and the same location.

"God damn you," Little John hissed under his breath. He clenched the ball, and threw back his arm as far as he could, and almost tore off his shoulder trying to hit Aaron's face with it.

Aaron had to run eight feet, and snap the ball off the ground before it hit one of the benches. The old people's heads shot up. Aaron held the ball in his glove, and walked carefully back to the center of the field. He had no idea what was going on, what had happened to Little John.

"Throw it," Little John commanded.

"Maybe you're tired," Aaron said.

"Throw it hard. See if you can throw it hard."

"How about lunch?"

Both fucking fathers, Little John thought. Both fucking fathers deserted you, the first chance they got. He suddenly realized how mad he'd been at Big John. He'd wanted to put his head down and charge into Big John's fat stomach, right there in front of both teams. And now this one. Sending him away two months out of the year. Not even fighting for him when Big John called up, every spring, to talk about his coming down. Not even saying, "Why don't I keep him one summer? Why don't I spend one summer with the boy? Why do you have to get him every time he's on vacation?"

They throw me from New York to Houston, and then from Houston to New York like I'm a ball, he thought. You won't throw the ball hard, will you, he said in his mind to Aaron. Why don't you throw the ball as fast as you throw me, you bastard?

He looked across the green field at the tall man in the old slacks and the sweater. He felt dark blood rise in his brain.

Southern blood. He heard a voice come out of his throat that he had never heard before.

"Hey, Jew," he yelled across the green field. "Throw me the ball. Hard. If you can."

What happened next was in slow motion. First there were the faces of the old people on the benches. No more talk, no more newspapers, no more memories. They were all staring at him, and their shock, and their fear—of him—made the air between him and them as thick as gelatin. Somewhere in the park a bird was singing, but the sounds of the bird bounced off the invisible gelatin. Then he watched the huge man's face across the field begin to change. He could see the ball drop out of the glove, like a white marble, into the enormous hand. He could watch the massive body set itself, one leg moving forward, one leg moving back. He could watch the arm draw back, the shoulder flowing with it, then the hand begin to whip up, to flash crazily forward toward him like a human catapult.

He never saw the ball leave the hand—it was moving too fast. He knew where it would have to hit, from the position of the other man's arm. He had half a second to set his glove to try to stop it. And he knew he'd remember, for as long as he lived, the hatred on the other man's face.

Then he felt the glove being ripped off his hand. He felt every inch of his hand turn into flame, as the glove was torn off and began spinning into the field behind him, traveling another twenty feet before it began to descend. He felt his arm fling out after the hand, and then his shoulder follow his arm, and then his body follow his shoulder, and then the hard grass of the field come up and meet his hand, which had no strength to cushion him, and then his face against the hard green scent of the field. Flames seemed to tear his thumb and fingers off his hand, and strange red shapes formed and dissolved in front of his eyes.

And then he was being turned over, lifted to a sitting position by an arm around his shoulder. His hand was being nestled in a far larger hand, but his hand, the right side of his hand, was now as large as that other hand. And somewhere, next to him, a man was crying. And he head a man's voice, Aaron's voice, say over and over again, "I'm sorry." And he looked up at Aaron's face, and he said through all the pain, "Why?"

"God forgive me," Aaron said.

"He'll have to forgive me first," Little John said. "I'm sorry. I shouldn't have turned you into that."

He looked at his hand, swelling up like a balloon, and realized that there'd be no game for him this Sunday, or any other Sunday for the rest of the summer. Then he looked up at Aaron again. And realized that at least part of the gelatin was still there. Had always been there. And then said, "No wonder you never get mad."

9.

The second time the dream came back that night, Melissa gave up trying to sleep. She stroked Aaron's hand through her hair till his face turned peaceful again, till the German words stopped, and then she continued to hold his hand in hers, and looked down at the huge slack fingers. She had clicked on the bedside lamp—she always turned it on when he began to dream, so that if his eyes opened it would be she, and not the dark one who was there—and she stared at the huge alien hand held in her own.

Two of the small bones in Little John's hand were broken, one in the forefinger and one in the thumb. The doctor had put splints on them, and told Little John that he'd be able to throw in three weeks. "Next time, play with a glove," he said. Little John had simply looked at the wall and said nothing, and Melissa had studied Aaron's face and seen nothing. Aaron had paid the doctor, and the three of them had got in the car and driven to the airport. Lacey was still at her friend Anne's. Melissa had called Anne as soon as she'd got the phone call from Aaron, and asked Anne to keep Lacy for dinner. There was no need for her to see Little John. He was leaving at eight, and when he came back the incident would be forgotten.

At the gate, she'd kissed Little John once, and then twice, and then three times. "Tell your father hello for me," she said.

"I will," he replied, and then he turned and looked up at Aaron. They stood there, staring at each other for a moment, while other passengers swirled around them to get onto the plane. Then, suddenly, with a cry, the younger man flung himself up against the older man's chest, and buried his head in that chest, and the older man held on to him, and ran his fingers through the blond hair, and kissed that hair, over and over again. And when Little John pulled away his eyes were glistening with tears but he was smiling.

Melissa got up from the bed, walked to the window, drew apart the draperies, and looked out at the river below. She had never seen the dream come twice on the same night before. She knew she should stay here in the bedroom, serving as sentinel against its coming again. But she had to get away from Aaron for a while. Had to get away. She left the lamp on so he wouldn't wake up to darkness, and kept the door slightly open.

She stood outside the bedroom door, leaning against the wall, seeing again Little John's face when the three of them had come out of the doctor's office, and when Aaron had gone for the car. It wasn't his fault," the boy had blurted out, before she could ask a single question. "I made him do it."

"How?" she had asked.

He turned away, and refused to look at her. "I made him do it."

"How?" she asked again, spinning him around. "How? I never saw him hurt anyone in his life."

The blue eyes stared up at her hopelessly. "I called him a Jew," he said quietly.

"Why?" She had known the answer before he had said it.

"I was mad at him. I wanted to make him mad. I wanted to make him throw the ball harder."

"He's not a Jew," she said.

"I don't care," he answered, and the planes of the face hardened, and she saw the man who was beginning to emerge out of the boy. "If he was a real Jew," Little John said, "then I'd become a Jew myself."

She stared at him for a moment, as she heard the sound of their car being driven up. And then she leaned forward and kissed him, and said, "I would too."

Still no sound from the bedroom. No more words. Jew, in German, was Juden. And that word was repeated, over and over again, in the dream, like some great sobbing chord. Because of that word, she had read the history books. In fourteen years she had read twenty books. And she knew that the stigma was sewn, as a yellow star, onto their clothes. That it was tattooed, as numbers, onto their arms. And that Aaron carried it burned, in fire, into his brain.

Five years before they had gone to a bar mitzvah of one of his clients. Aaron had sat through the service as stiff as a tree, as remote as a stone. He had never picked up one of the prayer books, or followed a single word, or muttered a single syllable for the entire two hours they had sat there. Finally, at the end of the service, when they reached the Kaddish, the prayer for the dead, Aaron had risen from his seat, and walked back down the aisle, and out of the temple. The client had called up at nine o'clock Monday morning and withdrawn the account. It had cost Aaron two million dollars in billing. It was the first crack in the agency. A crack that had now turned into a flood.

Her eyes could now see in the dark. The huge blue eyes, which she had learned as a child could function like a cat's. There was enough light from the bedroom and from the sleeping city outside, that she could see the railing, and the stairs, and the shadowed furniture of the living room downstairs. She was standing in the second story of a haunted house—haunted by fourteen years of love, and parties, and children, and growth, and triumphs, and failures, and gentleness . . . and silence. Fourteen years. Arlene had said what? No, she herself had said, "It's like you turned around, and it was a day." And then Arlene had said, "A long day, with kind of blurred memories. Nothing's changed except your face. And the kids have grown up. And you're still at square one."

It wasn't true. But it was. Arlene had said that. The two of them had sat, and talked, and got drunk—when? Yesterday. It was impossible. But it was only yesterday. Aaron had picked her up and carried her to the bedroom—yesterday. And he'd smashed Little John's hand—he'd let the anger come out for the first time—today.

Two days. Forty-eight hours. How could forty-eight hours be longer than fourteen years? How could you reach back through those forty-eight hours, and grab hold again of those fourteen years?

She felt panic begin to creep through the bedroom wall. She moved away from the wall and reached out carefully and took hold of the railing. She had to walk down those stairs and touch that room. She had to make that room real, make the life that she'd lived in that room real, make the man that she'd lived with in that room real . . . before she too was forced to run the risk of losing it all.

10.

She turned on the coffee table light. That was all the light she needed.

She went over to the Giacometti sculpture—the towering, compressed man—and she ran her hand up and down its muted bronze. He was real. Now, for the first time, she was beginning to understand how real he actually was.

She refused to look at the walls. There was nothing real for her on those walls anymore. The great Jackson Pollack was gone. The Kline was gone. The DeKooning was gone. The Gorky was gone. The Picasso was gone. She looked at her left hand. Her diamond was gone too. All gone to feed an agency of forty-four people, that should have been cut to ten or fifteen people three years before.

Too gentle, she thought. Too gentle to compete now, and too gentle to fire those who could no longer help him compete. In the sixties, advertising had charmed people into the stores. They had bought what amused them. And Aaron was one of the great charmers—one of that handful of New Yorkers whose wit could be transformed, in campaign after campaign, into profits—as long as people had spare money to spend. But when the sixties ended, when the stock market began to topple, when overtime evaporated, then the charmers were overwhelmed by the screamers. It boiled down then to who could yell loudest, who could promise more, who could lie best. It became an era of violent advertising, of advertising that whipped you into the stores. She loved gentleness, but gentleness was being trampled to death in a marketplace of elephants.

And so the accounts began to go, and the paintings followed. Six months of agency life for the first painting, eight months for the second, and finally two full years for the

Pollack. She begged Aaron to sell the country house instead, but the Pollack was worth six months more.

And so the weak, pretty paintings came into the house instead. If someone had never been in the house before, if they entered the room for the first time, then it would still be beautiful to them, with its pink and orange and pale blue clouds floating where masterpieces had been. Only the Giacometti remained—compressed in his nonviolence as Aaron was being compressed, day after day, lost client after lost client, in his nonviolence. And she refused to look at the walls anymore.

Under the coffee table were the photograph albums. Most women had one album, but every model had two. The first album—the important album—was the family, the life. The second album—thicker, really—was the career, the image. She took out both of them and laid them on the coffee table. The fourteen years were buried there. She had to unearth them.

The career album was the easier. There was almost nothing to prove, and it took less than five minutes to run through. First there were the flyaway assignments. She kept them grouped together in the front of the book. Especially Jamaica, where she'd gone for a *Playboy* fashion special for a week, where she'd spent most of her time warding off the men on the crew, where the final shots had been of her straddling two rocks in a whitewater stream, in a bikini, with a long pastel silk skirt, slit open at the waist, and its bottom soaked and darkened by the water. She was facing the camera hungrily, openly. She'd been without Aaron for a week. She'd never been more than two days without him in the six years before. The fashion editor told her later that those photographs had pulled more mail, more requests for another shooting, than *Playboy*'s full year's center spreads. But she never allowed the magazine to photograph her again.

The photograph transfixed her now. It warned her what her world would be like without Aaron.

Then there was Paris, twice with Aaron. Tahiti, with Aaron. One magnificent, sun-drenched week in Greece, three years ago, with Aaron. San Francisco, with Aaron . . . New Orleans, with Aaron . . . Los Angeles, with Aaron . . . Disney World, with Aaron . . . Mexico City, with Aaron . . . Bermuda, with Aaron . . . Easter Island, with Aaron . . . Machu Picchu . . . with Aaron. All of them—with Aaron.

Behind every one of these location photos, for all these years . . . Aaron. And in the New York shots, the studio shots—hundreds of them—it was the same. Leave Aaron in the morning, sometimes an hour before he got up . . . rush to the assignment, make up, shoot all morning . . . call Aaron around twelve . . . sometimes, if there was a long enough break in the shooting, if both of them were free, cab across town for lunch with Aaron. Then run back for the afternoon's shooting . . . then home to the children, to dinner, to homework, and—above all—to Aaron.

She closed the career album, and slid it back under the coffee table. She looked up at the darkness above her. Still no sound from the bedroom. The man who dominated those photographs—and her life—was still sleeping without the dream.

The darkness was quiet now. She reached for the second album. Its first page was filled with pictures of their wedding. The huge handsome man now emerged into the photographs, alongside the glowing woman. She studied the joy on her face. The love on her face. The complete contentment on her face. In photo after photo after photo.

I've never been happier in my life, she thought. In my entire life, I've never been more blessed.

11.

Somehow, by some desperate power, he managed to wake himself up. The dream which had been choking him to death vanished in an instant, into nothingness. Not a shred of it was left in his mind. All he felt was the suffocating emptiness in his throat. The deadly emptiness in his hand, which had reached out, and found nothing.

His lungs were about to explode, for lack of air. But he controlled himself with an iron will, and took in his breath so slowly that even he could hear no sound. No sign. Nothing to tell them he was still there.

The room was lit by a single lamp. He looked out the window and saw that it was still night. But how could it be night and the light on and the curtains open? How could the lamp be lit at night and the curtains not be drawn? His mind began to swim. He had to close his eyes. It was as though the dream had followed him, into the cold reality of the room. He fought down the panic that had been building in his chest, and he forced himself to pry open his eyes. Where were the bricks on the walls? Why was he not in the cellar? The last thing he had remembered, they had left him in the cellar.

He had lost a day. He looked around the room, and realized that he had lost a day. A day had vanished out of his life, disappeared into nothingness, been buried inside his brain, because it had been too much. The boy was dead. And he had killed him. He, Aaron Koblinski, had killed him as surely as if it were he, and not she, who had taken the scarf in his right hand.

He looked down at his right hand. It burned, with the pain of giving death. He had run from it. He had fled from it. He had given up a day of his life to escape from it. And now the running was over. The hand burned. He could have stopped the death. And now he knew—as they knew—as everyone of them knew—that the guilt was not hers alone, but his.

He bent forward in the bed, pressing his chest into his knees. The pain in his stomach, in his chest, in his back, was going to break him in two. He wanted to snap in two, like a used match. He wanted to join the boy in death. He wanted to pay for the boy's life with his own.

He looked around the room feverishly, still not quite sure where he was. Fine furniture. A rich house. The smell of a wealthy woman. Was it deserted? Had the owners fled south too, or had they broken in? Was that why the light was on? Because they had broken in, and the Germans would expect a light to be shown after dark?

He was still afraid to leave the bed. What if someone outside saw him cross the window in front of the light? Only his eyes could search the room. And the gun was not there. They had taken the gun with them. And there was no way his hand could reach the gun, and use it on himself.

The hand burned, waiting for the gun. They would be back, he knew, before the dawn. She would be back, before the dawn. And she would not go on. Nor could they leave her, to talk, or to die screaming.

He sat in the bed, and waited. Waited for her to come back. Waited for the moment, that night, to kill her.

12.

She had forgotten the five pages of photographs near the front of the album showing Aaron with Little John. That first spring together, they had taken Little John on picnics all over Connecticut and Pennsylvania. She watched herself swell in these photographs, as the spring passed; here she was sitting on a blanket, gnawing at an oversized turkey drumstick; there she was in front of a red and yellow rose garden with the two men in her life—one towering above her, the other barely able to put his arm around her hips. And always in these threesome photographs, Aaron's great arm would reach behind and beyond her, and his hand would emerge on the other side, resting lightly on Little John's shoulder.

Five pages of Little John . . . and then Lacey.

She had never seen a newborn child quite as beautiful. Lacey's face was round and plump and delicately pink. She had full dark-brown hair. There were no birthmarks, no signs of travel or travail. The happiness that had coursed through Melissa during the nine months of her pregnancy—that unremitting joy of being doubly a woman—had transmuted itself into flesh that was breathtaking. Lacey was, Melissa thought with an ironic smile, a model infant. She could have gone to work in front of the camera the instant of her birth.

But all Aaron could say, when he walked into her room after viewing Lacey in her crib outside, was, "Her hair is dark."

"But what about her face?" Melissa asked immediately, suddenly terrified at expecting joy, and discovering only disappointment.

"It's flawless," he said tonelessly. "Are you all right?"

"I'm perfect, Aaron," she said. "And your daughter is perfect too. She has your nose and your hair. And I couldn't be happier."

"She's healthy," he said. "That's the important thing. And there was no ordeal for you."

"Aaron," Melissa said. "Come here. Please." He sat next

to her on the bed. She reached out and took his hands and kissed them. Then she reached up and stroked his head. "You have beautiful dark hair," she said. "She's your daughter. She has beautiful dark hair too."

He took her hand away from his head, and kissed it. Then he reached out, and gathered Melissa's hair in his right hand. "But you have magic hair," he said.

"She has your hair," Melissa replied, gently removing his hand. "It's newborn hair. It's you—Aaron Carpenter—being reborn in her. That makes it far more magic than mine."

"She's healthy," he repeated. And then his face broke out into a genuine smile. "And you've come back to me. To stay."

She turned the album page quickly, and left the birth behind her. Now she went on, photograph after photograph, into thirteen years of children and growing. She saw Little John flash up like a sunflower—the smile grow wider and more mischievous, the eyes grow bluer and deeper, the hair grow more golden and more sparkling, the shoulders grow broader and more assured. On the next-to-last page of the album, the one filled with pictures from this past spring, Melissa froze. There they were, Little John and Aaron, standing in the park, lined up for the camera, their arms around each other, their hands wrapped in their baseball gloves, and the ball—the white, hard, deadly baseball—being held in Aaron's hand.

Melissa snapped the album shut. What if Aaron had not been able to control that ball? What if that ball had smashed, not into Little John's glove, but into his face? What if that ball had crashed into Little John's chest?

Her mind stopped thinking in English. Instead it repeated slowly, word by word in German, the description in Aaron's dream of the young child's death. There was a phrase in that dream, a phrase that had been repeated over and over through all these years—"the boy's lungs . . . no more breath . . . no more air in his lungs . . . and then there is silence . . . nothing but silence."

Oh God . . . Oh God, Aaron, she thought. Please. You didn't . . . you couldn't have connected the death all those years ago, with what happened to Little John today.

She looked up, past the tiny pool of light surrounding the coffee table, into the darkness. The light was still on in the bedroom; she could see a splinter of it spilling out down the stairs. He was still sleeping, protected from the dream. You're safe, she thought. Safe from the dark-haired one, who won't . . .

And then, again, her mind stopped. She picked up the album again. As she flashed through its pages once more, she traced the photographic history of Lacey.

Lacey at one. Her first birthday party. Melissa standing behind her, showing her how to blow out the candle. The tiny face so exquisite there was no way she could stop pinching it. Aaron taking the picture. But no picture of Lacey and Aaron.

Lacey at five. The first day of school. The outfit was deliberately plain. The face was irrepressibly radiant. One hand locked in her mother's, the other hand held by her brother. Her father again behind the camera.

Lacey at eight. Ten. Twelve. Thirteen. The face slowly lengthening, till it was all cheekbones, and eyes, and pointed chin. The profile now defined, till it was not Melissa's profile any longer, but that profile perfected, that profile made Egyptian, that profile transformed, when it was combined with that dark hair, into an identity, into a nickname that even her classmates at school used occasionally . . . Nefertiti. Her Egyptian daughter. Her dark-haired, dark-eyed, devastating daughter, who was irresistible to every man and woman she ever met . . . except her own father.

Melissa tore again through the album, checking every single photograph with Lacey in it. There was not one in which Aaron touched Lacey.

Could she ever remember when the man had picked up his child, and held her? Never. And never a kiss that wasn't formal. Never a touch that wasn't necessary. Never a contact that wasn't prompted by someone else. It was always Aaron and Little John, and never Aaron and Lacey.

She looked up again at the darkness—at the sleeping man who held the key. The dream had come out of the night, and had coiled itself around all of their days. And she had been too blind, until this night, to see. Unless the dark-haired one was drawn out of Aaron's dream, and brought into the light of day, and forgiven, and sent back to rest in the past—unless all of that was done, then the dark-haired Lacey would never receive the father-love she needed to come out into the warm clear light of her own day.

Tears were dropping from her eyes on the cover of the album. They were staining its brown leather. She was crying because two dark-haired women were crying as well. One dead—she was sure the first was dead. And one just beginning to live—crying out for the right to live.

She put the album away. But inside that album, there were women who were also crying out to her. One of those women, too, was dead—Victoria. The others were alive—Arlene, and all the rest—trapped inside the covers of that album.

Albums are graveyards for most women, she thought, where they bury their youth, and their looks, and their promise, and their sexuality. Albums are graveyards they're terrified to walk through, after ten or twenty years have passed. Albums are black mirrors where they see what time has done to their faces and their bodies. And the women in that album—all those women—needed her.

She leaned over and turned out the light. Now she too had given way to the darkness. Now Aaron and she shared the same darkness, and the same guilt. For not reaching out. For not listening to the cries. For not daring to give what they could.

She stood up. She could now begin to see in the darkness. Aaron had to face his dream. She had to face hers. No matter what the cost—no matter if the darkness swallowed up the album and the life—the cries must be heard. There was no other choice.

She moved through the darkness to the stairs. And began to climb her way up toward Aaron, and the light.

13.

He was sitting up in the bed, waiting for her. When she entered the room, he simply looked at her, his face as calm as she had ever seen it, his eyes absolutely blank.

"How long have you been awake?" she asked.

"I don't know," he answered. The words sounded as though they were being filtered through his brain twice, before he allowed them access to his tongue. "Where are we?" he asked. "Where are the others?"

"What others?" she asked in return. And then she went

on, knowing deep inside her gut that her words would make as little sense to him, as his words suddenly made to her. "Little John?" she said. "Lacey?" And then, when his eyes showed no recognition, "Alice?"

"No," he said. "David. Saul. Hans." And then, leaning forward, and looking behind her, through the door and into the darkness. "Esther."

After all these years, Melissa thought; her name. She had a name. And Aaron was sitting here now on their bed, waiting for her to come back through their bedroom door.

"She's not here," she said. "She's not coming back . . . ever."

"Why?" he asked, and Melissa saw raw anger rising in his eyes.

"Aaron," she said quietly, moving slowly toward the bed. "You're not awake. Think for a moment. Look at me for a moment, and think who I am." She sat down next to him, carefully, on the bed. "Here," she said, taking his hand and raising it to her hair, feeling it slide over the surface of her hair. "Try to remember who I am."

He pulled his hand away from her hair in disgust, and flung her hand out of his own.

"Where is she?" he demanded.

She had only one word for a reply. "Gone."

He stared at her, his eyes opening wide in amazement. "You did it," he said. And his huge hands came out and grabbed her shoulders. "In the field. Tonight. With the boy."

"No," she said instantly, suddenly terrified at the strength of his hands on her shoulders. "Nothing happened. Nothing."

"Then where is she?" He shook her as though she were a puppy. "Where is she?" He looked again at the black open door. "I have to do it."

"Do what?" she asked, speaking now through the pain that his hands were inflicting on her shoulders. "What?" she asked again.

"Give me the gun," he said. She watched the tears begin to form in his eyes. "Go south for an hour. I'll do it then. I have to do it myself."

Pain is red, she thought. She hadn't known that before now, but pain is red. She looked at his face through the red, and she watched the tears stream down his face. "Aaron," she said softly, keeping the pain out of her voice, "you didn't. You couldn't. Not her. Not her too."

He grabbed her forearms now. "I've got to do it before they find her. Before they touch her."

"Aaron," she whispered, closing her eyes, "you're breaking my arms." And then the pain became intolerable, and she opened her eyes. "Aaron," she cried out, "Don't do to me what you did to Little John."

He dropped his hands, and then raised them again to cover his face. The face inside the hands was sobbing. She picked up her own hands and lifted them six inches, to see if she still could. And then she hit him . . . hit him . . . hit him . . . hit him as hard as she could. Drew back her arms with all their pain and hit him. Hit him until she couldn't lift her arms again. And then sat there, sobbing alongside his sobbing, with her arms powerless to hurt him. She could no longer even lift them.

But then there was a way. There was a way to lift them, and she took it. She raised her arms slowly and gently, and wrapped them around the back of his shoulders and head. And then began to stroke that head, and kiss those hands, crying alongside him. But whispering through those tears, "It's all right. It's over. It's gone. You're here. You're here with me now. And it's over. It's gone."

14.

"What do you want to know?" he asked finally.

"Everything," she said.

"There's nothing."

"Everything," she repeated. "Her name was Esther. Esther what?"

"Esther Rochlitz. No. Esther Koblinski."

"How old was she?"

"Sixteen."

"It was her baby? At sixteen?"

"At fourteen," he said.

"She killed her own baby? At sixteen?"

"I don't want to go on," he said. "I'm tired."

"We have to go on," she said. "We should have gone on years ago."

"No," he said. "Let her stay dead."

"She's not dead. She's alive. Every night she's alive."

He looked up at her. She was standing by the window, framed by the night sky. He could see two of her. The blond woman in the room. The black shadow in the window. He stared at the black shadow in the window. "Let her stay dead," he said.

The black shadow spoke to him again. "You killed her," it said.

"There's nothing more to tell," he said.

"You killed her," it repeated.

"Yes," he said. "Of course."

"Why?"

"Because I loved her. I still love her. Now let her stay dead."

"You have to talk about her."

"No," he begged.

"Why?"

"Because then," he said, "she'll come back to life."

"She comes back to life already. She comes back to life every night."

"Yes," he said, watching the black shadow, waiting for the dawn to erase it. "But only at night."

"That's not true," it said, and he closed his eyes. "That's not true," the shadow said, even though he couldn't see it. "She comes out in the daytime too. She lives in this house in the daytime, as though she's still alive."

"Go away," he said to the shadow, his eyes still closed.

"I won't go away," it said. "I won't go away till you tell your story. All of it. To me. To a therapist."

"No," he said, clinging to himself. "No."

"You've got to tell your story . . . now. Just as I've got to tell my story . . . now."

He opened his eyes. Next to the black shadow was a blond woman. He looked at the blond woman. He looked at his wife. He asked, "What story?"

Melissa stopped . . . suddenly trapped. "No story," she answered.

He looked at the blond woman. Read her feelings across the room. "What story?" he repeated.

"I wasn't going to tell you tonight," she said.

"When?" he asked.

"Tomorrow," she said.

"This is tomorrow," he said. He was fighting for his life. "Tell me."

"I've been writing a book," she said, waiting for the reaction.

He turned his face into a smile. He turned his voice into that of a husband. "Really?" he said. "How marvelous. For how long?"

"I didn't think you'd approve."

"Of what? An exposé of our sex life?"

"Of course not. It's a book on beauty."

"By the world's most magnificent example," he said. "But why not? Your friends have been begging you for it for years."

"You don't mind?"

"I love it. But when, darling? And where?"

"An hour here. An hour there," she said. "On scraps of yellow legal paper." And then her smile turned crooked. "I had them in drawers, because I was afraid to show them to you."

He laughed. His laughter filled the room. His laughter shook the shadow in the window behind her. "May I perform an act of contrition," he asked, "By asking to see them now? Please."

"Tomorrow. You must be dead tired."

"Tomorrow is now," he said. "I can't wait to see them. Get them for me now, darling. Please."

She wavered. Her arms had stopped hurting. She was trembling with excitement. He was himself again. And he wanted to see them.

"A frightened child," he said, "terrified to walk across the room to the teacher's desk."

"Not at all," she said.

"Then . . . darling . . . please."

He watched her walk across the room to the bureau. He watched the dark shadow in the window grow smaller and smaller as she moved.

She brought back fifteen pieces of yellow paper. He swung his feet off the bed, and turned on the second lamp. He sat for a few moments reading the papers. She sat down next to him, reading her own fumbling words far more slowly than he skimmed through them, page after page.

"You write abominably," he said. "But what you have to say is vitally important. I know at least three of your friends who would sell their souls for these pages." He went on, not expecting an answer. He finished all the pages and looked up at her. "Style can be learned," he said, looking directly at her. "You think you have to write more formally than you speak, but that can be corrected. I can teach you how to make these words sing in just a few months—if you work."

"I'll work," she said.

"I mean five, even six hours a day."

"Even if I have to give up bookings."

He took her hand in his. "I'll be as hard on you," he said, holding her hand gently, "as I am on myself. As much of a perfectionist."

"Agreed," she said, looking into the soft brown eyes.

"We start in the morning, then," he said. And then he shook his head. "But no more now, darling, please. I can hardly sit up."

"I want to talk to you about Lacey," she said.

"Of course. Tomorrow."

"And you have to go into treatment, Aaron."

"No one realizes that more than I. But tomorrow, darling, please. Or I'll faint in your poor bruised arms."

She reached up defensively. He put out his left hand, and almost imperceptibly stroked her arms. "You're right," he said, his voice ocean-deep, "I have no choice now but to go into therapy. But tomorrow."

He bent down and kissed her arm. "Tomorrow." Then he swung back on the bed, and laid his head on the pillow.

"I'll be there in a moment," she said.

She started to put the papers in the drawer, and then stopped and left them on the top of the bureau. Then she went inside to the bathroom.

He lay there with his head swimming. The walls of the room kept changing before his eyes—one moment velvet, the next moment brick. He waited for the woman—and the shadow—to come back into the room.

They both came out together, and stood for a moment at the window, looking out at the night. Now he could see the blond hair of the woman. But that blond hair was false. He had discovered that earlier in the night, when he had reached out from the dream for it, and realized that it wasn't there.

Suddenly the woman closed the blinds to the night, and the

shadow disappeared into violet silk and blond hair. Then she turned around and smiled at him and walked toward him in the bed.

How clever of her to find the blond hair, he thought. No one in the world, he thought, would ever know now who she really was.

No one in the whole world. Except the two of them.

BOOK FIVE

1975—1976

1.

Their lovemaking grew crude.

For two nights after the breakdown, after the recovery, after the revelations, Aaron did not touch her at all, except for a brief, perfunctory kiss before they went to sleep. When she undressed for bed, he refused to look at her—unable to view the bruises that covered both her arms, unable to witness his own anger, embedded in her flesh.

But the third night they had gone out with friends to dinner, and he had drunk far more than he was accustomed to. When they came home, and she slipped in bed next to him under the covers, there was no perfunctory kiss. Instead he lay there rigidly for a moment, and then she felt his hand scrape slowly across the silk sheet between them, and then edge up against the side of her thigh, through the nightgown.

But his face had not turned to meet hers. His head was straight up on the pillow . . . his eyes closed . . . his only contact with her—his hand. Suddenly the hand reached down and began to gather up her nightgown. When he had bunched it up beneath her ribs, he threw off the sheets, and she could see that he was painfully erect, towering straight up out of his sprung-open pajamas.

He rolled over her in a second, his face sunk into the pillow alongside hers, his eyes still tightly closed. She shuddered at the iron rigidity of him, at the shock of forced entry, at the immediate penetration to the very end of her flesh.

His hands buried in her hair. His cheek slid roughly up against hers, his hardness moved in and out of her at full length, his pelvis circling back and forth, up and down, in one liquid powerful thrust every two seconds, like an animal, with no perceptible connection at all to his brain.

It took less than sixty seconds. She began gasping, and then softly screaming, in less than sixty seconds. And his moans muffled and echoed in the pillow beside her. She felt his pelvis tremble like a leaf on top of her. She felt the contractions—the vertical spasms of his penis—inside her.

She felt herself circle and clench and clutch at that penis again and again. And then she heard his voice in her ear, whispering, "Shush . . . shush . . . shush . . . shush" to her. And then he slid out his glistening penis, still fully erect, and rolled over on his back, onto his pillow—his eyes still closed, but his face now wrapped in sleep.

She lay there trembling. The echoes of the contractions slowly faded inside her body. But where were the stroking, the gentleness, the after-caresses? Where were the words, the consideration, the love? She looked again at her husband—her suddenly alien husband—sleeping alongside her. His face was relaxed, blissful, far younger-looking than she could remember it in years. He had taken everything he needed. He had given everything she needed—except accustomed love.

There were no words. Only the whispered command not to make words. It was a silent love, a hurried love, a hidden love. She shuddered. It was a love that was made in a forest, by two animals, at night.

At night. Quickly. By two hunted animals.

2.

The dream never came back again. After the first month, she realized that the dream was never going to come back.

He continued to wake her at night—in the dark of night when, before, the dream had awakened her. But this time— night after night, week after week—it was always to make love.

At first she had tried to snap on the light. But his hand always stopped her. By the third week, he was turning off the light the moment they got into bed. They no longer made love in the light. But he was endlessly potent. He was inexhaustible. And she adapted—learning to see his face with her fingers in the dark, learning to take sounds for words, learning to match the new rhythm of his body with her body, learning to rush to his rush, to explode with his explosion, to sleep with his sleep.

And at the end of the month, one solitary word emerged

from that blind love. He whispered it deep one night as he stroked her unseen hair, as he penetrated her unseen body. It was "Liebchen." And he whispered it over and over again in the dark: "Liebchen . . . Liebchen . . . Liebchen." And she knew then, beyond any doubt, where the dream had gone. She knew then why the light was out. She knew then the depth of his love for the dark-haired woman, and she knew how he made love to the dark-haired woman, and she knew that he was now making love again to the dark-haired woman—in her body, in her room, in her marriage, in the night.

3.

But then, after all her years of waiting, there came the book.

She could have written it downstairs, at the dining room table or at his desk. But she chose to write it in her own bedroom, on her makeup table, with the mirror staring her directly in the face, so that she could check at once every step, every instruction, every result.

Each day at ten, after Aaron left, she sat down at the table with a mug of tea. She looked at her face, studied it as though it were a piece of sculpture to be endlessly duplicated, and began to scrawl large firm letters across one of those pads.

Five yellow pages ended up in the wastebasket for every one she kept. Her fingers ached from grasping the pencils. Every half hour she would get up and go downstairs and get more tea, simply to clear her mind. The clock began to accuse her. Three hours passed . . . four hours passed . . . five hours passed—and there were only a few half-finished pages.

And then she would wait for Aaron to come home at night. They would have dinner together, watch television with Lacey, and then, after Lacey went to bed, attack that day's pages together.

She wrote in pencil, he corrected in pen. First he read the entire day's work. Every so often he would grunt or nod in approval, and she devoured every one of those nods as though they were the offer of a twelve-time-a-year contract for the cover of *Vogue*. At his desk, with his pen in his hand, he was the beautiful familiar Aaron—brilliant, warm, considerate, completely professional. He was the teacher, she was the student. She had carved the first rough images; he then began to turn them into polished marble.

Words would be crossed out of her sentences, and better words, stronger words, more revealing words would appear in pen on top of them. The sentences themselves began to be shortened, and made simple. Whole paragraphs were moved from place to place. Order was added. Logic was built in. Word-pictures—mental images—began to emerge from the sentences. Where before she had seen only a knotted chain of words, now she saw a million women's faces, with concrete explanations of their problems, concrete remedies for those problems, concrete results from those remedies. And when he had finished—an hour or two later—she was utterly, hopelessly, ecstatically in love with him all over again.

Then, when he was done, when the reading glasses finally come down from his eyes, and they'd kissed, she bent over and gathered each one of those golden sheets of paper together in a pristine pile. And the next morning she taped a list of new word-tools to her mirror, so that each day she could incorporate them into her own brain, and use them to mold her own sentences across those stubborn yellow pages—and make more and more of those sentences work by herself, before he came home and made them work for her.

By the end of the first month, sixty pages were done and typed. And even the nights—the dark nights—were tolerable to her now. And then, one Sunday, when she was out at a movie with Lacey, Aaron took the carbon copy of those pages, and prepared to give his wife the greatest gift of her life.

4.

He had never been happier. In his entire life, he couldn't remember a single moment in which he had ever been happier.

For two weeks, every time he closed the door to his office, he sat for the first few moments at his desk grinning, and doodling obscene abstract sketches on the pad, rather than writing. He had fallen in love, all over again, with his wife. He felt like an adolescent again—a man-child who suddenly discovers the right woman's body, and has free, glorious access to it, anytime he wishes, over and over again.

How do you work, when you've just fallen in love? Days passed, and then weeks, when he didn't write a single line of copy. He had enough discipline left to sit at his desk, but not to write. The only writing he did was the writing he did on top of her writing—just as his body now was constantly on top of her body. One love for the dark, one love for the light. His body on her body, his words on her words. No time—no time at all—for anything but love.

Deadlines began to be missed. Phone calls came in; excuses were given. Old copy, tired copy, second-rate copy was dug up and sent out. The faces around him changed, first to sullen, then to frightened. He heard fright in their pleadings. He knew he should be frightened himself. He knew he should block out the bed, the body, the night from the office. He knew he should make love to the paper, as he'd made love to the paper all these years. But paper was not flesh—soft, dark, night flesh.

He was in love. And even though the storm around him was growing, the love left him no room to fear it.

Or even to notice it, for more than a fleeting instant, between the doodles on his pad.

5.

Five days before Little John came home, when Lacey was at a friend's, he gave Melissa the present.

He brought it home with him in the file folder, the same file folder he carried home each evening from the office, with the retyped pages that she'd written, and he'd corrected, the day before. He laid it on the side of the desk, exactly as he'd always done before. He said nothing at dinner. He said nothing while they worked over the new, handwritten pages she'd created that afternoon.

Then, when they'd finished the corrections, she reached for the file folder. But his hand stopped her from opening it for a moment, and she looked up and saw a huge grin on his face.

"It's Rita's fault," he said.

"What?" she asked.

"She started it," he went on mysteriously.

"She didn't type them today?"

"No. They're there all right."

"She's in love again. Hopelessly. So they're full of typos."

"No. Perfect in every way."

"What, then?" she asked. And when she got no response but the grin, she went on: "Move your hand, you elephant, and let me see."

"All right," he said, "but I want you to realize, right now, that it's really her fault."

She looked again at his face, and then at the file folder. And then she opened it—very slowly.

The first thing she saw was the check. It was very long, very important looking, with that rippled green background, and with the name, Irving House, printed in its top left corner. On the check her name was written, "Melissa Carpenter." Next to it, there was the figure of $5,000—and then the same number written out in words on the line below. At the bottom were two scrawled signatures she couldn't read.

She looked up speechlessly at Aaron. His face was sparkling. "Pull it out," he said.

222

"What?" she asked dazedly.

"Pull the check out from under the paper clip. The real adventure starts there."

She slipped out the check, very carefully so the paper clip wouldn't tear it, and saw the word, "Contract." Under it, in the first paragraph, were other strange words, such as "Irving House as publisher . . ." and then "Melissa Carpenter as author . . ." and then finally "a work to be tentatively entitled 'MELISSA'S STAY-YOUNG, STAY-BEAUTIFUL BOOK,' the length still to be mutually determined."

"How in the world?" she asked.

"All Rita's fault."

"You'd better explain, or I'll . . . kiss you to death."

His shoulders moved in an innocent shrug. "She got beautiful," he said.

"Rita?"

"I'm afraid so," he went on. "A rather bad case of beauty. Advanced, I'd say, in the last few weeks, beyond all recovery." He sighed dramatically. "We finally traced the source of infection," he said, "to a series of paper invasions that were carried into her office every day by her employer. She was ingesting these as she retyped them. And then sneaking carbon copies home, and reingesting them again that night." He pursed his lips, and shook his head slowly from side to side. "Truly a tragic development in every phase.

"But," he said quickly, before she could interrupt him, "we nipped the epidemic in the bud before it could spread through the populace as a whole. We caught her at the critical moment, at the Xerox machine, spewing out deadly copies by the dozen . . . and, worst of all, stealing our stamps to send them out to her friends."

She began to giggle. She wanted to cry. She wanted to make love. She wanted to jump up on top of the desk and scream. She wanted to open four bottles of champagne and get dead drunk. She wanted to pound him with her fists for not telling her sooner. But all she could do was sit there and helplessly giggle.

He lapsed back into pure innocence. "And so," he said, "I just called Steve Spencer over at Irving House, and told him the story."

"You told him what you've just told me?" she asked in wonder.

"No," he answered slowly. "I told him that my wife—

for whom, as you may know, he has been horny for, for years—has just begun writing a beauty book. That she's finished sixty pages of it. That those pages deal mainly with lifting sagging facial skin by exercise, rather than surgery. And that my forty-five-year-old secretary, whose jowls used to hand down to her breasts, typed it up from rough draft. And that that secretary now looks like her own daughter, and got a proposition last week from the new mailroom boy. That's pretty much what I said.''

''Did he really? The mailroom boy?''

''Yep. Honest.''

''My God.''

''I thought so too. So did Steve. He asked me to send it over.'' Now the grin turned shy. ''I brought it over. Sat there while he read it. Sort of collected on that resumé I wrote for him five years ago.''

''How long ago was that?''

''Five days. Then he had to show it to an editorial committee. They ate it up. And he pushed a little—because he's no fool, and he can read a secretary as well as I can. And we got the contract, and the check, today. You still have to sign it, of course, on the back page. Read it first, though. But the terms are rather good.''

''I don't know what to say.'' She looked up at him. ''I don't know what to do.''

''How about going to the kitchen,'' he said. ''There's a bottle of Dom Perignon in the refrigerator. It's been waiting for us all day.''

''Hey,'' she said and then realized that the word sounded like Arlene. She wondered what Arlene would think about Aaron's reaction to the book. ''Hey,'' she said, ''I kind of love you.''

''I kind of love you,'' he said, ''very much.''

It was the first time he'd said it since Little John was hurt. She wanted to grab him, and pull him to the floor, and make love.

''But I just finished a long speech,'' he went on, ''and I am very thirsty. And''—he reached out and took her hand, and slowly kissed it—''I think we need a celebration . . . first.''

''You are incredible,'' she said. ''Incredible.'' She half-ran, half-floated into the kitchen.

He watched her leave, and then smiled. It had worked. But he wondered why he had been so terrified when he thought she might want to make love in the light.

Two days later, on Sunday, the three of them—Aaron, Melissa, and Lacey—were sitting in the living room. He was reading the magazine section of the *Times*. Melissa was reading the front page. Lacey was lying on her stomach next to her, her legs bent up, her ankles crossed at the slippers, reading one of her summer assignments from school.

Suddenly, the girl looked up at Melissa and asked, "What's a churl?"

"A what?" Melissa replied.

"A churl. C-h-u-r-l."

"Use it in a sentence," Melissa said.

"Oh churl!" Aaron said suddenly. "Drunk all, and left no friendly drop to help me after?"

Both of them looked at him in startled silence.

"Do you know the rest?" Lacey asked.

"Of course," he said. "I will kiss thy lips. Happily some poison yet doth hang on them, to make me die with a restorative." He looked at his daughter, brown eyes meeting brown eyes openly, unashamedly. "And then she goes on," he said. "To say what, Lacey?"

There was no need for the girl to look back at the book. "Thy lips are warm," she said slowly.

"And who is it that comes in then?" he asked, trying to remember. "Was it the guard?"

"The chief watchman," Lacey answered.

"Yes," he said. "Of course. 'Lead, boy. Which way?' "

Lacey's gaze was riveted on her father. Melissa sat on the couch, the paper lowered to her lap, watching her daughter interacting with her father for the first time in her life, through words that were written almost four hundred years before.

Again the girl did not look back at the book. "Yea, noise,"

she said. "Then I'll be brief. Oh, happy dagger! This is thy sheath; there rest, and let me die."

When the sentence was finished, there were tears in her eyes. Melissa had never seen a drop of moisture in Lacey's eyes before. Were they tears, she thought, for Juliet? Or for herself? There was no way of knowing. But she was now sitting up on the carpet, leaning on one arm, the book forgotten behind her, waiting for her father to go on, to keep the spell intact.

"I'm not sure what comes next," he said.

"Try," Lacey begged.

"I'll skip some lines," he said. "They're not important. But then . . . Pitiful sight! Here lies the country slain; and Juliet bleeding, warm, and newly dead, who here hath lain these two days buried."

Now Lacey turned to the book. "Go," she said, and her tone deep and resonant, suggested a full-grown man, "tell the Prince; run to the Capulets; raise up the Montagues; some others search."

"Perfect," he said. "The words come alive."

"And the end?" Lacey asked.

He smiled. Melissa could never remember him smiling so warmly at his daughter before. "Would you settle for the last four lines?"

The girl thought a moment. "For anything," she finally said.

He blinked. His face, for the first time in weeks, looked its age. Looked even older than its age. "Go hence," he said slowly, "to have more talk of these sad things. Some shall be pardoned, and some punished. For never was there a story of more woe, than this of Juliet and her Romeo."

His words faded out, and then there was silence in the room. The curtain had been lowered; the play was over. He was Aaron again, and she was Lacey, and Melissa was watching the two of them.

Lacey still waited for him to get up and leave the room, as he had always left the room before. But when he made no move to go, she asked, "When was the last time you read the play?"

He shook his head. "Before you were born."

"And you still remember the lines?"

"They're very beautiful," he answered.

"Will I remember them as well?" she asked.

"You're my daughter," he said. "I guess that means you will."

She sat there on the floor before the two of them for a moment, completely silent. Then she said, very softly, "Thank you," to her father. She got up from the carpet, and picked up her volume of Shakespeare, and said, "I've got to be over at Sarah's at one. So I guess I'm late."

She went over and kissed her mother. Then she wavered for a moment, looking at the giant man sitting in front of her, who, she knew, had not the slightest idea of what to do or say next. She walked over to him, and put out her hand. "Hello," she said, "I'm Lacey Carpenter."

He hesitated for a moment, and then took the hand. "Hello," he said, "I'm Aaron Carpenter."

"I'm pleased to meet you," she said.

"I'm more than delighted."

"I hope I'll see you again soon," she said.

"You will," he said. And then, as she raced up the stairs, he said again, "You will."

7.

Ten days later the two largest clients in Aaron's agency pulled out their accounts. The calls came through directly to Aaron. They lasted less than a minute apiece. Each of them cost him two and a half million dollars in billings. In less than three hours, half of the income of the agency was ripped out.

He put down the phone after the second call and sat paralyzed at his desk. It was like the war again. War without warning. Blitzkrieg. No notice—no sign—till you looked up at the clear blue sky and saw the first enemy planes diving straight at you.

Half of all income. Lost. In a single day. In an agency that was already running in the red. That was already spending five thousand dollars more a week than it earned.

He did not come out for lunch. He did not move, did not even pick up a pencil, till the office was empty and he heard the cleaning lady begin to bustle outside.

Ten thousand dollars a week. From this day on, they would lose ten thousand dollars a week.

No warning, he thought. No chance to retaliate. To recoup. To survive. No new prospective clients. No real reputation left. Nothing.

How long did they have? How much blood? How much money?

He walked out into the main office, into the emptiness where the staff had sat. Like a deserted battlefield. With the smell of defeat—and despair—everywhere. He had wanted to come out earlier. But how? How could he bear their faces—their eyes—especially when they knew that he had done her work—her work—instead of theirs? That he had sacrificed them to her.

He began to feel the cold rising inside him. Winter was growing again inside his soul. The spring had passed. The summer had passed. The winter was coming again.

He went to the bookkeeper's desk and pulled out the checkbook. Thirty-three thousand dollars left. Left from the Pollack. Left from the sale of the last major painting. Enough now for three weeks.

He put the checkbook back in the drawer, and then slammed it shut. For one brief moment he wanted to run. Run out into the darkness. Run out into the night. He didn't want to wait the three weeks. He wanted to run. But there was nowhere to go. Wherever he'd run, they'd come after him.

The cold now was taking over his body, and his mind. Winter had come again, and his mind could function again, without the heat of the sun. Without the heat of feeling.

He commanded his body to walk inside his own office again. To pick up the briefcase. He looked at the photographs on his desk. He reached out and touched one of them—of a beautiful dark-haired girl whose name was spring. But spring was over, and winter had come.

He commanded himself to turn and walk out the door again. To smile at the cleaning woman. To pretend the world was in place. To pretend that he had somewhere to go.

He thought of the sculpture. The Giacometti man, standing, waiting for him in his living room. The last remnant. The last defense. He had three weeks. Three weeks to trade it in for more time.

Melissa would scream. Melissa would cry. Melissa would fight. It didn't matter. He would do what he had done before.

Thank God he had done it all before. The sculpture would go to keep them all alive.

It was now a case of survival. Pure, agonizing survival. And those who could not—who would not understand this—simply must go as well.

8.

She pleaded. She reasoned. She begged. She screamed—yes, screamed, like a maniac. Both the children's bedroom lights went on, above them, on the second floor. Both their bedroom doors opened. She saw the light spill out from those doors, she felt inside her what those two children must have felt, and she went right on. For hours. While he simply stared at her—sitting, arms folded, hardly moving, answering everything she could say in a calm, even, conversational tone.

No, he would not sell the country home instead. No, he would not fire even a single employee. No, he would not take her money—the few thousand dollars she had saved over all those reckless years—if taking that money meant keeping the Giacometti. He had already called the dealers; he had already put up the sculpture for sale. One man had offered him a hundred thousand dollars for it. Aaron had asked for more. He was going to hold out over the weekend, and wait for the man to call him back on Tuesday. Perhaps—just perhaps—he could then get a hundred and eighty thousand for it.

"How long does that give you?" she asked.

"Fifteen weeks," he said quietly.

"For what, Aaron? For what?"

"To find new clients. To attack new accounts."

"How long has it been," she asked, "since you've got a new account?"

"It doesn't matter?"

"How long? Face the fact," she said. "How long?"

"Two years. But we've stopped running now. We'll fight now."

"You're going to accomplish more in fifteen weeks than you have in two years?" she asked.

He stared at her. Then he smiled. His face cut itself in half, horizontally, into a new kind of smile. The smile froze her, riveted her, fixed her to the floor in the middle of the room as though she were a butterfly on a pin.

"I'm going to do nothing but work on new accounts," he said quietly. "Day and night." Again, the smile. "Absolutely nothing."

"Don't sell it," she begged again.

"That's a promise," he answered. "Nothing but work on new accounts. Day and night."

And he kept his word. He had gone to war again. And that war captured every bit of energy, every thought, every act of his waking hours. He enlisted one confederate in that war— Little John. The boy alone shared his thoughts, shared his food, shared the one hour every Sunday he gave himself to relax. The others were excluded.

It was, for all of them, war. And Melissa was the sole witness to the first fatality.

The Saturday after the fight, three men from the moving company entered their apartment and removed the Giacometti sculpture. Aaron was not there; he was downtown working on a new campaign for an unknown client he had never met. The only person in the house to see the statue go was Melissa herself. She opened the door silently, let the three men into the room, and then watched them wrap the huge bronze sculpture in polyurethane and then plastic. Watched them seal it up from her forever. And then watched them raise it slowly and carefully onto a dolly, and open the front door to wheel it out.

"Just a minute," she said to the first of the men as they began to move it. "If you don't mind, I want to say good-bye to it."

She stood a few feet away from it—this piece of art, created by a man in torture, in a tortured world, and yet expressing beauty so deep and so profound that she had loved it more than any human being except her two husbands and her two children. She walked slowly over to it, now entombed in its plastic and polyurethane covering, and she threw her arms around the living bronze metal within that covering, and she rested her head against its chest, and unashamedly, she wept against the metal contained within it.

The three workmen watched her in complete embarrassment, afraid to say anything, afraid to pry her away from the shrouded statue. She had no concern at all with their witness, or their reactions. And then she pulled herself slightly back from the sculpture, and looked once again at the huge covering. "Go," she said silently, "to a good home. May those who inherit you know, and respect, and love you as much as we did."

She included Aaron in the sentence. And in that sentence she articulated the pain, the humiliation, the anger, the defeat that he must feel—but could not allow himself to feel—at this last parting moment. The final pain, the final defeat, the final loss of greatness that he could not even stay at home to watch.

Then she stepped back, and the three men took the burden without a word, and carefully wheeled it out of the front door. The door closed silently behind them, and she was left in her ghost home with its huge emptiness where the sculpture had been, and her ghost family, her ghost husband and, above all, her ghost marriage.

Aaron Carpenter went to his office every morning at six o'clock, sat at his desk without food or drink until the rest of the staff left at five, and then continued until twelve. He filled page after page, pad after pad, ream after ream, with brilliant campaigns—all for imaginary clients.

He realized that what he wrote was his most creative, daring, brilliant, and saleable advertising copy. Each evening when he left, there was a towering stack of this copy on Rita's desk. Each day thereafter, she would turn it into neat, handsomely typed pages, which would then be put into embossed leather presentation notebooks, and sent out to one prospect after another, most of whom had not even heard of Aaron Carpenter and his shrinking agency.

Week after week after week, the procedure continued in exactly the same way—the blind pursuit of accounts that had not requested new ideas, new campaigns, new solicitations.

At the end of ten weeks Aaron saw two of his own campaigns reproduced by the clients he had sent them to, done in slightly different forms by their own agencies, stolen by men who had every right to steal unrequested presentations.

That was all. Outside of the two stolen campaigns, there was no reaction, and no response. Not so much as a single echo in return.

Each night when he arrived home after twelve, he would sit down to dinner and devour whatever Melissa or Alice had prepared and kept warm for him. Every night for those ten weeks, Melissa was there to talk if he wanted to talk, to listen if he wanted her to listen.

For the first five or six weeks, he was filled to overflowing with the ideas. He would spend hours telling her what he had written, how he had developed it, the potential billings it must create. But as the weeks went by, and there was not even a hint of interest from any potential client, his conversation grew quieter and quieter. And by the end of the ten weeks, he had almost nothing to say to her each night, and she found herself filling up the time with tales of her modeling adventures during the day; or Little John's adventures, which produced a slight gleam in his face; or Lacey's episodes, which struck almost no response.

Their lovemaking had ended. Two or three times in the weeks that ensued, she had reached out and touched him or tried to kiss him. He had always gently pushed back her hand. The man was at war. He could not make love unless he had done something to deserve the erection that proved his manhood.

She began to wonder what it had been, during the long escape south during the war, that had allowed him to make love, over and over again, to the dark-haired one. After a few weeks, when her entire body began to tremble with need for him, she began to envy that dark-haired woman who had fled south with her husband so long ago, but had shared some mysterious bond that allowed him to make nightly love to her.

In that dark remnant of his past, there was at least shared love as well as shared danger. Here, there was only intense, obsessional, overriding fear. She could bring him nothing to comfort him or to spur him on. She searched her mind for a substitute victory; she called all her friends, all her contacts, every source she knew for a possible client, but they could promise her nothing but telephone calls or tepid leads, which amounted, one after the other, to absolutely nothing.

Absolutely nothing. Even his frame was shrinking—he had lost fifteen pounds in the ten weeks. He had aged fifteen years.

The fight was failing. Time was running out. He was being driven into a corner again. And this time it might be a corner from which he could never escape.

10.

One thing she did not mention to him during those ten weeks was her book. It had become evident, the first day after the fight, that he was not going to work with her on it any longer. She accepted this without question. However, if he himself was gone, techniques that he had taught her during those precious few weeks were still there. She never broke pace with the book itself. At first it was agony doing not only the writing, but the rewriting and editing herself. But, within two or three weeks, Irving House had assigned a rather bland, dumpy, but thoroughly professional editor to work with her. So that, once a week thereafter, she would take all the pages she had handwritten on her yellow pad, send them over to Irving House, and the editor would have them typed up, corrected, and sent back to her within five days.

The editor did not, of course, have Aaron's fluent, precise style. But even crippled in style, the book did go on, day after day. And soon there were a hundred pages, a hundred and twenty, a hundred and fifty. Little notes came back from the editor, saying, ''Fine,'' or, ''It helped me, and it will help a million other women.'' She was exhilarated by those notes. She had found an ally, who was helping her build a weapon in the neverending war against age.

But there was still the loneliness of doing it without Aaron's help, the loss of those soaring evenings when he had caressed her as lovingly with his pen as he did with his hands or his body.

Twelve weeks passed this way, and they had not gone out to a single party, a single dinner, even a single movie. And then, one evening at six o'clock, he reached her by phone at a photographer's studio, and asked whether she could be ready at seven-thirty for a dinner party at an old friend's.

His voice had a bounce to it, a hopefulness that she had not heard in all these weeks. Leave the studio at once, he said, abandon the shooting in midsession, and make herself look absolutely devastating. She knew of course that there was a dream hidden somewhere in that party, and that she was going to help him make it real. But it didn't matter in the slightest. They were going out again—going out as a couple. Perhaps this meant a crack in his mood, a break in the war, even a new beginning.

When she arrived home, he was already there, paying more attention to his hair, his clothes, than she had seen him pay in three months. When he was dressed, he looked again like the Aaron she had known before—thinner, yes, but with a radiance and competence in his face that she had almost forgotten. She had almost forgotten how tall he could stand, if he made up his mind to do so. She had forgotten how massive his shoulders were. She had forgotten how alive and witty and exciting his eyes could be, when he gave them the chance. She had forgotten how dignified the gray hair—along his temples, and now peppered throughout his hair—made his face seem. She had forgotten that he was still among the handsomest men she had ever seen.

But she had not forgotten that she loved this huge, gentle, embattled man more than she could give words to, more than she could give reason to.

By the time they were halfway to the party, she was dreaming that if he got what he was searching for there, perhaps, when they were home again, when the lights went out in their bedroom, when the darkness crept in, perhaps his hands would touch her body again, perhaps he would strip her nightgown from her body, perhaps she would know the giant dark thrust of him inside her, and the ultimate release which was now becoming almost an obsession to her.

She played with his fingers one by one as they sat in the cab, and he did not object. But she realized then that the most dangerous gamble a woman could take was to allow herself to be helplessly in love with a single man. To stake her entire sexual fortune on one love, and one desire. She knew now why most women never attempted it; they feared that the man's passion might focus itself upon a new object, and that they would be left alone, helpless, insatiable, with a need that could be satisfied by only one body, one organ, one man alone.

Then they were at the Rickovers' building on Park Avenue, and were whizzed up to the eighteenth floor, high above the city. A maid opened the door, dressed in a caterer's outfit that Melissa knew as one of the best in New York.

They hadn't taken two steps into the enormous living room, filled with English antiques, when George Rickover spotted them, grabbed Charlotte by the hand, and rushed over to greet them. So it was a plot between George and Aaron. The repayment of some ancient favor. But aimed at whom? And how could she help?

Melissa had long before learned to read New York parties, first by marking off the social status of the people who attended them. Usually, there were several honored guests of equal prominence, placed throughout the living room during the vital cocktail hour before dinner, so that each could receive old friends, and at the same time be introduced to profitable new aquaintances. But tonight, one glance told Melissa that this was not a multistar party. It must instead be a tribute to a sole prince of vast magnitude—the master of a commercial empire so vast that the ordinary run of multimillionaires spread across the room had come to pay humble homage to him.

Toward the front of the room, under two windows which looked over the shining lights of Park Avenue, George's customary armchair was occupied by a short, slightly balding, extremely distinguished Jewish man, to whom everyone in the room was being presented. He evidently ruled the party. Its entire purpose was to introduce this one man to as many of the Rickovers' friends as possible, and to make sure that, by tomorrow, everyone in New York knew that he had been in their apartment.

Melissa and Aaron were immediately marched into line, and spent the next seven minutes waiting their chance to meet him. Melissa leaned over to Aaron and whispered, "My God, who is he?"

"Not here," he said. "I'll tell you later."

Finally, they were face to face with him. He must have been at least seventy years old, Melissa thought, but his eyes were as bright and clever as any she had ever seen. And with that face so soft and pink and and plump, he looked like everybody's grandfather—the most intelligent and worldly-wise grandfather imaginable. He had a mustache and a goatee, perfectly trimmed, and her immediate reaction was that he looked like a Hebrew Lorenzo de Medici; decades of culture had left their indelible traces on that exceptional face. But there was genuine friendliness there too, that made her like the man, feel comfortable with him, before they had exchanged a single word.

"Albee Lauder," Charlotte's voice proudly announced, "I'd like you to meet Melissa and Aaron Carpenter."

"It's a great, great delight," Aaron said at once.

"Aaron Carpenter," Mr. Lauder repeated, holding up a small, plump, dignified hand, and giving Aaron's huge paw a firm handshake. As he did so, Melissa saw his eyes shift focus almost imperceptibly, as though he were speed-reading a computer printout located somewhere in the front of his brain. "The pleasure is mine," he went on. "I've admired your ads for years. But I think the car rental campaign you did—"We pay you to rent our cars"—has never been excelled in my lifetime."

Perfect, Melissa thought. Complete preparation—instant recall. He must have had George send over the guest list this afternoon. And what, she thought, does he have ready to say to me? Or does he take as much time preparing for the women as he does for the men?

Then, suddenly, Melissa caught the look on Aaron's face, and her stomach plummeted. At the first mention of his own work, Aaron had shown, for the flicker of a second, absolute surprise. Then, when Albee Lauder quoted his most famous campaign, done almost fifteen years before, Aaron's face took on a glow of positive delight.

Now Melissa knew why they were there. The man in the chair evidently controlled millions of dollars in advertising. And this first exchange—the mention of Aaron's work in almost the first breath—confirmed in Aaron's mind that his incredible dream might come true. This, by some miracle, could be the rescue operation, the counter-blitzkreig that Aaron was searching for so desperately.

Now she began to watch a response form on Aaron's lips; she could practically read the words before they were born in Aaron's mind. He was about to respond to a mere social trick—a formal courtesy that he himself had used a dozen times—with the reply that he had created a new presentation for Mr. Lauder's company. A presentation so gripping that he knew Mr. Lauder would like to sit down with him at once and discuss it. And such a reply would be an unforgivable social blunder, completely self-defeating.

"As a matter of fact—" her husband said.

"As a matter of fact," she interrupted, "I am Aaron's wife. I've heard so much about you from Aaron that I just can't keep quiet for another second. It's such a pleasure to meet you in person."

The sophisticated brown eyes moved from Aaron's face to her own. She had the feeling, when she met them, that this man knew exactly what Aaron had been about to say. There was an intellectual voltage behind those eyes that gave them the impact of a man thirty or forty years younger. She was amazed at the overwhelming physical appeal of a brain that commanding.

"And I am delighted to meet you at last," the perfectly modulated voice replied. "I've heard women all over New York say that you are a walking miracle, that there is no way that mere human eyes can tell your age from your appearance, not within fifteen years." He smiled. "One of the few truthful statements you hear at dinner parties these days."

"Thank you," she said quietly. So he did prepare for the women as well as the men.

The formal exchange was now over. They had had slightly more than their allotted sixty seconds. Somehow, they had escaped unscathed by Aaron's rashness. And now Charlotte began to move the couple behind them forward into the receiving position, and Aaron and Melissa turned to go.

"But," Mr. Lauder continued, ignoring Charlotte, and etiquette, and the entire line standing behind them, "I believe that no sane women in New York would also mention the fact that there is no other face in this city to compare in sheer perfection with yours. I must say, even from my first glance at you, that I somehow feel like the Bishop of Rome, at the beginning of the fourth century."

Melissa and Aaron had stopped moving. Charlotte and her couple had stopped moving. Every man and woman within earshot had stopped moving. All were riveted in place by the quiet tone of complete authority in Albee Lauder's voice.

"What a lovely compliment," Melissa heard Aaron say.

The permanent sparkle in the older man's eyes deepened. "Your husband and I," he said, "evidently have a great deal in common."

"I'm sure you do," she replied at once. "But I'm afraid that you both possess a knowledge of history far beyond mine." She silently begged Charlotte to forgive her. "I confess ignorance, but I admit utter fascination." Her eyes were fixed intently on the seated man's face, but she could feel the waves of approval—the first approval in twelve torturous weeks—radiating to her from her husband.

"Shall I tell the story," Albee Lauder asked Aaron; he was almost rubbing his hands in pleasure.

"Please do," Aaron said.

"The tale is told in several sources," the guest of honor went on, while the entire party stood frozen around him, "that one morning the Bishop of Rome was at Ostia, Rome's seaport, during the last great days of the Empire, in the fourth century, A.D. A shipment of slaves had just arrived from Great Britain. Four of these young slaves—two male and two female—had just disembarked from the boat, dressed in their typical blue tunics, and were standing before the bishop on the dock."

He stopped, looked at Aaron, and asked, "Am I correct so far?"

"Not only correct," Aaron replied, "but letter-perfect."

A chuckle issued from Albee Lauder's throat. Then he went on. "The bishop was literally stunned by all four faces. And come to think of it, I believe they were all blond." He turned to Aaron. "Isn't that right?"

"Precisely."

"Good. So he turned to the captain of the boat and asked, 'And what tribe do these young people come from?'" Then he paused for a moment, and Melissa suddenly saw the gentleness flow out of the eyes, and the smile change from one of pure enjoyment to the still greater pleasure of inclusion—or challenge. "But why not let your husband tell the story along with me? Would you like to give the captain's reply, Mr. Carpenter?"

"It would be my pleasure," Aaron said without hesitation. "The captain replied, 'They come from Britain, Sire, and they are called Anglos by their own designation.' Do my sources agree with yours, Mr. Lauder?"

"You have a photographic memory. I would have forgotten the last phrase of the answer. Remarkable."

"Thank you," Aaron said. And Melissa felt her heart start beating again. Albee Lauder was no prey to flattery; he challenged without warning.

"And now, of course, the point of our story," Mr. Lauder went on with even more relish. "'I am sure,' said the Bishop at once, 'that if any man who heard such a designation,'" and he nodded to Aaron, "'had listened attentively enough, and used the God-given sight of his eyes, he would have changed it at once—to, not Anglos, but Angels.'"

There was a pause. All eyes in the room were on Melissa. It was the most marvelous game of all, she realized. A game transformed into art, far more complicated than chess, where words were used as kings and queens, where there were no losers, and where the mutual prize was sheer creativity on the part of every person playing. She had been trained by a grand master for fourteen years. And now it was her obligatory turn.

"I feel," she said slowly, "as though I'd been given a . . . priceless necklace, fourteen hundred years old. And"—she smiled gratefully at Mr. Lauder—"because of your generosity, told that I could wear it, quite proudly, for the rest of my life." From the corner of her eye, she saw the incredible smile break across Aaron's face. "But," she went on immediately, "I'm afraid that I'm all too human an angel. A working woman, and the mother of two children."

Suddenly, from her side, came Aaron's great voice. "And also a budding authoress."

She turned, startled, to her husband. In twelve weeks, this was the first time that he had even mentioned her book.

But Mr. Lauder was completely intrigued. "On what subject?" he inquired.

Before Melissa could answer, however, her hostess broke in harshly. "I'm sorry, Albee. I'm sure you want to continue your conversation with the delightful Carpenters. But there are only a few minutes left before dinner, and there are several other couples who simply must meet you."

So the two of them were hustled away. As soon as they were out of hearing distance, Melissa asked, "All right, for God's sake, who is he?"

"He adored you," Aaron replied.

"Thank God. Evidently an acknowledgment from him is equivalent to a medal from the Queen of England."

"He makes more calculators and calculator parts than anyone else in the world."

"I knew he had to make more of something than anyone else in the world. But are there that many calculators sold?"

"Well," Aaron said, "if you add up the scientific calculators, the engineering calculators, the business calculators, the personal calculators, plus a dozen different companies that sell everything from copiers to minicomputers to software, then that little giant over there spends approximately eighty million dollars in advertising every year. Eighty million dollars. And George tells me that four or five million dollars of it has just left one of his agencies, and is up for grabs."

Four or five million dollars, she thought. Exactly the amount Aaron's agency had lost.

"But isn't he past the age of running the business himself?"

"He's seventy-six. But he runs the entire operation as though it were a grocery store. Not one penny of advertising is spent without his signature."

She was about to ask which of his products represented the four to five million dollars in billing, when suddenly Charlotte grabbed her arm, and wrenched her away into a corner of the room.

"You have probably ruined my entire social career," she said. "Mr. Lauder took an overviolent liking to you. He refused to meet anyone else after the couple that replaced you in line, and he's demanding—and I mean demanding—that you sit at his right at dinner."

"I'm sorry."

"You're delighted," Charlotte said. "And he is too. And Violet Schlesinger, who flew all the way in from Los Angeles to sit at his right tonight, is now going to be placed at the bottom of the table. And that means that the article about me in her magazine will simply be thrown out tomorrow."

"Oh God."

"Forget it. If she throws it out, I'll get it in *House and Garden* three months later. Besides," she grinned, "I simply had no choice. And I'm glad for your husband."

A sudden spasm of insecurity struck Melissa. "What do I talk to him about? I don't know the first thing about calculators."

Charlotte chuckled. "I'm sure he'll take care of that. His wife died four years ago, and he's been batching it ever since—not very successfully, I'm afraid."

"Batching it? At seventy-six?"

"Watch him, honey," Charlotte confided. "He's a horny old goat, and rumor has it that he has at least three mistresses stashed away in this country alone."

And then she was gone. The butler announced that dinner was served. And out of the crowd which immediately parted to let him through, Albee Lauder appeared at Melissa's side, to escort her to the table. It was an outright gesture of regality, and it conferred instant regality on her. She looked at Aaron. He was beaming. The old smile. The precious smile.

She smiled back, took the outstretched arm of the man beside her, placed her hand tenderly upon it, and was escorted to her seat of honor—feeling, from the gleam of Aaron's smile, as though she had just won the Oscar, the Tony, and the Emmy . . . all in a single night.

11.

Once again, at dinner, the two of them broke every rule of party etiquette. Albee refused even to notice the lady on his left. And Melissa, transfixed by the story of his life that she had coaxed him to tell her, hardly had time to touch her food, let alone say a word to the man on her right.

He had first wanted to talk about her. She had refused. He then offered to talk about Aaron and his career. She refused again, knowing the timing was wrong, and informing him that Aaron could tell him far more about that subject than she herself could.

Now it was her turn to choose a subject. And she chose what she called "the core" of his life. Not his business success, since she could read that in a dozen magazines, but the most memorable moments, the lessons, the personal growths that these years, and these opportunities, had given him.

He remained silent for a moment, and she realized two

things. First, that he was evaluating whether she was genuinely interested, or whether she was merely enticing him into the most treacherous form of self-flattery—that of telling his own history to a beautiful woman. And then she realized that she was intensely interested in learning those moments and those lessons—exploring that mind and, behind it, that spirit.

Why, she wondered, do I need this man's wisdom so much, now that he has chosen to spend dinner with me? Perhaps—perhaps because I sense a healing in it, not at all monetary, that can help close up the wounds of these past twelve weeks.

"It is not," he said with a faint smile, "a very heroic life."

"I don't care about heroism," she replied. "I care only about the truth."

"Then I shall give it to you, my dear, for whatever worth you may find in it. Where do we start?"

"At the very beginning."

And he started for her at the very beginning. With his father fleeing Russia in 1894, coming to America, selling rags and sundries from a backpack till he reached Palo Alto, where Albee was raised. He told her of walking to the boundaries of Stanford University everyday, seeing the ivy-covered buildings, and knowing that he would never sit in those buildings, or read the books they contained. But one special day he had the "temerity" to walk into one of the university halls, and hear a professor lecturing on Spinoza, the great Jewish philosopher of the seventeenth century. He stood for twenty minutes, listening to a Christian professor lecture on a Jew, and suddenly realized that the mind was more powerful, in at least some segments of this world, than wealth.

"Spinoza is now one of my favorites," he said, "to be read over and over again."

"I have read only fragments of him."

"You are the first woman I have ever met at a dinner party who has read him at all. You are to be congratulated."

"Thank you," she replied, deliberately not mentioning that the true praise should go to Aaron.

"I sometimes read Spinoza to my wife," he went on. "She had trouble with his words, but she listened attentively." Now the smile saddened. "She was a lovely woman whom I adored, with whom I had three quite marvelous children, and to whom I remained married for forty-seven years, until she died of cancer four years ago.''

''I'm sorry.''

''Thank you. In any case, this is not the time to take up my marriage. Instead, shall we concentrate on my rather checkered business career?''

She nodded, and he went on. With the two hundred dollars he had saved in high school, he started a small hardware store. There he spent twenty-three years, making at most five thousand dollars a year. And he would have stayed there for good, had it not been for his Thursday night poker game.

''A poker game?'' she asked involuntarily.

''Yes, the source of whatever little fortune I have was that game, in 1949. I shall explain,'' he went on, just as the first course plates were taken away. The Thursday night game was Albee's only vice. There were five regulars and two every-so-oftens in the game. The every-so-oftens were graduates of Stanford Electronic Engineering School. The only trouble with them, he said, was that they won every time they showed up. Statistically impossible—and absolutely enraging.

And then, one October night, Albee's chance came. Incredible hands were dealt that night—straights and higher, almost every fifth hand. Bets were far heavier than usual. And Albee was carried away with excitement at receiving four full houses in only seven successive hands.

He looked at her questioningly. ''Do you know what a full house is?''

''Oh, yes,'' she said, smiling. ''I play a mean game of poker. Plus chess. Plus backgammon.''

''I'd like to test you at them,'' he said.

She felt the allure fade out of the smile. She had been honest with him in everything else tonight; she wouldn't stop here. ''I'm afraid it would be an unpleasant test for you. I play well; and I'm afraid I play, always, to win.''

Albee's face changed to match hers. He was no longer the harmless chipmunk. His eyes instinctively narrowed, and she saw, for the first time, the teeth beneath the mustache. She felt again the sexuality of an intelligence that vast, of a will that strong. And she felt some impossible response to a man that age, move irrepressibly within her. For a second she glanced over at Aaron at the other end of the table. He seemed to be fascinated by his dinner partner. But Melissa knew that his eyes were taking in every emotion that registered on either Albee's face or hers. She knew that he saw what she had just felt. And the smile—the new smile that had been born on his face tonight—deepened.

When Albee spoke again, it was as though her eyes, and her attention, had never left him. "I, my dear," he said, "also play to win—when winning is allowed, and there is something worth winning." His tone was openly aggressive now, and he looked directly into her eyes. Then he resumed his conversational tone.

Four full houses within seven hands, he repeated. He bet fully on all of them. He lost all of them to the same two men. A total loss of three hundred and fifty dollars—three hundred more than he had brought with him.

He immediately offered to pay the balance by check. The offer was refused. Instead, one of the two strangers asked him why he didn't make the three hundred and fifty "respectable" by adding another four thousand six hundred and fifty dollars to it, and investing in a new company the two of them were about to start.

"I looked at him as though he were crazy," Albee said. "I had never even invested in the stock market. I was outraged. But I was also overcome by curiosity. I asked immediately what kind of company they planned to start."

The fish plate was removed, and the meat course inserted in its stead. Albee never saw the exchange; his eyes were focused twenty-seven years in the past.

It was calculators, of course. Very small, very smart calculators. Albee asked if they thought they could sell many. The man answered that he estimated about ten million the first year.

"I was amazed. I had never sold more than three thousand of a single item in a single year—namely carpet tacks. The idea of millions—of anything—suddenly seized my imagination."

He had asked the man for living proof that such calculators worked. The man produced one from his pocket, showed Albee how to work it, and let him experiment with it for fifteen minutes. At the end of that time, Albee knew that he was witnessing the dawn of a new era.

"There was only one more puzzle to be solved," he said.

"I know," she interrupted before she was fully conscious of doing so. "Why you? Why not someone else?"

Again, his eyes deepened with respect as he looked at her.

There were four reasons, he said. First, they wanted to concentrate on improving their "tiny mechanical brains," and not on manufacuring or selling them. Second, they had "cased" his hardware store, and were pleased at the net profit he made. Third, they felt the safest and smartest insurance policy was to make certain that their new partner was Jewish.

"And you felt?" she asked.

"Amused," he replied. "And reassured again of their intelligence."

She smiled, glancing again at Aaron. "And the fourth reason?"

"Money. They simply needed my five thousand to get started. As it so happened I had just enough in my savings account. Finally, I asked how much of the new company I would get for that figure. When they said one-third of the company—one-third—my fate was sealed." He looked up suddenly and smiled politely at his hostess, who was grim-faced. "I went home that night and told my wife. She wept for three days. She refused to sleep in the same bed with me. She went to the rabbi of our temple, and he spoke to me, not once, but four times. The president of the temple spoke to me. It did none of them any good. Within a week the papers were signed, and we were on our way."

He took a bite of salad. "But the numbers had been mistaken, you see. The first year's sales were not ten, but twenty million. The second year we sold fifty million. And from then on, it was as though I were in Las Vegas, standing at the most expensive crap table in the world. And all I did, from that moment on, was take my stick and rake the money in."

"I don't believe that," she blurted out.

He looked at her, bewildered. "Why?"

"Because it belittles your own contribution to the business," she said at once. "In 1949, how many people did your hardware store employ?"

"Four," he said.

"And how many people do you now employ?"

"About fifty-seven thousand, all told."

A flush shot through her body. That much power, over the lives of that many people. Again, she felt her flesh react as strongly as her mind. "Then how did you learn to go from managing four people in a local store, to fifty-seven thousand people all over the country?"

"I've never put it into words before," he said. "I went back to school at night, and took the usual courses in administration, and so on. But, every year, as soon as I learned enough to handle the people we already had, we needed more. So I got a list of the best firms in the industry. I found out who were the best people in each of them. And I bought them—at any price."

"At any price?" she asked, thinking suddenly of Aaron.

"Any price," he repeated, looking directly at her. "Like art. For the best—any price at all."

"And did it always work?"

"Nine times out of ten."

"And so your two partners gave you the finest products in the industry to sell. And you gave them the finest executives in the industry to manufacture and sell them."

"Quite possibly," he said. "I've never quite looked at it that way before."

"Let me ask you one last question," she said. Time was running out. The dessert was being served. "You evidently made a great deal of money from this transformation of careers. What was the most satisfying thing you bought with it?"

"My education," he replied immediately.

"The education you couldn't have when you looked over at Stanford University as a child?"

"Exactly."

"Strange," she said. "My second marriage did the same for me."

"How marvelous," he said, and looked at Aaron for the first time during the dinner, "for you both. In what way?"

"No," she answered. "These are still my questions. What education did you buy for yourself?"

"Those things I wanted most to know. But to know them, I also had to own them. For instance, I love art. Therefore I gained a rather thorough education in the arts of Europe, Asia, and the pre-Columbian civilizations—not by studying them in books, but by researching and acquiring them."

"I'd love to see them someday," she said.

"You shall," he said. "I promise you that."

And then, because they would soon be moving into the next room for coffee, she asked the man beside her what she knew must be her parting question. "And that was where your education stopped—with art?"

"No." He looked at her suddenly, very quizzically. "After my wife died four years ago—after a one-year period of mourning—I began to study, as a neophyte, the art of women. I have already devoted three years to this study, and I must admit that I am still a complete amateur."

He lifted his wine glass, and saluted her as he drained the last red drop from its bottom. "But," he went on, "there is hope. Now I realize that until tonight, I had never known, had never talked to, a woman of the beauty, of the quality, of the uniqueness of a Monet, of a pink period Picasso, of a Gauguin Tahitian. In fact," and he looked down at the table, so that his eyes no longer met hers, "I have now learned that there is a Metropolitan Museum of Feminine Art, contained in this city alone, and consisting of at least one impeccable example."

She whispered, "Thank you," at the exact same time that her hostess's frenzied voice echoed above the entire room.

"Shall we now have coffee—in the drawing room—everybody?"

In moments her hostess was at Albee's arm, had drawn him up and away, and Melissa was left alone again, to join Aaron. She knew that she would never be invited to the Rickovers' again. And she knew that she didn't give a damn. As she approached her husband, whose arm was outstretched to take hers, she looked up at his rugged face, and his proud, ecstatic smile, and she knew—gut-deep—that he didn't give the slightest damn either.

12.

For the rest of the party, it was impossible for them to get near Albee again. And then suddenly, an hour later, there he was behind them, dressed in his coat, saying good night to the rest of the guests.

When he reached them, he took Aaron's hand in both of his. "You have a magnificent wife," he said. "But I'm terribly sorry that you and I had no chance to chat privately for a moment. Perhaps, if you give me a call Thursday, when I'm back, we can have lunch together.''

Melissa felt the glorious shiver of good fortune run down her spine. She looked up at Aaron. His face had broken into a smile, but only she noticed—only she could notice—that the smile had not quite reached his eyes. Instead, in those eyes, she saw the brief passage of an emotion that she would never have believed could show there—self-doubt. The result of twelve weeks of repeated rejections, without even the courtesy of a single acknowledging phone call.

''I would love to,'' Aaron replied. ''I'll call you Thursday afternoon for an appointment. However,'' he went on, ''I couldn't help noticing that you had a most remarkable time with my wife at dinner. Perhaps you would like to take her out to dinner sometime in the future, and continue the conversation.''

Melissa stood there, stunned. Albee's face, sophisticated as it was, turned red. He turned to Melissa, looking for some qualification, some excuse. She had none to offer. She saw a dozen emotions flash through Albee's eyes—some of them she did not wish to remember. And then he held out his hand to her. ''A pleasure to meet you,'' he said.

''We had a grand talk. Thank you.''

''Thank you,'' he said, and he was gone. They waited five minutes to make sure he was safely away. Then they followed him into the dark street.

She did not speak till they had walked out of ear reach of the doorman. Then she said, ''Why in the world did you say that to him?''

He looked straight ahead, his expression perfectly calm. ''Because the two of you seemed to have such a meeting of minds.''

''So you invited him to have dinner—not lunch, but dinner—with me. Alone. So we could have a meeting of . . . what?''

''I have no idea what you're talking about.''

''Every implication you gave with that remark was wrong. And not only wrong, Aaron, but—tragic. Don't you understand? You had everything you could want. He asked you to call him—for what? To discuss his account.'' She stopped, and seized his shoulder. ''For Christ's sake, look at me! You had what you wanted. And then you took it, and threw . . .''

It was a moonless night. But there was a street lamp twenty

steps away. In the yellow light that bathed his face, the eyes said everything.

Eaten away, she thought, looking at the eyes. She had seen these eyes before, in the history books, in the photographs of Jews being rounded up for the concentration camps, for the ovens. Their bodies were still alive, but their hope was eaten away.

She said nothing more. ''I don't know what you're talking about,'' he repeated. ''If you feel there was the slightest thing wrong with my remark, then for God's sake, simply forget that I made it.''

''Please get a cab,'' she said, foresaking talk, foresaking touch. ''I'm desperately cold.''

13.

He came roaring through the door Thursday night. In a bellowing voice he summoned her from her writing desk. Then he picked her up and swung her around, announced that Albee had called him—had called him—before twelve o'clock.

Aaron had sent the presentation; Albee had just seen it. He'd liked it well enough to send it on to his vice-president in charge of advertising. The purpose of the phone call was to set up lunch for the three of them the next day at Le Cirque. They would discuss the four and a half million dollars in accounts that were still unplaced.

Aaron bolted down an entire chicken at dinner, drank a full bottle of wine. He recited from memory the exact headlines and copy and strategic planning and media schedules and product positioning for each of the three campaigns. It was as though the proposals had already been accepted, had already been placed in the newspapers and magazines that would carry them. There was no doubt in his mind that all four and a half million dollars was his.

He drained the cup of coffee at a single gulp, then threw down his napkin. ''What about bed, my raving beauty?'' he said.

Waves of resentment, of remorse, of accusation flooded

Melissa's mind. She never verbalized a single one of them. Her brain knew every one of the deprivations, every one of the insults she had suffered. But her body—the flesh and blood that her mind pretended it ruled—was trembling.

In the bedroom, he closed the door immediately, turned her around so that she was facing him, and snapped off the light so there was only the flow of the moon in the room. He began to strip every shred of clothing off her, dropping it on the floor next to her, and then slipped gracefully out of his own clothes. He ran his naked fingers over her body as though he had never touched that skin before, lowered her gently in the moonlight as though he were lowering her to the floor rather than the bed, then knelt above her and studied her body, touched her body, licked her body as though he were learning it from the beginning. Then, spreading her knees reverently, he brought himself slowly down till he could penetrate her, and then, when he was deeply inside of her, he gave out a sigh so long she thought it lasted for a full minute. Finally he began to move in and out of her, slowly, slowly, slowly, as though he were entering and leaving, again and again, some pagan, vine-covered temple.

She had no idea how long it was before they exploded together. She only knew that after that explosion he never withdrew from her, he never lost his rigidity, and he began the same act of animal worship all over again.

And then another joint convulsion. And then a longer pause, without withdrawl. And then a third silent ceremony in that pagan moonlight. And then sleep. And then awakening. And then love again. And then sleep, and then awakening, and then love still once again.

It was still dark, but now she was awake for good. She lay flat on her back, next to the sleeping eighteen-year-old boy in the fifty-year-old body, and she reached up and touched her own hair. There was no light in the room, so the hair she touched could have been, not blond, but black. Could have been—if she did not move her hand—not long, but short.

And she knew, with the touch of that hair, the question she had asked for all these twelve torturous weeks. How could he make love to you, she had asked, in his first war, when he could not make love to me in his second? And now she knew. It was the small victory, that lasted one day, and one night. The rabbit caught for dinner, the German patrol evaded, the crossing of some wire-fenced border. One day's fragile victory, that earned him one night's worshipful love.

And he did love you, she said to the night and the past. He did love you, as animal, as wife, as goddess. And he still loves you, in my bed and in my body. We are sisters, she said. We are born from the same love. I serve for you now. And I am proud to know the depth of that love; and I am proud to share that love, since it was so tragically cut off for you.

But I ask, Melissa Carpenter said to the past, only one favor in return. That you forgive him for what he did to you—as I have learned to forgive him for what he has done to me. For he has no other choice.

14.

The day of the lunch with Albee, she called Aaron's office four times in the afternoon; he hadn't come back. She held Alice till ten that night to serve dinner, then she let her go. She sat at the table till twelve, knowing what he had to tell her, waiting only to hear the details.

When he came in, she couldn't look at his eyes.

"He brought not one, but two morons with him. Two of his ad managers. They did the best hatchet job I've ever seen."

"But why?" she asked.

"A dozen reasons," he replied wearily. "It hadn't been created by them. Or by their agency buddies. Or their golf partners. Perhaps there were kickbacks somewhere—I tried to suggest it when Albee went to the bathroom—but there was no response. Nothing helped. Everything I mentioned—every headline, every phrase, every slogan—was simply shredded to pieces."

"But what did Albee say?" she asked.

"Nothing—either way." He was the king presiding at a court of petty thieves," Aaron said. "He showed no more support for their arguments than for mine. Of course, they took the proposal with them; they said they'd review it once more. Albee—the king to the end—said he'd contact me when he returned from vacation in two weeks.''

''Do you think he will?''

''Probably. There'll probably be the customary formal letter of 'no thanks.' '' He refused to look at her; for the first time in her life, she was grateful. ''Do you know,'' he asked, ''what the worst thing was? I felt like a fool. The ideas were good; I know they were good. But the man was paying me a courtesy call. He was being kind to me, but he brought along men who would counterbalance that kindness with just the right kind of unkindness to turn me into a complete fool.''

''Maybe that's not true,'' she said immediately. ''He's the kind of man who makes up his own mind, but who hears everybody's opinion before he does.''

''What makes you think that?'' he asked, a trace of life in his voice for the first time.

''From the conversation we had that night. I can assure you,'' she half-lied, ''that he'll go over it again in the next two weeks. And he'll let nobody else make that decision for him.''

He still wouldn't look at her. ''I'm sure of it,'' she repeated, dredging up some little hope to help him survive the next two weeks—the last two weeks of the money from the sale of the Giacometti.

They went through each day like puppets who had lost their strings, but somehow still remembered how to move. Aaron went to the office, prepared proposals, sent them out—without hope. She, thank God, had her book. She was now working on it from the time he went to the office till he came home late at night. She had neglected her modeling for half a year now, to give the book her full attention. Her income had suffered drastically.

She had taken the supreme gamble. A forty-year-old model had decided that something else was more important than her bookings. But fickleness is as much a trait of the modeling industry as any other. Now, new assignments dwindled down to a mere trickle. If Aaron did not rescue the agency, could she make enough to keep them in the penthouse?

Finally, the book was completed. The editor sent her a letter of congratulation. In six months the public would receive it.

But she was alone. The days were suddenly empty. She was serving inexpensive meals now. She had drawn up a plan to save every penny—including letting Alice go and doing the housework herself—if nothing happened in the next five days.

And then the phone call came.

15.

It was exactly three thirty-five in the afternoon. She was alone in the apartment, preparing a special cake that Aaron had once loved. When the phone rang, her hands were covered with the white dust of the cake mix. She picked up the phone, didn't wait to hear who was on the other end, but simply said, "I'll be with you in a minute, let me wipe off my hands." When she had cleansed her hands and the phone, she said, "I'm sorry. Go ahead."

The man's voice—the exquisite, mellow man's voice—said, "Do you have a minute, Melissa?"

She flushed. "For you, Albee," she said, "all day. How was your vacation?"

"Quite beautiful, and, because of the lady I took, quite disappointing. But I really would rather not discuss that."

Now she could pick up the tension in his voice. "Whatever you like," she said.

"Before I left," he said, "I promised your husband that I would review the advertising proposal he had submitted to us."

Hope—sudden, impossible hope—formed itself into a suffocating lump in her throat. "How did you like it?" she managed to say.

"It was good," the voice came back at her from the phone. "Clever. Ingenious. Cost productive. Excellent product positioning. However . . ." And there was a small silence at the other end of the phone. Again she stopped breathing.

"Yes?" she said as calmly as she could.

"I'm afraid the vice-president in the division didn't care for it nearly as much as I did," Albee said. "I could have overridden him, but there would be—I'm sure you understand—repercussions. So I would have to be very sure of the man I was hiring, if I did so."

Melissa could finally stand the suspense no longer. "And what would you have to know," she blurted out, "to be thoroughly certain of such a man?"

"First of all, what type of man and, indeed, what type of offer I was really participating in."

There was such a long pause that Melissa finally said, "Go ahead, please."

"I called your husband just now," he said. "I explained that the presentation was technically brilliant, and that it had a very good chance of working. I also explained to him, however, that there was a good deal of in-house resistence."

"And then?" Melissa asked.

"I told him that we might want to reconsider the decision a month or two from now, after we see the last of the other agency presentations."

My God, thought Melissa, a month or two from now . . . when there is no more agency. When my husband may be alive or dead. How beautifully ironic.

Again there was a pause at the other end of the line. Then she said, quite calmly, "And that was all?"

"No," Albee said, his voice suddenly returning to the sophisticated, businesslike tone that he had first used when they met at the Rickovers' party. "Your husband made quite an unusual offer to me on the phone."

"An unusual offer?" she asked. "Would you mind repeating it to me?"

"Not at all," he said. "I was about to hang up, and he said, and I believe the words were these: 'One other thing. As I said to you at the party, I thought that you and my wife seemed to have a marvelous time chatting together. So I just want you to know, despite the fact that we may not be working together, if you ever want to call her up and have dinner with her, alone, our invitation still stands.' "

Melissa felt as though her world were coming to an end. But the man expected an answer.

"Did that remark surprise you?" she said, amazed at the evenness of her own voice.

"My dear Melissa, in seventy-six years I have seen some rather unusual arrangements between husbands and wives, even the most affectionate types." He hesitated. "Your husband's words gave me to suspect that the arrangement between the two of you might be one of these unusual kinds."

Melissa tried to fight down the rage inside her, a rage directed not at Albee, but at Aaron.

"And if it is such an unusual arrangement?" she asked.

"Then I wish to let you know that I am driving up to my Connecticut home this Friday. I should be pleased to invite you there for dinner, for a look at some of my European art, and, the next morning, for a walk through some of the most beautiful forests I have ever seen."

"I see," she said.

"We shall return late Saturday night, since I have important business in town Sunday morning. And I think I should add at least one more fact."

"Which is?"

"There are three accounts for which your husband proposed advertising plans. They total four and a half million dollars in advertising revenue per year. If you will accompany me on this brief sightseeing excursion, I shall see that all four and a half million dollars of advertising accounts are turned over to your husband's agency, starting next week."

"Have you ever paid that much for a new painting?"

"I beg your pardon?"

"Have you ever paid that much for a new work of art?" she repeated.

He laughed—an old laugh, a pre-sophistication laugh, a Jewish laugh. "I once paid three million dollars for a Velasquez," he said. "The Metropolitan wanted it, but I outbid them. But you must know the truth of our arrangement. Despite the value I place on your accompanying me, I would never offer one of my accounts to an advertising agency that could harm us in any way."

"Nevertheless, there's no way you would make the decision in my husband's favor—even though Aaron's campaign might be far better than the other agencies'—if you did not receive an additional reward?"

During the long pause that followed, Melissa waited without saying a word.

"No," he said at last. "You are the only woman of your age I can look at today, and not wonder what she was like ten or fifteen years ago, since it is simply impossible for you to have been any more beautiful than you are now. You also engaged me in the most penetrating, most joyful conversation I have had since my wife died. As I told you, I have had very poor luck with women since then. I have been looking at

Greenwich Village art, when I never realized that I could find a Picasso. You are, my dear, a masterwork of womanhood. Therefore, if there is the slightest chance of my having a . . . more extended relationship with you, then I would consider myself the worst blunderer on earth to have missed it.''

"Thank you for being so honest with me, Albee," she said. "Now let me be as honest with you.''

"Of course," he said.

The next speech—the rejection speech—was already in her mind, the sentences composed and ready for immediate delivery. But all she could do was clutch at the receiver.

"Hello?" said Albee. "Is there something wrong with the connection?"

"No," she said, recovering her voice, and recovering her senses. "There's nothing wrong with the connection. But I'd like to call you back.''

"Of course," he said.

"Then you will hear from me''—she looked at her watch—''at approximately five o'clock.''

"Agreed. I shall clear my lines for your call." He gave her his telephone number, and they hung up.

She stood for a moment, looking at the white cake batter in its green bowl. Then she knocked the bowl off the counter and into a hundred pieces all over the kitchen floor. She reached behind her and took off the apron, crumpled it into a knot, and threw it down into the cake mix, which had settled everywhere.

She stalked from the kitchen to the hall closet and pulled out a fall coat. It didn't matter that she had traces of white cake mix over her shoes, her stockings, her dress, her hands. She had no further use for the appearance of a wife.

Right now, she was going to find out whether she was a wife at all.

17.

He was sitting with his jacket off and his shirt-sleeves rolled up. The top of his desk was strewn with dozens of yellow sheets. Each of these sheets was filled with his careful writing—campaign after campaign after campaign; all the dream worlds he had been churning out for the past weeks.

He glanced up at her as she threw open the door, and then, without saying a word, bent his head and continued to write.

She slammed the door shut behind her. His pen never wavered from the pad. "Look at me," she said. "I've just received a call from Albee."

"I know," he said. "Didn't he tell you that I asked him to call you?"

"He told me exactly how you asked him to call me," she said. "To take me out, if he cared to, by himself."

He put down the pencil. "Exactly," he said. There wasn't the slightest trace of emotion in his voice. But his eyes were not hopeless now; they were on fire.

"But you had promised me, last time, that you would never do that again."

"I agree," he said. "I did promise that. And now I've violated that promise—knowing the full implications of what might happen."

"You're insane," she said.

"No," he said calmly. "I'm drowning. This agency, which has been our lifeline for the past fourteen years, is drowning. We are all, my darling wife, on a death march together. If we do not survive, it will be because not all of us have made the maximum effort."

"And you knew that—"

"I had hoped," he corrected, "that he would call you immediately after. I had hoped that he would extend the terms of my proposed contract, beyond the usual agency-client relationship."

"So you decided to sell me too, like the Giacometti?"

"I decided to sacrifice you too, because there was no other alternative—like the Giacometti."

"As though I were made of canvas or metal."

"As though you were as precious to my life as they were. And had to be sacrificed, at a cost to my life far greater than their sacrifice."

"When did you decide this?" she asked.

"This afternoon. The exact moment when the call came, and I saw that his executive-pygmies would triumph."

"After fourteen years."

"After fourteen superlative years."

"And you decided . . ."

"I decided nothing," he said. "I am not a god who makes decisions for other people. All I did was to raise the possibility to Mr. Lauder, to see how he would react. The rest of the decision—whether you will contribute, whether you will sacrifice yourself as we have all sacrificed ourselves—is completely up to you."

He was talking insanely. She struggled with her words, to bring some semblence of feeling, of being a husband, back into his mind. "Do you know what he suggested?" she asked.

"I have absolutely no interest."

"But you do," she said. "You have a monumental interest in it. And if you expect me to make a decision, you'd better hear every detail."

He folded his arms, leaned back in his chair, and said, "Then tell me every detail."

"He wants me to go away with him this weekend."

"All right."

"He wants to take me to his Connecticut home."

"All right."

"He wants me to stay overnight with him this Friday." She slammed her fists down in front of him on the desk. "Do you understand the full meaning of that sentence?"

"And what did he offer you in return?"

She looked down at the man she had thought she had known for fourteen years, and she wanted to tear at his face with her fingernails. Instead she slowly—very slowly—smiled at him. "That's unimportant," she said.

"What did he offer you in return?" Aaron asked, suddenly leaning across the desk. "There must have been some quid pro quo."

"He offered to show me his collection of paintings," she said. He offered to take me, the next morning, to a beautiful patch of woods. That's what he offered me in return."

He said nothing. He turned his face away from hers, and she saw agony distort every line and muscle of it. She was surprised that she could still feel pity.

"If he had offered me twenty million dollars in agency billing," she asked, "would you let me go?"

There was no answer.

"If he had offered me twenty dollars in agency billings, then would you still let me go?"

No answer.

"What's the exact figure you'll take to turn me into a whore?"

He glared up at her out of his agony. "I do not—I never had—I never will have the answer to that question. In two days this death march of ours will be over. The only person in this universe who knows another possible outcome for that death march is you. I did not create the man who offered that alternative to you. I did not create you, who must accept or reject that alternative. The answer is yours. Entirely yours."

"But you did create the marriage that forms the basis for that answer."

"Yes. And I have treasured every moment of that marriage, even during the last fourteen weeks." He leaned forward across the desk, and she could see how much firmness his face had lost. "Tell me, Melissa, when the agency is gone, when we are left penniless and begin to liquidate the last of our assets to keep us going for a few more agonizing months—what will our marriage be like then?"

She said nothing.

"Will we have a marriage then?" he asked. "What will we use to build it up again? A man who can't even get a reply to his presentations? The laughing stock of a very small, very incestuous industry? Would you like to see me go back twenty-five years, and take a job as a hack copywriter, perhaps spending the rest of my life grinding out the same deodeorant commercial over and over again? I think the going rate for washed-up has-beens is approximately twenty thousand a year.

"And what about the children?" he said. "Do you have enough money to keep them in school, now that you are seldom modeling? Little John goes to college in two years—a good Ivy League school will cost about ten thousand dollars a year. And Lacey, your lovely Lacey, eats up at least eight thousand a year."

She could say nothing.

"No agency," he went on, "No future. No summer home. No school. Nothing but wave after wave of shock after shock for us all. And you stand there, in all your amazing beauty, in all your innocence, and ask me why I asked a man with four and a half million dollars' worth of advertising budget to spend, whether he would like to take you out to dinner alone one night?"

"Fourteen years of faithful marriage," she said.

"That will be the same, after you return home from Connecticut. Will you carry scars on your body? Will there be some horrible sign to you and the world that the transformation from faithful wife to . . . whatever it is, has taken place? What exactly, Melissa, will be lost?"

"Our marriage," she replied quietly.

"Then it was lost before," he suddenly shouted, so loudly, she was sure the secretary outside the door could hear it. "Then it never really existed before—except in the good times, in the plush times, in the years when the grain bins were full." The tears began to flow down his cheeks. "I have seen women," he started, and then stopped himself.

"Yes, go on. You have seen women—what? Sacrifice what part of themselves to keep you going?"

"It makes no difference," he said, turning away from her, facing the back wall of the office.

"What did she do to keep you going?" she asked.

"Shut up!" He did not turn to face her. "This is not what we are talking about. Get out of here. The subject is over." He spun around. "I told you—and I'll tell you again—I am not a god who decides other persons' lives, or takes those lives or their fidelities away. You have made up your mind. You have your honor intact. We have our defeat intact. Now go, and let me get on with my work."

"No," she said. "You have your victory intact. I'm due to call him in exactly five minutes. I'll make that call. I'll tell the children that I have an out-of-town shooting for Friday night. I can't guarantee what will come of it; but you have your second sacrifice."

She moved to the door of his office. "I only hope," she said, "that it gives you as much comfort as your first one."

Two days later, she had packed a suitcase, told the children the necessary lies, said nothing at all to Aaron, and was about to leave the bedroom. But she had forgotten one vital act.

She walked to Aaron's side of the bed. She lifted her left hand, and looked at the jade wedding band that had been on it, day and night, for fourteen years. It gave way without a struggle. She laid it neatly beside his bed lamp, where his hand would have to cross it to turn out the light before he went to sleep.

Then, without emotion, without hope, she picked up her suitcase and went to keep her appointment.

18.

The limousine was, of course, a Rolls-Royce. It was so large that it had to have been custom-built. It was waiting for her in front of the Pan Am Building, an anonymous meeting place, and the chauffeur got out of the front seat as soon as she stepped out of her cab. He walked over to her, and said, "Mrs. Carpenter? May I help you with your bag, please?"

She nodded, and he scooped up the bag and carried it to the huge limousine. The bag was smoothly and almost silently deposited in the trunk, and the chauffeur had reached the side of the door nearest the curb before she could even walk the distance between the cab and the limousine.

She stepped inside, the door was closed behind her, and she was seated next to an Albee exquisitely dressed in a camel's hair overcoat and light brown fedora, with his face trimmed and primped and massaged into regal perfection.

He turned and looked at her. The face was as paternal, almost grandfatherly, as it had been early in their dinner conversation. There was no sign of triumph, or suggestion of any situation other than a quite ordinary meeting on a quite ordinary street. When she sat down to the right of him, his right hand touched hers, lightly patting it once or twice and then withdrawing, as he said, "My dear Melissa, I'm so glad you could make it."

"I believe I'm on time," she replied.

"Perfectly."

The chauffeur had slipped into the front seat, the engine had started effortlessly, and they were already pulling away into the stream of traffic.

"I'm glad you were able to be prompt in this heavy Friday evening traffic. I want us to have plenty of time for a leisurely dinner, and for you to see every detail of the house."

She sighed audibly, and looked out the window of the massive back seat, at the other cars joining the flood of traffic, and the other passengers trying to see past the window blinds, trying to guess who might be riding in the magnificent limousine.

"You're well?" Albee asked.

"Perfectly well," Melissa replied.

"And the children?" he asked.

"Both fine," she said.

"I'm glad." And for the next half hour he said nothing. Melissa was occupied with the changing scene as they slowly moved over the bridge, across the river, through the miles of rotting slums, and then into the wonderful, quiet, protected enclaves of trees, lakes, and rivers that marked the homes of those that ruled the city, and could afford to escape it every weekend.

At last he spoke again. "Perhaps I should acquaint you with a little of the history of my European collection."

"I would rather you didn't. I've had a very good teacher," she said stiffly, despising the teacher, "and I'd like to test that knowledge against your paintings."

"Wonderful," he said, his face fairly glowing with glee. "Even more delightful. But I warn you, I may have a few surprises for you."

The act is cracking, she thought. I can't keep it up for even an hour. "Nothing could please me more," she said automatically. And then, hopelessly, she felt her face erase the over-polite smile, she felt her eyes look ruthlessly into his, and she heard her voice turned stringent by raw challenge. "But we shall see how many surprises you can provide me."

He stared at her for a brief second in utter surprise. His face flushed. Then he said grimly, "I shall prove to you—I promise you—before this night is over, just exactly how many surprises I can deliver to you." And then he turned away from her to look out the window again.

She sat there in mute shock at what she had just said. A seventy-six-year-old man, she thought, whom I happen to like immensely, and I've just dared him to play the twenty-year-old lover.

Why? Because he agreed to do what Aaron proposed to him, and I confirmed the agreement less than two hours later! He is willing to turn over four and a half million dollars of agency billing to have me come with him tonight—and what I'm now telling him is that he's going to receive, in return, nothing more than demands, intimidation, and possibly outright sexual humiliation.

I'm playing the bought and sold and delivered bitch, she thought. The woman who is worth nothing more than her price. Who gives, and punishes, at the same moment. To whom all life is a negotiation. And cheating—in every possible way—the only rule she can understand, or respect. All her life, Melissa had hated that kind of woman. And now she had just become her. She looked outside at the pure-white fields of snow gliding past her, she saw the window-image of herself in the car driving past those fields, and she suddenly realized that the fields and the car and especially she herself were all real.

The script she had unconsciously been playing was suddenly scrapped. Aaron had said to her, over and over again, that the choice was hers. She had made it with her eyes open. And she was going to fulfill it, not as a half-woman, half-bitch, but with every ounce of grace, of affection, of honor—her honor—that she could summon.

This man had bargained for a masterpiece of a woman; she was most certainly not that. But, whatever she was, he was going to get all of it. It was not Aaron's bargain now; it was not Albee's bargain now; it was her bargain. And God help her—yes, God help her—she was going to give this man the finest bargain he had ever made. Before bed . . . during bed . . . after bed.

She laughed. The man next to her turned in surprise. It's almost too bad, she thought, that I haven't had a hundred affairs before now. Then I could give him everything he expects for his four and a half million dollars.

And then she looked at the man beside her, and she reached out quite naturally and took his hand in both of hers. And she thought: No, it's better this way. As I really am. My third lover. The third man to whom I shall give love.

19.

They held hands, not talking, for the remainder of the way. Albee understood immediately. Touch had spoken louder than words.

Then, at last, they swung through the huge old stone gates and began to wend their way up the crooked driveway, until they saw the front of the house, with the sculpture on the outside already lit up in the early evening.

The sculpture garden was impressive. There were massive Henry Moores—four of them, seated figures of kings and queens staring out at the landscape, as well as a giant reclining woman. There were the Barbara Hepworths, the Jean Dubuffets, and three magnificent hammered iron pieces by David Smith. There was a giant Tony Smith, almost as tall as the house itself. And more. But she gathered at once, though every piece was magnificent, that it was merely a welcoming collection. The collection of a man whose real eye vibrated to painting, and not sculpture. The real treasures would be inside.

The Rolls pulled silently up to the front door. The moment the engine was turned off, the door clicked open and a butler and a maid stepped outside. Before she knew it, she was helped out onto the terrace and into the spectacular house itself, with Albee following behind her.

"Well," he said, hardly able to conceal his overriding enthusiasm, "would you like to go for a minute and freshen up?"

"No thank you," she said, her smile matching his.

"Shall we sit in the living room for a second," he said, "and have a brandy, or a coffee to warm up?"

"No," she repeated, the smile even larger and lighting up her face.

"Then what would you like to do?" he asked.

The smile broke into full glory. "Look at the paintings, dammit," she said. "Every single one of them."

He clapped his hands together. "Perfect!" he said. "Let's journey first into the front room."

It was evident that he must have had the most spectacular, the most expensive designers do the front room for him. In that room alone there must have been over half a million dollars' worth of antique furniture, fine rugs, and glorious fabrics. But she gave them all only a passing glance, and then riveted her gaze on the pictures that were spotted along the walls. Never in her life, in a private home, had she seen such a dazzling collection of Impressionists, Postimpressionists, and Fauves. There must have been eighteen paintings from the period of 1890 to 1908 represented in the room—most of which would be the glory of any museum in the world. She went to the first of them and stopped before it.

"Dazzling," she said. "It's Gauguin, of course. From the Breton period. But I've never seen one done with such complete naturalism, and so little flattening effect."

"Oh, my goodness," Albee said. "I'm afraid I'm out of my league tonight. I'm sure that this room—this house—holds no mysteries for you at all."

"Perhaps. We shall see," she said consumed by excitement, and moving on to the next painting. "Van Gogh. Arles. Very late, probably a month or two before he committed suicide." Then she turned directly to Albee, and stared at him for a moment. "I'm sorry," she said bluntly. "It would take me over an hour of looking to really see this one painting alone. If I go through the room, and simply name what you have here, I will have done nothing at all. May I ask a strange favor of you?"

"Anything at all."

"I know you have a dinner prepared, somewhere, in a spectacular dining room. But, since I imagine there are only the two of us, is it possible for that dinner to be turned into a moveable feast? May we have the first course in one room, the next in another, and the next in still a third room? That way, I'll be able to spend at least half an hour in each of these rooms of magnificent paintings."

"I agree," he said. "We shall have our moveable feast. Henry!" he called loudly, and the butler appeared from nowhere. "It shall be done as my guest suggests."

"Of course, sir," Henry replied, the puzzled expression on his face belying his nonchalant tone.

"Now," he said, and she imagined he was swollen with pride, "I want you to see something you will not find in any other private home in the world." He led the way into a small anteroom.

She looked into the room, and stared at the three medium-sized radiant paintings that hung by a huge Hepplewhite credenza. She exploded in admiration.

"My God," she said. "You have three Monet *Haystacks*. Three! And all of them absolutely gorgeous!" She went over and looked closely at them. "Do you mind if I touch their surfaces? I've seen his work at so many museums and I've always wanted to touch one, but have never dared."

"One of the privileges of owning great art is to come into

living contact with it—skin to skin," he said, and then suddenly blushed. She laughed and he joined her. She bent and kissed his cheek. And then she reached up and touched the living painting. Each dot of color was alive with energy, as though it had been painted the day before. Suddenly, she realized her definition of wealth and power. It was the ability to own precious, irreplaceable objects like these. And to be able, any time she wished, to reach out to them with her fingers as well as her eyes.

As they progressed through room after room, passing wonder after wonder, she experienced one masterpiece after another, through the feel as well as the look of its color. And by the time they had reached the den, the sensuousness that flowed through her fingers had filled her entire body, and the modern Lorenzo de Medici walking beside her was the most attractive man—with the exception of a man she would not even let her mind summon up—that she had ever seen.

But then, everything—everything—changed with one brief glance into the den. For there were three huge *Walking Men* by Giacometti—brothers of the sculpture she had loved so much. One of them was actually fourteen feet high.

She stopped for a full minute at the door, with her hands dangling at her sides. She gave out a cry of profound joy, almost a weeping. Then, forgetting Albee, forgetting the occasion, forgetting everything except the large and welcoming statues, she rushed across the room, threw her arms around the fourteen-foot marvel, and clasped it to her breasts, leaned her head against its metal skeleton, and began to cry.

Albee stood in shocked wonderment. She was like a little girl clutching a lost father, afraid to let go of him lest he evaporate into nothingness again. She was ashamed, felt that she had betrayed her mission, but she could not for one moment stop the flood of tears that was pouring from her eyes.

After a few minutes, he came close to her, and touched her shoulder. "Have you owned a Giacometti?" he asked.

"Yes," she said.

"And what happened to it?"

She took her face away from the emaciated metal figure that she still clung to. "We had to sell it," she said flatly. "Fifteen weeks ago. To buy enough time to attempt to recoup the fortunes of the agency. And I'm here today," she said, her voice warmer and more familiar now, "because that loss, that sacrifice, didn't save us."

She looked into the eyes of the small man standing opposite her. "He was the next to last sacrifice," she said. "I am the last."

And then she released the statue, and the tears stopped. "Now," she said to the master of this magnificent house, "I am ready to see more."

20.

At eight o'clock that evening it began to rain—a dirty rain that mixed with the snow, still pure and white on the penthouse terrace, so that within an hour it had washed away any vestige of that purity and that whiteness.

Aaron was in the apartment, alone. He had gone to one of the least-opened closets off the dining room, edged open a door that had not been used for years, and taken out a bottle of Hungarian red wine. It had been years since he'd even seen this wine offered for sale in New York. It was not a good wine. He wasn't even sure that it would still be sold in the homeland. Nevertheless, he had kept it for twelve years, since he had discovered it in an antique wine dealer's. This night was the night to open it.

He sat in front of the huge terrace window, drinking glass after glass of the cheap red Hungarian wine, letting it wash away the scene in front of the window even more thoroughly than the rain was doing. And taking him back, irretrievably, to that night in the cellar, when they had all left him to go out and bury the boy, and when he waited for them to return—and to bring her with them.

Now, in the rain-soaked drunkenness in front of the window, there was no longer any reason to search for the gun. He had it, in his right hand; he was holding it, turning it, opening it to see that it contained its five live shells.

Finally, after dark, they came back into the cellar, one by one. She was among them, her beautiful black hair soaking wet. The last to come in was Joseph.

They looked around the cellar to find their belongings, and then strapped them onto their backs. There were no last looks at the place where it had happened, no recollections of what had gone on that day. Just the gathering of what few possessions each had, and the filing out again into the night.

Now only he was left, and Joseph, and the girl . . . and the gun. The girl had sat down on the cellar floor next to him, legs crossed wide under her long plain skirt, her hands crossed between the cross of the legs, her head down, no trace of life on her face. She was waiting for him to use the gun. Joseph stood above the two of them, reaching for his knapsack, fastening it onto his back, tucking the belt lock in the front.

"Will you change your mind?" Joseph asked the girl.

"No," she answered calmly. "I want to stop running now. I want to stay here with the boy, forever. Go," she said. "God bless you. Survive. Leave me here with the boy."

"Will you make her go?" Joseph asked Aaron.

"I cannot move her feet for her," Aaron replied.

"He will do what I want," the girl said to Joseph.

"Yes," Aaron said. "I will do what she wants."

"Then there is nothing more I can say," Joseph muttered. "We will travel due south," he said, handing Aaron a compass. "We will travel for four hours, then we will hide. Use your eyes. You will find us."

"Good-bye," Aaron said to the man above him, who now kneeled beside the raven-haired young woman, kissed her head gently, and said, "Good-bye, Liebchen. Sleep well. You did no wrong. You had no choice. So sleep well until we meet again."

"I shall, Father," she said. "Thank you. But now, please go."

The older man looked down at the snakelike gun coiled in Aaron's hand. Then he walked out of the cellar door into the rain.

Now they were alone. The girl still sat with her legs and her hands folded—sat at Aaron's side, so much smaller than he, subservient and waiting, as she had sat a hundred times before.

Aaron—the eighteen-year-old man-child called Aaron Koblinski—reached out his hand in the penthouse bedroom, and touched the shoulder of the beautiful young dark-haired woman who had died that night thirty-five years before. The wine was gone from the old Hungarian bottle. And only the memories were left. Only his left hand, reaching out and touching that sparse young shoulder, and his right hand holding the coldness of the gun.

"Hello," she said, when she felt the massiveness of his hand on her shoulder. Then she raised her downcast head, and she looked at him with the dark eyes that had served as twin moons to a thousand of his nights. "Hello," she said again. "You're God, aren't you?"

"No," he said simply. "Just Aaron."

Her hand came up and touched his hand on her shoulder. "No," she said, feeling his hand, "this is God's hand. Just as it's been God's hand to me, at night, for three years. But now the man has left this hand, and it's solely God's, isn't it?"

"I don't know what you're talking about," he said blankly.

She picked up the hand and held it in both her tiny hands. With her fingers, she explored each of his huge fingers.

"How lovely," she said, "that God's hand should be so very beautiful. Touch it to my head, and my hair. Let it take out all the pain."

He let her guide his hand through the black, wet tresses.

"That feels so good," she said. "Do you feel the pain going out through each finger?" she asked. "Maybe if there were all the years left in the history of the earth, and we never stopped running your fingers through my hair, then, some-day, all the pain would be drained out."

She looked at him again quickly, with her dark brown eyes. They were black tonight, the color of death. They were the most beautiful eyes he had ever seen—the most beautiful objects this eighteen-year-old boy had ever encountered.

"But we don't have all the years, do we?" she said. "We have only tonight. And just a few minutes before you have to run, too, don't we?"

So she took the hand in both her hands again, and drew it from her hair, and held it a bit, and then leaned forward and kissed it.

Then she put his left hand down, and reached across to the right hand, which held the gun, and picked it up, too—gun and all. Then she bent down again, and kissed the front of the right hand, and then turned it over and kissed the back of the right hand, and then turned it over again and kissed the cold metallic object that it carried between its palm and fingers.

"Now, hurry," she said. "And be God to me. And make

everything go away. Now, quickly. Before it hurts so much that I can't breathe anymore.''

''I'm only Aaron,'' he said. ''Not God.''

''Be God to me now,'' she said. ''I need God.''

''I'm only Aaron,'' he repeated.

''But I don't need Aaron anymore. All I need in the world now is God.''

''I can't do it,'' he said suddenly.

''I need God now,'' she said. ''I need God to forgive me. I need God to take it all away. I need God with hands like yours, hands that will never let them come and take me, hands that will be strong enough to keep my hands from doing what they did.''

He felt her nails burn into his right wrist, and he felt her arms raise his right hand to her temple, just below where the exquisite black hair started to spring.

He had never fired the Mauser before. He had never fired any gun in his life. Its barrel reached her temple, her finger pressed harder on his wrist, and his fingers pressed in turn upon the trigger. There was a small sharp snap heard in the cellar. That was all. The gravel, the dirt bricks, the wooden scaffolding, all muffled the shot. Her head snapped back away from the gun, as though it had been hit very hard. She fell forward at his side.

He caught her as quickly as she fell, and she never touched the bare ground of the floor beneath them. He held her in his left arm, protecting her against the cold wet ground, giving her some little love, some little warmth against the rain and the darkness and the night. It was a very clean shot. In her dark hair, at the top of the temple, there had appeared a small red hole. It was hardly bleeding. He did not turn her head around to see what the other side looked like, although he could feel her blood beginning to run down onto his left arm.

She lay there in the crook of his arm. She was sixteen. She was dead. She was smiling.

He started to weep for her, to bury her first in tears. Just as he was now burying his new wife—with the same tears.

He sat there crying in the penthouse bedroom, with the glass and the bottle of cheap Hungarian wine lying at his feet. He had killed again—the second murder. Two loves—two deaths. He struck his right hand against the edge of the chair and the chair arm splintered. He watched as the palm of his hand began to bleed onto the bedroom rug.

Then he got up, and went to the bathroom to dress the wound, because Melissa would never forgive him if the rug were seriously stained.

Would there ever be a woman he could love—truly love—for as long as he wanted to love? Would there ever be a world in which he could love—truly love—without death? Where there was no penalty? No choice of sacrifices? No ultimate murder? No betrayal at the end?

21.

Finally, Albee broke the silence at the dinner table. "Shall we talk about it?"

Melissa looked up across the antique china, across the Baccarat crystal, to the man opposite her. "If you mean that ridiculous speech I made at the Giacometti," she said, "no. I don't think we should talk about it. Let's simply assume that I was carried away by the sight of an old friend, and babbled on for a moment. Please," she asked him, "why don't we just let the matter drop there?"

Albee paused in reflection. Then he said, "I'm sorry. To drop the matter would violate all our rules. We agreed on honesty; this would be dishonesty. We agreed on openness; this would close all real conversation. That sculpture which you 'babbled' about is at the very center of your life at this moment. What you said about it disturbs me greatly. And to pretend that you never said it, does an enormous disservice to both of us."

"I'm afraid there's far too much at stake," she said. "And I don't care to gamble it on a single moment's insanity."

"Ah, that," he said. "You're quite right. The sum of four and a half million dollars does seem directly concerned with this evening's meeting. And if you tell me the truth, you risk—I imagine—every cent of it."

"Please forget the entire thing," she said. "As a gentleman."

A smile broke out over his entire face. Not a chipmunk smile. Not a patrician smile. But a warm, immeasurably ancient, and open Jewish smile. "Who said I was a gentle-man? I said I was rich. I said I had good taste, and you would enjoy the house. But a gentleman—I never said I was."

Startled, she put down her fork and pushed away the plate. "Then, as a friend."

"A friend you have in me," he said. "I'll give in to that one. But which one of us two friends—you or I—shall judge how the one friend shall benefit the other most?"

"I think that, in this case, I'll have to."

"I don't agree," he answered immediately. "For the very simple reason that I have some thirty-five years more experi-ence than you." Again the smile reflected thousands of years of laughter and suffering and endurance and warmth. "And also because four and a half million dollars means slightly less to me than it does to you." He pushed the buzzer with his foot. The butler appeared before the sound had died. "Henry," Albee said, "we're pausing here for a few mo-ments to savor your excellent trout. We wouldn't like to be disturbed till I ring again.

"Now," he said when the butler had gone, "something emerged in that den that I had not anticipated, and that I have no way of understanding unless you explain it to me. There-fore, I make this promise to you. No matter what it is, no matter what happens because of it, I will give you the chance to see that your husband does not lose a single cent of that billing—not a single cent—if you tell me the truth."

She said cautiously, "Do you mean that?"

"Unalterably," he said. Then the smile broke out again. "But," and his shoulders shrugged slightly, "perhaps I should first explain to you exactly how I mean it. We made an arrangement, you and I, before you came here, that was based on a series of assumptions. If those assumptions are not true, and the arrangement does not work out as we agreed, then I promise you that you will have an entirely different way of gaining the four and a half million dollars for your husband's agency."

"I don't quite understand," she said.

"Well," he replied, "it is a little complicated. Therefore," and now the chipmunk was sneaking back into the smile, "let me explain. As I told you at the dinner party, I enjoy chal-lenges. I also enjoy giving them. As things now stand be-tween us, I am enough of a ruffian—and enough of a friend—to withdraw my offer of the agency billing." Then, before she could say anything, he went on. "You may stamp your foot, be infuriated, and the chauffeur will immediately take you home. Or you may trust me, tell me what you meant, and we shall then have two choices. Either we shall consummate our pact in its agreed-upon way, or I shall provide you with another way—a difficult but not impossible way—of taking home every penny of that billing."

She stared at him for a moment; the little mustache of his cherubic face was fairly twitching with glee. Suddenly she broke into laughter. "And what is your riddle, Rumpelstiltskin?" she asked, still laughing. "Do you have a hall upstairs with eight rooms and eight keys, one of which I am not allowed to open? Or do you always involve young ladies in fairy tales, with the promise of a pot of gold at the ending?"

He folded his hands over his stomach. "I shall give you a definite answer to that, if needed, after you tell me the truth."

"All right," she said. "Now what do you want to know?"

"I take it that you owned a similar statue to the one inside."

"For fourteen years."

"Which you loved very much. And which you had to sell recently to keep your husband's agency alive." She nodded. "And when you saw its brother here . . ."

"I went into renewed mourning. And I acted out that stupid little scene in front of you."

"It was not stupid. I would have reacted the same way. But no matter. I take it the sacrifice was in vain."

"Yes. The money from the sale of the sculpture ran out, as all the other monies from all the other sales had run out."

"But that was the next to last sacrifice," he said. "And you said in the den that you were to be the last sacrifice."

"Yes."

He spoke to her across the razor-sharp atmosphere of the room. "And what was that last sacrifice to be?"

She had waited patiently for the question. Let it all be real, then. "The sacrifice," she said, "was to end fourteen years of absolute fidelity."

"But I had thought—"

"You had assumed. Aaron had given you a series of implications, and you had leaped to their conclusion."

"Touché," he said. "He said nothing more than that I

might care to have dinner alone with you. And I assumed that you did what so many other modern couples do.''

"And I agreed to let you keep that assumption.''

"As the last sacrifice?''

"As the last sacrifice.''

"And, if you had not seen the Giacometti, if we had not had our little discussion just now, would you have gone through with it?''

"The answer is that I would still go through with it,'' she said at once. "In fact,'' she added, looking straight into the balding man's eyes, "proudly.''

"Despite the violation of vows.''

She flushed. He knew more about her than she had dreamed. "Despite the violation of vows,'' she answered.

"Despite the shame?''

"Thank you,'' she said, "for knowing how terrible a barrier that would be to me. But—despite the shame, yes.''

"Despite the effect on your marriage?''

"Despite the possible collapse of my marriage. Yes.''

"But why?'' he asked. And she sensed the disbelief and vulnerability in that question. "It's by no means only for the money.''

"No,'' she said. "Nor for vengeance against Aaron, if that's your next question. The answer is far simpler than that.'' She reached her hand across the table and took his. "Because, of all the men in New York—and I know hundreds of them—you would be the only one with a heart big enough, and an attraction great enough, to make that sacrifice tolerable.''

"Beautifully phrased,'' he said, "but I can't believe it. Look at me. I am hardly any woman's fantasy.''

"But listen to yourself, and you are. When you exhibit that mind, you stand a hundred feet tall. When you talk about business, or art, or Spinoza, the look on your face makes younger, more conventionally handsome men fade into the background. And when you take a woman's hand—my hand—and lead her gently into that immense universe you inhabit, then she becomes by your choice the most desirable woman, and the most desiring woman, in that universe. You give your magic, for that moment, to her.''

"I could even believe you,'' he said.

"Please do.''

"I thank you. I truly, I deeply thank you. But I am a Jew."

"I know that. But—"

"And there is a commandment in our religion—I believe it is the sixth—which says, 'Thou shall not commit adultery.'"

She looked at him in astonishment. "You weren't intending to commit adultery with me tonight?"

"No. I was going to commit intercourse with you tonight— with a woman who had committed adultery, for the first time, years ago." He looked directly at her. "It would have been very good intercourse," he said. "I am quite accomplished and quite virile in bed."

"I am sure of that. Instinctively," she said.

"But I do not take faithful woman away from their husbands."

"Even if they are masterpieces of women?" she asked, ironically.

"Even if they, alone, would fill the Metropolitan Museum of Art," he replied. "I went to a synagogue before I went to an art museum. And I am afraid that the previous training holds domain over the second."

"Then—" she asked.

"We can leave for home in my car at once," he said.

"Or?"

"We can finish our dinner."

"Or?"

"We can finish our dinner, and then play a little game," he said.

"Of what?" she asked.

He reached for the buzzer under the table. "My dear," he said. "We are slightly behind schedule. My chef gets terribly angry at me if I spoil his dinner. I am afraid we shall have to move to the next course—and then we shall take up the matter of what the little game shall be, and how we shall divide its stakes."

21.

"Have another chocolate truffle," Albee said seductively. It was a strange seductiveness, preparatory to—what?

"No, thanks," Melissa replied warily. "I've had three already. One more and I'll pop."

They were sitting in the living room now. Neither had discussed the game since the trout. Neither seemed to be in the slightest hurry. The evening was passing gently, conversationally, leisurely.

He took a last sip from the coffee. He glanced at the watch on his arm. "My, my," he said. "It seems to have reached ten-thirty already."

"Has it?" Melissa asked.

"Getting a little late, don't you think?" he said.

"Not really," she said. "It's Friday night. I always seem to become more and more awake as Friday night proceeds."

"Awake enough to attempt a little divertissement?" said Albee charmingly.

"Of course," she replied. "If you wish."

"What will it be?" he said, with a false tone of musing in his voice.

"Why," she replied, "whatever you would like it to be."

"But I'd like something challenging," he said. "Something close and"—his smile became piratical now—"vicious," he said. "Something positively brutal."

"Is that really so hard to arrange?" she asked mockingly.

"I'm not sure," he remarked. "I think you mentioned the other night at dinner that you play three games particularly well—chess, poker, and backgammon."

"Only for fun," she admitted, with a smile. "Never for much money."

"That's fascinating," he said. "Tell me. What is the highest stake you've ever played a single game for?"

"Well, there was once a backgammon game with Terry Radcliffe, in which we started at one dollar."

"One dollar?"

"Yes—a full dollar."

"And how high did the bidding get before the game closed?"

"Well—I'm not sure I remember, but I think I won thirty-two dollars from her that game."

"Very good," he said. "And you consider backgammon your best game?"

"Well," she said. "They're all pretty good. But, truthfully, I like it the most."

"And would you consider playing backgammon for a slightly higher stake?"

She smiled, took another bite from a truffle, and put it slowly down on the plate. She licked the chocolate from her fingers. "Yes," she finally decided. "I might try you for a slightly higher stake."

"For what amount?" he asked.

"You're the host," she said. "You suggest the stakes."

He smiled. A thin smile, a smile she supposed he had used in a hundred business negotiations, and won every one of them.

"What do you say to a series of three games—no more," he said. "That should fairly well rule out luck."

"All right," she said. "Three games."

"And we set a fixed stake for each of the games."

"No doubling?" she asked.

"No doubling," he replied.

"Perhaps," she said, "if the initial stakes were high enough . . ."

"Shall we say a million and a half dollars per game?" he asked.

She wanted to whistle. She blocked the impulse instantly. No change of expression moved across her face. "Let's see if I understand. You bet one and a half million dollars per game. And I bet?"

"Nothing. Your presence here is gamble enough."

"And if I win each game?" she asked.

"I doubt you'll win all three games," he said.

"But if I do?"

"Then, my dear, your husband will have four and one half million dollars' worth of advertising billing."

"Very nice," she replied. "Very tempting indeed, I must say." Then she frowned slightly. "And if I lose all three games?"

"That's more like it," he smiled. "If you lose all three

games, you will spend the night in the guest bedroom. I will spend the night in the master bedroom. We will see the forest tomorrow, as we planned, and you will go back to New York with nothing but what you came with. Nothing at all.''

"And if I win one of the three games?'' she asked.

"Then you'll take back one and a half million dollars with you."

"And if I win two of the three games?'' she asked.

"Not likely, but, if it happens, then you'll take three million dollars with you."

Now the situation was clear to her. He had gambled on a state of affairs between her and Aaron and lost. Now he was offering her a second gamble that he felt *she* would lose just as badly. He probably played backgammon two or three nights a week. She wouldn't doubt that he'd had a professional come and teach him. He was a man who allowed himself to do nothing badly. Therefore, he was confident that he would win.

His strategy was laid out before her like a map. The first game would be a triumph, a thorough display of his masterly playing. He would watch the expression on her face when she saw the first million and a half slip away. Then the second game would go just a little slower—with a little sloppier playing on his part—and offering just the smallest ray of hope for her. But it would inevitably end the same way, her realization that three million dollars in losses had just occurred. He would be masculine, triumphant, dominant. He would have his damaged ego intact again. He would have given her her chance to win back what she had given away, and she would have lost it.

The third game, however, was the question. She knew that if his plans and estimates were correct, then there would come the trade-off between his desires and his generosity. If he felt that she still needed the four and a half million dollars in billings that badly, perhaps he might listen to a last plea, a last request, and he might end up with the Metropolitan Museum in bed after all—with his honor assuaged. Or, if no such offer was made—if she preferred to go home faithful but penniless, and if he preferred to be remembered with gratitude rather than resentment—then he could horribly misplay the last game, bungle any one of a number of moves, and let her leave the next morning with her own comfort assured, and a million and a half dollars in her pocketbook.

There was no way for him to lose. The money meant nothing to him. It was like giving a head waiter at the Four Seasons fifty dollars for a special dinner, or a cocktail waitress in Las Vegas a hundred dollar chip. It was a gratuity of no meaning to the person who gave it. It simply made a grand night even grander.

However, she knew that all this would come true if, and only if, he had the talent and skill he thought he had. And if she had the amateurishness, and the feminine panic, he was so evidently counting on. She was immediately, overwhelmingly eager to find out if he was anywhere near as good as he thought he was. And she couldn't wait to see how much difference money made—if any—in that marvelously nasty little game of backgammon.

"All right, Albee boy," she snapped, "get down the board. And for God's sake, take off that jacket, and roll up your sleeves, will you?"

The look of astonishment that crossed his face was the most unguarded expression she had ever seen on it. But a brief second after, it was replaced by the usual chauvinist's air of superiority. "My dear," he said, "in this house we do not pull out the backgammon table. We go to it."

He rose and took her by the hand, and drew her to a small sheltered alcove that she had not even noticed as they first moved through the house. There he snapped on lights, and she saw in the center of the small, velvet-covered room, a backgammon table that must have been made by a master English furniture designer of the eighteenth century. Perfectly proportioned in shining, dark mahogany, it was a board designed for the wagers of generals, lords, and princes to the throne. She imagined it must be worth over a hundred thousand dollars. It was the ultimate setting for a battle worth one and a half million dollars a game. She smiled. "How appropriate."

"Would you care for a glass of brandy," he said, "as we play?"

"No, thank you," she said.

"Shall I set up the board for you, my dear?" he asked.

"Of course not." She took one brown man and one yellow man in her hands, put them behind her back, shuffled them briefly, and presented her two closed hands to him in a flash. "Pick," she said.

He hesitated a moment, then reached out a well-manicured

finger and touched one of the hands pointed at him.

She opened it. "Brown," she said. "I'll take the yellow." Before Albee could remove his jacket, before he could draw back his chair in a stately manner to position himself at the table, she had scooped up her pieces from the various places they had been left during the last game, and had set up her board. She did this with all the sleight-of-hand, all the speed of fingers necessary to mark the true backgammon wizard. She had scarcely looked at the board.

He stood there, watching her hands flash across the board. She did not sit down until all her pieces were in place. Then she looked up at him and smiled, ready to begin.

She was smiling. He was not.

He still hesitated. Then, he took off the impeccably tailored jacket, and hung it over the back of the chair. He did not, however, unbutton the vest. But, as he sat down intently at the gaming table, he unconsciously loosened his shirt-sleeves to give his wrists the maximum freedom of action. In thirty seconds—not as quickly, not as precisely, not as automatically as she—all his pieces were arranged in their starting positions.

At each of their places was a set of dice. They both flung a single die from their antique leather cups. The dice came to rest with an imperious sound. He had thrown a one, she had thrown a six. She gave a tiny chuckle, reached out instantly, and rearranged two of her men at once to block the seven-point on her inner board.

"That was luck," he said under his breath.

"That was brain," she replied. "Move please. I can't stand a slow game of backgammon."

He threw miserably, studied the board to pick the least vulnerable of his alternatives, and moved the pieces carefully. No sooner had he picked up his dice, when hers came spilling out of her cup again, across the board, and into a perfect throw that she followed up with an instantaneous move of two more men—blocking another point on her inner board.

And so the first game went. It was not a game—it was a massacre. He had been rattled, and his temporary confusion projected itself in the dice. Almost every throw he made was bad. The game was little more than a triumphant march of Melissa's pieces across the board. Less than fifteen minutes later, she lifted her final man from the board, and was one and a half million dollars richer.

He stared down at the board for almost a minute. "I can't believe it," he said. "I have never seen such incredible luck, such a run of perfect throws."

"Nor," she interrupted, "such clever picking of the advantages they offered me. That was the real secret of the game, and I admit that I enjoyed it, even though . . ." and her voice trailed off.

"Even though what?" he asked.

"Nothing," she said.

"Even though what, please?" he repeated.

"Well," she said, looking up at him innocently with her lovely large blue eyes, "You missed two or three good moves about the middle of the game, my dear." Her smile had never been more radiant.

She watched the well-kept skin grow red with anger. For a moment, she thought the dapper little man sitting across from her was about to have a stroke. He controlled himself with the greatest of willpower. He stumbled on several sentence-openings before saying, under his breath, "It's not possible."

She said, "I'm probably wrong. Have you got a pad?"

"Have I got a what?"

"A pad, a scoring pad, some sort of piece of paper where we can write down the score, so we can't forget it."

He looked wildly around the room. Finally he pushed another button on the floor, and the imperturbable butler appeared.

"Henry," Albee said, "I imagine we have a backgammon pad here."

"Of course, sir," the butler said, seemingly noticing nothing wrong in his employer's face. "It is right here." The butler went to a desk and took out a pad and a small gold pen. He handed them to Albee.

Melissa looked at Albee wide-eyed. "Shall I keep the score, or will you?"

"You don't trust me to keep the score of three games?" he said.

"Of course I trust you," she said. "But I do so like to do it myself."

"All right, then," he snorted, pushing the pad across to her. "You keep it in any manner you see fit."

She looked at the backgammon pad for a moment, and then shook her head. She tore off the top sheet and turned it over to its blank side. At the top of it, she wrote: Albee and

Melissa. Then she drew a heavy line down the center of the paper, and three horizontal lines directly dividing it. The horizontal sections were labeled one, two, and three. "There," she said, holding it up for him to admire. "I think this will do the trick."

"Anything you wish," he muttered.

"Now, let's see," she said. "You lost the first game to me, so we'll just mark the fact that you owe me the sum agreed upon." She picked up the pen and began to write under her name, "one and a half million dollars." Suddenly, she looked up at him with complete mystification clouding her face, and said to him in a syrupy voice, "How many zeroes are there in a million and a half dollars?"

"Five," he said, hardly able to restrain himself a second longer. "Now, for Christ's sake, let's get on with the second game."

She put the pad down in front of her, and placed the pen diagonally across it. "Of course," she said brightly. "Anything you want."

Albee shook the dice, his hand trembling slightly, and the second game was underway.

This game was far more difficult. She moved instantly each time the dice revealed themselves. He reviewed the board between every move as carefully as if he were playing in a master chess tournament. He made no mistakes whatsoever. He played an air-tight defensive game, trying this time to strangle her. He played brilliantly. In twenty minutes, it was clear that he was ahead and would win.

She had only one chance, and she knew it. This time, despite herself, she rolled the dice more slowly. On the entire board, he had only one man exposed. She, on the other hand, had spread out her men in desperation; she now had three men equally vulnerable. And he had five points in his home board sealed off; she had only three. When her dice came up with a three and a five, she realized that she could protect two of her three vulnerable men, and at least make a decent fight out of the game—or she could hit his one lone unprotected man and send him to the bar; and then her opponent would probably roll that man out of his prison on his next throw, put one of her men in the cell next to it, and turn the game into a sure rout.

She had misplayed throughout the game. She had gambled recklessly, and the dice had refused to back her. For the first time, her facade was cracking. Now this last throw—the three and the five she was staring at—meant the difference between three million dollars . . . and only one and a half million. Panic began to flood its way up her spine like a paralyzing poison.

"Well, beautiful one," his sarcastic voice floated across the board at her, "are you a little baffled? Would you like some fatherly advice on which move gives you the best odds now?"

Thank you, she thought at once. You sense fear the instant it speeds up the other person's pulse. If she hesitated now, she would lose—not only this game, but the game after. There was only one way out—sheer bravado. Take the amateur's chance, the beginner's chance, the idiot's chance. There was no more hesitation. With a brilliant smile, she hit the man and sent him to the bar, to his temporary prison.

"Are you crazy?" he exploded at once.

He was right. At her club, she would have been ridiculed unmercifully. But at her club, they had never dreamed of risking over a million dollars on a single move. "I beg your pardon," she said, staring at him open-eyed.

"That's the worse play I've seen committed on this board in twelve years."

"Then why not take advantage of it?" she replied sweetly.

He looked at her in open astonishment. There was no humiliation on her face. She simply sat there, smiling, as though she had invented a new rule which guaranteed her the game.

Disgusted, he picked up the dice. Slowly, he let them rattle in the cup. Regally, he let them clatter across the board. He knew, as well as she did, that nine out of ten throws would have blasted her hopes right off that board. And then he sat there, and sat there, and continued to sit there as the realization sank in that those dice had just delivered the improbable ten percent. And that he was still trapped in that bar, without the ability to move a single man.

"Well," she said, "they didn't come up the right way for you at all, did they?"

There was no sound from him. She picked up her dice and rolled, and made another point on her board.

"Try again," she said politely.

He threw four times in a row without coming up with a single one of the numbers that would liberate his man from that miniature prison, while she kept covering points on her board. Each time he failed, his face grew redder and redder, darker and darker. And each time she looked at the dice, smiled pityingly at him, and then continued to roll, and to walk away with the game.

On the fifth roll he was out, and hot on the chase again. Man after man, on both sides, came off the board. But when the game was over, and she had delicately picked her last man off the board, two of his still remained.

She had won again. She had played the imbecile, and with luck she had stolen the prize. She noticed tiny beads of sweat forming on his forehead, on his beautifully textured mustache, and beneath the armpits of his one hundred dollar shirt.

She smiled sweetly at him again, and picked up the pen resting on the pad. "Isn't that funny? I seem to have won the first two games from you," she said. "Now let me see. There are, as you said, five zeroes in one and a half million dollars. Therefore, I imagine there would be six zeroes in three million dollars, headed by a three." She looked up at him demurely. "Isn't that right?"

"Six million dollars," he contradicted.

"I beg your pardon?" she said.

"Six million dollars," he repeated. "We play the last game for that."

"Six million dollars?" she asked. "But the agency business isn't worth that."

"Worth what?" he asked. "Worth four million, five million, six million? You're asking me what part of eighty million dollars a year I should give you? You're talking about small change. Chicken feed. So, instead of giving your husband this account, I give him that account. A little shift here, a little piece tacked on there, and he's got six million dollars. Six million dollars we can do easy. That's no problem."

"Six million dollars," she said.

"Or nothing," he said.

She looked up at him, startled, now genuinely frightened. "But I have three million dollars now," she said.

"I know," he answered.

"And if I lose it—"

"You lose it."

"But I can't—" she began.

His face changed. Suddenly, the anger drained out of it. It

became again the Jewish Santa Claus, the wise old man from the East, everybody's uncle.

"Look Angel," he said, "let's face it. I'm really sort of an old man—even though I don't look it," he added rather suddenly. "It's not my age. It's my heart. It's a little funny now, and every so often it goes off the hook and does strange things."

She started to say something, but he brushed aside her remark with a quick wave of his hand.

"Now," he said, "I'll be frank with you. I like to go to bed with beautiful women, but"—and he shrugged—"I have to admit that sometimes—a little of the time—I would rather beat them at backgammon. Angel," he said, "I like backgammon. I like bed, too, but a bed partner you can always find, and a good game of backgammon is a good game of backgammon. Besides," and he reached out and took her hands in his, "you're playing for money, I'm not. Money is real to you. It's not real to me, so let me do this. Let me play you the last game for double or nothing. If you win, you bring home your husband six million dollars in agency business. If you lose, you lost all of it—every cent of it."

"But—"

"Please, don't interrupt an old man when he's talking. Show some respect for your elders. We'll play winner-take-all, loser-take-nothing, or else it's no game. Right? Right. But, because you've been a nice girl, because you look like a dream I might have had forty years ago and wanted to devote my life to, and because you make an old man sort of believe again in God . . . for all those reasons, I'd like to give you a little farewell gift for spending this evening with me. In fact"—a smile crossed his face—"I'll give you one of two gifts. Not for going to bed with me—we've already agreed on that—but for making my night so beautiful. If I win, and I'm going to win, I'll give you three million dollars of billing for your husband. Give it to you, you understand—not lose it to you. I won't owe you a thing. You understand?"

"I understand."

"But—if the impossible should happen, and you win the six million dollars, then you'll have that as your due. But if you win, I'd also like to give you a little present, for being here. Perhaps you saw the small sketch by Giacometti near the *Walking Men*. You'll take that, too," he smiled, "for showing an old man that there's nothing more dangerous than a beautiful woman who doesn't look up when she sets up the pieces for the next game.'' His eyes gleamed with anticipation. ''What do you say?'' he asked. ''Have we got a deal?''

She looked at him, picked up the container with the dice, and began to rattle them. ''All right, hotshot,'' she said, ''six million or nothing. Brace yourself for a fight. And for heaven's sake, tell Henry to bring in some brandy.''

Twenty-five minutes later, four glasses of brandy had been drained to the full. There were nine pieces left in their home boards—five of them Albee's, four of them Melissa's. It was Albee's move; his hand sweated so much that it was making the leather of the cup dark brown. Finally, with a small, silent Hassidic prayer, he released the dice, and they fell out on the board in a perfect double two position.

''A mitzvah,'' he yelled, flinging his hands to the air. He reached down and carefully removed four of his five markers. Then he looked up at her and sweetly intoned, ''Your move, my dear.''

She had only one throw of the dice left; if he received another throw, the game would be over. There was one roll—one roll in the entire world—that would let her scoop off all four markers with the same gesture. It was a double six. It was next to impossible. His smile told her that. He had risen now from the table, and stood glowing over it. ''Roll, my dear,'' he said. ''Let us get it over with and, shall we say, crown the new champion.''

Somehow, she didn't care about the extra three million dollars in billing. Somehow, all that mattered to her was the Giacometti drawing. Gone. Lost forever, since she knew he would keep his word.

''Roll,'' he said above her. ''You have to roll sometime,'' he said. ''It might as well be now.''

She looked up at the chipmunk face, at the sweetness and generosity now turned into glowing victory. Her hand reached out across the wooden table, and picked up the cup with its two fateful cubes. She lifted her hand, and felt the rumble of the dice within the carrier.

The dice spun crazily out of the container, rattled across the board, bounced off the far side, quivered slightly, and then came up with a single six, and then another six.

For one moment, both players looked down at the dice. Neither moved. And when their eyes finally met, they burst into laughter together.

For a full sixty seconds, they remained there, she sitting and giggling, he standing and roaring. Then, without a word, she pushed herself back from the table and stood next to him. She must have been four inches taller than he, at least, but it didn't matter in the slightest. Then she moved forward, and she found those welcoming arms of his around her waist. Her arms slipped effortlessly around his shoulders, and she found her hands touching the back of her arms. Without a word, she leaned over, and suddenly, she was kissing him.

The kiss was passionate, friendly, exploratory, but entirely loving. When it was over—when the kiss was done—they came apart just as naturally again. He looked up at her, his face beaming now, his eyes twinkling, and he said, quite simply, "Congratulations."

"But it was all luck," she said.

"But what magnificent luck," he said. "Six million dollars and the Giacometti sketch. And I'm so glad you have it."

"I can't believe it," she said.

"You will when you go home tomorrow with the sketch under your arm, and when Aaron receives the phone calls Monday morning."

She searched his face. There was no anger, no hostility, no rivalry left there. He was genuinely happy for her. She had beaten him, and he was joyous about it. She had not given him what he had bargained for that evening, and he couldn't have cared less. He had lost, and he had a magnificent time losing.

She looked at him and she said, quite simply, "I love you."

His expression changed to astonishment, and then to some deeper, more complicated emotions that she could not read. "I thank you," he said.

"I love you," she said. "And I've told those words to only two men in my entire life."

"I believe you," he said. "And I appreciate them, for everything they're worth." Then he let his arms drop from her. "You know," he said, not quite looking at her any longer, "if it weren't quite so late, and if we hadn't expended so much energy in the game . . ." And then his voice trailed off.

"And I," she said in turn, "might very well be tempted to join you."

Then he looked up at her again, "But it is late."

"Yes," she said.

"And we should go to our separate rooms."

"If you wish," she said.

"But—" he said.

"Yes?"

"Some other day—some other night—some other occasion —I might very well . . ."

"You might very, very well." She picked up her empty brandy glass, and raised it. "To that occasion," she said quietly, and reached out her tongue and licked the last drop of the brandy from the inside of the glass.

"To that occasion," he repeated, and did the same with his own glass.

Then he turned around and pushed the button that would summon the butler, to show her to her room.

23.

The next morning, after breakfast, the two of them wandered, mittened hand in mittened hand, through the vast expanse of woods north of his house. The forest was covered in unsullied white—a Christmastime poster of acres and acres of tree and snow, the way few New Yorkers see it. They spent almost two hours walking through the trackless woods, laughing with wonderment while a single bluebird scurried from one snow-lined branch to another in front of them.

When they returned, both were soaking wet, and they went upstairs to change. Then it was time for steaming cups of chicken soup and a magnificient lunch, then the ceremonial pulling down of the Giacometti sketch, and the handing of it by Albee to Melissa. Finally, they were settled once more in the limousine, for the trip back to the city.

Neither said much on the way. Somehow their hands found each other again, and remained intertwined for the full hour and a half back to the city. Then they were at 46th Street and Vanderbilt again, exactly where he had picked her up the day before.

"What do I say?" she asked.

"I think the most honest thing you could say," he replied, "is 'you're welcome.' "

"For what?"

"For the 'thank you' I had ready to say for each of the enduring memories you've given me."

"But it's I who should—"

"I could go on with a list of them for a full hour," he smiled. "But it's late, and I think you should be home with your family." He reached out and touched the Giacometti sketch, a little regretfully. "Love it well, as I know you will. I would only have given it up to you."

"I'll adore it, every day of my life," she replied.

"And," he said, as the great door was opened, "perhaps, in a few weeks, if you have a lunch open, and an old Jewish voice calls up and offers to fill it—"

"Then I'll be the luckiest woman in the world," she said. She leaned forward and kissed his ruddy cheek.

In ten minutes, she was home. When she walked into the apartment they were all reading the newspapers. They looked up, and the three smiles were identical.

Aaron rose from his chair, strode across the living room, and placed both his hands on her shoulders. As always, he leaned down and she kissed his cheek. "Did you have a successful trip, darling?" he said.

"Quite successful," she said, and then turned to grasp Little John and Lacey.

"What's that?" Lacey asked, when she saw the sketch.

"A prize, of sorts, that I won on my trip," Melissa said.

"It looks like our statue," Little John said.

"It does, doesn't it," Melissa said, staring directly at Aaron.

He picked up the sketch, and turned it to the light. In seconds, he had evaluated it completely. He looked back at her squarely, and said, "It's magnificent." Then he handed it to her without another word, and said, "Hadn't you better clean up for dinner, darling?"

The rest of the evening passed slowly, as if in a dream. They sat down and had dinner, and made meaningless conversation. Then Lacey recited the new part she was learning for the school play. Little John disappeared to see one of his girl·friends. Lacey went upstairs at the regular time for bed.

And the two of them were now alone, in the living room, not looking at each other.

Finally, she spoke. "What do you want to know about it?" she asked.

"Nothing, really," he answered.

"Not even the size of the billings?"

She studied the face of the man she had married fourteen years before. It was quite composed. They might, at that moment, have been discussing an ordinary business deal. "If you want to," he answered, nonchalantly.

"It's not four and a half million dollars billing," she said at once.

His face darkened. "No?"

"No," she repeated. "It's six million dollars."

She had the reaction from him that she had hoped for, and that she hated herself for hoping for. His face, reddening, looked as though it had just been slapped. She saw—thank God—jealousy and shame fight their way across his eyes.

"Six million dollars," he repeated.

"Exactly," she said.

"That is quite a bit more than we had discussed."

"That's true."

"You must have been very persuasive," he muttered.

"Very. Would you like to hear how I did it?" she went on.

"No." He spat the word out. "No," he said quite a bit more calmly. "I'll take your word for it that you were . . . persuasive. And we'll leave it at that."

"It's quite a story," she said.

"It's getting late," he said. "I'm a little tired tonight," he went on, suddenly rising. "Are you going to bed now, or are you staying up and coming later?"

"Later," she said. "Much later." And then she watched her husband walk away, and leave her abandoned in a living room that she could no longer call her own, and go up, by himself, to the gravelike bedroom, where her wedding band still rested like a tombstone on his night table.

"You should have listened to it," she said to the emptiness of the room around her. "It's quite a story. You see, the man didn't touch me. Do you hear?" she silently shouted to the empty stairs in front of her. "The man never touched me. Never made love to me. Simply gave me the six million dollars after I had won it in a game of backgammon. Would you believe that? Would that fit into your nightmare world of war and sacrifice?

"Do you hear?" she moaned to the light going off on the cemetery floor above her. "Lie there in the dark now, and imagine to yourself what I must have done with him to have been worth the extra million and a half dollars. Torture yourself with those pictures, as I could never torture you. Believe those fantasies, and live with them, till you declare that this insane war is over. Know that you won the battle, but lost me.

"Choose," she commanded. "Cancel your war, and come back to sanity and me, and I will give you back your clean wife.

"Or continue your war," she promised. "Continue to live out your past one more time—and offer to sacrifice me, one more time—and I swear to you that there will be no more me left in this house—no more—ever to sacrifice again."

24.

Monday morning, at exactly nine o'clock, four separate phone calls came into Aaron's agency. Each of them represented a different subsidiary of Albee's. Each operation carried advertising worth approximately one and a half million dollars. When the last call was finished, the sum was just over six million dollars in new billings.

She had been right, he thought. She had brought back what she had said. The war was over. They had won. They were alive again. The agency had money now even to expand, to fill in the gaps of the unfaithful who had deserted during the long siege.

It was complete victory. It was perfect triumph. But why—he wondered—did he sit there looking at the figures on the large yellow pad, and feel as though he had lost, and not won, the war. As though those numbers were not agency billings but—somehow—casualty lists.

Within minutes he had shaken off the mood. First, he went out and announced the news. Responsibilities were assigned.

Copies of the original presentations were made. Details were added, and production started rolling on the first finished proofs. No one left their desks. No one bothered to look at the clock. There was work to do again. New campaigns, new ideas, some of the most brilliant work ever done by Aaron.

By that afternoon, Aaron was on the phone with the head hunters, seeking new staff to handle the job. New account executives for each of the four initial accounts. A new art director. A new coordinator. A new media buyer.

Within one week, although he had earned an additional twenty thousand dollars a week from Albee's accounts, he had brought the total of the agency's expenditures up to thirty thousand dollars a week. And he was still interviewing. He did not tell Melissa a word about it, of course. He was going to keep it as his great surprise. He knew how astonishing, how advanced had been the advertising he had created during this crisis. He knew that once it appeared in the papers, it would dazzle the advertising community. He knew that other advertisers would see that he had not lost his touch, that he had gained new power during the intervening years, and then they would flock to his bandwagon. And when they came, he wanted to be ready, to have the personnel on hand, trained, stationed, to put their excitement to work immediately.

And so he continued to hire. And hire. And hire. Finally, he found himself as far short in meeting his payroll as he had been before Albee. Every week they stayed in business—unless they got new accounts, and got them now, immediately—they were losing ten thousand dollars per payday.

The war was not over. Only a single battle had been won. He looked at the figures, and waited for the despair, the anxiety, the overwhelming panic to envelop him again. Instead, he felt nothing. No emotion whatsoever. He was as cold, as impersonal, as disembodied as the freezing wind outside.

A cutting wind, he thought. So sharp that it could almost kill.

25.

Five weeks later the call she had been dreading came through. It was from a man called Eastman, who was president of a huge dress manufacturing company that spent approximately three million dollars a year in billings. He had met her once or twice at parties, years ago. She remembered the guarded passes he had made each of those times.

Now he was calling her at home, with a new confidence in his voice.

Yes, he said on the phone, he and Aaron had discussed the account. Yes, it might be moved, under the right circumstances. She waited, without being able to say a word, for the final, fatal line.

There was a pause. Finally his words came through, distinct and clear. "Aaron says that—uh—he would have no objection if—"

"If what," she asked, speaking with surprising calm. "Please be specific, Mr. Eastman. I would like to hear every detail that my husband suggested."

"If we had dinner," Eastman's voice continued. Then he waited for a reaction. Got none. And pressed on. "Alone, that is. Just the two of us. You and I." Another pause. Another wait for a reaction. And then, "You know?"

"I really don't know, Mr. Eastman. What?"

"You know—afterward—"

"Did Aaron say that?"

"Not exactly, but—"

She waited for him to complete the sentence. When he did not she asked, "But what?"

Anger. Trapped anger suddenly came into Eastman's voice. "Mrs. Carpenter," he said sharply, "I think you know exactly what."

"Just as Aaron knew exactly what. Is that right?"

"Yes."

She couldn't believe the calm in her voice, in her mind, in her body.

"Mr. Eastman," she said. "My husband implied that I would screw you for your account. Now I'm telling you that you can go screw yourself, and your account." There was dead silence on the other end of the phone. "And if you wish," she added, "you can even include my husband in that offer."

She hung up the phone. Then she walked smoothly to the closet, took out her coat, and caught a cab to Aaron's office. This time, when she opened the door, she thought she was on the wrong floor. Where before there had been empty desks, and tired, disheveled people sitting behind the few that were occupied, now every square inch of space was occupied by neat, trim, aggressive young men and women, bending over desks, arguing into phones, pounding typewriters, making sketches, all seemingly in a life-or-death race to grind out ads by the bushelful. A new army, she thought, preparing for a new battle, in the same mad war.

She burshed past the secretary before the woman could buzz Aaron. He was again stooped over his desk, again scrawling out dreams on his sheets of yellow wish-paper.

He heard the door snap shut behind her, looked up for a second, then went back to his scribbling.

"I've spoken to Mr. Eastman," she said quietly.

"Good," he replied, his hand not missing a word.

"I told him to take his account, himself, and, my darling, you—and screw them all, as best he could."

The pencil stopped. "In those words?" he asked, looking up at her.

"In those words," she said.

"He bills three million dollars a year," he said.

"Not with me," she answered. "And, I imagine, after today, not with you."

"All right," he said, picking up the pencil again. "You've decided."

"I have," she replied. "About much more than Mr. Eastman."

"Tell me tonight," he said.

"No," she demanded. "I'm going to tell you now. Right now. And, by God, Aaron, you'd better listen, because you're never going to have the chance to hear it again."

The pencil wavered.

"All right," he said. "But quickly."

"He never touched me," she said.

"Who?"

"Albee Lauder. He never touched me. He never had intercourse with me."

"First of all, I don't care. And, secondly, I don't believe a word of it."

"But I care. And it's the living truth. The man gave me the money; he didn't trade me for it. We became friends, not lovers. The six million dollars in billings meant as little to him as one of those legal pads means to you. He gave them to me—literally gave them to me—as a friend."

"I don't believe you," he said, his eyes as hard as metal.

"Aaron," she said, "listen to me. Try to hear what I'm saying. I'm still your wife. I still belong to you. I'm untouched. I'm still faithful to you, still yours. You still have that. Don't—please—for God's sake—don't throw that away."

"Don't tell me fairy tales," he said.

"By God's name," she said, "it's true. The man never touched me," she screamed at him.

"Lie," he said.

"On Little John's head. On Little John's life, I swear to you, the man never touched me."

Words died in his mouth. The face turned gray. Eyes, dead eyes, stared into her frenzied ones. The hand on the pencil began to tremble. She watched the pencil move under the weight of that hand, slide off the yellow pad, and then drop to the floor.

"Run," he muttered, almost inaudibly.

"What did you say?" she asked.

"Run," he said, more loudly. "Run, now. Get out of here. Get out of the apartment. Run. For God's sake. Run for your life."

"Aaron?" she said.

"Get as far away from me as you can," he said. "Take the children, if you must. But run—go—now. Get out of my reach. Get away from my voice. Get away from my hand." And then the head came down, and there were no more eyes to look at hers.

"Run," he said one last time. "Now."

"Aaron?" she said softly, not daring to close the space between them. "You need help."

"No," he said.

"You need treatment."

"No."

"You must—"

"Get out," he said, from the lowered face. "Get out now."

"Aaron, let me help."

"Stay," he said, "and I'll kill you. One way or another."

"I can help."

"You can die."

"Aaron—"

"Goddammit," he said, rising to his full towering height. "Leave. Or I'll pick you up and throw you out that door myself."

"You're a sick man," she said.

"No," he replied. "I'm a dead man. And you'll be dead too, unless you go now."

He started to move across the room toward her. She felt her hand behind her turn the knob, and open the door. She felt the door slip open just wide enough for her to squeeze through. The office staff must never see him like this. She backed out through the crack in the open door, shielding with her body what was inside that room.

The door snapped shut again. She turned and looked at the men and women looking at her. Somehow, through some social reflex, she smiled . . . managed to walk through them all to the outer door . . . and gained the privacy of the hall outside.

She would be gone from the apartment before he came back from work. She knew that.

But she also knew this. Before, he would have sacrificed her to save himself. But now, somehow, he had just sacrificed himself, to save her.

26.

Her conversation with Little John was brief, and came out exactly the way she had anticipated.

He was aware, of course, of the strain between Aaron and herself. It came as no great surprise, therefore, when she said that she was leaving, and that he had the choice of going with her, or remaining with his stepfather.

She adored him for both decisions he instantly made. The first was to reassure her that he realized she must have a deep reason for deciding to go. And he told her that his first love, his primary love, belonged to her.

But then, when he was sure that she had understood that he would always love her, he looked frankly into his mother's face, and said, "Hell, I don't even know if he can get dressed without you."

Then he smiled the not-quite-so-innocent smile that had already become famous all over the East Side of Manhattan. "Somebody's got to keep his shoes shined." Then he looked at her penetratingly. "At least until you come back. And I guess it has to be me."

"I guess so," she said.

"I love you. I'll love you no matter what happens," he said. "But I kind of worked too hard to find him. And he's just too big and vulnerable to be left on his own. So you see, I'm elected."

"I know," she said. And her arms went around him, and she kissed the cheek of the beautiful young face.

"I love you," he said again.

"I love you."

"Don't make it too long, huh Mom?" he said.

Fifteen minutes later she told Lacy. Her daughter asked only one question: "Will I have my own room in the new place?"

"Yes," Melissa said, "I promise you that."

"Two against the world," Lacy said.

"Won't you miss him?" Melissa asked.

"Horribly," Lacy replied, "but I've been missing him all my life. This will just make the gap a little larger, that's all."

And the conversation was over.

That same afternoon, Melissa called Pamela Haas. Although she hadn't seen Pam in years, she'd thought of her many times, and occasionally heard some news of her through a mutual friend. Now, some instinct told her that turning to Pam would do them both good. It took three calls, till after five-thirty, when Pam returned home from her job as a salesperson at Macy's, before the phone was answered.

"Hello, Pam," Melissa said. "It's—"

"Good Lord," Pam said, "It's Melissa." And then, suddenly, "What's wrong?"

"I need your help."

"Of course. You have it. What's wrong?"

"I'm leaving Aaron."

"I have three extra beds," Pam said, thinking that she'd take the skinny little cot herself.

"I only need two of them," Melissa said. "Little John is staying with Aaron."

Pam didn't allow the hurt to make itself known. "Then I have two real beds," she said. "I have a kitchen, some food, not very good conversation, but lots of love. The address is the same. When are the two of you coming over?"

"This evening, if that's all right."

"It will be the hurt leading the hurt," Pam said.

"I need a helping hand," Melissa said.

"You can have a whole arm."

"It won't be for long," Melissa promised.

"I don't care. It can be for as long as you need," Pam said. "I'll welcome every second of it."

"Then I'll be over there as soon as we can catch a cab."

"Fine," Pam said. "I'll have my last bottle of champagne chilled and waiting," she added with a laugh.

"And I'll steal a can of caviar from the kitchen here to go along with it," Melissa said.

"A celebration," Pam laughed. "A reunion of sorts."

"A reunion of sorts," Melissa agreed. "Thanks."

She put down the receiver, and paused; then she picked it up, and began to dial again. She had one last phone call to make. A necessary one, she had decided—to Albee.

27.

She had talked steadily for almost an hour and a half, and was scarcely aware of the meal she had ordered. Now that she was finished speaking, Albee looked down at the red wine in the glass he was holding, and said, "Two weeks."

"Two weeks, what?" Melissa asked.

"Two weeks earlier than I'd thought we'd have this lunch," he went on.

"You knew?" she asked.

"Angel," he said softly, "your husband was asking you to do something you couldn't do. Some men do it subtly, with innuendo. Others do it brutally, with command. Either way, either the wife bends and breaks, or the marriage bends and breaks."

"I still love him," Melissa said.

"They always do," Albee went on. "Especially after the break."

"Albee," she said bluntly, "I'm going to sell the Giacometti in order to get the kind of place Lacy and I need to live in."

He took a sip of the wine. His shoulders moved almost imperceptibly in their gesture of a perpetual shrug. He smiled—the smile of an ancient confirmation. Then he said quietly, "That's why I gave it to you in the first place."

"You what?"

"I gave it to you as an escape hatch, in case the situation should reach a real bend or break," he said. "Angel," he went on, "you just don't look like the kind of woman who does a lot of saving. You might not have been able to get out as easily as you wanted. If everything turned out fine, then you had a beautiful sketch to look at on your walls. But if it didn't," and the shoulders rose another inch, "people pay funny prices for such small things." He looked up across the crêpes suzette. "I'll buy it back from you myself, for forty-five thousand," he said.

"I checked with Perle's," she said. "Their best price is thirty-five thousand. That's what I'm going to sell it to them for."

"Ten thousand dollars buys a lot of curtains," he said.

"You gave me one gift. That's enough."

"It's really worth forty-five thousand," he said.

"I'm selling it to Perle's," she said finally.

"Tell me the day you sell it to them," he went on. "Then I'll buy it from them for forty-five thousand. I miss it. It belongs with its brothers."

"They'd charge you a ten thousand dollar markup for a day's transaction?" she asked.

"Of course."

She thought a moment. Then she said, "Forty thousand."

"Forth-two five," he replied immediately.

"Forty thousand dollars, and not one penny more," she answered, smiling.

"Sold," he said. "But you are the hardest businesswoman I have ever dealt with," and he reached out his hand, and took hers, and kissed it lightly on the back.

"Do you need anything else?" he questioned.

"Yes. Your friendship."

"You can have much more than that," he said suddenly.

"I know," she replied. "I adore the thought. But I don't want it now."

"It comes in several packages," he continued, smiling.

"Like a calculator?"

"Like a calculator," he nodded. "Would you like to hear the full line?"

"Yes."

"Well," he said, "there is the bottom of the line, which is available to you, but which I do not really recommend. It's called the friendship loan. It's given," and his face turned deadly serious, "out of the gratitude that you exist in the world. Nothing more. And it entails whatever amount of money you need, and it has no payment terms, no sexual down payment at all, no obligation, and absolutely no carrying charge."

She looked at him, and reached out her hands to take his. "Thank you," she said. "But you know that's impossible for me to take."

"Maybe now," he said. "Maybe not tomorrow. You might have ideas I'd like to invest in as a businessman. Why not, then, as a friend?"

"Because I don't want to owe you money," she said. "I love you too much to owe you money."

"Owe?" he asked. "Who said anything about owe? Angel," he said, "I have so many bank accounts that I can't keep track of them. What difference does it make to me if one of them got lost?"

"It makes a difference to me," she said. "The answer is definitely no."

"Good," he said. "I was hoping you'd say that. So now, shall we look at the second model in the line?"

She again involuntarily broke into a smile. "I imagine it should be far more interesting."

"It is," he said, a leer replacing his usual smile. "This is called our love, lust, and loot model. In this—quite bluntly, and we are getting to be very old friends—you share my bed from time to time, and you share my pocketbook from other times to other times.''

"A very attractive model," she replied at once. "But I am only separated, and not divorced."

"What does that mean?" he asked.

"That means, for the beginning at least, I am still married to my husband in bed."

"For how long?" he asked in astonishment.

"I'm not sure. Perhaps a month or two. Perhaps longer. Until I'm sure that he won't go for treatment. Or . . ." and her voice trailed off.

"Or what?"

She looked up at him, and her eyes began to well up with tears. "Until I can't stand it anymore," she said. "Believe it or not," and she searched for the right words before finally saying softly, "I need a man."

"God be thanked," he said. "Then I'll wait."

She looked up. "It may be longer than you think."

"No, Angel," he said. "Even at my age, even with my heart, it won't be longer than I think." And then his voice thickened, and she heard in it the uncle, the father, the lover, the businessman, and the friend—all at once. "My dear, beautiful one," he said, "you are forty years old. You look twenty-five. This city, though you have no idea of it, is waiting for you. It's at your feet, just waiting for you to reach down and scoop up whatever part of it you fancy." Suddenly his face became somber again. "And there is a third line in the model, which perhaps you should examine."

"Which is?" she asked.

"That old-fashioned, silly, nonworking, excruciating, but unavoidable institution called marriage," he said. "I have a few years left—despite this strange ticker of mine. I imagine they could be very good years, with you, if you'd like to share them."

"That's the most beautiful model of all," she said quietly. "And the one that is simply impossible for me to afford right now."

"This is not a one-time offer," he said.

"I know. And I thank you."

"None of the line, then," he said.

"No," she replied. "None of them—yet."

"Then remember not to shop at our competitors," he went

on, and the eyes glanced sideways at her, with the knowledge that almost forty years stood between them. "If you do, think of us as an auxiliary to your own operations."

"Thank you, kind sir," she said. "I can't imagine operating anywhere in the future without you."

"Then I haven't lost a sale yet," he said, "and my record is still perfect."

He motioned to the captain for the check. As the man approached with it, Albee looked at the beautiful woman sitting across from him and nodded.

"One month," he said. "Two months. Three months. I'll bet my Monets on it. Some idea. Some project. Some crusade. Some man."

He handed the check to the captain, and prepared to leave the table with her. He smiled, at her, at himself, and just a tiny fragment to God. "I only hope," he said, "that he happens to be me."

28.

She woke again, reaching for him.

Her right arm moved out slowly, and felt nothing. Half-asleep, half-puzzled, she moved it another inch to the right, still encountering the emptiness of the bed beside her. Now, slowly growing into more and more awareness, the hand thrust out, and found nothing in the bed beside her.

She was now fully awake in the darkness of the room. She was alone in Pam's guest bedroom. The luminous face on the clock said four-thirty. But there was no need to turn on the light. She was alone. Alone at four-thirty in the morning on the twenty-ninth night.

Twenty-nine nights. Twenty-nine empty nights. Her right hand slowly retreated to her own side. There was nothing to reach out for. No warmth, no closeness, no security, no sex, no love . . . no man.

His wife. Still his wife. There had been no other man. No other flesh. No other touch. Still his wife—so very far away.

She could get up. She could read. Or work over the final

galleys of the book. Or she could just sit and stare into the emptiness.

But tonight, she did not turn on the light. She did not want to see, for the twenty-ninth time, the empty room. The darkness was bad enough. The lighted emptiness would be even worse.

She lay in the darkness, her body on fire. She lay in the darkness, trapped in her loneliness, knowing no one in the city of New York, in the entire world—whose hands would set that body free.

BOOK SIX

1976—1979

1.

She had moved to a two-room apartment on Fifth Avenue and Sixty-fifth Street, the third floor of a once grand whitestone, which she had furnished with the generosity of Albee, the immense resources of Bloomingdale's, and her own good taste. Lacey had the bedroom; Melissa worked and slept in the oversized front room. There was a tiny kitchen in between.

The book had finally been published. It received two marvelous reviews—one in the *Little Rock Gazette,* and the other in the *Des Moines Tribune.* Melissa went on a two-week whirlwind tour to eleven cities—twenty-seven radio and television programs in all—with absolutely no results. In the first month, the book sold only four thousand copies. After three cocktails, her editor revealed that it would probably sell eight thousand copies in all—not enough to pay Melissa any royalties.

The years of hope and dreaming, the months of agonizing work, the help that lay hidden in the book for unknown thousands of woman—all seemed in vain. She remembered a phrase of Aaron's about dropping rose petals down the Grand Canyon. She had dropped her first petal, and was now listening to its resounding silence.

She returned home that night, ready either to kill herself, or laugh all evening at her own madness in thinking that she could ever become a writer. But when Pam got home from the store, phoned Melissa, and heard the pathetic story, Pam said, "Well, there's only one sane course of action to take."

"I can't drink that much," Melissa answered immediately

"Nonsense," Pam retorted. "There's a huge party on the Island tonight. Tony is taking me. So why don't you just come along with the two of us? He says the place is so big, and there'll be so many people there, that the host will never notice another face." And she smiled, "Except, of course, in your case. And I don't think they'd turn that face away."

Pam was right. She'd been acting beaten, and she knew that was no way to act when you were beaten. So, for the first time since she had left Aaron—with the exception of a few quiet dinners with Albee—she put on a night face and a party dress. She climbed into Tony's car with the two of them at seven o'clock, and was on the grounds of a huge estate—what was her host's name?—by eight-thirty.

It was a massive Georgian house in Kings Point. At least eighty cars had already driven up, and there were two Long Island policemen to direct and park them. The place was exquisitely furnished in modern contemporary furniture, without a single piece of art to recommend it to a cultured eye, and the people churning around in the stylish rooms were the stylish people that were churning around that Wednesday night in a thousand New York parties—all strangely distant from her, all good-looking and well-kept and uninteresting in the extreme, all trying to pretend they had something to do with their lives, or someplace to go.

She wandered around in the house for half an hour. She had one glass of fairly good Chablis. Man after man made an attempt to start a conversation with her. Their faces all looked like the faces she had posed with hundreds of times in ads. She wasn't looking to live in an ad tonight. She She broke off the conversations rapidly, and kept drifting. Finally, seeing a small door that led to a side porch with no one on it, she went out and sat down. She looked out over exquisite rose gardens, freshly in bloom, their smell scenting the night air. For a few moments she would drink in the peacefulness, before she waded back into the melange of people to see if she couldn't persuade Tony and Pam to head back to the city, or at least got another ride for her.

Suddenly, there was a man at her side, and his quiet voice in her ear. "Lousy party," he said, "isn't it?"

She looked up at the man standing above her. The first thing she noticed—that she always noticed about a new man—was his height. After the six foot two of Johnny, and the six foot six of Aaron, he definitely seemed short. Actually, she thought, he must be about six feet tall, a perfectly normal height.

Second and almost instantaneously, she registered the fact that, standing in the porch doorway with the light glancing off only one side of his face in the darkness, and with that face a mass of dramatically defined shadows and brightnesses, he must have been the most beautiful man she had ever seen. In fact, his face looked as though it had been lit for a 1930's movie. Some swashbuckling episode. Some kidnapping of the female lead in which he was about to scale a twelve-foot wall and had paused in front of the camera for five seconds before beginning the ascent.

She said nothing. And he smiled. "May I sit down for a minute?" he said.

No, she said inside immediately. You're far too dangerous.

"I'm afraid it's somebody else's party," she said on the outside.

"And you have no control over who sits next to you?" he asked.

She laughed. "I don't arrange the seating list," she said. "Sit where you please."

"I please here," he said, and sat down on the chair facing her. Now his face caught the full light, and he was no longer in a 1930's swashbuckling film at all, but in a picture by Eisenstaedt that she had seen in the pages of *Life* magazine. It was a full-face photograph of the aging Tyrone Power—a year or two before he died. He must have been forty or forty-two years old at that time. Tiny lines of age had spread across his eyes. There were slight black circles under those eyes. A line or two had deepened around his mouth. His face, because it had aged, was now human, instead of perfect.

And, tonight, this man, now sitting three feet away from her, resembled that photograph so much that she felt herself compelled to ask, "What is your name?"

"That's an unusual question for a woman to ask a man she's just met at a party. Aren't I supposed to ask your name first?"

"I'm Melissa Carpenter," she said. "You simply remind me of someone. Someone impossible. And I'd like to dispel the illusion immediately."

He laughed. "Was it someone you liked very much?"

"Yes."

"And I remind you of him?"

"Impossibly."

"Good. I'm not him. But I am here. And my name, unfortunately, is Michael Black."

"Why unfortunately?" she asked.

He looked at her with sudden surprise. "You don't know?" he asked.

"No," she said quite frankly. "I don't."

"Marvelous," he said. "Even more perfect." And he

leaned slightly across the space separating them. "Then you'd be perfectly willing to agree with me that this is a lousy party?"

"I imagine so," she said.

"I imagine so," he said. "Or you wouldn't be sitting out here by yourself, smelling the roses. What happened to your escort?"

"They're in there," she said, "churning with the others."

"They?"

"My girl friend—and her boyfriend."

"There are over a hundred and twenty people in there," he said.

"I know," she answered.

"It would take almost an hour to find your escorts," he said.

She laughed. "Not if I hurried, or was lucky."

"But such a waste of time," he suggested.

"But what better use of time is there?" she asked, looking down at her glass that was empty.

"I can think of several," he said. "For example, there's a marvelous little Italian restaurant on Houston Street, just off West Broadway, that makes the finest Chicken Romano in New York. Tonight is Thursday night, and they only have family, a few guests, and nice people—like us."

"It's nine o'clock," she said, looking at her watch.

"We could be there in three-quarters of an hour," he said.

"We couldn't be there from Kings Point," she replied, "in three-quarters of an hour if we flew."

"Wanna bet?"

"Are you going to take a 747?" she asked.

"No, strictly four wheels."

"You're insane."

"Perfectly."

"You'd kill yourself in the process."

"Haven't yet."

She laughed. "Or get both of us thrown in jail."

"You said both of us," he replied. "C'mon, it's better than burying yourself for the rest of the evening with the hundred other corpses in this mausoleum."

He got to his feet. The lighting changed again on his face. Tyrone Power, yes. Long slim planes of cheek and nose and mouth and chin, that were far too beautiful to belong to a man, but that somehow added up to a complete virility, and—surprisingly enough—a completely unselfconscious attitude about his own appearance.

"I'd have to let Pam and Tony know," she said.

"Nonsense," he said. "It would take far too long to find them. Besides," he said, looking at her, "if they have any sense at all, they'll be able to figure out what happened."

It had been four and a half months since she had left Aaron. This afternoon she had heard of the book's complete collapse. The party was unspeakable, he was right, but neither Pam nor Tony would probably want to leave until the dinner was over. She was doing nothing, she was giving nothing, except permission to go on a breakneck ride, probably with the handsomest madman she had ever seen. She smiled to herself; there was probably more danger of fracturing her hip than getting kissed.

"I'm married," she said.

"Congratulations," he replied. "So am I."

"I'm separated," she went on. "But I'm faithful to my husband," she added.

"We differ there," he said. "But I'm really not asking you to go to bed with me. Only help me escape from this Long Island purgatory, and get some good Italian food instead."

She set her glass down on the table beside her. In an instant she was on her feet, standing beside him.

"How tall are you?" she asked, able to say anything, at any time, on this utterly lost night.

"Do I have to qualify for a height test?" he asked.

"No," she said.

"Will six feet do?" he asked.

"No." She laughed at herself, mockingly, then shook her head, and said to his surprised face, "I mean, yes. Six feet will do very nicely, and it isn't important anyway."

"You have an aversion to men who are less than six feet one?" he asked.

"Not at all," she replied. "It's only that my first two husbands . . . well, my present husband . . ." Flustered, she tried to catch herself with the sentence. "Anyway, he's six feet six."

"Oh," the man said at once. "I'm afraid that's much too big to fit into a real sports car. Poor fellow."

She smiled again. "I'm afraid it's you," she said, "who has the prejudice against men bigger than six feet tall."

"Would you like to see the sports car that he wouldn't fit into?" Michael asked suddenly.

Melissa was wavering. But there was a full moon, and a whole new evening of craziness. "Why not?" she said.

He directed her through the house to the front door. He did not gesture to one of the attendants who were still parking cars, but simply led her straight across the driveway to a magnificent black Alfa-Romeo—brand new—looking exactly as though it had been parked at eighty miles an hour. The door opened at his lightest touch.

"Madam," he said, "your pumpkin is ready."

She paused for a second. "How fast do these mice really run?" she asked.

"One hundred and forty miles an hour, when they're warmed up, but we may not reach that figure tonight."

"Perhaps I should go back inside."

"I promised you we'd be in the Italian restaurant in forty-five minutes. Remember?"

He smiled. Even in the shadowed driveway the smile was dazzling. It was, she realized immediately, an irresistible smile, a deadly smile, a mind-blanking smile. God, she thought, to meet a man who looked like this when she hadn't been with Aaron for over four months.

She climbed into the streamlined sports car, half-wishing that it wouldn't start, half-wishing that it would go in reverse immediately, and smash itself against the Rolls-Royce parked behind it.

He got in beside her, and casually said, "Fasten your seat belt, please."

Both did so. The engine purred almost silently to life. He back-shifted, turned the car with immaculate grace, and in two seconds they were out of the driveway, and down the shady tree-lined lane, already roaring past the half-a-million dollar houses at a speed that caused her to gasp.

"You're not really going to do it!" she exclaimed breathlessly.

"I promised you," he said, next to her.

"I take back the challenge," she said immediately.

"Too late," he said. "There's a bar on the front of the dash. If you feel the need to, just hold on to it. But believe me, you'll have more fun if you don't."

Kings Point is one of the wealthiest suburbs in the United States, but its roads have been kept purposely old, rustic, not terribly well-paved or straight, with dozens of hidden driveways and unseen streets. He moved down these streets and these roads at eight-five to ninety miles an hour. He handled the car perfectly, with the instinct of a racing driver—seemingly able to see other cars coming from nowhere, without even a trace of their lights showing; bluffing some of them to a screeching halt, swirling noisily and dustily around others; leaving one after the other screaming and swearing in the background as the car raced through the night.

"You'll be arrested in two minutes," she said desperately.

"If they can catch me," he said. "They haven't so far." And he pressed his foot a tender touch deeper on the accelerator.

Suddenly, the road widened, and they were in a main thoroughfare, now screaming past lines of cars rather than single automobiles, still going two to three times the legal speed limit, still causing other cars to swerve out of their way, still majestically gliding through the now neon-lit night, free and in command.

Then the car banked sharply, swerved to the left, and they were on a huge throughway, leading into the city. Now the car shot instantly into the left-hand lane. He lowered his foot on the accelerator, and she saw the speedometer rise leisurely over 100 . . . 110 . . . 120 miles an hour. He was veering in and out of traffic, changing lanes every twenty seconds, flashing by cars before they even had time to react to the glare of his headlights coming up on them, and then leaving them behind him.

Despite the speed, despite the swerving course, there wasn't a whisper of a sound inside the Alfa-Romeo. They were traveling far faster than she had ever gone in a car before, yet he was in such control that it simply seemed silly to let the slightest tremor of fear enter her mind.

She turned and looked at his face. It was alternately illuminated and then cast into absolute darkness again. Each time it emerged, it was serene and beautiful. There was a faint smile hovering about his mouth, which became more appealing each time he swerved out to pass another car. He himself was part of the metal bolt of black lightning speeding down the highway. His face was absolutely in ecstasy, as he pushed the great machine to its utmost. She felt then that she knew exactly what he would look like at the moment of orgasm.

As they flashed up the entrance to the tunnel—as the great

skyline of New York erupted in front of them in all its dazzling glory—she finally turned to him and said, "Have you never cracked up one of these things yet?"

"Not one of these, no," he replied, without letting his eyes leave the road ahead of him for an instant. "Something far faster, far more dangerous, that makes this feel like standing still," he said. "But that's another story, for another time."

His foot began to leave the gas pedal and come down effortlessly on the brake. Now she felt herself being pressed against the back of the seat with almost monumental force. He watched the speedometer drop crazily from 140 to 120 to 100 to 80 to 60 to 40 to 30 to 20 miles an hour as they approached the toll booth to the tunnel. By the time they reached the attendant, his window was down, they were traveling at the ordinary speed of everyone around them, he had the coins in his hand, and she watched the reaction of the woman attendant as she reached out her hand to take the fare, and saw the incredible face of the man who was handing it to her.

The window rolled up, and they were in the tunnel, traveling at a normal speed.

"Have you looked at your watch lately?" he said.

"Thirty-one minutes exactly," she answered. "I wouldn't have believed it. Nor," she quickly added, "will I ever do it again."

"Why not?" he asked. "You weren't afraid for a moment."

"How could you tell?" she asked suddenly.

"I can smell fear the same way a dog does," he said. "You liked it. I think you'd like any trip I could take you on."

The car screeched to a halt in front of a fire hydrant on Houston Street, directly before a small, seemingly run-down and half-darkened Italian restaurant. He switched off the motor with a single motion. Then he turned and looked at her. "How many minutes?" he asked.

"Forty-three," she replied. "Do you always get everywhere you're going as fast as this?" she asked.

"Only when getting there is half the fun," he answered.

She hesitated. The words tried to clamp themselves down in her throat, but there was no stopping them. "Would it be—this time?" she asked.

"No," he answered immediately. "I think that getting

there, this time, would be far too much fun to hurry by even one second."

"Maybe there's no place to get," she said.

"Then it would still be great fun to get to that nowhere," he said. "I hope to prove that to you before we're done."

2.

The owners recognized him the moment he came in. Within seconds, she was introduced to a dozen members of their family, all of whom made her feel at home at once.

Three or four tables were occupied when they came in. It was startling for Melissa to see where their eyes traveled, when they first looked at Michael and her. Whenever she had been with Johnny, or Aaron, all faces at a table—both men's and women's—had always traveled to her face first, and had noticed the man only later. Now, for the first time in her life, she watched the eyes at each table jump between the two of them, unwilling to leave either amazing face.

His face and his car—that was all she knew about him. And that was all she was going to find out about him for the next two hours, because the man had the same genius for listening—for drawing the other person out—as Aaron had. After he had greeted everyone he knew, his eyes were focused on her alone; for him there was no one else in the room. The food came—delicious course after course of it. The wine came. Questions—dozens of questions—came also. Questions not about her personal life, but somehow, unerringly, about her just published work, her goals, her message, her failed crusade.

In those two hours, hypnotized by the bottomless depth of his dark eyes, and the unceasing flow of leading questions, she had practically recited the book, page by page, to him. His very nod at the end of each new thought or sentence was like the applause of a vast audience.

Then, finally, he made her describe in detail the publicity campaign she had just returned from—every city she had gone to, every interview show, what she had said, what the host had asked, the questions that the audience had phoned in. After the first few minutes of this recital, his face turned suddenly puzzled, and then grim. Every now and then there was a bewildered shake of the head, and every so often a question on whether she had described this technique, or had guided the interviewer into that chapter.

Then she was finished, and the restaurant was practically empty. He said without emphasis or bitterness, "You were taken."

"I don't understand."

"Your publishing house," he said, "or the public relations agency they hired to do the tour with you—were no good. They prepared you in the wrong direction, away from the book, rather than into the heart of it. You had something unique to say—something every woman is waiting to hear. At least every woman I know," and he smiled disarmingly. "Instead, you've talked as though this were another rub-some-cream-on-your-face-and-wait-and-see kind of book. None of the unique points came out."

He threw back his head and laughed. It was the first time she had ever seen him laugh. When he did it, he gave his full attention and being to it, exactly as when he drove a car. She watched the beautiful head lean back, the mouth suddenly open, and the dazzling teeth appear.

"Christ!" he said suddenly, explosively. "I could have done a better publicity campaign for you myself. In fact, I could sit down tomorrow, if you give me your book, and write an ad for it that will sell a hundred thousand copies."

She wanted to shake herself out of the dangerous spell of concentrating too much on that mouth. So she flippantly asked, "Of a book that one of the largest publishers in America has sold only four thousand copies of?"

"Of course," he said. "But, again, you're not believing me." He leaned over the table and touched her hand. She was shocked at the power of that touch, but did not draw back her hand. "One hundred thousand copies it is then. I'll do the copy over the weekend."

She looked at his face across the candlelit table. A Tyrone Power face, telling her that he was going to set sail with the first morning tide, and bring back the treasure of the Spanish galleon. She could practically see the blade at his side, and all she had to do was wait until he returned, until the sail was sighted on the horizon, and he came through her door bearing the emerald and ruby cross from the Spanish queen. Everything was suddenly so simple. The plot had been written by a grade-B scriptwriter. The cameras were grinding away. He had said he was going to have the ad for her Monday, and he would. She knew that, just as clearly as she knew that each of his cheeks held a dimple that you could lose your eyes in for an entire month.

The ad would be perfect, of course. She would approve it at once. It would run soon thereafter, and a hundred thousand copies would be sold immediately. Wasn't it all in the plot? Hadn't it all been approved by the director? Things were so simple, she thought, in grade-B movies. Nothing to worry about, now, except how to spend the royalty money.

"It's getting late," he said. "Let me drive you home."

The check came, was paid, there were a few quick hugs with the family, and they were out on the street again.

He was unlocking her side of the car, when she suddenly said, "But I don't know anything about you. Except your name is Black. You're six feet tall," she laughed. "And you drive a car as though it were a wingless plane."

He paused a moment at the opened door. His face turned suddenly serious. "Thank you," he said. "I like that phrase."

"But what do you do?" she asked.

"I chase genes," he answered. "The little things inside your body that tell you what you're going to grow up to be."

She caught her breath, and said, "God, and I've been doing all the talking tonight. Let's—"

"Some other time," he said. And then he reached out in the deserted street, and touched her—this time on her bare shoulder. It was only the lightest possible touch, but she felt it through every inch of her body.

"Things need time to develop," he said. "That's one of the first things you learn in gene-chasing. And if you don't give them time"—his hand pulled away from her shoulder and indicated she step inside the car—"they can't develop in the right way."

"You promise you'll tell me more?" she said.

"I definitely promise," he replied. "Nothing could stop me the next time."

"All right," she said.

The sleeping city whizzed silently by. In what seemed seconds, they pulled up in front of her door. He went around

the car and held the door for her. They stood there looking at
each other on the sidewalk.

"Shall I unlock the front door for you?" he asked.

"No," she said. "I'm perfectly capable of doing that."

"As you wish," he said. "Thank you for a glorious evening. I'll get the book tomorrow. I'll have the ad for you
Monday."

"I know you will. I thank you for that, and I thank you for
this evening." She turned and walked up the front steps.

He leaned back against the Alfa-Romeo and watched her
unlock the door. As she pushed it open, she turned to him,
and said, "How long will it take you to get home?"

"Forty-three minutes," he replied at once.

"Forty-three minutes?" she answered. "I don't understand."

"The house where we met," he said. "It's called the
Black house—and not because of its color. I was sure you
really didn't know." And he laughed. "My wife and I were
your hosts this evening. But I'm so glad you came along. It
was really a lousy party."

3.

The ad, as promised, was delivered to Melissa Monday
afternoon—completely set, laid out, photo in place, and ready
to insert in a newspaper.

It was delivered in white and red gift wrapping, with a
white and red bow tying it.

She knew it was the ad. She knew it came from Michael.
She was as excited as a young girl when she undid the bow,
and literally ripped away the red and white paper.

But she had no way to prepare for the sight that greeted her
then. It was a full page ad that would fit in the *New York
Post*. On its top, in letters big enough to go on a Broadway
marquee, were the words: WHY MODELS DON'T GROW
OLD TILL 60. Underneath was a photo of her, blown up
from the book, showing her at the age of thirty-nine in a
small, red, hip-high disco dress, with her hair long and kinky,
and with a come-hither expression on her face that might have

been used as a cover for either *Cosmopolitan* or *Playboy*. Underneath the photo were the words: THIS WOMAN WAS EXACTLY 39 YEARS, 3 MONTHS AND 6 DAYS OLD WHEN THIS PICTURE WAS TAKEN.

Then the entire page was filled with a condensation, and dramatization, of the contents of her book. He had evidently read every word of it several times. And he had boiled them down into such tantalizing individual sentences, that it would be almost impossible for any woman, with any kind of beauty problem at all, not to read the ad and then order the book.

It was an irresistible ad. She herself, who had written the book, felt that she wanted to run right out and purchase another copy for herself.

Along with it, in a small brown envelope, and so small that she almost missed it, was a brief handwritten letter from him. It said:

Hope you like this crude attempt. The book is even more valid than you suggested. It *must* belong in the library of every woman over twenty-three. Call up Irving House and tell them they have to run it immediately—or I'll buy the mail order rights myself, and do it for them.

You made the party for me.

Michael

P.S. Everything you say in the book is absolutely correct, except your night cream. It only works halfway. There is a much better cream available, as of three months ago. But I'm afraid I'm the only man on earth who knows what it is.

What will you give me for it?

Curiously,

Michael

She read the last paragraph of the letter—the P.S.—eight times. It wasn't true. It couldn't be true. She knew every cream—old and new—in existence. He was playing games with her. Besides, how would a gene-chaser know . . .

Something totaled up deep in her mind. Something made sense—too much sense. Something whispered itself in a part of her mind she had never heard from before.

She took the letter and very calmly tore it in half. Then she tore it in fourths, then eighths, then sixteenths. And then, when she could not tear it in thirty-seconds she wadded it up and threw it quickly in the wastebasket.

She rushed to the phone, and picked out the number of her editor at Irving House. The phone rang once, twice . . .

The perfect face cream, she thought. The answer to any woman's dream.

And then, from that dark, unknown side of her mind, the whispered reminder: the perfect double answer to any woman's dream.

Irving House was by no means stupid. Her editor sent for the ad the very next day, took one look at it, met with the advertising department, and scheduled it in the *New York Post* for the following Sunday.

The continuity acceptance man at the *Post* saw the ad on Wednesday, demanded to see Melissa herself an hour later, checked for himself at a glance that she really looked like the photo, and then demanded to see a copy of her birth certificate. She roared with laughter, ran home, got the certificate, showed it to him, and the ad was scheduled for four days later.

She wandered in a daze those four days. She knew that sooner or later she was going to have to pick up the phone and dial the number that was on his business stationary. It was burned indelibly in her mind. She couldn't believe that it was she—Melissa Carpenter—not picking up the phone, not thanking a friend for a towering favor, not even letting him know whether or not she had received the ad.

But the phone turned hot to her touch when she picked it up. There was no way she could talk to him without discussing the P.S., and that P.S. was too hot for her to touch right now. She wondered if he expected an immediate response. She wondered if he'd called the delivery service, and made sure the ad was delivered.

She wondered—most deeply of all—whether he knew that she wouldn't call him for a while. Whether the last paragraph was there to keep her from calling him too soon. Whether getting there was really more than half the fun.

Nevertheless, each day blurred into the next until, finally, it was Sunday. All day Sunday her phone was busy with friends and relatives, calling about the ad. Universally, they thought it was a sensation. Each time she put down the phone that Sunday, it would start ringing again almost instantly. Each time, when she picked it up, she was waiting to hear one of two voices at the other end.

One of those voices was Aaron's, asking her who had written the ad. Congratulating her. Asking her to come home. Asking her anything—just breaking the silence.

The second voice she waited for all day Sunday was a different man's voice, calling for a different reason; it was a voice she had spent only one evening listening to, and could never forget. It was a deep voice, a laughing voice, a voice that had presented her with two challenges the very first night, and then a third and larger challenge three days later. But she had to wait for the voice itself to state the challenge in warmer words, in more personal words, in more intimate words, than those contained in the letter.

She waited for both voices during the entire day and night. Neither of them was ever on the other end of the phone.

4.

At ten-thirty the next morning, the advertising director from Irving House called. The woman's first words were explosive enough to bring down the barriers that had walled Melissa in all her life.

"We had 1,139 phone orders for the book yesterday! More than a thousand orders on the phone in one day! Do you know what that means?" And then she answered her own question. "That means we'll do ten thousand orders this week alone, through a single ad in the *New York Post*. Ten thousand orders in a single week! Eighty thousand dollars in revenue from an ad that cost five thousand. Think of it, Melissa. Think of it."

"How many did you say?" Melissa asked.

"Ten thousand this week. At least a hundred thousand before the primary campaign is over. Good God, we're rich!"

Melissa said nothing. Her eyes were looking elsewhere—at flashing white teeth, at eyes that were certain, sure, and yet never stopped laughing.

"We run next week in Detroit, in San Francisco, in Los Angeles, in Chicago, in . . ."

"Thank you," Melissa said. "But I've got to go now."

"Wait a minute," Jane went on. "I've only begun the list. There's San Antonio, and Miami, and . . ."

"That's nice," Melissa said. "Why don't you send me a list?"

"Nice?" The woman's squealed on the other end of the phone.

"Very nice," Melissa replied. "Congratulate the space buyer," she said. "I've got to go now. I have to—"

"You have to what? What's more important than selling ten thousand copies a week?"

"Telling somebody that if he said he could fly off the roof of a house by waving his wings," Melissa replied, "I'd be the first one in the world to climb right up on his back."

Melissa dialed the number on the stationery. She first got a secretary, who asked her name, and then clicked off for ten seconds. Then the girl's voice came back on, saying, "Mr. Black is on a long distance call to California. He'd like you to hold on for one minute, please, or he'll . . . he'll cut off his ear and send it to you in a wooden box."

Melissa smiled back at the puzzled voice. "Please tell him I'll hold on. I wouldn't want to put him through the expense of the box."

And then his exuberant voice came thundering over the phone. "Thank God," he said. "I thought you didn't like it."

"I loved it," she said, "but—"

"I thought you thought the picture was pornographic in that context," he said.

"It was perfect," she replied. "It had just the right flavor."

"I thought you didn't speak to male copywriters who were married, and gave away your age in print."

"Stop it," she said. "I should have called you the day I got it," she said.

"No," he answered. "The moment you got it."

"I should have called you the moment I got it," she went on, "but—"

"Did you like the wrapping?" he questioned quickly.

"It was very pretty," she replied.

"I did it myself, including the bow. First bow I ever tied, outside of my shoelaces."

She laughed. "It was a masterful bow. It was a masterful ad. Did you like it when you saw it in the *Post* yesterday?"

"I thought it was pretty good."

"Pretty good?" she said. "It pulled over a thousand telephone orders yesterday alone."

"Is that enough?"

"Sensational," she said. "It means, they tell me, that we'll probably sell," and she let her voice lower in acknowledgement to him, "about one hundred thousand through mail order."

"Oh, my God," he said. "You think . . ." and his voice trailed off.

"I don't understand," she said.

"I have two questions," he asked. "First, if you liked it when you first saw it, why didn't you call me then?"

She hesitated. Then she spoke the truth bluntly. "Because of your P.S."

"Good," he replied immediately.

"Good?" she asked.

"Good," he repeated. "Second, will you have lunch with me?"

"When?" she asked.

"Today," he said. "Tomorrow. Thursday. Friday. Anytime. Anyplace. You choose it."

"I'm available when you are," she said, and then turned beet red.

"You have no idea," he answered. "But I have another question as well. A little harder question." Then she actually heard him take a deep breath before continuing. "Tell me, beautiful one," he said, "will you have lunch with me anytime, anyplace, under any conditions—after you've learned that I lied?"

"Which lie?" she asked.

"The ad," he said. "I didn't write it. I couldn't write it in a million years. But if you'll have lunch with me, I'll tell you who did. And I'll actually introduce you to her. And," his voice smiled impishly at her through the phone, "also show you how the two of you, together, can make a million dollars next year."

5.

She arrived at the restaurant the next day, one and a half minutes past the appointed time. She had spent over two hours on her hair, her face, and her clothes, and she was delighted to see the face of every man in the restaurant reflect her success. But he was not there.

A woman got up from the bar and walked over to Melissa. She was short, dark-haired, unattractive. But she had marvelous eyes—and, as Melissa was about to learn, an incredible mouth.

"Hi," she said to Melissa. "You've been stood up for a virus. And I'm hardly an adequate replacement."

"Michael?" Melissa asked.

"Exactly," the woman replied. "In Boston since nine o'clock this morning. Said to tell you this: that there's been a breakthrough on what he calls an axe-virus, that splits big genes into little genes. He needed to see how they worked, and wanted to pick some up and carry them home in his pocket. He said they'd make his P.S.—at least that's what I made him say twice—his P.S. ten times as powerful. So he asked me to reverse the order of our lunches, and meet you here myself, today. So look what you've ended up with," she said. "My name is Sally O'Toole—honestly."

Disappointed though she was, Melissa's recovery was instant. Her hand shot out, and she said, "It's a pleasure to meet you."

"It's not," Sally replied immediately, "but we're here, and let's get a table." She motioned to the headwaiter, and they were seated at once.

"I guess I'm surrogate hostess," Sally said, "so what will you have?"

"White wine, please," Melissa replied.

"White wine," Sally repeated to the captain, "and there's a near-empty martini glass belonging to me on the bar. Don't bother to revive it. Just mix up a new one the way I like it, Tony, and get both of them over here as quick as you can."

Then she turned to Melissa, and smiled again.

"The reason I'm here, in case you haven't guessed, is that I wrote the ad that Michael sent you."

"You wrote the ad?" Melissa asked.

"Yes, in two days," Sally said. "Thanks to that handsome bastard promising he'd fly into the Empire State Building if I didn't have it for him on Sunday."

"It was marvelous," Melissa said immediately. "Thank you."

"No," Sally replied. "It wasn't marvelous at all. All the content, all the claims, came from your book. It was a purely mechanical job, except perhaps for the headline, and the inclusion of the exact number of years and months you were when you had that sexy photo taken." Sally shrugged. "I simply became you for a day or two," she said, "on paper. And I let the world read, in condensed form, what you had to say."

"I can't thank you enough," Melissa answered.

"Michael says you can," Sally went on. "That's why I'm here. That's why we're both here, I guess. Michael says you'll sell ten thousand copies a week through the ad. Is that correct?"

"Yes," Melissa said at once. "And I want to know what I owe you for it."

"You don't owe me anything," Sally said. "Michael paid me for it, a long time ago. I was simply paying him back last weekend. End of transaction."

"But why should he—" Melissa started.

"You really don't know?" Sally said.

"No," Melissa replied, blushing suddenly. "Yes," she added hastily. "Of course I can guess. But it just doesn't quite add up."

"Right," Sally said quickly. "It never adds up with Michael." And then her smile turned sad, and she said, "It never will add up with Michael."

The captain returned to the table, carrying the menus. Both women took one, and stared at it, welcoming the break in the conversation.

Finally, Sally looked up. "You have two choices," she said.

"On the menu?" Melissa asked.

"No," and her smile mixed sweetness with sadness, "for the conversation that's wrapped around the menu. We can either talk how you can make five to fifty times as much money—even build a permanent business—as you'll make from the sale of the book. Or,'' she said, ''we can talk about Michael Black—why he'll never add up, anytime, in any situation, with any woman.''

6.

They sat till three-thirty, till the restaurant emptied out, and they were alone.

''I don't know whether I'd rather be him, or me,'' Sally had begun. ''He's magnificent. He's unforgettable. Women spend their entire lives telling themselves that someday they're going to marry him. I'm completely forgettable. I call myself a Kleenex girl—men use me like a Kleenex and then throw me away and forget me. He can have almost any woman in the world he wants—even you, honey. I get the absolute bottom of the barrel as far as men are concerned, the apples that are so rotten that you can't even get enough substance to pull them out of the barrel with your hands. But there are some nights, when I'm alone, and I know he isn't, that I'd still rather be plain and expendable like me, rather than like him.''

''Why?'' Melissa asked.

''Because I still believe in something he doesn't. And won't. And perhaps never will.''

''Which is?''

''That stupid word that destroys all of us sooner or later,'' Sally said. ''The greatest four letter word of them all. Love.''

''He doesn't believe in love?''

''He makes love,'' Sally replied, ''constantly, magnificently, impeccably. He acts at love, as naturally as his cheeks dimple when they smile. And he inspires love—my God, does he grow it; just like Johnny Appleseed in his heyday. But he's never experienced it. And I really don't think he knows it exists.''

''But his marriage?'' Melissa went on.

''A mutual acquisition,'' Sally said. ''Been together fifteen years. She got the handsomest heterosexual male in New York—the perfect dinner companion, bright, a war hero, who can always be depended upon to go to bed with other women, and leave her alone, which is exactly where she wants to be—alone in bed.''

''And he?''

''Got, I guess, independence. The facade of marriage and the liberty of nonmarriage. The freedom from financial care, and plenty of time to chase his little genes—and his little girls.''

''He sounds pretty bad,'' Melissa remarked. ''But you've completely lost me. Would you mind explaining a few basic terms?''

''Fire on,'' Sally exclaimed.

''A war hero? When?''

''In Korea,'' Sally replied. ''He fought in one of the first jet combats in Korea. Shot down seven MIG's and was shot down himself. He was trapped behind enemy lines, with a broken hip, for twenty-three days.''

So he flies, Melissa thought, remembering the conversation in Michael's car.

''I take it he cracks up relationships as well as planes,'' Melissa said, quite suddenly, quite recklessly.

''To smithereens, honey,'' Sally said. ''I've counted fourteen of them in the last three years. I've sat up with five of those fourteen all night, trying to piece those girls together, actually trying to keep one of them from killing herself.''

''Just a minute,'' Melissa said, quite bluntly, ''how do you know so much about his love life? How have you kept such careful track of his fourteen women in three years?''

''Do I hold his pants?'' Sally laughed. ''Am I his towel girl? No, sweetheart, I'm not there. I don't watch. But I do make appointments, schedule the trips, send the flowers, saying both hello and good-bye, pick out the right rooms with the right views in the right hotels, and even make sure that he shows up at the important occasions with his wife . . . I'm his secretary. I've been his secretary for the past three years.''

''But the ad?'' Melissa questioned.

''Is the third ad I've ever written. Beginner's luck, honey. I've been going to advertising school at night—he paid for it,'' she laughed quietly. ''Since then he's been getting me copy assignments from his friends in the advertising field. Now, because of your ad, he's running all over town, trying to get me a job as a copy junior with a real advertising agency. He knows I can't remain his secretary forever.''

"You're his secretary?" Melissa said out loud to herself.

"I'm his secretary," Sally repeated. "His left hand. The one person in the world who knows more about him than God himself—I hope. Certainly far more about him than his wife knows—or cares. All the secrets. All the hideaways. All the hidden landing fields all over the world—which I'll talk about on special occasions like these, but which I'd never identify by name."

"Why is this a special occasion?" Melissa asked. "Wait a minute, before you answer that. Have you—"

Sally's eyebrows rose slightly. "Have I what?" she asked calmly.

"Forget it," Melissa said. "Let's go on to the—"

"Have I slept with him myself?" Sally interrupted.

"It's not important," Melissa said.

"It's terribly important," Sally said, "because you see, that's the key. He's marvelous in bed. Spectacular in bed." She leaned forward across the table, her eyes blazing, her face now dominated by a streak of cruelty. "Would you like to hear the details of how good he is in bed?" she said.

"No," Melissa said immediately.

"Sure," Sally went on. "I went to bed with him. If you worked for him for three years, wouldn't you—even you— dream of going to bed with him? And I made it once, just once. Out of his pity. Out of kindness. Out of saving me from slitting my wrists.

"I told you—I'm the Kleenex girl. Man No. Thirty-eight—I keep track of everything, don't I?—man No. Thirty-eight was particularly good in bed. He was a performer, honey. He worked at his trade. He took me to bed four times, and then, I guess, had proved everything he wanted to. So he broke it off with a three-minute phone call. Just the usual, 'There's some- one else' and 'Good-bye.' Half of them do it that way—you wouldn't know. I thought it was the end of my little sexual universe. And I was staring at the vial of sleeping pills when Michael walked into my office to give me some new reports to go over."

She laughed.

"He took one look at me and asked me out for a drink. I told him what had happened—and that the son-of-a-bitch was the greatest lover in the world, and I'd never be able to find another. And that's how it happened. He thought, I guess, that it would be better for me to spend the night making love than popping sleeping pills. So we went to a hotel. We made love. God, did we make love! And I learned that the other bastard was a tenth-rate performer. I learned the difference between champagne and vinegar. And I knew, from that evening on, that I'd never pop sleeping pills over vinegar again. We never talked about it later. We've never done it again, either. But, you know—''

She looked up at Melissa, and Melissa swore that she herself would never show eyes that hungry to another living person.

"You know, I keep waiting for another chance." She smiled down into her empty glass. "Call me number fourteen and a half, if you want to."

"I'm sorry," Melissa said, not knowing if that was the right thing to say. Not knowing what she should be sorry about. "But now I have to ask you my second question. Why in the world are you telling me all this?"

Sally looked up. "That's a cinch," she said. And a shy smile appeared on her face. "Because I read your book."

"The book?"

"Yes, the book. The book was good, honey. Damn good. And I realized, from the very beginning, that it was an act of love, from you to millions of American women like me. You shared secrets most women would rather sell their soul than reveal. That made me respect you, even before I met you. And I guess—I just wanted you to know what you were getting into. I wanted you to know that the plane you were boarding—the plane called Michael Black—has just one little spark plug missing in its motor. So that motor sputters when you hit a certain altitude. And the parachute works. But believe me, Melissa Carpenter—there's no place to land. You just hang there, suspended in mid-air, and keep hoping, and hoping, that the plane will turn around and scoop you up for one last ride.''

7.

Melissa called Little John at five and discussed the day's events with him, as always. She welcomed Lacy home at six-thirty, and spent until nine that night thrilling to the new part the child had learned in Tennessee Williams' *Glass Menagerie*.

Then, by ten, she was alone, and replaying the entire conversation with Sally in her mind. It had been a stupid lunch. An insane lunch. A disastrous lunch.

She thought of Sally's image of herself floating high in the sky, unable to land. Melissa knew that feeling, had known it for the past few months. The airports she was familiar with were closed off to her, and now the pilot's loudspeaker system was saying:

"Michael Black has been closed in. Visibility is now zero. We are being diverted to another landing strip—we don't yet have word on how long it will take us to get there."

Where was the other landing strip? How did she reach it? When did she touch solid ground again, instead of this endless circling . . . circling . . . circling . . . in the fog?

Aaron? Closed in because of dreams.

Albee? Frozen over because of age.

Michael? Sunk beneath a sea of other women. Erased from the map—her map—forever.

8.

Michael didn't call Thursday. Or Friday. Or Saturday or Sunday. Michael didn't call again until the following Thursday. She had a small speech memorized for the occasion, but she never used it.

330

"Hello," he said on the other end of the phone. "I'm sorry, but I wanted to wait till I had it for you."

"There's no need to be sorry," she said automatically. "But what 'it' are you talking about?"

"The cream," he said. "The face cream I promised you. I'll give you a sample of it when we have lunch today."

"Lunch?" she asked. There were fifty ways to say no. She knew each one of them perfectly. They were all useless.

"Now that I've got it for you, you've got to try it at once," he rushed on. "How about twelve-thirty at Le Cirque?"

"You'll have the cream?" It was half a question, half an excuse to see him again.

"I'll have the cream. And I think you'll be amazed by it."

"All right. See you then," she said.

"Yes," he said. "You'll see a lot of me then."

She hung up the phone. She looked up at the antique clock above her mantel. She had one hour and thirty minutes. They were going to circle in the fog for another hour and thirty minutes. Then they were going to come down—a zero-visibility landing. On a landing strip she didn't even believe existed anymore.

9.

He hadn't seen her come into the restaurant, and she stood for a second watching him talk to a male friend, his profile turned full force toward her. She, who had grown numb to the idea of female beauty by viewing it in the mirror each morning, noon, and evening, was now stunned by the overwhelming fact of male beauty in the living, glowing, articulate flesh. She stood stock still in the entrance for a moment, knowing for the first time in her life what a hundred men must have been thinking as she raised her eyes from some table, or some conversation, and saw the same look on their faces that she knew must be on her own now. And she was no longer repelled by the look in their eyes, which she had hated for years.

Beauty, she thought suddenly, is a crime if it is unownable.

Just imagine, if there were a Renoir that refused to be purchased, a Monet that was willed never to have an owner, a
Degas that was to spend its life always on the auction block,
with an infinite reserve, so that no matter how high you bid,
the house would always bid one step higher—so you could
only look at it in vain, and never touch it, never possess it,
never take it home to call your own.

She laughed silently at herself. Her own eyes were now her
own retribution.

"Well," he said, coming over and taking her hand gently.
"Now we're all here. The three of us."

"Your other guest is invisible," she replied.

"Yes," he said. "And a trifle shy. He's waiting for us in
the checkroom, until I give him the proper introduction, and
then I think he'll join us for dessert. Meanwhile," he said,
motioning to the captain, "why not enjoy ourselves? Let me
sit you down, feed you, and tell you about him."

After they had ordered, he said at once, "We've got a lot
to cover. Shall we start right in?"

"Of course," she replied.

"Good. First of all, exactly how much did Sally tell you
about me last Wednesday?"

She thought a moment, and then said, softly, "Fourteen
women in three years." There was no change of expression in
his face, and she added, "Or should I number them exactly at
fourteen and a half?"

"That too?" he said.

"That too."

"Good," he said suddenly. "Then you know my romantic
background and I won't have to go into it deeply. Did she
also tell you about the planes?"

"Korea. Of course."

"And that I fly in air shows every month?"

"We didn't get around to that. But I can certainly believe
it."

"Good," he said. "You know my entire relevant background. Now, do we fill the rest of this luncheon with
trivia—and I'm one of New York's leading experts on mealtime
trivia—or do we get down to the core of the subject?"

"Are you talking about the face cream now?" she asked.

"I'm talking about the face cream," he said. "And what
the face cream means to millions of women—and men—who
are watching their faces grow old. And about us"—he looked

up at her face as he said the word—"and about God, and about hatred, and a few other choice, forbidden subjects."

"All here and now?"

"All here and now. Unless you'd like to duck out of this restaurant, and go to my midtown flat."

"No."

"Excellent," he said. "We'll start. How old am I?"

She was startled by the question, and took a moment to think it through. Finally, she said, hesitantly, "About forty-two years old."

He flinched. The twitch in his face was so imperceptible that it took a trained professional eye—the eye of a doctor, or a photographer, or a model of long standing—to detect it. If she had been staring any less intently, or if she had been a foot and a half farther away from his face, she would never have noticed it. But it was there. She saw it. He saw her seeing it, and then he immediately smiled.

"It's the most accurate guess I've ever had," he said. "You're six months off—I was forty-three last November."

"But most people say thirty-two or thirty-five, don't they?" she said.

"Exactly," he replied.

"Just like they say twenty-eight to me," she said. "But you asked for a professional, and not a—"

"Don't apologize. You're possibly the only woman in the world I could discuss this with. Every woman, every man, knows how it feels to grow older, and have someone guess their correct age. We are all of us—all of us—continual shoppers for guesses that are five to ten to fifteen years too young. In fact, the world is full of professional misguessers—people who make a profession out of underguessing others' ages, so they can win either social or business favors from them. It's universal. Try it on any of your friends. But you and I, recipients of the cruelest gift of all, are especially vulnerable."

"The cruelest gift of all," she repeated, and her mind flashed immediately to Victoria.

"Am I good-looking?" he went on.

"Incredibly," she said at once. "Impossibly." And then she thought for a moment, shook her head at her own newly discovered feelings, smiled, and said, "Devastatingly."

"Do I show the signs of my age?" he said.

"Professionally, yes," she replied. "Nonprofessionally, no.

But you're a man, Michael. Those signs of age work for you now, where they wouldn't work for a woman. The lines around the eyes, the small furrows between the nose and chin, all of them add up to strength and character on you. Make you mature, shall we say? Irresistible to females of the entire age range that you must be interested in. I don't think they'd do that for a woman.''

"And now the payoff question," he said. "Do I worry about those signs? Just like a woman?''

"Fourteen girls in three years? I would guess the answer is yes. Excessively.''

Again, the almost invisible flinch. But the immediate reply, "If I didn't have the fourteen girls in three years, but looked the same and was happily married?''

"You mean, would you worry about the aging of your face? Yes. I'm sure you would. But," she asked suddenly, "why are we discussing this?''

"Because we're talking about a face cream, and why I'm developing that face cream for you. Why it does what it does, and I imagine, most important of all, what I want from you in return.''

"You intend to give me the face cream?" she asked.

"I intend to give all sales rights of the cream to you. Lock, stock, and barrel," he said. "Or, to be more precise, to give them to a new company that you're going to form on the basis of the success of the book.''

"And the cream does what?" she asked.

"Makes the ordinary woman look five to ten years younger in approximately one month. I'm afraid it'll make you look only two to three years younger in a month, because of the shape your face is in today. But it will still do enough to amaze you," he said.

"And a cream like that—?''

"Would be worth millions, if it were handled correctly.''

"And you're going to give it to me, instead of to one of the giant cosmetic companies?''

"I don't like giant companies, or the animals who inhabit them," he said immediately.

"To my company?" she said again. "Which isn't even formed? And as far as you know now, has absolutely no capital?''

"You can get all the money you want," he said slowly. "As a loan. As a gift.''

She looked at him sharply. "How do you imagine that?"

"I know Albee," he replied, smiling.

"And he told you—?"

"Never. I performed a small, logical operation called deduction, based on the gossip that's now circulating around the city concerning your husband, yourself, and Albee."

She blushed. She felt as though Michael were taking off her clothes, one by one. His smile remained unchanged. He was still as beautiful as a cameo to all the women staring at him across the room. Only one person in that room knew the real danger in that exquisite smile.

"And if I were not financed at all, would you still give this miraculous cream to me?"

"Absolutely."

"For what?"

"A very small exchange," he said quietly.

"Which is?" she asked.

He looked at her across the table. To the eyes across the room he might have been discussing his latest golf score, or the play he had seen open last night on Broadway, or even a mutual friend who had just had her third baby. His voice was as calm and as low as before. Not the slightest trace of emotion passed through it as he said, "I want you to go to bed with me. Without romance. Without love. Without seduction or courting of any kind. Simply and purely on a business basis—nothing else. A new product," he said, the smile now dazzling in its effect, "in trade for a simple fuck."

10.

"Why did you use that word?" she asked.

"Which word?"

"You know perfectly well."

"I know perfectly well. But I want you to say it."

"No."

"Say it. Fuck. F-U-C-K. Fuck. Say it."

"Absolutely no."

He smiled. "That's exactly why I chose it," he said. "Because I know you wouldn't say it to a stranger like myself, over a luncheon table, in a civilized resturant like this. Even though it's probably being used all around us, five times a minute." Now the smile remained, but his eyes were no longer smiling. "And I want to help you. I genuinely want to help you."

"What?" she exploded. "By using your language?"

"Yes," he said, no longer with a smile "But forget the words. All I'm talking about is coming into the real world, where that language fits."

"Your world is not the real world."

"Is yours? Without thinking—right now, from your gut—answer yes or no. Quick."

Aaron. Lacy. The separation from Little John. Loneliness. There was no answer. There was nothing she could say.

"I'm going to tell you something," he said. "And then we'll go on with our . . . business conversation." "When I saw you that first night on the porch, sitting there in the half-shadows, it took me three minutes before I could be sure that you weren't a fantasy. And when I discovered that you weren't, then I violated a pact with my wife that I had stuck to for years—and I ran out on that party because I had to be alone with you."

She watched the eyes of a man who had had fourteen women in three years, and she believed every word he was saying.

"And then," he went on, "in that restaurant that night, when I listened to your dreams and your ideals, I felt twenty-six again. And I hated that feeling—hated it—because I worked so hard to break out of that twenty-six-year-old idealism. Because I live in the real world now, and that real world—with all its hazards and all its compromises—is the only world around to live in, and the only world in which you, yourself, can be productive and real."

"I don't agree," she said.

"I know," he said, and smiled charmingly. "So now we're back to our business conversation, aren't we? Would you like to hear about the cream, and what it does?"

She nodded.

"Well, then—do you know anything about the molecular structure of protein?" he asked.

She let her mind run over the dozens of introductory texts in chemistry, physiology, and biology that she had struggled through with Aaron's help. And then she said, "A little."

"Marvelous," he replied. "Then I'll still talk in terms of your future customers, and you can fill in the gaps as I go along. You have a face. That face has a skin. That skin is made of protein. The most important type of protein in that skin, to my way of thinking, is called 'collagen.' Collagen is the building material of those tiny organic ropes that hold that skin firm when you're young, but began to sag, deeper and deeper, when that skin gets old. And there you have the number one source of the wrinkles, the sags, and the bags that we call aging."

"Go on," she said, fascinated.

"End of technical discussion," he said. "The rest is very dramatic, but very simple. When you're young, the body is strong enough to weave new supports for the skin, and so it doesn't sag. When you're old, the body just can't do that as fast, and the skin gradually collapses. It's all a matter," he said, now talking more to himself than to her, "of protein absorption."

"Explain that, please."

"It's simply a matter of how much food your skin gets from the food you eat. When you're young, you can eat enough protein for your skin. But when you get older, you can't."

"And that's where your face cream comes in."

"Exactly. Every face cream manufacturer has been dreaming about this for years. But, until now, the protective surface of the skin has always stopped them from accomplishing it. The holes—let's call them holes—in your skin were simply smaller than the proteins in the cream. So the proteins couldn't squeeze through those tiny holes, and your poor skin couldn't absorb that protein, as it desperately needed to."

"You make it sound like a war," she said involuntarily.

"It is a war. A never-ending war against age. I fight on another battlefield of that same war. But then I saw that I could chop up the proteins the skin works with. I can chop them up into small, easily digestible bites. And, in essence, create a baby food for your skin, that it can swallow right up."

"A baby food for your skin," she repeated wonderingly.

"Not quite," he replied, the seductive smile creeping back into his face. "Melissa's Baby Food for Your Skin."

She felt a chill run up from the bottom of her spine to the

base of her brain. "Melissa's Baby Food for Your Skin."
She listened to it in silence for a moment. And then she
acknowledged another feeling—this time in her gut. A strange,
marvelous, tingling feeling at the bottom of her stomach. And
it took a full minute before she recognized it as pure greed.

She ran from it instantly.

"I've never seen that expression on your face before," he
said. "What are you feeling?"

"Nothing."

"Nothing that exists in your world," he corrected. "But
something you bump up against a dozen times a day in the real
world. That's one of the fuels of that real world. And God
help you if you don't recognize it in yourself and others."

"You're not only acting as my teacher now," she said,
"but as my analyst."

"Only my first two roles," he said. "The others are
better."

She couldn't stop the blush. He went on. "But let me make
you taste a little more of that . . . unacceptable emotion, right
now, so you can feel more comfortable in the real world, if
you ever decide to enter it. Just think of the consequences of
your baby food for the skin. Rich new protein reaches those
old cords under a woman's skin. They begin to tighten up.
They're replaced much easier, much faster. The skin looks
younger, day after day." His voice was so low now, so deep,
that his words were almost lost in the physicality of that
voice. "Think of it, Melissa Carpenter, think of *years* disappearing from even your face in a single month. What would
you pay to lose those years in that month?"

He's making love to me, she thought. He's making love to
me with his words instead of his body. And—God help
me—I want it.

"It sounds like . . . a commercial success," she said,
hating herself for hiding behind those conventional words.
"If it works."

"It does," he said, without the slightest shift in voice. "It
works very well indeed. You can try it yourself, starting this
evening."

"I'm going to hate you," she said. "Why are you doing
this to me?"

"For two reasons. One, because if I give you this cosmetic, and you go into business selling it, I don't want you to
lose either the cosmetic or the business six months after you

get started. And you will,'' he added, ''if I don't toughen you up before I give you my little treasure in a jar.''

''To protect your investment?''

''To protect a far more important investment than a cosmetic or money. You. I'm trying to show you what the real world is like, because you've been too beautiful, too lucky, too gifted ever to find out for yourself. And I'm trying to use this new perspective of the world to make you into what you can be.

''Yes,'' he said. ''What you've secretly dreamed of becoming all these years. A giver—a source—a fountainhead. The woman of impossible beauty and youth—in other words, to borrow from mythology, a physical goddess—who gives impossible beauty and youth to other, more mortal women.

''I want to take what you are today—a female Prometheus bound—and I want to rip off those chains, and release that bound power. You, my dear, are a reluctant goddess, a self-imprisoned goddess, who refuses to come down to this flawed earth, and take part in the brutal battles that are the only workshops of creation that this earth offers. I want to take away the chains of self-perpetuating fantasy that now bind you. And I want to make you hard enough, and strong enough, and tough enough to survive the vultures of this earth who will see you in the cosmetic business as mere food, rather than the provider of food.''

The blinding smile returned to his face. ''And to do that, as a start, I have to get you to agree to fuck me—yes, fuck me—without loving me, or being infatuated with me, with your self so repelled by what I tell you that I'm not even attractive to you any longer. Simply and solely as a commercial trade-off—the handshake made over a signed contract. The physical act that says money is changing hands.

''In other words,'' he concluded, ''this is the deal Albee wanted to make with you. This is the deal Mr. Eastman, who called you four months ago and shattered your marriage, wanted to make with you. This is even the deal Aaron wanted to make with you. In fact, this is the deal the whole world wants to make with you—because you have to become as real and as flawed as the rest of the world, or else you'll never really be part of it.''

He gave her a last dazzling smile. But his words had made her dazzle-proof.

11.

She came home with a jar full of white cream, and a mind full of turmoil. She didn't even bother to open the jar. She put it on her bathroom shelf, somehow hating the thought of putting anything related to him on her skin.

She hated him now. She hated his trying to draw her into a false world—a world called "real" only by those unfortunate enough to be trapped within it. She had spent her entire life fighting that world. It was the world of all the parasites she saw crawling over the body of New York, trying to gnaw a little piece of it for themselves, before they starved to death from the impoverishment of their souls.

At last she called Pam, and asked her to come over. Then she went again into the bathroom, and picked up the fatal jar. Its white top unscrewed easily, and she stared down at the soft, white cream underneath. She put one finger in it, tentatively. It was smooth as silk, cool to the touch. She could feel it being absorbed into the skin of her finger the instant she touched it.

She raised a dab of it to her nose; there was no odor to suggest that anything artificial had been put into it. In fact, it had no odor at all. She let her tongue touch the very tip of the dab—a sweet taste. But the taste meant nothing; only the performance on the naked skin itself would tell.

She took an empty jar, and divided the contents of Michael's jar in half—half to remain in the original, and half to be kept in the empty jar. Then she sealed both jars, and waited. When Pam arrived, they chatted for a few minutes over cups of tea, and then Melissa shoved the second jar across the table toward the other woman.

"I want you to try this as a night cream for one week, as a favor to me. It's essential you use no other treatment cream but it. And I'll call you one week from tonight, to see if there are any results."

"All right," Pam said. "What is it made of?"

"I don't know," Melissa said.

340

"The plot thickens," Pam replied. "Will I be allergic to it?"

"I don't know," Melissa said again, quite bluntly. "Actually, I'd be happy if you were. But if you are, call me at once."

"Are you trying to help my skin or poison it?" Pam asked. "Did you buy this cream or steal it?" And then she looked hard at Melissa. "There's something more than cream going on here, honey."

":Will you try it for me for a week?" Melissa asked.

"Absolutely," Pam replied. "I'd put a bottle marked strychnine on my face if you told me to. But are you sure you don't want to tell me the real story behind it?"

"No. Not now."

"Okay." Pam sniffed the jar once more. "Something tells me," she said, "that one week from now I'm going to look like a twenty-year-old."

12.

The cream worked. Melissa knew that the first night she stood in front of her mirror and spread the first few dabs of it around her eyes—the most vulnerable part of the face, the part that all her knowledge, all her skill, all her discipline had been unable to protect. With her makeup off, in the harsh bathroom light, there were crow's-feet spreading out relentlessly around both eyes. In the daytime, with the proper makeup, through the proper lens, the lines could not be seen. But now she ruthlessly exposed them to the full glare. She took her tiny camera and photographed them, time after time. Then she carefully measured every single line and crease and wrinkle.

She opened the jar, reached in two long tapering fingers, and removed some of the pure white cream. As she stroked the cream gently into the areas around both eyes, she felt its smoothness and softness on her flesh. She noted immediately that it left a small, greasy residue; that meant it would not do as a night cream, since it would stain her pillows, and whatever parts of her sheets that it touched. This was Michael's first mistake. Its greasy residue must be removed before it would be commercially successful.

Then her eyes opened wide in astonishment as the greasiness began to evaporate in a matter of seconds. In less than a minute it was completely gone. She touched her skin where the cream should have been, where indeed it had been only seconds before. There was no feel of cream there at all. The cream had simply penetrated the outer protective layers of her skin, submerging itself deeper than the eye could follow.

Her fingers flashed into the jar again, and more of the pure white cream began to be applied to her cheeks, to her chin, to her entire face, to her neck. If there was really protein in that cream, and if that "baby food" protein were now at work below the protective layers of her skin, and if a feeding and nourishing and rebuilding process were actually taking place deep in the cords that held her skin tight, then . . .

It was a dream, she thought. A dream as old as all women. Only the next days would tell whether that dream would turn out to be a fantasy.

13.

Five days later, Pam called. "You swear you don't know what's in this jar?"

"Only theoretically," Melissa said.

"Can you get more of that theory? Say about two barrels full?"

"I don't know if there is any more."

"For Christ's sake, Melissa, you've got to get some more. Do you know what my face looks like? Do you have any idea what my face looks like in just five days?"

"Yes," Melissa said wearily. "I probably do. I've been watching the same changes on my own skin."

"What's in it?" Pam asked again. "Some kind of subtle acid that eats away the wrinkles around your eyes? And leaves the rest of the skin looking baby plump?"

"It shows up that much?" Melissa asked.

"On my neck, too," Pam said. "Those awful lines on my neck. They're beginning to dissolve. They've been there for fifteen years, and I can see them beginning to fade away. But the jar's going fast," she added. "For Christ's sake, honey," she said, "get me more—please."

"I don't know whether I can get you more," Melissa said bluntly. "How many days' supply do you figure you have left?"

"About a week, I guess, if I stop bathing in it."

"Then I'll let you know if I can get more, before you run out," Melissa said.

"Honey," Pam said. "Don't tell me if you can get it. Get it. I don't care what it costs."

"I do," Melissa said. "Speak to you in a few days."

"Oh, my God," Pam said.

After Melissa had hung up the phone, she went into the bathroom and examined her face for the tenth time that morning. The edges of the wrinkles around her eyes had begun to fade away. There were perceptibly narrower. The skin under them was beginning to tighten. She could see the tightening effect in the mirror. She could feel it now, just this last day, with the sensitive tips of her fingers. And she could swear she felt the skin of her face begin to tighten from the inside. Michael was right. And she knew that she half-worshiped him, half-hated him, for that proof.

She looked at the half-empty jar, and held it in her hand as she might hold the Holy Grail itself. She knew what this jar would mean to millions of women. And suddenly her hand shook as her eyes painted the outside of the jar with a visionary label—a pink and white jar with a picture of her own face engraved on its outside, and the words "Melissa's Baby Food for Your Skin" in gorgeous Gothic letters, right next to that picture. And then she was shocked—shocked—at the involuntary act her eyes had performed without her brain giving her the slightest warning. "Melissa's Baby Food for Your Skin." Again, greed. Again, ambition. Again, a self-glorification that she had never known before.

Then she caught herself, and stopped. "Never known before? Bullshit!" she said out loud. She suddenly remembered the home in Houston—the tiny prison she'd lived in for five years with Johnny, completely unaware of where her real emotions lay, where her real dreams were stored. She remembered the post-midnight trips, after Johnny was safely asleep, into the small dressing room, with its mirrors and its *Vogue*s. It had taken her twenty-six years to begin molding her life around her dreams and fantasies. And it took Johnny—poor, pathetic Johnny—to shove her up to New York where she could give that ambition, and that hidden need for self-glorification, a chance to actualize themselves.

And what had her fourteen years in New York really been like? Over two hundred magazine covers. Over two thousand spreads, advertisements, and features in newspapers and magazines. Dozens of television commercials. Billboards. Posters in cheap stores all over Broadway and Lexington Avenue. Till at one point there was no way she could escape her own reproduced face. Melissa's smile. Melissa's profile. Melissa's new hairstyle. Melissa's endorsement.

Someone had once defined a prostitute as a woman who sold her body, and a model as a woman who sold her face. The only difference, he had remarked, was that the prostitute served only a few men an hour, and the model served millions. She had kept the body for herself—not for purity, or religion, or chastity, or faithfulness—but for herself; she had sold the face to anybody who had the money to buy and use it.

She thought of Pam, and of a dozen other women she knew who had not had the luck or the face to find the right love. She thought of the women she knew who had never known true love, who had never had the power to capture—even for a brief moment—the kind of love that served them, rather than their having to serve it. She thought of all the women who struggled most of the day to make a living, who faced each night with the certain knowledge that they were growing older and more vulnerable, who took whatever semblance of love they could get at that moment. She thought of the women who fought love, who suffered love, who tricked love, who trapped love—even for one brief night or two. She tried to count how many women she had known, in all her life, who had found true love for at least one year out of all their adult lives. She stopped when she reached the number three. Love, she realized, was rarer than great beauty. And you had to be luckier to capture it.

She thought of Albee and the six million dollar backgammon game. She thought of the moment that game was over, and she had won, and they clasped each other, and she still hadn't had the good sense to lose, as well as win. She thought of the times since then that she had seen him, and the dinners, and the talks, and the strange marvelous love between them . . . and her own incredible stupidity in keeping this towering figure of a gentleman away from the body he should share with her.

She thought of the people she had loved in this world. The people who had died—such as Victoria. The people who had been crippled, such as Pam and Arlene. The people who had won, but still had not won what they really wanted—such as Albee. The people who had won, but were too bound by the past to claim what they had won—such as Aaron.

She thought of the trade-offs that life demands of you. The trade-offs that she had ignored. She had lived in a modern Garden of Eden, where the fruit stood ripe and low enough simply to pick whenever you were hungry. Some trees were called glory. Some were called money. Some were called happiness . . . and marriage and love. But there was one tree in the center of the garden that you didn't even glance at over your shoulder. It was called by many names—the tree of knowledge, of life, of suffering, of imperfection. And now an apple had fallen off that tree, and landed, right at her feet. There was a gate at the end of the garden, leading out to the world, and it was marked with a slogan—"YOU HAVE TO GIVE TO GET." Live. Come out from the garden. Become as human as the people you want to help.

Damn perfection, and false purity, and false nobility. Damn self-lying, and hiding behind your face. Damn Michael Black, and his version of the Garden of Eden. But take his cream, and your newfound womanhood, and go out into that "flawed, real" world—Michael's words—and help those millions of women who need you—in whatever flawed way that you can.

14.

The next day she made two phone calls, one to Albee and one to Michael.

Both calls were brief. She asked Albee if he trusted her enough to lend her—yes, lend her—fifty thousand dollars to start a new cosmetic business. He asked no questions. He simply said that there would be no interest charge, and that she would sign a personal note of which he would have the only copy. The loan would be an open one, with no due date, and she should determine the time when she would return all, or part, of it. Then he asked, ''Is there anything else you need?''

''Yes,'' she said, ''your love.''

''You have it,'' he replied.

''I needed that more than the money,'' she said. ''Thank you.''And then she hesitated. ''Albee,'' she said, ''I owe you something. Something I've owed you for a long time. The next time we see each other, I'm going to pay it to you— gladly.''

Then she made the second call. She told Michael, immediately upon his picking up the phone, that she was accepting his offer, and wanted to know where and when he wished to collect.

''Do you want a paper drawn up by our lawyers?'' he asked.

''Later,'' she said. ''Right now, I'm naive enough to take your word. That hasn't changed yet.''

He laughed. ''It may,'' he said. ''But then again, it may not.''

''When and where?'' she asked.

''Tomorrow night,'' he replied. ''At my apartment.'' He gave her the address.

''Fine. What time?''

''Shall we say eight o'clock?'' he said.

''Dinner?''

''No. Strictly business.''

''Agreed,'' she said. ''Any special makeup? Any special clothes? Any special accoutrements?''

''None whatsoever,'' he said. ''I need nothing but you.''

''Very good. Any other instructions?''

''No, just looking forward to a successful transaction—on both sides.''

15.

Promptly at eight o'clock the next evening, she rang Michael's doorbell. The door was opened at once, and he was standing there, dressed in a pair of tight-fitting slacks and a white dress shirt, with the top two buttons undone. The room behind him was the brown of dark leather—matching the color of his eyes—and she was startled at the feeling of vitality and health that flowed from his body.

"Good evening," he said. "I wasn't at all sure you were coming."

"I told you eight. It's eight now. I'm here. As agreed."

"As agreed," he said. "Come in—please."

She walked into the single room, with its two huge windows overlooking the side street between Madison and Park Avenues, with its large bed-couch, neatly turned down to make a double bed, complete with crisp, newly laundered white sheets. The rest of the room was standard bachelor, New York—except for a series of remarkable, iridescent, beautiful photographs lining the wall over the ancient mantelpiece. They were each three feet tall, about two feet wide, and she could tell at a glance that they were pictures of some exotic cells, taken through a microscope, blown up to giant size, and lined up, one next to the other. They were almost as powerful as any abstract painting she had ever seen.

The other wall was lined from floor to ceiling with hundreds of books. Many had been used so often and so roughly that their spines were cracking. Others were filled with sheets of yellow paper on which he had evidently taken notes.

There was a tiny kitchen which looked unused. And then a bathroom at the end of the apartment. That was all. It was mainly a study room, and a bedroom, serving both his passions simultaneously and neatly. It was in perfect order; there was no mess anywhere to be seen. Even the desk at which he had been working had its books piled neatly in a semicircle around the paper he was writing on. She couldn't help notice the top page of the paper. It was filled with the most graceful

347

and mysterious hieroglyphics. She looked longingly at the scribbles on the paper. Of all he could have shared with her, the key to those hieroglyphics was what she craved most. Life's book of instructions. The commands to the body, stored in the body itself. And now unraveled, at last, by men like him, with their electron microscopes, their super-chemicals, their tame and obedient viruses.

He stood there silently, watching her gaze wander around the room and come to rest on the work sheets he had just abandoned. Then his voice quietly broke into her reveries.

"Someday, if you'd like me to, I'll show you how those drawings work. How they let you see things inside your body that you can't see with any other device besides your brain."

"I'd love to know them," she said.

"You will," he answered. "Soon."

Then he put his hands on the white blouse covering her shoulders, and drew her closer to the desk. It was a nonsexual touch; all he wanted to do was draw her face closer to the light. He had seen at once that she had worn no makeup but her lipstick and mascara. There was no powder, no highlight or other model's trick to cover the lines around her eyes. He swiveled the head of the study lamp on the desk until it beamed directly up into her face, almost blinding her with its glare. Then he put gentle hands on her skin around the eyes, and let them run, almost imperceptibly, over that skin.

"Remarkable," he said. "Much better even than I had hoped. And on the eye lines too."

"You were right," she said.

"No," he answered quietly, "nature was right." And then the smile returned. "Nature is always right."

Then his hands reached down and touched her blouse again. This time they were not gentle, but masculine. She felt the shock of them penetrate the silk as though it were not even there. The hands were alive. They were electric. They had an energy, a current, all their own. In another age, those hands would have glorified him as a saint, or had him burned as a warlock.

"Would you like a little wine?" he asked.

Suddenly she forgot the books, the work papers on the desk, the six magnificent photographs over the fireplace. She saw nothing but the open bed, the chilled bottle of white wine, the man standing next to her, holding her like a new possession between his hands.

"No," she said bluntly. "I've eaten and I've drunk. I'm here for only one thing—the transaction. And I think we should get it over with as soon as possible."

His face was less than two feet away from hers. He stared at her for a few seconds and then he threw back his head and laughed.

"I see," he said. "The transaction. Of course. My simple and uncomplicated little act." He looked down at the watch on his wrist. "It's eight-fifteen. Do you have a time schedule for the act itself?"

"No," she said. "As long as you like."

"As long as I can tolerate your indifference," he corrected. "Your coldness." Again he laughed. "My dear girl," he went on. "I'm afraid you don't understand the hidden terms of the agreement. These things are always done with a certain degree of aplomb. They are not endurance contests. They are not assaults upon the flesh. The woman usually acts, from the very start, as though she enjoyed the entire transaction. There is a certain degree of pretense here, as there is in all business."

"I—" she started to say.

"It doesn't matter," he said. "You are what you are. You feel what you feel." He turned away from her and poured a glass of wine for himself, then took a sip.

And then he turned around again, and he snapped off the main light, leaving them both half in shadow, half in street light. His face was devastating in this muted light; he had known this before. "Now we shall see exactly what you are and how you feel," he said calmly, beginning to unfasten the buttons of his white shirt.

Slowly the brown chest emerged from beneath the white shirt. His eyes continued to stare directly into hers. Now there was no smile on his face. It could have been carved in granite by Michelangelo—the face of a dark angel, strong as marble, insanely beautiful in the half-light that streamed in from the street, so awe-inspiring in the strength that flowed from its majesty that she wished it *had* been carved in marble, so that it would never change.

"Would you like to sit down?" he asked.

"No, thank you," she whispered hoarsely.

"As you wish."

He slid his shirt out of the pants, and dropped it to the floor. There was very little hair on the upper half of his body.

She could feel with her eyes that his skin was almost as soft, almost as smooth as hers, but that the muscles that gleamed in the half-light from the street were a thousand times as hard.

He stared at her, watching her stare at him. She stood there motionless, waiting for the next motion of his hands or arms. And again she had a sense of being in a grade-B romantic movie. The pirate captain had just taken the Spanish galleon by storm, and now had his prisoner safely locked up in his cabin belowdecks. She—proud royalty, unbending; he—the renegade Englishman, the former slave, the man who had sunk a hundred ships and burned a dozen towns. She could almost hear the whirring of the cameras behind her. She knew that she should collapse into subservient moaning when his hands touched her again, when his lips closed upon hers. She knew that she should let her body be crushed against his, and slowly and willingly and helplessly he pulled down on the great captain's bed. She knew, also, that in grade-B movies nothing ever happened after the two bodies touched. At that moment the cameras would stop grinding, the action would terminate. But she also knew—this time—that it would not.

He reached up slowly, and again touched her blouse, but his hands did not stop at her shoulders. This time his fingers slowly traced a path of excitement down the front of her blouse, to the buttons that held it together. His hands moved so softly that she hardly felt them. All she felt was the blouse open, and the brassiere underneath slowly show its lines and its curves.

Suddenly his head bent forward and he slowly began to blow his hot breath between the cleavage of her breasts. His hands hadn't even touched the brassiere, but when she felt the warm intimate air on her flesh, suddenly her breasts began to tingle, and she felt her nipples tense and swell.

Now she watched his head bend even farther toward her skin, until she could see only his jet black hair. And she involuntarily gasped as she felt his tongue explore the spot between her breasts. She felt the electricity of that tongue begin to work deep chemistry in the breasts, and down to her stomach, and then farther down to all the secret fortresses and hiding places of her body, traitors to that body, fifth columns, beginning to lubricate the opening hinges to swing open the gates, long before the final siege was waged.

Then suddenly his fingers reappeared at both sides of her slacks, slipping neatly into the top of the slacks and her panties in a single smooth motion, and then just as smoothly pulling them down. In seconds, she stood in the half-shadow of the room, with her slacks and her panties around her heels, and watched his head descend after them, until he was on his knees in front of her. Slowly, she felt his hands lift up one leg after the other, and slip off the slacks and the panties and the shoes.

Then he raised his head, and the beautiful half-angel, half-devil face looked directly into hers. With a small, masculine moan his hands forced aside the lips below, till the clitoris was exposed, raised unwillingly to absolute uprightness, stripped of all flesh protection; and in the same moment his head followed, and before she knew it his lips and tongue were wrapped around her clitoris, biting gently, sucking, licking, tasting, feeling, arousing, thrilling, owning, and controlling.

She could no longer keep her hands away; they came down to the top of his head, touched at last the soft silken hair of that head, grasped the back of that head to keep her from collapsing, massaged that head in rhythm with the rhythm of his own mouth and tongue.

The screams started at the bottom of her throat, and were trapped there by some last fragment of self-control. All she could do was hold on to his hair, feel that smooth hair move through her fingers, as she spasmed against him, as she felt her own clenchings, as she felt him press her closer and speed up the action of his tongue and his mouth to make her even more frenzied. Her knees had begun to buckle; his hands were now encircling her hips, holding her upright so she did not fall, pressing her against him as his sexual prisoner, allowing his tongue to draw more spasms from her body, until she was sure that there could be no more involuntary reflexes left. Then she felt his arms slip from her hips to her back, and raise her off her legs and carry her soundlessly across the rug to the bed.

He said nothing as he undressed. She stared only at his face, not at his body. There was no need to look. She knew what was there. Then she saw his magnificent body flow above her and between her legs. She saw his head bend forward and kiss her shoulders; she felt his teeth take the shoulder straps of her brassiere, and lower them, one by one, until her breasts were finally exposed. And then she felt the very essence of him, the god within him, the most beautiful part of this incredibly beautiful man, slowly enter her.

Months had passed. They were all forgotten now. The emptiness was gone. The loneliness was gone. All she felt now was full, was complete, was woman, was goddess. She began to feel him move inside her slowly, exquisitely, commandingly. At first she managed to hold herself still.

And then it broke. The dam exploded. Her mouth opened by itself, and she heard her breath rush out in a great liberating cry. She felt her legs and arms come up by themselves, felt her mouth explore first his eyes and then his cheeks and then his mouth. Her tongue met his tongue automatically, and the juices of her body mixed with the juices of his. But, most of all, she felt herself lying there, penetrated by the man lying above her and in her—her mouth half-kissing him, half-tasting him. And then she was throwing her head back on the pillow, to escape the now-limiting effect of that sweet mouth, and exploding into the night, into the half-darkness of the room, into the new reality of orgasm after orgasm—all the passion, all the tension, all the sadness, and all the struggle she had felt—and all now supremely, esctatically, insanely worthwhile.

16.

They made love until the light outside the window changed from the yellow of the street lamps to the gray of the dawn. They made love half-bathed in the red of a new rising sun. They made love while the red faded away and a new, brighter yellow streamed in through the venetian blinds, and marked their bodies with the unshielded light of the new day.

Finally, their bodies slowed, and then stopped. She found her mouth closing and touching his no more. She found her vagina closing, and touching him no more. She found her eyes closing and seeing him no more. Soon, the sun was blacked out by sleep—the first relaxing sleep she had had in months. And then suddenly she heard his soft voice at her ear, and it was shaping sounds into words.

"It's two o'clock in the afternoon," he said. "Do you have to be home?"

She opened her eyes languidly. His face was immediately above her, his head resting on one elbow on the pillow. She smiled slightly at the shape of his hair; it was completely mussed; a jumble of black curls.

"Two o'clock in what afternoon?" she said.

"Friday afternoon."

"How marvelous," she replied. "I've never slept till two o'clock in the afternoon in my life. How marvelous that it should be a Friday afternoon when it happens."

"I agree," he said. "But should you be some place?"

"No," she said simply, and then she rolled softly over on her side, and closed her eyes, and began to see softly glowing lights, purple and green. "Just here," she mumbled softly, grateful that her daughter was staying with a friend through the weekend.

Then she felt his tongue gently lick the back of her neck.

"Are you sure you want to go back to sleep?" he asked softly.

The tingling that was traveling down her spine was now turning the purple and green lights into red and blue. She could feel the tongue leave the hairline at the back of her neck, and follow the tingling down her spine. She could feel his hand slowly draw down the sheet from her naked body, until it fell far below her knees. Through the multicolored lights that were flashing in front of her eyes, she heard his voice drift up to her. "Are you absolutely sure?"

"Not absolutely," she answered. The tongue began to play now with the small circle that marked the very top of the opening where her buttocks met. The lights were now flashing more and more red, with the blue colors moving slowly out to the very edges of her vision.

His hand slowly slid down her stomach. When it reached her belly button, one of his fingers made a series of slow, gentle circles there. Her body was now marvelously trapped between the two slow circles—his finger on her belly button, his tongue on the very beginning of the crack between her buttocks. She lay there completely unmoving, unwilling to disturb the electric circuit set up by his finger and his tongue.

The tongue paused for a moment. His voice drifted up to her ears again.

"We have no place to go, then?" it said.

"No place at all," she replied.

The finger slid down her skin. The tongue slid down her

skin. Her eyes opened automatically when the finger and the tongue reached their final destinations at exactly the same time. The red inner lights changed to a burst of yellow outer lights, a huge circular spot of sun resting on one of the photographs of a cell, mounted over the mantelpiece. She lay there on the bed, with her mouth wide open, gasping for breath every five or ten seconds, feeling the waves of psychedelic orgasm pass back up her spinal cord to her brain again, one after the other.

She lay there sideways on the bed, at two o'clock in the afternoon, on some date she could not remember, and waited helplessly for his finger and his tongue to stop—and hoping they never would.

17.

She awoke at four-thirty that afternoon. Michael was sleeping next to her, flat on his back, no motion, no sound but his breathing. Her bare arm was lying on his bare arm, and she withdrew it gently. He did not stir. She was alone now in the room, isolated by his sleep, by his removal into his dreams. Watching the reflection of the late afternoon sun, she began to think her own thoughts, and make her own judgments.

It was done, she thought. It was finished, and paid for. And it had been marvelous. She lay there with her head on his pillow and marveled at the quality of it. Close to fourteen hours of continuous lovemaking—less three or four throwaway hours for sleep. No sense of time. No sense of exhaustion. No sense of repetition or boredom or endurance. Hungry bodies—his as hungry as hers—why? Flesh raised to the highest limit of sensitivity, and kept there for hours. Sex raised to the level just below love. It was true, everything that Sally had said. Women who had never known true love would surely mistake sex like this for real love. Given a man who could constantly provide them with sex like this, they would never age, never grow sick or sad, never wake up one morning to see death standing at the foot of their beds.

She had never known such a lover existed. She had never

known such a love act existed. In bed he put Aaron to shame. In this very bed, she had let him put Aaron to shame.

She was now a traded woman. What Aaron had tried to do to her, she had done now for herself. She no longer belonged to Aaron, or to any man, or to any human being but herself. The jade band around the second finger of her left hand was now simply a jade band and nothing more.

She lay next to the man who had given her more orgasms than she had dreamed possible in the course of a single night, and she looked again at his beautiful sleeping profile, and mourned the one ingredient whose absence made those orgasms meaningless, and made that profile as incidental as the head on a statue of stone.

She mourned love. She mourned the world of reality that did not include love. She was now in a new world that transcended faithfulness, that violated fidelity, that ate away like acid the marriage bonds and left you in some beautiful stranger's bed. And didn't even tell you what to say to him when he woke up.

They had won. The world had won. Johnny had won. Aaron had won. Michael had won. They had all brought her—triumphantly, ecstatically—into the real world. She was cast out of the garden forever. But she had never known how empty the real world would be. What did a woman do, in this new real world, when her self was reduced to nothing more than a brain and a body? Where there was no garden. Where there were no flowers, or trees—only orgasms.

She laughed out loud, loud enough to disturb the sleeping profile alongside her. Because the thought struck her—what you do is plant a new garden. In the desert of this new, real world, she thought, you remember those trees and flowers. And you plant those old memories, those old hopes and dreams. And you build again—to value, and to commitment, and to love.

His eyelids began to flutter. His body began to awaken. He rolled over on his left side, toward her. As he rolled, the sheet fell off his naked body, and exposed it. She looked at the magnificent shoulders, the broad, flat chest, the slim stomach, and then stopped—eyes paralyzed with shock—at his right hip.

It was a map of scars. White scars, red scars, ragged scars, smooth scars. The hip, the side of his leg, the back of his right buttock—all were covered with scars. It was a map of pain. She stared at it with horrified eyes, until he rolled over on his back again, and opened his beautiful brown eyes.

He looked around the room. "It's four-thirty," he said dazedly. "Of what day?"

"The same day," she said softly, reaching out and touching his shoulder. "Still Friday."

"My God," he said. "Only two hours since we woke up the last time?"

"About that," she said.

"After that," he said, still not moving his head off the pillow, "we should have slept through the entire night."

"After that," she agreed, "we should have. But we didn't."

His eyes were gaining more clarity as the two of them talked. Suddenly they blinked in an instant realization, and he looked down and saw that he was nude, that the map of pain on his hip was fully exhibited. Almost instinctively, she thought, far too fast for it to be a reasoned action, his hand shot out and pulled the sheet over the bottom half of his body.

"I'm a little chilly," he said at once.

"I saw it," she said. She thought of glossing it over. She thought of a dozen different subjects to pursue instead. But none of them held the honesty she desperately needed. "What is it?"

"I told you about it before," he said. "My hip—"

"Yes," she replied. "You said—Sally said—something about your hip being broken in Korea. But that was no sign of a break. There must have been almost a dozen scars there. You must have had almost a dozen—"

"It's a rotten subject," he said, pushing himself up on the pillow with his elbows. "This is the least appropriate time to discuss it." He jumped up from the bed, tearing the sheet off the bed behind him, and wrapping it around the lower part of his body like a sarong. "Besides," he said, "I'm famished. Will you eat a ham omelette?"

There was no road left but to retreat. "Do I have any choice?" she asked.

"Not the slightest," he said, smiling. "Not in this apartment, with this kitchen, and this cook. Unless you'd like just plain English muffins, orange juice, and coffee. That's all we eat here."

"How about two ham omelettes?" she asked.

"For both of us?"

"No, for me. Start working on them now," she said,

getting up awkwardly from the bed and gathering her things from several corners of the room. "I'm going to try to make myself presentable by the time you've finished them." She managed to walk barefooted and bare-assed into the bathroom, and close the door after her.

Ten minutes later she put on her quite creased clothes from the night before—she hadn't even thought to bring a change of clothes for the next day—and used what little instruments she had in the tiny cosmetic kit in her handbag to repair her make-up. She stood for three minutes before the closed door of the bathroom, not quite daring to come out in the apartment again, not knowing how to look, how to smile, what to say.

"Hey," he said from the kitchen right next to her. "Going to take all day in there? There are four ham omelettes sitting on the table, growing cold."

Her hand shot forward and threw open the door. "A fate worse than frigidity," she said, far too flippantly, and let herself be led across the kitchen and then across the room, with its bed now neatly made and folded back into a couch, to the chair at the bridge table, directly in front of the window.

"Everything look all right?" he said, pointing down to the food.

"Scrumptious," she answered. "Just don't expect to get back the plates. I'm going to eat them."

"Dig right in," he said. "Don't wait for me. I'll be right back." And he was gone, to reappear in moments, fully dressed in his slacks and shoes, and a fresh white shirt. He threw one leg over the back of the chair opposite her, was settled in it in seconds, and had his first forkful to his mouth before she could even finish a sip of orange juice.

"I like to do one thing at a time," he mumbled through the full mouth of ham omelette. "I do them well that way."

"So?" she asked.

"So, I'm going to spend the next five minutes gorging myself and nothing else." He looked at her plate. "You have a dainty little head start on me," he said, "but I'll still race you through the two omelettes, and two English muffins apiece. No talking; just jawing. Starting now," he said. "The first one to make a sound, or the last one to finish every scrap, does the dishes. Okay?"

"Okay," she said.

"Here we go," he said. "Let us have a reverent silence."

He was good at gorging, she had to admit, but so was she.

Her hands worked smoothly and automatically, and her jaw was in fine fettle. In four and a half minutes she had popped the last little scrap of English muffin into her mouth, and he was still lowering his fork on the last remaining sliver of ham on his plate. Instantly, she threw down her napkin, pushed back her chair, and laughed. He looked up and swore, then grudgingly began carrying plates off to the kitchen.

"What do we do now?" he said.

"Talk," she replied.

"Good enough," he said. "And what then?"

"Let's let the talk decide that."

"Fair enough," he said. "Go ahead."

"Is that all there is of our transaction?"

"What transaction?" he asked. Then his eyes lighted with a fond awareness, and the great smile broke across his face. "Oh, yes," he said. "Our simple fuck. Yes," he went on, "I think you can say that end of the transaction has been completed, and"—he nodded in silent salute to her—"completed very well."

"Nothing else?" she asked.

"Nothing else. I hereby give formal notice that I consider the transaction completed."

"Then I assume that the formula for the face cream is mine?"

"You consider right. Would you like to call up your lawyer"—he looked up at the clock—"tomorrow, and have him draw up the papers to your satisfaction?"

"I think tomorrow is Saturday," she said.

"How nice," he said. "What do you usually do Saturdays?"

"Which brings up the next point," she answered. "Am I under any continuing obligation to repeat this transaction?"

His face grew surprised and then grim. "None whatsoever."

"Good," she replied, then she smiled. "I'm just trying to get the terms of the transaction clear in my own mind. I believe it's what you call 'being tough.' I guess my father would have called it 'speaking your mind, so that both of you know where you are.' "

"Fine," he said. "Here we are then. Now what do you want to do?"

"Anything I want?" she asked quiety.

"With me?" he asked in return.

"Definitely with you," she replied.

"A day full of surprises," he said. Then he looked at the newly made couch. "I don't imagine it's over there, is it?"

"No," she said with quiet determination.

"But with me?" he repeated again.

"Yes," she said. "With you."

"All right," he said slowly. "I'll buy it. Yes, anything you want."

"Good," she said. And her face became far more serious than it had been at any time since he first touched her the night before. "I want to learn everything you know about genes and creams—"

"Everything?"

"Everything you can teach me in a single weekend, even if we don't go out to eat, walk, take a breather, even stop long enough to—"

"Not even long enough to—"

She looked again into the limitless brown eyes. Her face smiled by its own volition. Her body trembled by its own instinct.

"Well," she said, "Two days is a rather long, lonely time."

18.

They spent the entire weekend together. She had no commitments. He had no commitments. They never emerged from his apartment, except to go out and eat, until early Monday morning. In between, in the time that they devoted to each other, they primarily did two things. First, make love. And second, learn. They spent as much time at his desk as they did in his bed. And he taught her an overview of what man had learned about the command system of the body—the gene—since 1953. Twenty-two years of intense scientific exploration were translated by him into glowing words and diagrams.

It was a cram course in how life really works. And she filled her mind as full as she filled her body. She learned the molecular structure of both RNA and DNA. She learned how genes were made up, how they were turned on and off, how they sometimes went wrong, and how to return them to normalcy again. She learned how tiny viruses could be used to cut into genes like an ax, and make them smaller, and digestible, like the proteins in her cream.

And, above all, she learned every single fragment possible about the manufacture, the workings, the possible hazards, and the testings of her own cream. Almost all day Sunday was spent exploring the genetic structure of that cream. How it worked on the collagen under the skin. How long it would last. How fast it would work on different women.

And here her own dreams began to interact with his stored-up knowledge. She must have asked a hundred questions on that Sunday—some of which he had not asked himself. Why could the active ingredient in the cream be used only at night? This was her first question. Why could it not be used in an invisible makeup base for daytime treatment as well?

Could it be added to a shampoo, or setting lotion, or some other treatment for the hair, so that the damage and aging of hair could be retarded in the same way as the damage and aging of skin?

Were there other parts of the body—for example, the hands—that could use the same direct skin-feeding as he had developed for the face? What, for example, caused the brown aging spots on the skin of women's hands? Were they also related to collagen breakdowns? If so, could this cream or an adaptation of it be used to wash away those brown spots?

At the end of that Sunday, she had drawn up a product chart that built his original inspiration into a complete business that could take over the entire counter of a department store, and furnish a woman with everything she needed to look younger, from foot cream to lipstick.

She had never been in business, but she had spent fourteen years of her life, at countless dinner parties, talking to New York's best businessmen. She had asked questions during those conversations. These men, flattered by her attention, had provided the answers. All these conversations—hundreds and hundreds of them—had somehow, she knew, stayed stored in her brain, with almost total recall. Conversations unrelated to such subjects had faded away the next day. And now she knew why. She had been waiting for this opportunity all her life. Michael was right. She was Prometheus bound, waiting for the chains to be loosened, and for the opportunity to give her gifts to the women all over the world who needed them.

They went to bed, to make their final love of the weekend, at three-thirty on Sunday night—Monday morning, actually. By that time, the entire business, its full product line, had taken shape under her fingers, with his encouragement and technical information. She noticed a new respect on his part in bed that night, combined, thankfully, with an increased sexual drive. When they got to sleep, it must have been close to six-thirty or seven. She awoke at nine, and left without breakfast, in the same shirt and slacks she had worn to the apartment on Thursday night.

But it didn't matter. When she got to her own apartment, she was floating. In her body she carried more sexual excitement and gratification than she had ever conceived possible. In her handbag, she carried the outline for—not a business, but if the first tests proved valid, and if her reasoning was right, which she believed it was—an entire industry.

No one was home in her apartment. She put her handbag down on her desk, opened it, and took out the scraps of paper on which her future, and her business, rested. She had just unfolded them, when the phone rang.

She picked it up and heard Pam's frantic voice.

"Where have you been all weekend?" Pam asked.

"Is Lacy all right?" she asked quickly.

"Yes—yes—fine," Pam said. "Little John's fine, too. And so is Aaron. But, honey, prepare yourself for a shock."

"What happened?"

"Okay—here it is straight. Albee's had a heart attack. Thursday night. They thought he wouldn't live through Saturday. But he has. He's still alive, at Lenox Hill Hospital. And he's been calling for you—I mean calling for you— every single hour since Thursday night."

19.

She dialed the number immediately, fought her way through the hospital operators, then past what seemed to be a private nurse made of granite, then directly to Albee himself.

"You're alive!" were his first words on the phone.

"You're alive!" she replied in return.

"You're alive; I'm preserved," he said. "It's not much, but it's certainly much better now that I know you're in this world, too."

"This world?" she asked.

"The world you come back to after you black out in one of these places," he went on, and his voice sounded a little weaker than usual, but still—thank God—like Albee. "When you come back," he said, "you find out you're still alive. Then you've got to start putting your new world together, to see how much it resembles the old one you left."

She shuddered at the thought. The same night—Thursday —both of them had entered new and different worlds. Hers had become magnificent. His was—what?

"Are you there?" he asked.

She had been lost in thought too long. "I'm here, always," she said. "When can I see you?"

"Do you mind elderly men in bed?" he asked with a tiny laugh.

"I adore elderly men in bed," she said immediately.

"Then you can see me tonight," he said. "The official visiting hours are from seven to nine."

"I'll be there at seven o'clock sharp."

"If you are," he said, "I won't see you. I want you here at ten minutes past nine, and not one second sooner." His voice speeded up. "Get to the hospital before nine, or they won't let you up. There's a waiting area about four doors down from my room. Wait till ten past nine, and then no one will stop you. All right?" he asked.

"All right."

"I'll see you then," he said, the voice fading slightly now. And then, "Thank God," he said. "Thank God you're in this world too."

At nine that evening, she walked into the hospital, went directly to the waiting area, and let eight minutes pass.

At exactly eight minutes past nine she got up and walked toward his room. A rather tall, impeccably dressed nurse was standing at the door. She looked at Melissa, snorted, and stepped into the room, allowing Melissa to enter.

The room was the largest one they had in the hospital. The first thing that assaulted you when you walked into it was the overpowering smell of flowers. There must have been seventy-five bouquets, filled with orange, red, yellow, violet, even multicolored flowers Melissa had never seen, and could not name.

He was waiting for her in state in his bed, the end of which had been raised to a semisitting position; his head and shoulders laying almost verticall on three beautiful down pillows. His beard had been trimmed, and his hair combed by a master barber. Aside from the stanchion supporting the two bottles of glucose, and their extensions piercing his right arm, it was impossible to tell by sight that the man had just suffered a serious heart attack. His face was slightly flushed, but the flush gave a healthy look to the lovable round contenance it colored. His welcoming smile when she walked into the room was even more dazzling than Michael's, and his left hand rose slowly into the air to bring her to his side, and to embrace her.

She walked past the nurse, dropped her bag on one of the tables, in the narrow space between two bouquets, and—despite the seriousness of his condition—almost flung herself into his arms.

"Oh God, Albee," she said.

"Hello, beautiful one," he whispered.

Her cheek was against his in an instant. She could feel the fuzzy beard and mustache, the slightly heated skin of his face, the softness and smoothness of that skin as her lips touched it. Her arms wrapped around his right shoulder, and under his left arm, holding his solid body, pulling herself as close as she dared to the little man's firm chest. His left arm reached around her shoulders, and she felt it stroking her hair as they embraced. She was crying, soundlessly, at the same time that her lips kissed, and then rekissed, and then kissed again the smooth skin of his face. She knew the nurse was looking, and she didn't care. Albee was alive, he was here, still in the flesh, still in her new world. And she was still in his.

She drew back and looked at him closely. Except for a slight tint of red in his eyes, she could see no facial difference. She reached over and grabbed her handbag, and pulled out a tissue, and began dabbing the mascara around her eyes. Then she took a new tissue and began dabbing his eyes too.

"You look marvelous," she said. "I know it sounds ridiculous, but you do."

"Miss Everet," he said, with the customary tone of command in his voice, "will you please go and take a long pee in the nurse's bathroom down the hall?"

The nurse glared at him. He went on: "Close the door when you leave. And don't let anyone—yourself most of all—come in, or open that door till I ring for you."

"Mr. Lauder," she said, "it's quite late."

"I paid five thousand dollars for this watch," he said, gesturing to the thin beauty strapped to his left wrist. "I am perfectly capable of reading it. I'll tell you when to come back in." He smiled at her again, the same commanding smile. "Have a good pee," he said, "and close the door behind you."

The nurse left. The door clicked silently closed behind her. His left hand came out, and wrapped itself around her right.

"Let me look at you," he said. "Let me touch you." "You're real. You're true."

"Of course I am, you marvelous ninny," she replied.

"But you weren't for three days," he said.

She turned her head away from him. "No," she said. "I wasn't for three days."

He looked at her for a moment. She could feel his gaze, but couldn't meet it. Then his left hand tightened on her hand beneath it. When he spoke again, it was in the same loving voice that she had luxuriated in so many times.

"Did you have a good time, Angel?"

She turned and looked at him. There was nothing but love in the bearded face.

"Yes," she said simply.

"I'm glad," he said. Then the eyes blinked once; something was filed away permanently inside of them, and again he said, "I'm glad."

She looked into the devoted eyes again. A conversation had just been concluded—a conversation of thousands of words, and four full months. It had been concluded in two words— "I'm glad." It was over. It was done. There was no need to go into further detail, and there would be no change—no change at all—in the relationship between them.

"But you," she said.

"But me," he repeated, with his magnificent shrug.

"Why did you have to—?"

"I didn't," he said very quietly, and very gently. "God did. And you don't question God—not even we crazy Jews—you don't question God about these things."

"But what did the doctors say?" she asked. "How are you?"

He looked at her through the same smiling eyes, and his left hand tightened a little upon hers. The smile never dimmed, but the shoulders shrugged again, when he quietly said, "I'm dying."

She almost pulled her hand away from his in distress, in shock, in negation. But his hand held on more firmly to hers, and she returned the squeeze more firmly still.

"I don't believe it," she said. "Get new doctors."

He laughed. "I've already bought the best doctors in New York," he said. "Yesterday, I had the best doctor in London—the man who kept Rothschild alive for three years after he should have been dead—flown over here to confirm their opinion. They all agree, my beautiful one," he said. "My heart has a rip in it. It won't even hold me up straight anymore. I'm going to be like this," and the eyes suddenly darkened, and she caught a brief glimpse of pain and outright fury in them for the first time in their relationship, "like this, for as long as they can keep it ticking. For two months, for four months, maybe even—if I'm lucky—for six months. Like this," he repeated, "until the heart stops."

He turned his face away from hers for a moment. She clung to his hand, as though she were clinging to the hand of a man on the edge of a cliff. Then his face turned back to hers again, and it was perfectly serene.

When he spoke his voice was calm. "That drawer in the top of the night table, there. Open it."

She reached out, and silently pulled open the drawer. "Underneath the stack of tissues," he said, "you'll see a small envelope with your name."

She found the envelope hidden between several layers of tissues. The envelope was engraved with Albee's name and address, and her first name was written on the front in his fine, miniature hand. She took the envelope, and began to pass it to him.

"No," he said immediately. "It's for you. Open it."

Inside was a check made out from the Melinger Corporation. It was made out to her. It was for the sum of fifty thousand dollars. It was signed by Albee.

"There," he said. "is the money for your cosmetics idea. May you use it in good health."

"Thank you," she said. "But whom do I pay it back to? You? Or this company?"

"Oh God," he said. "You pay it back to no one. That's who you make the check out to when you've made your first fortune—N-o o-n-e."

"I don't understand," she said, looking up from the check to his face.

"One day," he said. "That's all it took them—one day. I got sick on Thursday night, right? My oldest son, Harry, God bless him, he was here with two lawyers at the bedside Friday afternoon. Flew in from San Francisco. They must have spent all Thursday night working. I never saw such powers of attorney with such details in my whole life. He had a different one for each of the companies I own." Albee smiled. It was a weasel's smile. A proud smile as the father of a younger weasel. "Some of the companies," he went on, "I didn't know he knew I had. He's clever, that one. He's going to make my money into more money—you just wait and see."

"But the check?" she asked.

"Oh yes," Albee said. "That's one of the companies Harry doesn't know about. I kept it for little emergencies like this. It's owned by another company, which is owned by another company, which is owned by still another company —you know. This check—they won't find out about it if they look for it with an electron microscope for twenty years. By that time, how are they going to justify getting it back? The corporation doesn't even have an office or a book." He chuckled. His left hand moved up and down on hers, in a patting motion. "Keep it, maidela. Nobody will ever miss fifty thousand or so."

"I can't," she said.

"Look, love," he said. "I wanted to give you something all along, in case anything happened to me. But there was no way I could put you in my will. I've got three kids. They're good kids, but they're tough kids. They'd fight a clause in the will, and besides, I don't want to battle with them, no matter what their faults, from the other side."

"But—"

"Nobody'll know. Nobody'll care. Beautiful one, there's ninety million dollars more sitting out there—that's what they care about. This is petty change to them." And he chuckled again. "One week's lawyers' fees—that's what they're going to find out. Leave them alone, maidela. Don't cause them any more trouble. They got enough already.''

"I—"

"Fold it up," he said. "Now. Put it in your purse—that's a good girl.''

He took her hand in his, and raised it gently to his lips. The lips were soft; her hand tingled at their touch. When he lowered the hand, his face was dead serious again. When he spoke, the Jewish accent was gone.

"Look, darling," he said, "I apologize—I honestly apologize—for acting like Santa Claus to you. But it can't be done any other way now. And you've been Santa Claus to me so many times in the last few months, that I had to play the role, at least once more, for you.''

She looked at the small, flushed, adoring face. She felt the delcate hand wrapped around her own. She heard the words, knew the love that stood behind those words, and quite suddenly, without warning, she broke down completely in front of him, and began to cry again.

"Don't," he said immediately.

"I can't help myself," she said.

"Beautiful one," he said. "Stop. Please. Tears I don't need now.''

"But I—" She looked up at the radiant face on the pillow again. "I failed both of us so completely." The tears dried up in an instant. They were replaced immediately by self-hate. "It's you who've played Santa Claus to me in the last four months. I could have played him once, just once. Oh God," she said.

There was silence from the bed. She felt the pressure from his hand slacken. A hundred different regrets crossed his face in a single moment. Then he smiled.

"Melissa." It was the first time she could ever remember him calling her by her real name. "Melissa," he said, "it just isn't your way of doing things.''

"I was an imbecile," she said.

"Was?" he asked.

She looked directly into his eyes. "Was," she said bluntly. "If I had the chance today—if I could turn the clock back—then," and she grabbed his hand with both of hers, "then I would have gone to bed with you that first night—right after the backgammon game. Right after the first kiss. Right after I first realized that I loved you.''

His entire face changed. A radiance came over it. A different glow. A happiness that she could feel pouring back to her through the contact with his left hand.

"Say that again," he said.

"I love you," she said immediately. "I love you, Albee Lauder. And if I had the chance"—she threw back her head—"oh God, if I had the chance, I'd go to bed with you now in a second."

He chuckled. Despite the tubes leading down from the glucose, there seemed suddenly to be no sickness or weakness anywhere in his body. "You mean that?" he asked.

"Yes. I mean that."

"Aren't I a little old for you?"

"You're young for me," she answered. "You've always been young for me."

"God's blessing," he said. "An angel," he went on. "An angel of deliverance." Then, suddenly, he took his hand out of hers for the first time that evening, and placed it over his heart. "It's the first time it's felt normal in four days," he said quietly. "Do me a favor, Angel. Say it all again for me now, will you please?"

"I love you," she said. "I've loved you for four months. And if I had the chance, I'd go to bed with you this second."

He threw back his head and laughed a wild laugh that she had never dreamed existed within him. His head turned upward. His eyes looked to the ceiling. "God's mercy," he said. "God's blessing." And now a wild impossible smile dominated his face.

"Who says you haven't got the chance?" he said quietly. "Now, the only question—the only question, my beautiful one—is whether you have the love to make use of that chance, now."

20.

She sat staring at him, clinging to his left hand, trying to understand what he was saying. His smile flickered. He waited to let his last remark sink in, and then went on.

"I'm going to be honest with you, Angel—possibly more honest than any other man has ever been with you before. Do you think you can take such a massive dose of honesty?"

"I don't know," she said candidly.

"The facts are these," he said. "I have had a—rather large—heart attack. It didn't quite kill me, but it came close. There's too much scar tissue on my heart now for it to function properly. Eventually it will happen all over again. But this time it will be final." He smiled. "Doctors don't lie to you, if you pay them enough."

"Go on," she said.

"Till then," he said, "the heart will keep on working in somewhat the usual way, but faintly. I won't be able to play golf, or fly in an airplane, or eat a great dinner, or drink a great wine, or—especially—make love to a woman.

"Angel," he said, "Can you imagine me here—or at home in a replica of this room? Lying in this bed all day, being shielded from all real life by that Valkyrie outside. Never dancing, never riding, never making love again?"

"No," she said to the man on the bed, with the tubes running into his arm. "I can't imagine you that way at all."

"They want to make me that way."

"They can't."

"They can't," he repeated. "Not for six months, not for four months, not for two months, not for two weeks, not for two hours. You know that, don't you, Angel?"

"Yes," she said. "I know that."

He smiled again. "So you have your chance—now."

She smiled back at him. "You offer me that chance?"

His face turned serious. "I beg it of you," he said. "I don't believe them—I want you to know this first. I don't care if an orgasm is the equivalent of jumping over a mountain at one bound. I've had too many of them to believe that one will kill me—now or ever. But if it does—if it does— that's God's will too, and it's all right."

"Is it really all right?" she asked.

"Perfectly satisfactory, and long overdue," he said. "Is it all right with you if it happens that way?"

Melissa's mind was moving at lightning speed now. She laughed inwardly at herself and at Michael. What real test had Michael put her to, in order to enter his "real" world? To sleep with a gorgeous man when she had been without a man of her own for four months? Michael's world was as far from real as her own former world had been. There was no true gamble in taking Michael's challenge.

But what if Albee was wrong? It had been only four days since his attack. The doctor's diagnosis was almost certainly right. If she agreed, and he died in the act, then what? Would she then be this beloved man's murderer? If another attack began, she wouldn't leave the room without obtaining help for him. Would she have any career, any name left, if it turned out that way? It was ridiculous. Insane. But it was the only thing in her new world that she wanted to do. It left him—either way—still in charge of his own life. It left her—either way—still in charge of her own life.

"God's angel," he said. "Now?"

"If you wish," she said, "now."

"Open the third drawer down in the night table," he suddenly commanded. "Underneath the nightshirts, there's a rather bulky envelope. Get it for me."

She found it almost at once and handed it to him. He slipped off the rubber band that bound the envelope. Inside, there were several dozen—she couldn't tell, at first glance, how many—hundred dollar bills. Each ten were joined by a single ordinary paper clip.

He pulled out one paper clip full. And then he reached back in the envelope and pulled out a second. Then he bound the envelope again, and handed it to her.

"Emergency money," he said softly. "You never know, in a place like this, when you're going to need a quick Nova Scotia and bagel sandwich. Put it back in the drawer where you found it, please."

She did. At the same time, he pressed the call button. Within seconds, Nurse Valkyrie was back in the room. They glanced at each other—she and Albee—for a second. Then he said, "Come here, please."

She walked halfway across the room, toward the two of them. "Come closer," Albee said, and she moved slowly toward him, till she was right next to the bed.

He looked straight up into her iron-hard face. He picked up one bundle of money. "This," he said, "is one thousand dollars. Please count it."

She looked startled for a moment, then unloosened the paper clip, and counted the ten hundred dollar bills. Then she put the paper clip back on the bills again, and said without expression, "That's right."

''And this,'' he said, ''is a second thousand dollars.'' He passed the money to her. ''Pease count it again.''

She did, and then he went on. ''I want you to take that money, and put it in the pocket of your uniform,'' he said. ''Then I want you to go out, and take a chair, and sit beside the door until I call you again. Until I do so,'' he said, ''I don't care who comes by—the night drug nurse, an intern, the doctor, the head of the hospital himself—I don't want any of them to get into this room. If they get in here,'' he said, ''the two thousand dollars comes back to me. If we are undisturbed until I call you, you take it home. Do you understand?''

The nurse looked at Melissa, looked back at Albee, looked at the two thousand dollars in her hand; there was not a single blink of her eyes, not the slightest change in her face. She folded the money, pursed her lips, and said, quite simply, ''I understand.''

''Then get out of here, please,'' he said.

''There'll be the head doctor coming through to see you at eleven o'clock. There nothing I can do to stop him. Everyone else I can put off.''

Albee looked at the watch on his wrist. There was over an hour to go. ''Fine,'' he said. ''Make sure the door is closed tight after you, and that it stays that way.''

Without another word the nurse left the room and closed the door behind her.

''I think an hour should give us just about enough time, don't you?'' he said.

His eyes were sparkling. Her eyes caught the sparkle and lit into fires of their own. ''If we hurry a little,'' she said.

''How''—and he looked about the room—''do we go about it?''

''Like this,'' she said, and stood up from the bed. She had worn a brown suit from Saks Fifth Avenue. She looked at the light above the bed, and turned it to a half-muted glow. Then, quite slowly, she began to unbutton the jacket of her suit. She watched his eyes with each movement of her hand. He had sunk back on the pillow, his face even more flushed than it had been when she walked into the room, and she saw with delight the excitement in his eyes when the jacket parted, and revealed the silk chemise that she wore under it.

Never once did the thought that someone was going to break the nurse's guard, and come into the room, even occur to her. It simply didn't matter. Never once did she question the authenticity of the act, or her sheer enjoyment in performing it. She was performing her first striptease, for an audience of one, and all that she cared about was his reaction to the performance, and the repayment of the love that he had given her all these weeks.

Within seconds the chemise and brassiere were on the floor. He was breathing heavily now. She reached down and took his left hand and kissed it. Then she lifted his hand, and directed it first to one nipple, and then to the other.

She straightened up again and stepped back three or four paces. She slipped her hands underneath her skirt and quickly removed her panty hose. Then her hands moved back to her skirt, and in a single motion the skirt fell to her feet. She stood in front of him now in white silk panties and brown shoes. She shook her head and let the masses of blond hair fall all around her shoulders and her back.

"Turn around," he whispered hoarsely. "Please turn around."

She smiled again and then slowly began to turn. When she had made the fourth full turn, her hands came slowly up to her waist and, without stopping the slow circular motion of her body, she lowered the white silk panties down to her knees and then, through their own weight, let them drop to the floor.

Now she was perfectly nude in front of him, still turning slowly, still letting him see every inch of her body. Never had she been more thankful for the gifts God had given her than she was at that moment, when she saw the pleasure in his eyes.

Finally she came to a slow halt directly in front of him. She shook her way out of one of the brown shoes, and then the other. The second shoe she kicked up in the air.

Then she sat down on the bed beside him, naked, and let his hand run over her entire body, wherever it wished to go. While he was doing this, she slowly began to pull down the sheet from the bed. While he was stroking her body, she began unbuttoning his nightshirt. Within moments, she had parted all the lovely white buttons, spread the nightshirt aside, and exposed the marvelous little body to her view.

He was small, but his body was still an object of beauty to her. He had a good chest, a still-solid abdomen, strong legs and, there in the center of his body, now fully erect and surprisingly predominant for a man of his size, was his ultimate instrument of love.

She looked down at it, and then slowly her hands joined at the very base of it. Then, without a word, instinctively, she lowered her head to it, and began rubbing it up and down her cheek, before putting her lips to it. This, she told herself, this was reality. To allow love was real. To make love physical was real. To let love blossom, wherever it might grow, under whatever conditions, no matter what the hazards—this, to her, forever, would be the only reality.

She felt his hand on her hair. ''No, Angel,'' he said. ''I love what you're doing—too much. Stop it now, please, or we won't be able to do what I really want.''

And so, moving smoothly and gracefully, she placed one knee on one side of his body, and the other knee on the other side.

At the moment of welcome, of coming home again, his eyes closed for a second, and he gave out a deep gasp. And then what should have been done, was at last done. And what should have been given, was at last given. And what should have been shared, was at last shared. They were together—at last.

The orgasm must have lasted—for both of them—over a full minute. Then, his head sank back on the pillows, and on his face there was a peace and a satisfaction that she had never seen there before.

''Angel,'' he said, raising his hand and touching her face. ''Angel. Angel. Angel.''

''I love you. Do you know that now?'' she replied softly.

''I've known that for months now,'' he said. ''Of all the things I'll take with me,'' he continued, ''that will be the most superb.''

There was nothing more to say. She bent down from the side of the bed, and gathered up her things, then dressed herself in front of him. Then she went to his private bathroom, and wetted a washcloth with soap and water, and came back to the bed and cleaned his body and dried it with a towel. She buttoned the nightshirt, and pulled up the sheet till he was covered as he had been before.

Then, when she was done, and was reaching for her purse, his left hand came out, and took her hand in it. His face was transfigured. His eyes were heavy, and she could tell that a deep sleep was only minutes away.

"I had forgotten God," he whispered heavily.

"And now?" she asked.

The hand left hers and came up and stroked her face. "He created you," he said. "Ergo, He exists." A faint smile crossed his face. "Do me one final favor?" he asked.

"Of course."

"Don't forget Him yourself," he said, "ever."

"Never," she said.

"There's no world," he said, "no world, without you and Him."

"No world. No reality at all," she said.

"Never forget," he said.

"Never," she said.

"Good night, Angel," he whispered again, more heavily. And then the eyes closed, and she looked down at his beautiful sleeping face.

"Good night," she whispered to the sleeping face. "Good night, Albee, who always was—and who always will be."

Then she walked to the door, and opened it, and walked past Albee's nurse to the elevator, and then down to the street, and the black night, and the glorious moon and stars that made it a heaven.

21.

The next morning, when she awoke, fully refreshed, she called the hospital to find out whether Albee was all right. There was a smile in his voice; he told her that he was fine, "better than ever," but that "twenty doctors" were there and he'd have to call her back. Routine was reestablished in her life. Albee was fine; there had been no physical consequences at all of the previous night. Michael had been incredible; but that episode was over. She looked down at her desk. She had Albee's check, and Michael's cream. Now her task was to combine the two of them into a viable business.

And then the thought struck her. Michael's cream. Albee's check. One man's product, and another man's money. And, she wondered suddenly, where was she in that combination?

Of course—the recipient, the beneficiary. Cinderella, with not one fairy godfather, but two. One furnishing the pumpkin-coach; the other furnishing the mice turned into horses.

Looking through her windows, she saw that it was a bright, blue, cloudless day. She sat down at her desk, and stared at the coach and the horses.

Cinderella, she thought. Always Cinderella. Always a fairy godfather, who gave her the tools she needed a build a new life. First Johnny, with his made-to-order subordinate house-wife role. And then Aaron, with his glowing gift of art, food, wine, learning.

And now, when she had been forced to leave those fairy tales behind, when she had set out, desolate and alone, in search of her own reality, what had she found? Nothing but a new, enlarged, super-Cinderella, with not one glass slipper, but two.

There before her was a jar of miracle cosmetic, sitting on a fifty thousand dollar check. There was no way she could break the spell by calling up Albee, and asking him to take back the check. Besides, there would be no future demands, no future obligations to Albee. But there might be from Michael. It was his discovery, and not hers. He might want it sold in a certain way. He had already laid out his plans for department store distribution with her. He had already told her to contact his friends at Bergdorf's, Saks, and Bendel's. He had already called the best packaging man in New York, to have the layout of the jar label done *his* way. And he had already made an appointment for this morning to contact his private label house, to begin the first prototype run of the cream.

All glass slippers had strings attached, she thought. Strings that ended in a male hand, a male will. That was why such slippers broke so easily, or were pulled right off your feet when you tried to turn in your own direction.

I can't get out of fairyland on glass slippers, she thought. I'd rather walk barefooted into reality, bruised and bleeding, if I have to.

She reached for the phone, and began to dial Michael's number. From now on there'll be one iron rule, she said to herself as the phone started ringing. No more pumpkins. No more horses. No more slippers. And—above all, no more—no matter how gorgeous, no matter how generous—no more fairy godfathers.

22.

He came on the phone immediately. His voice—even the electronic reproduction of his voice—turned the sunlight brighter, turned her room larger and lonelier, turned the flesh of her body warm and yearning.

The first words he said were, "How is he?"

He knew. Of course he knew. And then she thought, the whole world—including Aaron—had to know.

"Better," she said. And then she added, "Much better—now."

There was no change in the tone of his voice. He was not a mindreader. It was not a mythical world, but a real one. "Thank God," he said. "I like him. I genuinely like him."

"So do I," she replied, "without limit."

"You've seen him?"

"Yes."

"And the prognosis?"

"Not good." And then, before he could go on with the questioning, she said, "Michael—Michael, I want to thank you."

"For what?"

"For caring."

"I do."

"For the weekend."

"I'm sorry," he said. "I don't understand."

"I simply want to thank you for the weekend."

"But it's I who owe you—"

"Michael," she said again, and the word was a charm, an incantation—the wizard's key, in and out of fairyland. "Michael, I can't take the cream from you."

"Now you've completely lost me," he said. His voice had changed completely. She had never heard that flat tone before.

"The cream is yours," she plunged on.

"The cream is yours," he contradicted. "It has been yours," and he paused for a moment, "it has been yours since the first evening I discovered you sitting on that Kings Point porch.''

"You invented it," she said.

"For you."

"It's the product of your brain."

"Waiting for your face to appear on its label."

"I have it now," she said. "But you still own it, as completely as you owned it last week."

Again, silence on the other end of the phone. And then he said, slowly, "Are we talking about a piece of paper?"

"No," she replied. "Much more than that. I don't want to own it your way. I don't want to sell it your way."

"But what other way is there to—"

"I don't want to sell it through stores."

"On street corners, then?" She had hit home, finally. His voice had turned sharp.

"No," she said. "Through mail order. First to the women who have already bought my book."

"A hundred thousand of them?"

"Perhaps as many as three hundred thousand."

"But that's a fraction of the women who want this cream." With each word his voice honed itself sharper.

"It's a start," she said. "From there—"

"But you can sell more cream in stores in a week than you can in all mail order media in a year," he interrupted.

"One customer will tell another," she said.

"As they will in stores," he added quickly.

"I want the women who bought the book to have the first opportunity to try it," she went on.

"But why?" he asked.

She caught her breath, stopped reasoning with him, stopped defending her position. "Because I want it that way," she said. "Because I'd want to introduce it that way—if it were my product."

When his voice finally came back on the phone, he said reluctantly. "It is your product."

"No," she said. "It isn't."

"Yes," he said, "it is. Irrevocably. You've proved your point. I was wrong, and I apologize."

"It's still yours."

"Not anymore, goddammit. If you want to take the god-damn thing, and pack it in a suitcase, and stand on the street in front of Bloomingdale's, and sell it to passers-by, then do it. We can settle it as simply as this. I'll send you two pieces of paper. The first will be a contract, giving you the full and exclusive right to do whatever you want with the cream. Anything at all. To make it, package it, sell it in any way you deem feasible. No approval necessary from me. Not even the right of consultation. Okay?''

She thought a moment. The flush of victory, equal almost to a slow flush of orgasm, was creeping up her body.

''All right,'' she said, ''I'll take it on those terms. But I'm afraid those are the only terms I can take it on.''

''You'll have them,'' he said. ''In writing.''

''And the second piece of paper?'' she asked.

''A diploma,'' he said. ''Shall we say, a certificate of graduation, marking your entrance into the world of independence. It should occupy a central place in your room. What about right over your desk?''

''Fine,'' she said. ''I'll put it there.''

His voice shifted again within a fraction of a second. Now it was the weekend voice—deep, throaty, masculine, sexy. ''I've never seen your apartment,'' he said. ''Do you need a strong, sure pair of hands to help pound in the nail for you?''

Now she knew what Pavlov meant by his conditioned dogs. They salivated when the lunch bell rang. A different part of her body now salivated with every slow, deliberate word in that sentence with its double meaning. ''I can use a hammer,'' she said.

''I would imagine,'' he went on in the same husky tone, ''that you would handle it very well.''

She blushed. Her entire body blushed. ''I think you'd better send the diploma, instead,'' she said.

''Not bring it?''

''Not yet,'' she said hurriedly. ''I want to see you—''

''Say it again, please.''

''I want to see you, but not''—and she hesitated, trying to fit her thoughts into civilized order—''but not until I get this business off the ground. Let me have that time, Michael. Please.''

When she heard his voice again, she knew he was smiling.

''You give a greater compliment,'' he said, ''by saying no, than any other woman I've ever met who said yes. Take as much time as you want. I'll be here.''

It was over, she thought. The first victory, the first defeat. Her will had won—she knew that. But her body had lost. A fair exchange, she thought. But for how many days? She shook her head, marveling at herself, and began the next call, to her editor at Irving House.

23.

It was a short, brittle conversation. She was told that the book was doing very well. She then told the woman that she had a new product which she wanted to sell to the buyers of the book. The voice on the other end of the line immediately changed from warm and welcoming, to icy. There was no honesty, no outright denial. The woman simply said that the subject was not in her department, that she would have to contact a vice president of sales, who would call Melissa back within a day or two.

Period. It was as cold, as final as that. The other phone clicked down in Melissa's ear, and she realized, for the first time, how quickly an unexpected twist in business could turn a former ally into an outright antagonist.

What have I done? she questioned herself. And the answer came echoing out of her brain almost immediately—asked a logical favor that wasn't explicitly stated in the original contract. Threatened this woman's corporate status. Expected business people to act like friends.

She shivered. Then she wrote on her calendar, two days in advance: "Bug Irving House." And then added, for emphasis, "and keep bugging them."

All right. It wasn't even ten o'clock, and she'd already made two torturous phone calls. Now she needed to hear the voice of a person whose reactions she knew in advance. "C'mon, Pam," she silently pleaded, "be home."

The voice that came on the phone, still sleepy, was like honey to her senses.

"Albee's all right," Melissa said first, putting herself into Pam's time frame. "I saw him last night."

"Thank God," Pam's voice shot back. "How long do they think it will take him to recover?"

"Not too long," Melissa lied. "But he's fine now. And that's the important thing."

"Agreed," Pam said. "And our other little problem?"

"I have the cream," Melissa said. "As much of it as you want." And then a smile crossed her face. "Would you settle for ten thousand jars as an opener?"

"Well," Pam replied. "There's my mother in Iowa. My sister in Seattle. There must be three hundred other women I like well enough to give it to. So that's a good start. One little question, though," she said. "How much does it cost me? As cheap as you can, please."

"Time," Melissa said immediately.

"That's all?" Pam replied.

"That's all."

"Sold," she said. "Time I've got plenty of. When do I start getting the cream?"

"Want to discuss it over dinner tonight?"

"You name the time, baby, and I'll be there right on the dot—even if it's MacDonald's."

Good. The first coworker. An old reliable. Now, not quite so certain, she tried for the second.

She called Sally O'Toole and set up a lunch at the Carleton Delicatessen. When she got there, Sally was already seated in one of the corner tables.

"We never got around to business at our last lunch," Melissa said immediately. "We were going to build a business, I think."

"That's right," Sally said. "Catalog products that we can sell to the people who ordered the book."

"How were we going to work it?"

"I don't know exactly," Sally said. "I guess you were going to get the products, and I was going to write the catalog."

"And we were going to split—how?"

"I don't know," the woman opposite her said bluntly. "Not fifty-fifty of course. Not even sixty-forty. It's your face, your identity, not mine. I can do it for you on a fee basis, or a percentage of gross, or . . ."

"You write everything," Melissa said suddenly. "I approve all copy and layout. You get ten percent of the company now, maybe more later."

"Too little," Sally said automatically. "Too much night work. Let's say twenty—"

"No," Melissa said at once. It was a simple no, an easy no. She had spent the first twenty years of her life listening to her father negotiate with the contractors, the builders, the homeowners he worked with. Sometimes she had sat in a corner and listened for three-quarters of an hour while two men haggled over a difference of fifteen dollars. By the time she was twelve, she could predict the price to be agreed upon, right down to the penny.

But she had no male ego to defend. And, even before Michael's first lesson, she had never expected, nor hoped, to be loved in business—only respected. Therefore, she said to Sally, "I don't negotiate. I make you what I honestly believe is a fair offer. You can take it, or you can walk out on it. But I'm not going to waste my lunch hour with you, dancing around the extra five percent figure that you think you'll end up with."

Sally blushed slightly. "Sold," she said quietly. "Ten percent it is."

"Of several million dollars," Melissa added.

Sally's eyes opened wide in surprise. "Not from the catalog sales of the book," she said.

"I'm not interested in the catalog sales of the book, except as a minor sideline," Melissa said.

"You have something better?" Sally asked.

"I have."

Melissa watched an invisible curtain come down over the other woman's eyes. It was made of mood, but it was stronger than steel.

"So he gave it to you," Sally said.

"Then you know about it?" Melissa asked.

"All twenty versions of it," Sally said, tapping her cheek with her right forefinger. "All of them have been tried here, including last month's version—the one that worked."

"Then—"

"Honey," Sally said. "The cream wasn't invented last week for you. He didn't whip it together, like a magician, to give you a bed-e-boo present."

Melissa flinched. "How much does he tell you?" She asked involuntarily.

"About you?" Sally said. "Nothing. About the cream—everything. I'm just another one of his human guinea pigs, sweetheart. All five girls in the office have been testing the variations of the cream for as long as I've been there, probably longer.'' There was a moment's pause, while Sally looked down into her glass of cream soda. Then she said, ''I can't drink any more of this rot. Let's go next door, to the hotel dining room, where I can get a real—''

''No,'' Melissa said again. ''I don't drink at lunch, especially at business lunches.''

''Then I drink fart water,'' Sally said, and looked up at Melissa.

''I think we should set another rule,'' Melissa said quietly. ''What happens between Michael and me is strictly his business and mine. If we work together, it stays precisely that way.''

Sally's eyes avoided Melissa's, but she said, ''You're tougher than I thought. I think you've got a chance—especially with that cream. Count me on board.''

''Now,'' Melissa said, and her face crinkled into a smile, ''when can you have the ad for me?''

Sally's face flashed back to normal. Her eyes were empty now of envy and unconcealed bitterness, and when they looked into Melissa's, they were as sharp and probing and New York-merciless as ever.

''How long have you had the cream?'' she asked.

''Almost two weeks,'' Melissa replied.

''It shows. Did you use it every night?''

''Yes. And every morning too.''

''You didn't happen, by any chance, to take photographs —for example, around your eyes—before you used it?''

''After reading your previous ad,'' Melissa said, ''I certainly did. In the bathroom mirror. They're not good, but I think they'll do.''

''Without makeup?''

''Without a spec of makeup.''

''Do they show—''

''Yes.''

Now it was Sally's turn. The two of them were all business now. Business is real. Business is hard. In business, as in medicine, you can hurt, as much as is required, as long as both parties agree that the hurt is necessary.

''You look twenty-eight, right now, with your makeup on. How old did your eyes look in the photograph, without that makeup?''

''Older,'' was all that Melissa could manage as an answer.

Sally was relentless. ''How much older?''

"At least thirty-five," Melissa finally answered.

"And now, after the cream, if we took those same bare photographs again, this time with a professional photographer, how many years would those eyes have lost?"

"Back to thirty," Melissa said. "At most, thirty-one."

"Good," Sally said, in her specialist's tone. "Now for the jackpot question. Do you want the world to see your face truly naked, without, as you call it, a spec of protection?"

Melissa instinctively looked around the small delicatessen, to see if anyone was close enough to their table to overhear the conversation.

"Let me make it clear," Sally went on. "I'm talking about running this ad, and these photographs, in perhaps one hundred newspapers and magazines. That means every newspaper and magazine that has ever run all your photos before, with no makeup, no camouflage, no protection—"

"And you feel—"

"That it's the only kind of ad that will really work. The oldest idea in the business, but the most convincing. Because it's the truth. The naked truth." And then Sally pulled out all the stops, and paid Melissa back for a lifetime of being plain, while the woman sitting across from her had lived a lifetime of being beautiful.

"A double truth," Sally said, as quietly as a surgeon's scalpel breaks the skin.

"Double in what way?" Melissa asked.

"First because women who read those newspapers and magazines know you. They've seen you on those covers, in four-color spreads, for . . . what—fifteen years? They know that face. They've envied that face"—again, the cutting smile—"for all those years. The face that doesn't grow old, while they do. And now," Sally went on, "they'll see that face again—that marvelous, unchangeable face—but this time without the makeup, without the photographer's professional lighting—shot in a bathroom mirror, with a crude camera. And that will be the first truth, Melissa. That your face has aged too, in those fifteen years—not as much as ours, but enough. Enough to prove that you're mortal and fallible too."

Melissa sat there silently, remembering suddenly a mirror she had looked into once, fifteen years ago. That mirror's name was Victoria. She returned Sally's biting smile with a soft one, and she said, "No more goddess, then?"

"No more goddess," Sally agreed.

Melissa's smile deepened, and, as it deepened, she could feel the skin around her eyes, even now, even after a month with Michael's miracle, crinkle in unison with that smile. And she said, gently, "Thank God."

Sally's smile vanished. "What?"

"Thank God," Melissa repeated. "So you think that if I run these photographs of myself, I can convince women, other women like you and me, that this," and she touched the softer, smoother, but still aged skin around her eyes, "that this can be softened . . . can be reversed for one, two, perhaps even five or ten years?"

"Yes," Sally said. "Yes, at least a hell of a lot of them."

"Then do it," Melissa said. "Tonight, if you can get started that quickly. I'll have the photographs over to you by messenger this afternoon. Blow them up as big as you want. No retouching. No softening of the blow. We'll make the first truth so strong, so convincing, that they have to go on to believe the second."

"It will be a hell of an ad."

"Good," Melissa said. "But one last thing. That Kleenex girl image you have of yourself. One of our first priorities will be to get rid of that. It doesn't belong to you. It belongs to the way you dress, make up, and feel about yourself. The first month," Melissa said, "while you're working on the copy for the cream, I'm going to work on erasing that image for you."

"The first month?" Sally said. "It will take ten years."

"It will take one month—that's all," Melissa said. "I promise you that. In fact," she said, "I'll even write it into your contract. We'll put in a little clause that ought to turn the male lawyer's head gray. Clause 17-a— whereas, Melissa Carpenter does guarantee Sally O'Toole, the employee being presently hired, that the party of the first part shall remove forever the party of the second part's image of being a Kleenex girl, by the time the first month of employment has concluded, or the party of the first part guarantees the party of the second part that she will turn over to her, at the end of that aforesaid month, an extra five percent of the stock of the named corporation."

Sally looked up at Melissa. The invisible iron shield in front of her eyes had melted away into tears. Then suddenly she looked down at the glass of cream soda in her hand, and took a large sip from it.

''You know,'' she said, as much to herself as to Melissa, ''this stuff isn't bad. It could even get to be a permanent habit.'' And then she looked up again at her blond employer-to-be. ''I might just start having three of these for lunch every day, instead of three martinis.''

She smiled. She had a good smile, Melissa thought. In a few weeks Melissa was going to show her how to have a great smile.

''Thanks,'' Sally said. ''You've made yourself a deal. And you've also made a friend. A jealous friend,'' she admitted, ''but, baby,'' she went on to finish, ''you'll never have a truer friend in all your life.''

24.

That night, Melissa made the same ten percent deal with Pam as the general administrative assistant for the new company. She now owned eighty percent of the stock herself. She had two trusted friends—one sure, one probable—in the only two positions she felt she herself couldn't fill at the beginning. She spent the entire evening with Lacy, thrilling to the way her daughter was perfecting the crippled girl's part in *The Glass Menagerie*, and she went to bed with a clear heart and an exhausted body, at the same time Lacy did. She slept til seven, when the phone woke her, with the news that Albee was dead.

She had no idea whose voice it was on the other end of the phone. She didn't even think to ask. It was a man's voice, and he told her tersely that Albee had died at six o'clock in the morning, that the death was quick and relatively painless, and that the funeral would be at the Riverside Chapel in two days. Until then, the man's voice had stated, the family was sitting shiva in the proper room at the memorial chapel, starting at seven-thirty that night.

Then the phone clicked dead, and there was nothing but emptiness on the other side of the line, on the other side of the world.

She sat there, half in, half out of bed, with the phone still

held to her ear, and listened intently to the electronic emptiness. It was like listening to the very silence of death, with
the suddenly sure knowledge that Albee's voice would never
again break that silence, that she would never see that glowing, loving face again, that she would never watch those
shoulders rise in that habitual shrug from wisdom to infinity.

All that was left to listen to was emptiness. All that was
left to listen with was emptiness.

Then she put down the phone, gently, on the hook. And
she sat there, on the side of her bed, completely alone, and
she wept. She wept for Albee. She wept for herself. She wept
for the world, which would never know his gentle smile
again.

No, never again.

She was still sitting in shock at ten o'clock that morning,
when the downstairs buzzer rang. When she answered the
intercom, she was told that she had a registered package
which she must sign for personally. When the delivery boy
came up, he brought a large brown envelope, sealed with
tape, and on the green slip he brought with him someone had
written, in a failing hand, "Hold for Delivery till 10:00 A.M.
Tomorrow Morning." When he left, she closed the door, and
threw the envelope on the couch without giving it a second
look. Then, suddenly, something about its feel alerted her,
and she turned again, staring at it on the couch, wondering
where the vibrations inside it were coming from.

She picked it up, and slowly began peeling off the tape.
Inside it was another envelope, with a large rubber band
circling it. She knew what was inside it before she took off
the rubber band. As she slid it off the envelope, her hands
shook, and as the rubber band came off the edge, it fell to the
floor and lay there.

The envelope was not sealed. Inside it were the neatly
arranged rows of hundred dollar bills, just as they had been in
the hospital, each ten bills bound by a separate paper clip.
Also, behind them all, was a small, neatly folded note.

It was in the same failing hand that she had seen on the
delivery slip. There were only two lines on it. The first was,
"If you ever need a good lox and bagel sandwich . . ."
Underneath it, probably as a hastily added second thought,
was the line, "Go out and spend it to look good for Mr.
Lucky . . . whoever the goddammit he is." There were fifty-

seven hundred dollar bills in the envelope. Her first thought was to start crying again. But she didn't cry. Her second thought was to send the money back to the family, or give it to one of his charities. But there was no way to explain it to the family, and she already knew that he had set aside millions for each of those charities.

Last night he must have known. He knew that nurse Valkyrie would rip apart the drawers, looking for the source of the bonus money. He could have called his son to come get it. He could have sent it to a dozen, or even a hundred, people. He'd already given her far too much anyway. But . . . there it was. And her third thought was to laugh—laugh with him, wherever he was, at the trick he'd pulled on all the others, at the lox and bagel sandwich he'd sent her, at his last command with what to do with the money.

She sat there on the couch, with the two windows open, with the hundred dollar bills lying all around her, and she picked them up and let them drop, turning them into green snow, and laughing, and laughing, and laughing with him. She knew she was laughing, and yet her eyes, at the same time, were crying.

Then she stopped, and looked at the antique clock, and saw that it was eleven o'clock. She picked up the green snow, flake by flake, and reassembled it into money. It had to be got rid of today. It had to be transformed into beauty today. Not a single trace of it must remain in her house, unfulfilled, by the time the sun went down.

She threw on brown slacks and a favorite silk blouse, and stuffed the fifty-seven hundred dollars into a good handbag. Then she grabbed her keys, and ran down the three flights of stairs to the landing, out the door, up the street to Madison Avenue, and three blocks to a favorite boutique.

In two hours she bought thirty-eight hundred dollars' worth of slacks, blouses, suits, and a man-tailored evening outfit. She counted out thirty-eight of the bills, and waited while the salesperson counted them in turn. She asked for no discount, and refused the girl's offer to put in another silk blouse for free. Albee was buying the clothes for her; Albee didn't know the meaning of the word "bargain"; Albee never looked for free gifts.

Then she walked slowly, in the sun-drenched day, the ten or so blocks to Bloomingdale's. There was nineteen hundred dollars more to spend on lingerie, on shoes, on boots, on accessories, on all the little complements that made the outfits complete. She spent every cent of it exactly as Albee would have wanted her to.

By four o'clock that afternoon, the fifty-seven hundred dollars was completely gone. The last little task, the last loving command, had been obeyed.

25.

The funeral service was held two days later, at the Riverside Memorial Chapel. She got there an hour early, and sat in the fifth row; the same row, by fate or by coincidence, as Aaron, five bodies away on the left. And four bodies away on the right, were Michael and his wife.

Aaron looked marvelous. There was more and more steel-gray in his hair. He physically dwarfed the other men in the room. His color had never been better, his profile never stronger. He saw her first when he sat down. He flushed. She had never seen eyes as penetrating as his eyes were then—not even Michael's. They looked at each other for a moment, the first time they had seen each other in more than five months, and then he nodded, and she nodded, and he picked up a prayer book—a Jewish prayer book—and actually began to read through it.

Seconds later, on the other side of her row, she looked up and saw one of the most beautiful, and blankest, women she had ever encountered. She was black-haired and violet-eyed, about Melissa's own age. With few wrinkles and no sags, as though they would be banished from her face upon first appearance. She was impeccably dressed; the dress had been worn all the way from Kings Point, without daring to collect the slightest crease. She was beautiful. She was ice. She was frightening. Behind her, dressed in a black suit, and perfectly gorgeous, was Michael. Their eyes met; he nodded, and as they both sat down she lost sight of him on the other side of his wife.

The service began. Albee's family walked in from the side waiting room. The one woman among them was crying a little. All three men seemed nothing more than embarrassed and impatient.

A rabbi, the smoothest-tongued rabbi she imagined the family could buy, mounted the podium, and conducted the final service. He spoke easily and beautifully; he repeated stanza after stanza written by men who had lived thousands of years ago, and who felt a passion for life, a commitment to life, that this man, echoing them now, would never feel. Melissa sat there, immobile as a statue, as decorous as a painting, making no sound or move that would call the slightest attention to herself, and feeling herself ripped open by the sadness inside her.

The chapel smelled of money, and the man she had known had been so much more than money. The people sitting here were celebrating the eternity of money, rather than mourning the loss of one exceptional human being. She didn't give a damn for his money; she knew that she would never be able to replace the human being in her life.

So, to drown out the flow of gold and honey, she forced her mind back to that Albee she had never known—but knew better now than anyone else sitting in that entire chapel. The one who had stood outside Stanford University's ivy-covered walls, and dreamed of someday being allowed to share in the wisdom that was dispensed there. She remembered the day that he had wandered into the philosophy hall, and heard, to his surprise, the lecture on another Jew, who had lived five centuries before—Spinoza. Later he had told her the words of Spinoza that he had heard that day, and instantly memorized:

"Blessedness is not the reward of virtue, but virtue itself. Neither do we rejoice therein, because we control our lust but, contrarywise, because we rejoice therein, we are able to control our lust."

Blessedness and rejoicing, she thought, they were yours. And you taught them to me, and you finally shared them with me. Leave us, she said, and be blessed, and rejoice. May you rejoin that woman you loved more than me; may you spend an eternity in blessedness with her, but may you always carry with you on your long journey just a bit of the love I have given, and continue to give, to you.

Her private service was over. The droning of the public service went on for a few more minutes. Then it too stopped, and the casket was carried out into the sharp sun, the family filing out behind it.

Albee was put into the huge black limousine, and the doors closed after him, barring her from him forever. Michael and his wife said good-bye to a few people—not to her—and then were swallowed up by a cab. Aaron stood, towering above the crowd, for a few moments, and then walked over to her.

"Hello, Melissa," he said, taking her hand.

"Hello, Aaron."

"Are you well?"

"Very," she said.

"And Lacy?" he asked.

"Equally."

"You look wonderful."

"So do you," she answered. "I understand the agency is doing very well."

"I understand," he replied, "that the book is doing very well."

There was a pause, and a thousand unspoken words died on both their lips.

"You look beautiful," he said. And then he smiled, and melted into the crowd outside the funeral parlor.

26.

When she returned home, there was a message from the subsidiary rights manager at Melissa's publishing company, or, more exactly, from her secretary. Melissa did not really have to pick up the phone and return the call to receive their decision. But, of course, she did.

The story was simple, and sharp. A vice-president of sales had been consulted about Melissa's using the names of the women who had bought her book by mail. The campaign had done far better than any of them had dared to anticipate. The projection was now for three hundred thousand copies to be sold by mail order. Therefore, this esteemed gentlemen, who was not named in the phone conversation, felt that she should be immensely grateful for the royalty moneys she was about to receive—at the specified contractural time, of course. As for letting Melissa use the list of names, this was, of course, contrary to company policy. The answer was therefore, "a reluctant no." The list would be available for rental at the proper time—somewhere between six months and a year from now—just as any other outside source could rent it.

Period. Her book, her ad. And the answer was no. Welcome, she thought, to Michael's real world.

Melissa turned from the phone, ran to her filing cabinet, tore out the folder with the contract in it. She read every word of it twice. She was no lawyer, but the meaning was clear enough. She got, for her life packaged in a book, only the royalties, and half the income from subsidiary rights. The names were theirs.

She took the contract and crumpled it up, and threw it across the room. Then she walked over to it and stomped on it. Albee was dead, she thought. Michael had not even said hello to her. Aaron was a statue who said nothing she wanted to hear.

She had the world she wanted. She had made the trade, she had made the transition. She had her independent world.

It hurt. Most of all, it hurt.

Five minutes later, her anger spent, she picked up the crumpled contract, smoothed it out, and put it back in her file folder. Then she returned to her desk, poured herself a cup of coffee, and thought about the matter of contracts. Michael had said he would draw up a contract. Now she realized she must dictate that contract herself. She looked up the phone number of a lawyer she had known for years; a rights contract to the cream was drawn up, giving Michael's firm a five percent royalty, assigning any and all decisions to her. The contract was finished two days later. She sent it with a brief note to Michael, asking him to contact his lawyer, and to set up a meeting between the four of them—herself, Michael, and the two attorneys—using this rough draft as a departure point.

The next day, the contract was back, without a change, signed and certified. With it was a note: "An excellent job. This man really knows his business. Tell me when you want the first production run, how many, sizes, labels, etc. See you soon, Michael."

Just that. No call. No contact. Just "See you soon."

She tore the note into tiny pieces, and then let them drop, one by one, into the wastebasket. And then she plunged back into work.

Sally had already given Michael her notice, and had received a leave of absence. The next morning, she showed up at Melissa's tiny apartment with a huge shopping bag full of her accessories: typewriter, paper, pencils, fifty-seven pages of scrawled notes, and her own bottle of gin for whatever emergencies might arise.

Pam had shown up two days before for her first day of work. She sat with Melissa on the couch, day after day, going over the cost of the first orders, the size of the production run, the names of cosmetic manufacturers they'd gotten from the phone directory, plus label houses, packaging houses, design studios, and thirty-five dozen other details—all of which were first agreed on together, over the clacking of Sally's typewriter keys, and then handed to Pam, who spent the rest of the day yelling into the phone to sort them out.

They worked past a call-in dinner from the deli, every night that week. Past midnight, till the other two women staggered home half-blind, till Melissa sank down on the couch too weary even to undress, to sleep the six or seven tossing hours until the front buzzer rang again, and the two of them marched in once more to begin the next day's task.

Three women against the world, doing everything themselves. Getting quotes. Designing the first rough sketches of labels. Cutting out type. Meeting with possible suppliers. Haggling prices. Judging odors and scents. Negotiating terms. Writing, then criticizing, then rewriting, then recriticizing, then re-rewriting, then re-recticizing the first ad, till it said everything Melissa wanted, everything Sally wanted, everything Pam could add as an afterthought. Until at last ready to run in the *New York Post*. And, that final Friday night, Melissa let the other two women go home early—at only ten o'clock. She had done several months' work in a week. She had done it with only two friends. She had risked the entire concept on a single ad. She had no idea what the results of that ad would be. But she didn't care. It had to be done.

She was bone-tired. Out of her apartment, a challenge was being fashioned to one of the most heavily promoted, heavily advertised industries in the United States—with an annual volume of billions of dollars a year. One woman with a dream. Two women sharing that dream. Three women making that dream become real. That, she knew, in America, was all it needed to confront such a giant industry. Now the rest was up to history.

But was it? It was ten-thirty. Her body wanted desperately

to crash down upon that couch, and sleep a dreamless sleep. But she stood there instead, looking at the new cream ad for the hundredth time. It was gorgeous, she thought. It was startling. It was convincing. It was, above all, true. But an irritating, upsetting thought had slowly crept into her mind. Did it have every element, every ingredient that had made the first book ad so successful? She realized suddenly that not one of the three of them had looked at the book ad again, during the entire period they were hammering together this new appeal for the cream. Yet, Melissa thought, both ads addressed themselves to the same vital problem. What if the book ad had one sentence, one promise, one word that could be used in the cream ad, and, because they hadn't checked, it had been left out?

Her eyes were so tired that they were fuzzy, even with her reading glasses. But she went back to the filing cabinet, and dug up the original book ad. There it was, seemingly a hundred years old. She remembered the day she had first received it, wrapped in its gift ribbon. She remembered the note that came with it, enticing her to make that fateful call to Michael. She remembered what finally came of that call in his apartment.

And she stopped remembering. Because that kind of memory was now her most deadly enemy. Instead, she forced herself to reread every word in the original book advertisement. To take a red pencil in her hand, and underline every word that struck her with its power, and then compare it to the cream advertisement, to see if it had the same power.

It was eleven-thirty when she was finished. The type on the two ads swam before her eyes. She was numb with need for sleep. But she had underlined parts of every sentence in the original book ad—except one.

It was a tiny sentence, set in the smallest type of the ad. It lay in the bottom right-hand corner of the ad, and it was set on its side, running vertically rather than horizontally.

It had only three words. The first of these words was a symbol, which she knew from her years with Aaron meant "copyright." And then the following two words simply said: "Melissa Carpenter."

That was all there was to the sentence. "Copyright Melissa Carpenter." That was all. Set so small, used in advertising in such a matter-of-fact way, that neither she, nor anyone else, had noticed them. Three tiny words, that meant nothing more nor less than that she owned the ad. That the ad was copyrighted in her name, and not in Irving House's. That they had been using her ad, her property, without ever getting written permission from her to do so.

She laughed. They had been sloppy as well as selfish. They had the contractual rights to the book, but not the ad. They were using her ad without legally compensating her.

She continued laughing. She couldn't stop laughing now. It was midnight. A new day. She could hardly wait the nine hours till their executive offices opened.

27.

She was up at seven, cleaned the apartment twice, had three cups of coffee. She could hardly wait until the hands of the clock crawled to 9:05, and she could call Irving House. She quickly brushed aside the arrogant secretary she'd spoken to last time. One sentence, one tiny little sentence, and there was blissful confusion at the other end of the line, a most cordial "hold on, please," and then the juicy silence that symbolized the frantic scurrying from office to office as her dear publishers looked for someone big enough, and daring enough, to stop the buck.

Finally, three minutes, four minutes later, a man's voice came on the phone.

"This is Charles Osgood," he said.

"And you are, Mr. Osgood?" she replied politely.

"Vice-president in charge of direct marketing."

"How wonderful," she said. "Then you're the gentleman who's in charge of selling my book."

"Trying to sell your book, Mrs. Carpenter," he said.

"I believe I was told the other day," she went on, "that you've just placed your second round of ads in *Family Weekly*, *Parade*, *Cosmopolitan*, and *Family Circle*."

"It might be true," he admitted. "I don't have the schedule right here in front of me."

"It doesn't really matter," she said. "You are, however, using the original ad I gave you some time ago?" She was measuring out each word by the quarter teaspoonful. She was in no hurry to force the conversation to its climax. She loved every little evasion, every little dodge contained in it.

"Well," he said, "as far as I know now, we are still using that ad. Though I might have to check the latest insertion orders to supplement my memory."

"Then, Mr. Osgood," she said, "if the ad is unchanged, it must have the original copyright line in it. Doesn't it?"

"I believe so," was the reluctant admission.

"Would you like me to hold on while you check?"

"No," he said. "It really isn't necessary. I happen to have a copy of the ad in front of me."

"How fortunate. Then I imagine you can read the copyright line quite clearly."

"I can."

"And?" her voice meekly questioned.

"I'm afraid it's copyrighted in your name, rather than ours. I have no idea how that could have happened."

"I do," she said, her voice rising slightly in tone. "I'm no lawyer, Mr. Osgood, but my husband has had an ad agency of his own for twenty-five years. And I believe that copyright makes the ad my property, rather than yours. Is that right?"

"I'd have to check it out with our legal staff," he replied, "but—"

"Go ahead," she said sweetly. "Take your time."

"—but I would say, offhand, without thorough checking, that you'd be right. At this moment the ad does seem to belong to you."

"And do you have a letter from me, giving you permission to run that ad?"

His voice suddenly turned angry.

"Mrs. Carpenter—" he began.

"Yes."

"I would assume," he continued, "that you are fully aware that you never made out such a letter."

The moment, she thought, when the trap snapped.

"Then," she said slowly, but firmly, "you have no legal right to run that ad."

"Mrs. Carpenter," he repeated, "we are running that ad— legal right or not—to sell your own book."

"Mr. Osgood," and now her voice picked up its pace, "I called last week and asked if I could use the list of names of buyers of that book. Are you aware of that call, Mr. Osgood?"

"It might have been called to my attention."

"I'm sure it was. And I'm also sure that you denied that request, quite flatly, as I remember."

"Mrs. Carpenter," he said. "we have an established company policy."

"So do I, Mr. Osgood. Quite established. And now there seems to be a clash of policies. Don't you agree?"

"I don't quite understand."

"Then let me make myself perfectly clear. What would happen, Mr. Osgood, if I forebade you, tomorrow, by letter, to open and fill any of the orders you received from now on, using my copyrighted ad? And let me remind you," she went on, "that would include all the orders from *Family Weekly*, *Parade, Cosmopolitan, Family Circle*—about one hundred and fifty thousand dollars' worth of media advertising, if I remember correctly."

"Mrs. Carpenter," he said angrily, "I don't believe you could legally do that."

"My lawyer believes I legally could," she lied. "And what would happen to the orders, Mr. Osgood, while we both waited for a judge to tell us which of our lawyers is correct?"

There was a silence on the other end of the phone. And then: "Mrs. Carpenter, we are selling your book. We are earning you a great amount of money in royalties."

"How nice. But, Mr. Osgood, let me say this. Giving me the royalties just isn't enough."

"All right," he said finally. "What is enough?"

"Just this," she replied. "Do you have a pencil and pad handy, Mr. Osgood?"

"I do."

"What I want, then, is this. First, I want a list, in chronological order, of the names of everyone who has ordered my book until now." She paused. "Am I going too fast for you, Mr. Osgood?"

"No," he replied. "My secretary's on the other extension. She's taking down what you say."

How fascinating, she thought. Always the masculine brain, and the feminine hands.

"Second," she went on. "Every week from this date on, I want a new addition to that list, giving me every single name that has come in for the book for that week. Every single name with the address, and the zip code."

"I understand."

"I want those names delivered to me by the Monday of the following week. That means immediately. Immediately, Mr. Osgood. Not six months or one year from now."

"There are thousands of names coming in every week," he pleaded.

"Every week," she repeated again, slowly. "The Monday following the Friday of that week. On my desk."

"All right," he said. "What else?"

"An exchange of letters, Mr. Osgood. One from me giving you the right to use the ad as you see fit, and as often as you please. And, in exchange, one from you, signed by you personally, Mr. Osgood, giving me the right to use the names as I see fit, as often as I want."

"Is there anything else?"

"No," she said. "I think that will be all."

"Did you get all that, Joyce?" he said.

And then, the voice of the anonymous female on the other end of the phone took on reality for two brief words. "Yes, sir."

"I'll expect the first list, containing all the names you've received up until now, on my desk by next Monday. Do you understand?" Melissa said.

"I understand perfectly, Mrs. Carpenter. Is there anything else?"

"Yes," she said. "Have a pleasant day, won't you? And," she went on quickly, before he could slam down the phone, "you have a pleasant day too, won't you, Joyce?"

"Good-bye," he said, and the phone then truly crashed down on his extension.

She sat there for a moment, staring at the deadly electronic weapon still held in her hand. Then she lifted the speaker up to her mouth and lightly, but passionately, kissed it.

28.

On Friday morning, the ad for the cream appeared in the *New York Post*. She remembered the day the original ad for the book had run, only one short lifetime ago.

When she received her first copy of the newspaper, about noon, Melissa simply sat on the couch of her apartment, and stared at the page where it appeared. There she was, with the tell-all close-ups of her eyes, stripped naked and revealed to the world. No pretense. No conventional disguise. Bare-skinned. Almost obscene.

By two o'clock seven friends had called her up. Four hated the photographs, three applauded them; but six of the seven left an order with her on the phone for an immediate rush order of the cream.

At three o'clock she received a call from the advertising director of one of the agencies she still modeled for. He had resented her, for some unknown reason, for years. Now his voice was glowing with outraged justification. "Do you know that we have a national campaign, featuring you, breaking this month? Do you have even the slightest idea what this insane ad you're running will do to that campaign?"

"No," she answered honestly.

"It will kill the image. It will practically kill the campaign."

"How?" she replied.

"By puncturing the illusion, my dear. The illusion we pay you five hundred dollars a day to provide for us."

"I'm sorry," she said. "We have no agreement—"

"My dear," he said. "You're certifiably insane."

"Perhaps, Alan," she replied, "but that is strictly my own business."

"Your own funeral," he corrected. "You're through, Melissa. Finished. Washed up. Like a spar from an old ship, washed up on a beach. You've been sinking, darling, for years. Now you've exposed your skeleton for all of us to see."

"Well," she said quietly, "I hope at least I've given you a little diversion."

"A costly diversion," he said. "Oh, I know I can't sue. Nor, if you still have any other clients, can they. But I just wanted to call and tell you, never to phone us again. And, rest assured, we shall never phone you."

The dead, empty click, and the deed was done. The stakes were clearly defined. In the advertising capital of the world she had dared to run the truth.

As she hung up the phone, she admitted to herself that the man was right. Her modeling income was lost from now on.

Sally teetered into the apartment, at least three martinis to the wind. Her hands were black with newspaper print. She plopped herself down on the couch, and looked up at Melissa with glassy eyes.

"I've been riding the subways," she said, "going nowhere. Watching people coming home from work. I've been looking over the shoulders of women reading the *Post*. Waiting for them to reach the page with the ad. Watching to see if they stopped, if they read the first paragraph, or the second, or the third. Suffering the tortures of the damned every time one of them turned the page before she'd finished the copy." She paused and looked around the apartment blankly. "Do you have a drink?"

"No," Melissa said.

"Thank God," Sally replied. "You know, I went to Las Vegas once," Sally went on. "I bet one hundred dollars on a hand of blackjack. This makes Las Vegas look like a game of jacks. All—everything—on one roll of the presses. Either your number comes up, either they buy what you say, or—poof—they take all your chips away."

"Go home," Melissa said, "Please. And stop worrying."

"I'll never live till Monday," she said.

"You will," Melissa answered. "But badly."

"Very badly," Sally said, and dragged herself out of the apartment.

But how will I live till Monday, Melissa thought. And then, as though she had a direct line to God, the phone rang.

This time it was Michael.

"I've studied the ad for three hours. Let me ask you a blunt question. Whose idea were the photographs, yours or Sally's?"

"I took them," Melissa said, "the first night I tried the cream. But I had no idea anyone else would ever see them."

"Till Sally saw them?" he asked.

"No, asked for them."

"And you actually let her run them like this?"

"Of course."

"Of course," he laughed. "Of course I flew planes in Korea when the Reds had rockets that could knock a mosquito out of the air at forty thousand feet."

"It's not quite the same."

"Of course," he said. "Let me say that I am awestruck.

My congratulations. It's the perfect advertisement. At the ultimate risk.''

"Do you think it will sell?" she asked.

"Yes," he answered immediately. "Any woman who doesn't try the cream after seeing that advertisement must be beyond hope."

Her entire body relaxed. She hadn't been aware, one second before, of the amount of tension it was carrying.

"How do you feel?" he went on.

"Tired," she said. "Drained. Exposed." Then she smiled. "I guess I feel like I'm flying at forty thousand feet, and wondering whether the enemy rockets are going to find me."

"Do you know what we did, every night, when we got back to Japan?" he asked. "To get us back into those cockpits the next day, even though we knew our loss rate was one out of five?"

"What?" she asked.

"Made love," he said bluntly. "Made wild, orgiastic love."

She had no words to respond. She was too unprepared, too aroused. She said nothing.

Then, in the same tone he had used before, he said, "What are you doing this weekend?"

"I'm going to bed now," she said. "Otherwise I'll sleep till Monday."

"And tomorrow?" he asked.

"I'm seeing Little John, exactly as I do every Saturday."

"For both lunch and dinner?"

"Probably not," she replied. "He usually has a date Saturday night."

"And Sunday?"

"Lacey, of course," she answered. "So it seems—"

"If Little John does have a date tomorrow night?" he went on relentlessly.

Suddenly she thought of what it feels like to take your first plunge into sea water so cold it turns your skin to fire, and you suddenly have enough energy to swim parallel to the coast for a mile. The exhaustion that had gripped her body moments ago was gone. It had been lost in the immeasurable depths of that male voice on the other end of the line. Depths to plunge in. Depths to swim in. Depths to drown in, and be reborn again.

"What time is it now?" she asked.

"Six forty-five," he answered.

"How soon could you be here?"

"Six fifty-five."

"Then be here," she said, and she put down the phone.

She turned, and looked at her clothes closet, full of Albee's new suits, and Albee's new dresses, and she waited for nine minutes to pass, and Mr. Lucky to appear.

But she made no move toward the closet, no move toward one of the new outfits. Instead, she turned slightly to the right, and gazed at her dungaree and old work-shirt image in the mirror. No time, not even any desire, for a bath. This was the way she was. This was the way he'd find her. This was the way he'd either reject her, or take her.

The first time, with Michael, it had been a trade. The second time, with Albee, it had been a gift. The third time—this time—it was neither. Nothing but sheer want on her part. Sheer need on her part. Sheer taking.

No excuses. No illusions. No fairy tales left any longer. The real world. Pam's world. Sally's world. Her world. Welcome, she thought, to the world of women. We fight. We wait. We suffer. And we need, so we take. Not what we dream, but only what we can get.

The buzzer sounded from downstairs. She pushed the button, long and hard. She heard the entrance door slam open. Aaron, she thought, you saw the ad—and you never called.

A man running up the stone stairs. A beautiful man. Bounding up the stairs two at a time.

She opened the door.

You never called, Aaron, she thought. You've become another fairy tale that I once believed in. And I need more than fairy tales now. And now, feeling the entire surface of her body tingle, she was going to take what she needed, and take and take and take it, from this magnificent, very real man, who seemed to need her in exactly the same way that she needed him.

Her arms and mouth reached out, and in a second they were filled by the real world. She moaned, she felt her belt being ripped open, she leaned back to let the tattered slacks drop around her ankles, and she left her last fairy tale a million years behind.

29.

Friday night—all Friday night—at her apartment, because Lacy was at a friend's. Saturday night, till two that morning, at his apartment, because Lacy was sleeping home, and thought her mother was out with Little John. Then Sunday night—all Sunday night—alone in her own bed, awake, remembering Friday and Saturday with him, and waiting for Monday morning, and the delivery of the first mail.

It arrived at eleven o'clock. None of them—neither Pam, nor Sally, nor Melissa—had done anything that morning except wait for the sound of the postman at the front door two flights below. They had left the apartment door open so they wouldn't miss him. And when they heard him walk away, whistling—all too soon, it seemed—Pam looked at Sally, who looked at Melissa, who looked at Pam.

"I'll get it," Pam finally said.

"No," said Sally. "I need to stretch my legs."

"No," Melissa snapped, grabbing the ring of keys from the table. "I couldn't live till you came upstairs again."

She forced herself to walk down the two flights of stairs slowly, as though she were in a fashion show. She watched her hand tremble as she brought the key up to unlock the bin. And then she pulled at the letters that were stuffed into that copper cage—far too few letters, so few that she could hold them all in her left hand, while her right hand scratched up against the sides of the copper bin, feeling for itself whether there was a letter or two her eyes had missed.

On her way upstairs, she counted the orders from the ad. There were eighteen in all. A fifteen hundred dollar ad, and all the orders it had brought in, on Friday and Saturday and Sunday, were eighteen. She stopped on every other stair, turned each letter around so she could study its face, held it up to the stairway lights so she could read the exact date, and hour, that it went through the post office. Most of them were mailed on Saturday, a few on Sunday. Then, by the time she had reached her door, she had torn open each envelope with her thumbnail, looked inside, seen the coupons and the checks, and discovered that seventeen of the letters were true orders, and one was merely a letter full of questions.

She walked in the door, looked at the other two women without a word, and threw the pile of letters on the couch in front of them. None of them said a word. She watched Sally and Pam repeat the futile procedure that she had just finished. And when they had stopped searching, and their faces began to look up, ashamedly, at her, she turned and walked out the door. Down the steps. Out of the brownstone. Down the street to Fifth Avenue. And then up Fifth Avenue, block by block, mile by mile. At some point she crossed Central Park to the West Side.

She had no purse, no money, no confidence. When she finally looked up and took notice of her surroundings, she found that she had walked all the way to Columbia Presbyterian Hospital, at 163rd Street—almost one hundred blocks, almost five miles. She had no watch. She had no idea what time it was. She didn't have a dime to make a phone call, a subway token to get back home. She looked up at the huge gray monolith of a hospital towering over her. The early autumn wind was cold, and she she suddenly realized that her bare arms were freezing. There was wetness under her eyes; her mascara must be smeared. She suddenly realized that old people, people sitting in gray and black coats on the park benches outside of the hospital, were staring at her.

She stopped at the entrance to the hospital. She didn't know why she had walked there. There was no one inside who could heal her. No one there who could bring the ad back to life.

It was cold, she thought. I'm going to freeze walking back home again.

Good, she thought, I deserve to freeze. Failure is cold.

She turned away from the hospital, put her head down, and forgot the eyes of the people staring at her. She began walking with her arms folded, shielding her bare arms with her hands as best she could. I deserve to freeze, she thought again. They didn't listen. They didn't believe. They didn't want.

Ten blocks . . . twenty blocks . . . forty blocks. Waiting for lights to change, being bumped by strangers, listening to the subway under her feet.

Maybe there's something wrong with the mail, she thought

for the five hundredth time, and then laughed at her own ability to lie to herself.

The ad didn't work. The cream worked. The ad didn't. The only question now was—what? Accept Michael's philosophy, and try the stores? Not in New York, after they'd failed so badly there. Send out the ad as a mailing piece to the three hundred thousand customers of her book? Fine. But why send them out a mailing piece that would lose at least $1,000 on its first test? Why—

She stopped, somewhere in New York City, lost, on a cold windy day. A hundred and fifty blocks, and the right question had suddenly popped into her mind.

Why wasn't it—why wasn't the cream ad as good as the book ad? Why didn't they believe it? The same woman had written both of them. She had been right the first time, but now was dismally wrong the second.

What was missing from that ad, that kept women from ordering it? She didn't know. Sally didn't know. Pam didn't know. Even Michael didn't know.

But there was one person who did know—who would know at a single glance. He had seen the ad. She knew he had seen the ad. But there had been no call, no comment, no word.

In the middle of Manhattan, a woman stood alone, on 80th Street and Broadway. She had no idea how she'd gotten there. She was standing stock still, her hands clasped around bare arms. Finally she moved to the front of a small stationery store, with its newspapers stretched out on a rack into the street.

The first reaction—the feeling she had to fight down with all her strength—was the urge to run home. Yes, run home, and call Aaron. After all these months, all the suffering and all the growth, to pick up the phone and break the promise she'd made to herself, and ask Aaron, her surrogate God, her primary fairy godfather, to reach out his hand and heal the bleeding wound.

Call Aaron! The thought repeated itself in her mind, ten times each minute. Call Aaron. He'll know. He'll help. He'll give. Call Aaron. Break your word to yourself. Throw away your independence. Give up the real world because it's too cold. Run back to fairyland. Make the first fatal move. Admit you're a woman, and sit, and listen, and be corrected, and take orders.

Oh God, how she wanted to obey that thought. How she wanted to make that call, and then make the trade that that call demanded. How she wanted to be Cinderella again.

Coins dropping into the tin container at the newsstand. Her body being bitten incessantly by the wind, being riddled incessantly by waves of failure. And no husband—no real husband at all—to call up, and say, "Make better." No magic wand permissible. No wonder-working Aaron. Only—only—only myself. Only my brain. Only my thoughts. Only my memories—yes, my memories—of Aaron, to help me now.

Aaron, she thought. I have fifteen years of memories of Aaron stored inside me. Aaron Carpenter, master ad craftsman. Welder of words. Magician of headlines. Who would come home every night, for almost fifteen years, and talk about those concepts, those headlines, those positionings, those ads, those campaigns, those results. And she had sat at the dinner table, and she had listened adoringly to those stories of persuasive triumphs. It was the woman's role, she thought—a good deal of the woman's role—to listen. And all the stories, she realized with surprise, all the techniques were still stored in her brain. They were there, sitting in a special Aaron Carpenter circuit in her brain, just waiting to be pulled out, and turned on, and skimmed over for help, just as though he himself were standing next to her.

Now her feet began to move again toward the apartment, but this time faster and more determined than before. Her hands came down from her shoulders, the cold against her arms no longer mattered. No sensation except the movement of her feet, the movement of her mind, could get through to her. She was going over five hundred dinners, five hundred ads by Aaron Carpenter.

She began to pass people, almost at a running speed. She no longer waited for the lights to turn in her favor; instead, she walked out into the crawling line of cars as they were moving against her, and threaded her way sideways past one fender after another.

Aaron Carpenter's eyes were now looking out of her head, and appraising an ad that she had read so many times, that she knew every word of it by heart. Aaron's mind was moving over the ad, paragraph by paragraph, whispering silently inside her head that this sentence was good, that this sentence was good, that this sentence was good, that this sentence was good. Good. Good. Good. Good.

And then, ten blocks from home, her body and Aaron's mind suddenly halted. ''No!'' She shouted out loud. ''Bad!'' And four passing people suddenly turned and stared at her.

No, she thought, using Aaron's mind. The cream is too good. The photographs are too good. The truth, Aaron Carpenter's voice said to her, will not be believed if it goes beyond common experience. Therefore, you cannot sell a true miracle. You cannot sell it; you have to give it away. Yes, give it away. You have to make sure that the person trying that miracle cannot lose money, and cannot lose face, to prove whether you are lying or not. You cannot ask her to pay you for trying it; instead, you have to pay her to try it.

''I have to pay them to try it,'' she said aloud, not giving a damn whether anyone passing by heard her, or looked at her. I have to pay them to try it, and I have to put that promise of payment in the very headline of my ad.

And then she laughed out loud into that cold wind. No, she said, I won't promise them their money back in that headline. I'll promise them *double* their money back if that cream doesn't work. ''Twice your money back,'' she thought like Aaron Carpenter, ''if every word of this ad doesn't come true for you.''

That was it, she thought. The final promise that the campaign needed to make it believable. Capture that line, she thought. Stop thinking. Say nothing else to yourself till you reach home. You have the line; now keep it.

Her feet began moving again. Her brain was like a broken record, thinking nothing, feeling nothing, seeing nothing, except the exact wording, and the exact spacing, of that one golden headline.

Down Fifth Avenue, along the park, running, saying the same words over and over again. Like a mantra. Like a hymn. Like a prayer that she, and Aaron, had devised—to move the real world in her direction, on that cold, dismal afternoon of marvelous failure.

30.

When she arrived back at the apartment, both women were waiting. She refused to allow either one of them to talk to her. She waived them into immediate silence, sat down at the desk, and scrawled the precious headline on the first piece of paper available.

Then she went to the tiny stove, and set the water boiling for hot chocolate. Then put a sweater around her numb shoulders. And then asked Pam, "How many letters this afternoon?"

"Thirty-three," Pam replied.

"That's fifty altogether," Melissa said. "That means," and she went back to the desk, and the small electronic calculator confirmed it, "that we'll lose almost a thousand dollars on a fifteen hundred dollar ad."

"That bad?" Sally whispered.

"Just about that bad," Melissa answered. Then she paused, and looked straight at the younger woman. "The headline's wrong," she said.

"Oh?" Sally said. And a pitched battle began with half an hour of logic, of reasoning, of arguing, of defending, and finally, of downright screaming on Sally's part.

"Tomorrow's mail will pick up," Sally insisted.

"Not enough," Melissa said.

"You don't put the guarantee in the headline," Sally screamed.

"We do," Melissa repeated.

"You do," Sally said, "I don't. You know exactly what to do now. You take over. It's your ad. You paid for it; now you ruin it completely."

"That's possible," Melissa said. "I may. But I'm going to try anyway."

"Not with me, baby," Sally got on her feet. She pulled on her coat. "Good luck. It's been a nice job. Call me when the new ad flops."

"She has quite a temper," Melissa said to Pam after Sally stormed out.

"She'll be back tomorrow," Pam said.

"I know," Melissa said, still shaking from the cold and from the argument. And then: "Sit down. We have a hell of a lot of rewriting to do."

The next morning, Sally was back at eight, was at her typewriter five minutes later, and took every crude sentence that Pam and Melissa had hammered together, and began to weave it into a professional rewrite, that was finished and ready to print before lunch.

Meanwhile, Melissa was glued to the phone, calling up one after another of Aaron's friends, asking them to recommend the names of the top experts in the mail order business. She had thought that the cream was going to be as easy to sell as the book. It wasn't. Now she was going to do her own kind of research, to help sell her own kind of ad, using every contact, every weapon, every tool of persuasion she knew.

And she needed them all. Because mail order was a man's business, and although it was easy for her to get to see the men she needed, it was far harder to get the information she wanted from them without giving the ultimate in return.

An endless stream of dinner and lunch conferences. She must have met twenty men who had made a million dollars or more in the mail order business. Of the first fifteen, ten propositioned her by the first night, two propositioned her by the third night, only three had the gallantry to give information without asking anything in return. Her great talent, she decided, was being able to get any information at all, and still maintain even her clothes intact.

She never deceived any of these men, even for a fleeting second. She told them she was married, temporarily separated —and faithful. The only lie—the implied lie, the forgivable lie—was that she neglected to tell them to whom she was faithful. They might or might not have believed her; it didn't matter, as long as they continued to take her out and feed her the facts she needed to know.

The new ad was run two weeks later, in the *Denver Rocky Mountain News*. Again, there was the investment of almost fifteen hundred dollars, to find out if women in Colorado would listen to her new version of the cream story. Again, there was the terrifying wait for the first mail to come, the scrambling down the stairs to count the now-larger number of pieces, the entering of the number of orders each morning and each afternoon, the slow build-up of income until the number of dollars received from the ad had passed fifteen hundred, then two thousand, then, at last, the golden three thousand dollar mark. Every night, after the other two women had gone, she spent a half hour alone with her calculator, before she dressed for that evening's date. Every night, she checked the growing stack of figures, to make sure that she had made no arithmetical error, that her estimate of the promised profit of the ad was completely accurate. Finally, when the orders dwindled down to just a few each day, she knew that she had made almost eight hundred dollars' net profit on a fifteen hundred dollar advertising investment. One dollar gained for every two spent. Still not as good as the book ad. But profitable. Very profitable.

The ad had proven itself. It was now as good as they could make it. It was ready to be converted into a mailing piece, and sent out to the three hundred thousand buyers of her book. It was now ready to insert in the great, and expensive, national media.

She totalled up the money she had, the money she could borrow from a mail order advertising agency, and the money that all those mailing pieces, and all those full-page ads, would cost. Then she threw in the number of jars of cream she would have to buy to fill those orders, plus the number of catalogs, offering other products, that she would have to print to go out with those orders, plus the cost of opening that much mail, packing that many jars and catalogs, and shipping them out as soon as possible through the United States Post Office.

The total figure came to one hundred and forty-eight thousand dollars. More than one hundred thousand dollars in excess of what she had in the bank. She would have to sign personally for the rest. If the gamble didn't pay off, she would lose every cent she had in the bank—and be in debt, for years afterward.

But millions of women out there needed that cream. When she had accepted the cream, she had taken with it the responsibility to tell those women about it, as truthfully as possible, as soon as possible. And she wasn't going to let a hundred thousand dollar debt stop her. She went down to the advertising agency, she spent thirty-five minutes reading and signing a series of iron-bound contracts that would haunt her for the rest of her life if the promotion failed. And then she rose, shook the owner's hand, and walked out into the street, feeling as though she'd just been given the moon as a present, and now had to wait only six weeks for its delivery date.

31.

One man. In all those weeks, there was, in bed, only one man. Michael Black. And he was all the man—all the man in the world—that she needed.

The second weekend, they discovered the one position that they came back to a dozen times during their meetings that followed. First, they would make love with her on top, or with him on top. And suddenly there would be sort of a mock-childish struggle, they would flail around the bed in a jumble of hands and arms, and then she would have him pinned on his back, with her hands holding down his arms, and her lips on his chest, tasting every part of the sweet, sweat-filled skin with her lips, her teeth, her tongue.

Then, time after time, she would murmer in a soft low voice, "Don't move." He would whisper up to her, "I won't." And she would slowly turn herself around on his body till she faced away from him, slowly pivoting with his beautiful erect penis still inside of her, never letting it slip out a fraction of an inch, making a complete turn on it till she was facing his feet, with his penis at an entirely different angle in her vagina, and with his hands now on her back, underneath the cascades of golden hair, massaging her shoulders. She would sit calmly that way for an unknowable amount of time—his penis trapped inside her, but not moving—his hands on the back of her neck and shoulders, softly kneading, caressing that fluid skin, with the feeling of her hair covering his hands and arms, and reflecting like waves in water every move of his fingers.

Then, sometime later, his left hand would slowly slide down her left shoulder, down her left arm, till it met her left hand on her own knee. It would grasp the hand and bring it softly and slowly back, till she could feel his tongue massage the inside of her palm. Then his left hand would leave hers, leave it to the mouth and the tongue, and slowly return to her left thigh. It would slide around the thigh to her spread-apart pubis, and slip slowly into place upon her erect and extended clitoris, facing away from him, but filled with the expectation, the need of that slow, lingering touch.

Then she would lower her body slowly back, till her gold hair rested on his stomach and chest, and she could feel the dimensions of his body with her hair. Now her clitoris was even more fully exposed to his gentle fingers, and she began to slowly rotate on his penis, while his fingers picked up the motion of that rotation, and fed it back to her at an ever-increasing pace. Soon, she was bent back almost parallel, resting her hands on his arms, completely comfortable, supported by the weight of his arms underneath her on the bed, feeling the triple flow of sensation into her brain like the tributary of three mighty rivers feeding into an endless sea. The wonderful sensations inside her, combined with the overwhelming tingling and response of her clitoris, combined with the somehow even more sensuous tracing of the outlines of his body with her full head of hair—all turned her drunk on top of him, made her body almost float parallel on top of him, built the nerve endings of her body up to a triple orgasm.

Slowly, nerve ending by nerve ending, all three tributaries broke into the sea and overflowed it at the same moment, and she dissolved into sound, and became the stormy, sweeping, endless ocean, and there was nothing in the world but the pounding waves of that endless ocean. And then he too dissolved into motion and sound, as he became the beach being pounded upon by that surf inside.

They repeated this ritual over and over again—day, night, sunrise, dawn, morning. She had never known that you could be drunk, mad, hopelessly insane on sex, and sex alone. That during these times nothing else in the world—not even love— could matter except the next act of sex. The next stroking. The next heightening. The next overwhelming orgasm. Sleep, on those nights, was only a pause from sex. Food was fuel for sex. Talk was a means of surrounding sex with intimacy and meaning.

Weekend after weekend, both of them were devoted to the worship of sex. She was its prime priestess. She was its willing slave. She was its mindless novitiate. She needed nothing else.

She was nature. She was beauty. She was feeling. And nothing else existed for them on those nights . . . or mattered.

32.

Eight days after the first mailing went out—to 296,513 customers of her book—Melissa Carpenter thought that she had imported Las Vegas into her tiny apartment, and every slot machine, every crap table, every blackjack board, every roulette wheel on the entire strip had all paid off for her at once, and the croupiers were simply shoveling stacks of money across the green velvet surfaces into her eager hands.

After two days of bending her friendly postman almost double with the weight of letters he was carrying to her brownstone, the post office called up and told her that they would send a special carrier to her, with a truck, once a day, or otherwise Joe Held, the postman on that route for fourteen years, would explode to the union.

Melissa agreed, and once every day, promptly at noon, the blue and white and red truck rolled up to the front of their house, and two burly postmen got out and carried three or four mail sacks up her two flights of stairs, and finally dumped them unceremoniously on her apartment carpet, which, by now, was noticeably dirty from their grime.

It took all day long, including Saturday, to open, to count, to total up, and to deposit all those money orders, and all that cash. And one day, when they had finished opening three thousand orders, Pam stood up, her arms black from ink and dirt, and gleefully held a stack of money orders and checks in her arm, as long as that arm itself.

"Look at me," she said, "I'm holding over twenty-five thousand dollars in my arm, and it's not even heavy."

Sally looked up from the count sheets she had been keeping of each individual mailing and newspaper, and said, "It will be, honey, if you try to walk out of the door with that money still in your arm."

Pam put down the huge stack of money, and said, suddenly, "I think we should all be searched, inside and out, before we're allowed to leave this place every night."

Before Melissa could answer, Salley immediately said,

"Agreed. But there has to be a new man every night to do the inside searching."

At the end of the second week, some one hundred and twenty thousand dollars later, Melissa suddenly realized that they were doing nothing but serving as clerks, and spending all their time opening the mail, depositing the money, and tallying up the results. The money itself was too magnetic. It riveted each one of them to it, and allowed them to do nothing but serve it.

Within hours, she had located the best mail-order fulfillment house in New York, had hired them to open the mail and tend to the money for her, and had notified the post office that, from the next day on, all that beautiful mail, plus all that seductive money, was to be sent to the professionals, rather than the obsessed amateurs that they had proved themselves to be.

So the next day, fifteen business days later, the three of them arrived at a mail-empty apartment, cleaned up the precious dirt that had seeped into every crack and crevice of rug, floor, walls, and desk . . . sharpened their pencils again, put aside their adding machines and calculators . . . and settled down to the humdrum existence of writing new ads for the catalog, ordering new products to fill the orders from those ads, checking out the day's results from the fulfillment company, and seeing exactly how much money they were making, and what the next step would be.

After five weeks of this they were flushed with success. Drunk with business. High on profit. One hundred and fifty thousand dollars spent for advertising. Another two hundred thousand dollars spent on product and fulfillment costs. But over four hundred and fifty thousand dollars taken in so far. As far as Melissa could tell, and she checked out her figures ten times daily, she had already made close to one hundred thousand dollars profit, in her first mail order campaign alone. One hundred thousand dollars sitting in her bank account. Over and above the fifty thousand dollars that Albee had loaned her. How proud he would be!

Then there was the day the reorders began coming in. At first, just a trickle, perhaps ten to twenty a day. But, about one and a half months after the first orders had been received, that trickle had turned into a small flood. And Melissa read every one of the reorder letters that contained any testimonials or information at all, just as she read every letter from someone who did not like the product, and filed each one of those pro and con letters away carefully in her file cabinet.

Every reorder was, to her, like a faint distant kiss from the woman who sent it. This was what she had dreamt about; this was what she had prayed for—that she would sell these women, not a product, but a real difference in the apparent age of their faces. The product was what they had paid for, but the difference in how old they looked was the cause of the second order, for one or two or three jars, so they would never fear running out of it again.

And then, as the magazine and newspaper ads and the direct mail piece grew old, the flow of orders slowly dwindled. The fulfillment house finished its count, not at four o'clock that afternoon, but at two.

The first attack on the mail order front had been overwhelmingly successful. Now her net profit stood at over one hundred and thirty thousand dollars. But the flow of new orders was shutting off, like a faucet being slowly closed. Only the reorder flow was building volume. What was she to do now? Go to other lists, outside lists, of women who did not know of her? Run ads in newspapers and magazines that the mail order experts she had consulted had not recommended? Had all her success been based on beginner's luck? Would she lose back what she had won? How much should she gamble again? All of it?

She had to speak to someone who knew. She had to keep moving the product. She had to reach the millions of women who still hadn't heard about it.

Once again, she needed help.

33.

The help came—but not, this time, from a man.

For weeks now, Pam had been coming into the office with the once-clear area under her eyes getting darker and darker, with her face becoming more and more haggard from the loss of sleep. She was never late. She never complained. Not once did she hint to Melissa that she would welcome one of their private lunches outside the office. She arrived at the stroke of nine; she stayed at night till there wasn't a scrap of paper left on her desk; she seemed more alive and more cheerful than she'd been since the two of them had joined forces once again. But there was no doubt that she was trading her sleep for something, and Melissa was sure that something wasn't sex.

Melissa had hinted interest, and got no response. So she waited, and hovered around receptively after hours whenever she could. Then, the fifth Friday night, when the two of them were alone, Pam suddenly said, without even looking up from the account book she was working on, "How would you like to make an extra quarter of a million dollars in the next few months, kiddo?"

"Sounds like it might be fun," Melissa answered, playing the game, not looking up from the pile of reorders she was reading. "Depends on what I have to do to get it."

Pam closed the account book. "Just let me pour out my guts to you for five minutes."

The reorders were pushed aside. "I'm listening," Melissa said.

"It's kind of a stupid story," Pam said.

"Let me be the judge of that."

"I've been meaning to tell it to you for weeks now, but I haven't had the punch line till tonight." There was a pause. The space between them dissolved. "All right. For twenty-five years in this town, I've been what? A face, a fuck, and a failure. Where was I when you pulled me out to work here? Clerking in a store, for a hundred and fifty a week. And then you started this business. And you tapped me on the shoulder and you said, 'Hey, you've got a brain. And I can use that brain. Come put it to work for me.' Do you know—do you have any idea at all—what that meant to me?"

"Yes," Melissa said. "I've been a face myself for years, remember? I had to prove, I'm still proving, that there's a brain behind that face."

"Honey," Pam went on, "you started a business, I started a new life. One week I was wrapping packages, the next I was giving orders for thousands of dollars' worth of product over the phone. And you know what? The men—yes, the men on the other end of that phone believed me. They took the orders from me, and they filled them. And they filled them on time, exactly the way I told them to fill them. And you know what happened?''

"Possibly," Melissa answered.

"I stopped going out to the neighborhood bar to get screwed every weekend. Because I was worth more than three beers, and a half hour of sloppy love. Because I was . . . important. How do you like that?''

"I can't tell you," Melissa said, "how much I like that."

"I've been working here," and Pam thought for a second, "an average of twelve hours a day. I haven't told you, but I've been studying at home six hours a night. Because I don't like to come down to this office not knowing exactly what I'm doing. Because now that I've got a brain, I want to see how far it can go.''

"It can go a long way," Melissa said. "So far that I can't even see the first turn in the track.''

"Really? Honestly?''

"You constantly surprise me," Melissa said. "You come up with solutions that would have never occurred to me. You shave costs. You make packaging work. You hound the poor slobs to death—and God forbid a single label should be missing. Lady, you're not only smart—you're tough.''

"It's called stubbornness," Pam smiled. "But really?''

"Honest to God.''

"All right, then I'm going to say what I'm going to say. I've told you about part one of my research—the reading. But part two is the listening—the smiling, the asking, the applauding. You do your research on the top brains in the industry—the Ken Brennans, the Jay Cogans, the Gene Gellers. I don't. I pick the follow-up men—the little guys who get the job done—the nice, intelligent, mediocre men who make the genius-ideas work, who figure up the profit and loss columns, and, most important of all, who know the nuts and bolts of this crazy, seat-of-your-pants business.'' Pam's face flushed. "Sweet Jesus," she said. "I sound like one of the books I've been reading.''

"To me, honey," Melissa said, "you sound marvelous. Go on.''

"Do you want to hear what I found out?''

"No," Melissa said. "I don't *want* to hear what you found out. I'm dying to hear it.''

"One," Pam said. "No one ever told you how much a mail order ad drops off, in orders pulled, between the first time you run it in a newspaper, and the second. The answer is one-third. If you wait one month—one tiny month, honey—you get two-thirds as many orders the second time as the first.''

Figures began to flash in Melissa's mind. There was no need to open the count books. She didn't have to; they were all in her mind.

"You ran a hundred and fifty thousand in advertising the first time around, didn't you?" Pam asked.

"That's exactly right," Melissa said. "That means I can rerun about ninety-five thousand again. At a damn good profit."

"Ninety-seven, to be exact. There's a sheet in your countbook, with every one of them listed for you."

"You're incredible."

"I'm just beginning. And you can do the same thing with the mailing to your own lists. Give those three hundred thousand women another chance to try the cream, and they'll give you back another seventy thousand in profit."

"That easy?" Melissa asked.

"That easy, when you know how. But now—now comes the real payoff. It's called percentage of reorders to total number of jars shipped. Ever heard of it?"

"No."

"But I bet you can figure it out, right now, in your head, down to the last percentage point."

Melissa could almost see those lovely reorders, every one of them, in front of her eyes. She'd gone over their counts sheets, every single day, since they first came in. It was a cinch. "About thirty-five percent."

"I'd say more," Pam said. "But I've always been a hopeless optimist. But let's play it safe, and say one-third. That's in just two months. Do you understand what that means?"

Again, the tingle at the bottom of Melissa's spine. The sudden turning over of her stomach, as though she'd just seen the most gorgeous man in the world. But this time she didn't run away from those feelings; she welcomed them. Because she'd fought for them. She'd gambled for them. She's suffered for them. And, by God, she'd earned them.

"That means," Melissa said slowly, "that one out of every three women reorder the cream in just two months."

"In just two months," Pam echoed. "Now work it out for six months. Figure out how many there are going to be in six months, and how much profit you're going to make on each.''

Numbers that tasted as sweet as candy. That you wanted to hold in your mind for a minute, and lick again and again. "Then we should make," and she blushed at the size of the results, "more than one hundred thousand dollars extra profit from those reorders alone.''

"One-fifty," Pam said. "But remember, I always see things a little too bright. But that's my two hundred and fifty thousand dollars extra profit, right?"

"Right," Melissa said. "Pam, I want to—"

"Don't interrupt me during the one chance in my life I've had to be a smartass. Because now, says the Herr Female Professor, 'Ve come to the crucial question. How many products, mein schoene schtudent, do you think get a reorder rate of one-third in the first two months?' ''

"I imagine very few."

"According to all my friends, almost none. And"—her eyes narrowed and she studied the potential reaction in Melissa's face carefully—"what would happen if you took that mail order profit, and that one-third automatic reorder rate—"

Now Melissa finished the sentence—"and presented them to the retail stores, as proof that the cream would do the same, or better, for them. My good Lord!"

"Precisely," Pam agreed. "End of lecture."

There was a moment of silence. Then Melissa said, "I'm proud of you. I don't know how to tell you how proud of you I am."

Pam blinked. "I've waited forty-three years for someone to say that. Thanks."

"I want to give you a commission."

"No, ma'am. I've already got a piece of the action."

"A raise then."

"No way. Not till you and Sally get one too. You hired me to do a job; I did it."

"What, then?"

An expression that was almost a smile, almost a grimace of pain crossed Pam's face. "My choice?" she asked.

"If I can give it to you—anything."

"I want you to build this business," Pam said, "to be so big and so good, that the whole country will know about it. And I want you to give me a chance to grow as big in this business as I can. All right?"

"More than all right."

"And then—someday—I don't know when, but someday, if I work out, some newspaper in this town's going to take a photo of me, as one of your top executives, shaking hands on a deal with some other top executive. As I said, I'm a hopeless optimist, but I can practically see that photo now." There were tears in Pam's eyes as she looked straight at Melissa. "There are eighty, maybe ninety guys in this town that I want to see that picture. I want them to see that photo, I want them to read that caption, and I want them to say, 'Jesus Christ, I screwed that woman. And I thought she was nothing but another dumb little broad.' "

Now the eyes turned away from Melissa's. "And I want them to know—I want them to know for the rest of their lives—that I'm not just another dumb little broad. That's payment enough—all the payment in the world—for me."

34.

The apartment below hers became vacant, and Melissa snapped it up with a one-year lease, moved in phones and some ramshackle desks, and hired five women to handle the ever-mounting flood of reorders, inquiries, paperwork, and record-keeping.

Each reorder came to the downstairs apartment, where the girls opened them, and sent up every question, every complaint, every word of praise to Melissa. This intimate contact with her growing army of customers was one function she would not delegate, for even a single letter, to anyone else. She sometimes spent up to three hours a day with this special mail, reading it, absorbing it, dictating personal letters whenever she felt that a difficult question deserved a personal answer.

The telephone number on the letter asking for the reorders was switched from the living apartment upstairs, to the working apartment downstairs. Between nine-thirty and five-thirty, at least forty or fifty phone calls were received from customers. And whenever she had the chance, when she was not drowned in direct business matters or meetings, Melissa would accept these calls, and hear the voice of her public, one-to-one, woman-to-woman.

But, after five-thirty, when the downstairs apartment emptied, and when she decided to take Lacy or Little John—or some supplier, or advertising rep, or media executive—out to dinner, then the calls were switched to an answering service; the women were asked to call back the next day.

On some of these weekday nights, however—as often as she could arrange it—Sally O'Toole would wait till Melissa and Pam had left the upstairs apartment, would slip down the one flight of stairs to the working apartment, would place herself at one of the desks, pick up the phone, tell the answering service to put the calls directly through, and would sit there—sometimes till ten o'clock at night—answering calls from women all over the country.

In the months that had passed since Melissa had hired her, Sally had written over twenty ads—face ads, hair ads, figure ads—for the corporation, all in the first person, and all signed with Melissa's name. She had spent hours interviewing Melissa on the way she used these products, and her own life experiences with these products. She had duplicated, down to the last turn of phrase, Melissa's own conversational style, so that now when Melissa read a new piece of copy, she could swear that she herself was taking to the customer on that piece of paper. Sally O'Toole had become Melissa Carpenter's hair, Melissa Carpenter's figure, Melissa Carpenter's hands, Melissa Carpenter's neck, and, above all, Melissa Carpenter's face.

During those same months, Sally had lost a good thirteen pounds. Her face was now properly made up, the strong jaw softened, the brilliant eyes highlighted, the missing cheekbones added by the magic of Melissa's skills. Her style of dress had progressed from Macy's to Saks, though she spent only ten percent more for her clothes.

A new Sally O'Toole had been created, as promised, by her employer. But though the outside had altered dramatically, there was no way the inside could be reached by mere clothes, posture, or makeup. There was more initial respect, less ultimate brutality, more-in-between spending for her favors—but she still instinctively chose the users instead of the givers, the scorers instead of the romantics, the men who responded to sex with enthusiasm, and any mention of love with immediate absence.

The phone on the desk in front of her rang. She waited for the third ring, and then picked it up.

"Yes," she said gently, confidently.

"May I speak to Melissa Carpenter," the voice on the other end said.

"This is she," Sally replied immediately.

"Oh, Mrs. Carpenter," the voice said, slightly flustered. "I didn't expect you to answer your own phone."

Sally had repeated the next lines over a hundred times before.

"It's after business hours in New York now," she said. "The staff has left. So I pick up the phone myself, to make sure that anyone who needs help from me, gets that help, without waiting another day."

"That's wonderful of you," the voice said.

"Not at all," Sally said.

"Oh, it is, it is." The voice took on a more intimate, a more confiding tone. "You know, I've read almost every word of your ads, and your catalog."

A thrill shot through Sally's back and shoulders, yet her voice remained unchanged as she said, "That's very kind of you."

"And I've studied your pictures, dozens of times. I just can't believe that you're actually over forty years old."

"I am though, really." The words came effortlessly out of Sally's mouth. "The photographs are completely unretouched."

"Mrs. Carpenter," the woman said. "I hope you'll forgive me for saying this, but you're a miracle. An absolute miracle."

"Not at all," Sally replied.

"But it's not only your youth," the woman went on. "It's also your beauty. Not just an outer beauty, but something more. An inner beauty, a beauty of the soul, that just shines through in every one of your pictures."

"Thank you," Sally replied. "That's most kind of you to say."

"Oh, Mrs. Carpenter, You must lead such an exciting life," the voice spurted out.

"I lead a good life," Sally replied. "There are moments of great adventure, and beauty in it, of course. But the deepest fulfillment, by far, is helping friends of mine—and I do hope you'll consider yourself my friend—find their hidden beauty, just as I've found mine."

"Oh, Mrs. Carpenter—"

"Call me Melissa," Sally said.

"Oh," and then there was a hesitation. And then the voice said, softly and tremulously, "Melissa . . . you could never have been less than beautiful for a single moment in your life."

"But I was," Sally corrected. "When I was thirteen," and now Sally's voice took on the genuine tremble of deep emotion, "I was impossibly fat. In fact," she went on, openly lying, interweaving her own story with that of Melissa's, "it was years before I had a real date," and then she caught herself and moved without a trace into the real story, "but then I began to look at myself, not as what I was at that particular moment, but what I could be if I took myself in hand. In fact, I think it was then and there that I began forming the philosophy that now guides this company."

"Wonderful," the woman said. "It's such an inspiration, just talking to you. I could go on all night, but you must be terribly busy."

"I would love chatting with you for hours," Sally said, "but I'm afraid there are some matters here I must attend to. And, besides, it must be costing a great deal of money to place this call. So, tell me how can I be of help to you."

And then the problem was explained to Sally, the orders taken and filed. And so it went, till eight, nine, even ten o'clock. Perhaps twenty calls, perhaps forty. Until finally the phones fell silent.

The room was now empty. The dream was over. Sally looked at her watch, decided that the Carleton Deli down the block was the only place where she could still have the semblance of a meal. And then to some bar—any bar—anywhere—for her gin. No conversation—no men. Just sitting there, and running over in her mind one conversation after another from that evening. Hearing those women's voices again. Thanking them. Instructing them. Inspiring them.

Every woman deserves to be beautiful, she thought, quoting from her last ad. Even if only on the telephone.

35.

Melissa waited a month to go to the stores. First she had to hire the finest artists for redesigning her jars and labels . . . then hone the ads so they would sparkle with a department-store logo . . . and, above all, to make sure that the reorder percentage stayed at that magic one-third.

Then she took those reorders figures, had them attested to by a public notary, put them under her arm, and marched off to Saks, Bloomingdale's, Bendel's, and Bonwit's.

The first three accepted; Bonwit's declined. The conditions were a thirty-thousand dollar advertising campaign in all three New York newspapers, all goods shipped to the stores on consignment, with no money down from the stores and no guarantee that they would buy a single jar that Melissa didn't sell for them, and a personal three-day appearance by Melissa herself, at each store, demonstrating the use of the cream, and the effect it had had upon her own skin.

Nine days of personal appearance, from nine in the morning till five at night. On your feet all that time, an open target, with one hour off for a quick sandwich, and your voice hoarse and raw at the end of each day.

Afterward, Melissa remembered the first day, a Friday; the other eight were only a blur in her mind. That first day was the test, the struggle, the proof, the triumph. The rest were only confirmations of that proof. And it was also that first day that she took Michael along with her, to personally see the reaction to his cream of a continuously changing group of women.

He arrived at the same time as she, at nine-thirty, half an hour before the stores opened. While she checked her face, and the counter displays, he was busy picking up jar after jar, unscrewing their caps, and tenderly sniffing the contents for absolute perfection of scent.

She was nervous. He was more so. She was merely afraid that her product would be rejected by the public, and her business ruined and her fortune lost. He, on the other hand, was terrified that one woman —just one—might not like the smell, or feel, or texture of his child, and might crinkle up her nose, and walk away with her money still in her pocketbook—and leave an unwanted jar sitting on the hard cold shelf, all alone, like an orphan.

It became apparent, almost from the first fifteen minutes, however, that almost none of the women wanted to reject a jar. Melissa answered endless questions, Michael hovered, and clerks rang up sale after sale.

By four o'clock that afternoon, she was bone-weary; he still looked as though he had knotted his tie only half an hour before. It was a day of crowning victory, of record sales; and yet there he stood, in all his masculine splendor, still fearing that first word of outright censure, still not reassured that he had produced a miracle treatment in a tiny jar.

And then, at four forty-six exactly, catastrophe struck. A woman about sixty-eight years old, with a face that looked like crumpled paper, poked her finger into one of the test jars, held it up to her nose, then stuck out her tongue and tasted—yes, tasted—the cream. Then she handed the jar back to the nearest clerk, and said, "It smells good, but it tastes terrible. Not for me, thanks." And she walked out of the store.

Melissa glanced at her, smiled, and went on to the next customer's question. She was deep in the explanation of the reason why the cream worked, when she suddenly noticed that none of her customers was paying her the slightest attention. Instead, their eyes were riveted to the gorgeous, broad-sholdered man who had hastily forced his way through the crowd of women, and had now arrived at the counter about three feet away from Melissa. This man, evidently a reincarnation of Tyrone Power, had picked up the rejected jar that old woman had put down, dipped his finger deep into that jar, and drawn out a huge dollop of cream. And there he stood, oblivious to the mob of fascinated women surrounding him, taking tiny nibbles out of the cream.

Melissa stopped. The clerks stopped. Now every woman for counters around was staring at Michael, slowly devouring his cream. And at last he looked up at them, and said in a puzzled voice, "It's not true. She's wrong. It tastes delicious."

The women burst out laughing. Melissa joined them, and even managed to say, in a dulcet tone, "Thank you, sir," and then went on with the sale of the cream.

When the day was over, and they had celebrated, at dinner and in bed, just before he rolled over to finally drop off to sleep, she cuddled gently behind his back, reached up her lips to his ear, and whispered gently, "Darling."

"Yes," he muttered, only half-awake.

"If you ever come down to a store again while I'm there demonstrating, and decide to eat your cream in front of my audience, then, darling, that night I'll bite off your testicles, and ask you to taste them too."

She felt him stiffen. Then nod. Then laugh. And then say, "Agreed. I'll stay in the laboratory. You stay at the counters."

36.

After nine personal appearances in two weeks, Melissa's fuel supply finally ran out. On Friday she had a dinner date with the vice-chairman of Consolidated Department Stores. There was no doubt that he was important to her future. But there was also no doubt that if she kept performing for one more hour, there might be no future to perform in. So, for the first time since she had started the business, she called him up at a quarter to six, apologized, and rescheduled the dinner.

So she was alone. Free. Ready to collapse from exhaustion. Her plans were simple—a piece of pie from the refrigerator. A hot bath, makeup off, and bed. Nothing more. She pulled off her suit jacket, and moved toward the phone just as it rang, to call up the answering service and make sure that no calls, except from the two children, were allowed to come in. When she reached the phone, it had rung three times, and then stopped. But the light was still on. She looked up at the clock. Ten minutes to six. Strange, she thought, as she picked up the receiver, and held it to her ear.

"—speak to Mrs. Melissa Carpenter," an unfamiliar woman's voice was saying.

"This is she." It was Sally's voice, speaking in a tone that Melissa had never heard before. Sally's voice—cool and collected, self-confident almost to the point of pomposity. Condescending.

And then the woman's voice went on. And Sally answered, and Melissa stood there, numb, unable to do anything but listen to the incredible exchange that had become an electronically produced nightmare. Sally, in that make-believe voice, was playing the woman like a hooked fish—drawing compliment after compliment out of her, submissiveness after submissiveness.

The call would have taken Melissa less than two minutes to have handled, the customer would have been completely satisfied. But Sally kept the poor woman on the phone, all the way from Oklahoma, for over ten minutes, coaxing out of her even more abject adoration. Then the call ended, the phone went dead and Melissa stood there, until a second call came through on the other line, and both she and Sally tuned in to it at the same moment, and the same game began all over again. This time Melissa could tolerate the exchange for less than a minute. Then her finger shot down to the hold button, she lowered the receiver silently onto its hook, and she flew out of the apartment, down the flight of stairs to the apartment below, and threw open the door. Sally sat there, phone to her ear, eyes enormous as they stared back at her.

"Put down the phone," Melissa said.

"It's a personal call," Sally replied.

"Tell Mrs. Crawford in Chicago to call back tomorrow. And do it right now."

Sally blinked, and she said, in exactly the same even, calm, patrician tone, "I'm sorry, Mrs. Crawford, but an important business call has just come through on the other line. Would you mind terribly calling me back tomorrow? Thank you." She slowly lowered the phone to the hook. "How long have you been listening?"

"Just this call and the last," Melissa answered. "That was enough."

"Did you enjoy yourself on the phone as much as you admire yourself in the newspapers?" Sally went on.

"That wasn't me on the phone," Melissa began.

"That isn't you in the papers either."

Melissa sat down on one of the folding chairs, by the desk opposite Sally's. "Are you drunk?" she asked.

"No, not at all. Not yet."

"How long—"

"For weeks." There was no fear and no guilt in Sally's

face. Only raw, naked hatred. "For hundreds of calls. Hundreds."

"Playing me?" Melissa asked.

"Being you," Sally replied immediately. "Being you, honey. Just as I've been you, every day, for the past five months. Only this time," she went on, "I got something out of it."

"What?"

"What you don't want anymore. What you never lacked, and I never had."

"You're crazy," Melissa said.

"Insane," Sally echoed. "Certifiably mad." And even more hatred blackened her face. "To have made you all that money—all those thousands of dollars—and got—what? Three hundred pitiful little smackers every week, almost as a handout, from you in return."

"Five hundred pitiful little dollars, starting last week," Melissa corrected.

"Five hundred miserable dollars, last week," Sally said, "while you made over ten thousand dollars profit. For what? Ninety percent of the work? One hundred percent of the brains?"

Melissa stopped. She held herself down in the chair. Then she said, as quietly as she could, "You're fired."

"No, I'm not," Sally said.

"Tonight," Melissa said. "This minute. Without severance pay. And we'll let our lawyers fight out how much it costs me to buy your contract back."

"You're kidding yourself."

"Get out. Now."

Sally smiled. "Aren't you cutting off your tongue to spite your face?"

"You have five minutes," Melissa said, "to go upstairs, clean out your desk, and get the holy hell out of here, for good."

"The ads will get old," Sally said.

"I don't give a damn."

"The mail order ads will be dead in a few months. And the department stores will want a new version every two or three months themselves."

"I'll give them what they want," Melissa said.

"You?" Sally laughed. "What will you do? Peck out the words on the typewriter with that beautiful nose?"

"Sally, God damn it, get out of here before I hurt you."

"Your face goes only so far, baby."

Melissa found her hand reaching out and encircling a large stapler on the desk. She picked it up, and then opened her fingers and let it drop noisily to the desk. And then she laughed. "How long has it hurt that much?" She asked.

"Shut up," Sally said.

"Since Michael," Melissa said. "No, not the first day I met him. But the first night we went to bed. Right?"

"Wrong," Sally said. "I've always hated you—long before I ever knew your name."

"Why?" Melissa asked. "Because I was born with a face as good as your brain?"

"Brains only count in men."

"And only faces count in women?"

"Screw you," Sally said. "Does your husband know?"

"I have no idea," Melissa said. And then, after a moment, "I have no concern."

"Does your son know?" Sally asked.

"Do me a favor, Sally," Melissa said, getting up from the chair. "Go upstairs and clean out your desk. Or I'll simply go upstairs myself, now, lock you out, and send you your things Monday morning."

"You'll be shot down as fast as you went up."

"Perhaps. It doesn't matter. If I am, then I'll deserve it. In any case," and again Melissa smiled, "you won't be here to see it."

"Oh," Sally said, "I'll see it all right. Send me my things. I don't want to go into that perfumed whorehouse again."

"I will," Melissa said, "the first thing Monday morning."

Sally began moving toward the door. "You'll crash."

"I'll fly. Now that I've dropped," and the words came out by themselves, "heavy ballast."

The pain, and then the surprise, showed on Sally's face.

"My God," she said, "the beautiful face can bite."

"If it has to," Melissa replied.

"I hope the cream turns into acid."

"I hope you turn into a woman someday." And then she added, "I think both our hopes have the same chance of succeeding."

"Fuck you," Sally said as she reached the stairs.

"He will," Melissa yelled after her. "Tomorrow, and probably Sunday."

And then there were only footsteps, and the outside door closing. Melissa sat back on the plastic folding chair, and watched her arms tremble. She wanted to run upstairs, and burn Sally's desk, with every scrap of contamination in it.

But all she did was sit on that cold plastic chair, and tremble. And then, look around the cluttered office, and realize, slowly and silently, that she had won. She had been in a cat fight with a young word genius, and she had won. She had been hit, and hit back in return. She could hurt. My God, she thought, I can hurt.

37.

Monday night. Thirty blocks away from Melissa's apartment, a man was sitting at a desk, lit by a single table lamp, tracing out the probable action of plasmid chains upon the operation of controlled genes, and having his work interrupted every two or three minutes by the dream of being God again.

Finally, he drew a giant X through the page he was working on, and threw the pencil down in fury on the desk top.

He looked up in despair at the photographs of the plasmid chains on the wall opposite him. "Help me, you little bastards," he said to them, and then laughed to himself. He got up from the desk, poured himself the third Jack Daniels and water of the evening, sat down on the couch, and continued to study the photographs before him, and think of Melissa.

Arbeiten and lieben, Michael Black thought. Freud was right. To be normal can be defined as the ability to both work and love. To be abnormal is as elementary as the inability to do one or both.

The plasmid chains seemed to be round rings of tiny teeth, laughing at him. For months now they would do nothing for him. All the circuits of his brain where inspiration and insight lay, had been filled by one trans-scientific thought—her face, or the feel of her skin, or the mystery of being deep inside her body.

Arbeiten—work. No work. No work at all. Yes, the routine administrative duties—the purely mechanical tasks that he did almost out of memory—these he could still do without mistake. But his real work—his arbeitin—his life—was stopped cold.

In the past thirty days he'd slept with three different women, all three as adventuresome and as accomplished as he was in bed. He'd spent hours with them. The *Kama Sutra* illustrated. He'd tried things he hadn't explored with a woman for years. They'd held nothing back. And he hadn't had a single orgasm.

Lieben, he thought—the wisdom of the body. No loss in potency. No loss in performance. But what had been joy before, had now suddenly become, for him, only grinding work.

He drank far too heavily from far too strong a drink. He wanted to be God again. With these women—with any other woman he knew except Melissa—he was only man. Only with Melissa could he be God. When he felt his body pour out into her, it was as though he added new life to her life, renewed her youth, her growth, became not only the moon, but the sun, the wind, the clouds, and the blue sky as well. Then suddenly, at that instant, he felt that he—Michael Black—was far more than any mere man had ever imagined before. That he was God himself.

He laughed out loud at himself. Something unforeseen had happened in his life. Something far more dangerous than he could ever do in a plane. He was suddenly in a dive, with the ground coming up fast. The sudden coming-up of the ground was always beautiful to him. But he needed divinity now more than he needed death.

Divinity and death—they seemed strangely akin to him. He had always known he hungered after one of them. And now he was finding a new and separate . . . what? He smiled. Was the proper word love?

A new kind of love? That banished his need for death? That made him feel like God? He laughed again. It would be as improbable as finding a new kind of gene.

38.

Some fifty blocks away in Manhattan's night, another man sat alone in his penthouse bedroom, looking out from his armchair at the red lights of Brooklyn, and drinking Harvey's Bristol Cream from a water tumbler.

He stared at the shadows in the window as he drank—shadows seen so long ago, shadows that turned gold into black. Shadows that were now choking him to death.

Michael Black. The name reverberated through his brain. The beautiful, black-haired Aryan. He thought of the anonymous phone call he had received that afternoon. He pictured Melissa's long tapering hands running through that black Aryan hair, and he felt the vomit rise in his stomach.

"Your wife," the woman's voice had said, "and Michael Black." That was all. Just a voice that knows it speaks the truth, and uses that truth as a razor to slash another's throat.

It was true. He had known it was true as soon as the words came echoing to him over the phone. But he also knew, deep in the hidden recesses of his brain, that it simply couldn't be true. It couldn't have happened. It hadn't happened last time. There was no way that she would give herself over to the Nazis. She would kill herself before she would let the Nazis come across her alive. She would never . . .

But she had. He had left her, as he had left her a dozen times before, and this time, this time, she had. None of the other times, when she had her black hair, had she given herself over. But now, when she had her golden hair, she had.

He looked down at the bottle. The sherry was almost gone. He was drunk. Drunk enough to think with both halves of his brain. Drunk enough to think in German and English. He stopped thinking in German. And he thought in English, smiling to himself, that he was drunk enough to know he was crazy.

This one is blond, he said to the window. She's always

been blond. The black hair, the black eyes, the black shadows were a lie. A lie of the windows. A lie of his own.

Not dead, he had said in German. He had left her lying on the cellar floor, sleeping, with a small red mark on the side of her head. And he had waited for her to be born again in the window, so there would be no guilt, no death, no killing, no unbearable pain.

And then he looked at the black window, and saw the second one lying in the black-haired man's bed. He could see her golden hair lying next to his black hair. And the vomit rose from his stomach.

"Say it," he said in English. "Say it. The first one is dead. You killed her. And she's dead. Dead. Dead. Dead."

The first one is dead; let her die. The second one is alive; call her up tomorrow and beg her forgiveness for what you've done to her, and beg her to come back on whatever terms she chooses.

But not to this window, he thought. Not to this window with its dark-haired woman sealed in its shadows. "Forgive me," he said in English to a woman who had never had the time to learn English, "for keeping you trapped this long."

He lifted the sherry bottle in his massive hand, and drew back that hand. "Go now," he said, "to the God you once mistook me for." And with a horrendous scream, he flung the bottle straight into the bay window, and shattered its blackness forever.

39.

The first call woke her up at seven-thirty. As soon as she heard his voice she was immediately, hungrily awake.

"Hi. This is Michael. Remember me?"

"Oh, yes," she said, slightly puzzled. "I remember you. I remember you very well."

The voice on the other end picked up the softness in her tone and carried it through to his own. "I just called," he said, "to tell you a discovery I've just made. You don't fit."

She thought about the statement, and then agreed. "You're right. I don't fit."

"You don't fit into my life at all," he said again.

"Again, you're right," she said. "Just as you don't fit into my life at all."

"Agreed?" he asked.

"Agreed," she said.

"Wonderful," he said. "Now we can get on with the real question—will you go to San Francisco with me next week?"

She laughed. "No," she said. "Of course not."

"Why?" he asked.

"Because I can't take time off now. Because it would mean spending at least five days with you—"

"Seven—"

"Seven days with you. And we've both just agreed that we don't fit into each other's lives."

"Don't distract me with superfluities," he said. "Let's get down to the real issues. You've just spent nine days standing on your feet eight hours a day, answering thirty thousand questions from half a million women."

"Not quite that many," she said.

"A mere incidental," he went on. "Perhaps there were only twenty thousand questions, from a quarter of a million women. In any case, if you stop and listen to your voice right now, you'll admit it is more than a little hoarse."

"Well, maybe."

"And, besides that, I don't believe you've taken a vacation in over a year."

"I've been building a business."

"You're absolutely right. You have been building a business. But that business has kept you in the city for nearly a year. Right or wrong?"

"All right," she admitted. "Right."

"And Friday night you had your—admit it—crucifying confrontation with Sally."

This time her agreement was instantaneous. "Yes," she said. "I had my moment of truth with Sally last Friday."

"Moments of truth cost," he said. "And they cost far too much in energy and stress when they're piled on top of everything else you've been undergoing in the past few months. Admit it."

She said nothing.

"Melissa," he went on, "I'm going to say something to you

I never thought I'd find necessary. I'm going to tell you the direct truth—that you look lovely, but tired. And that this business of yours is essentially your face. And if you don't protect that face, then you can't protect or maintain that business either.''

"I don't like it," she said, "but I have to admit it's logical.''

"Good," he said. "Finally. Now we've defined the problem. Now let me give you at least a partial solution.''

"I am a little tired," she admitted cautiously.

"There's a marvelous place in Carmel," he said, "called the Delmonte Lodge. There's a room in that lodge, room 106, that's parked on the eighteenth hole of the most beautiful golf course in the world. That room has three sides made of windows. One side looks over the green. One side looks over the most gorgeous cypress trees you've ever seen. And the other side—the long side—has nothing outside it but the Pacific Ocean. It's the most marvelous room in the world to make love in at sunrise and sunset.''

"I need to plan the rest of the line," she said weakly.

"You can plan the rest of the line when you come back. *Or* out there," he said immediately. "It won't make any difference—you know damn well it won't make any difference.''

"I can't go, though. Not just now. It's crazy.''

"There's a room in the Fairmont Hotel, in San Francisco," he went on, "room 1127, where you see the entire Golden Gate Bridge from the city. When you wake up in the morning, you just draw back the curtains, and watch the fog come in over the bridge, then over the water, then over Alcatraz, then over the hills beyond. Pretty soon, if we're lucky, and we'll be lucky, there's nothing outside the entire room but that gorgeous white fog. We're floating in fog. We're making love in fog," he said, "with no time limit, no place to go in a hurry, no interruptions at all.''

"Do you do anything else" she said, "when you get there?''

"Lots," he said. "For one thing, I fly. There's an air show on the fifth day that I'd like you to see. I'm bringing out a souped-up P-51 fighter plane with me, and I think you'd enjoy seeing some of the tricks I've told you about.''

"How do you get the P-51 out there?" she asked. "In a suitcase?''

"No," he said. "A friend of mine flies it out. And then I simply take it up that day. It won't interfere with us for more than six to eight hours."

"When is the show?" she said.

"Two weeks from today," he replied.

"You still don't fit into my life," she said.

"For seven days?" he asked. "And seven nights?"

She stopped, caught her breath, and then let it explode again in a burst of laughter. "Yes," she said. "You fit for seven nights."

"We go then," he said with a note of triumph.

"God help me," she said. "We go."

"We'll leave next Wednesday," he said. "But—"

"No," she said, "not before. Not this weekend. I've got to make up for the time we'll spend between now and then."

"Agreed," he said. And then, thinking of the work he could get done now, and the ideas that were flooding his mind already, he added, laughingly, "And you don't fit into this weekend for me either. But next weekend, I'll think we'll fit. And fit. And fit. And fit."

She put down the phone quickly, or else she wouldn't get any work done for the rest of the week.

The second call came fifteen minutes later, while she was frying herself some ham and eggs. While the call went on, she watched the burning pan emit streams of black smoke and fill the kitchen with deadly air, but she never interrupted the conversation to stop the poison, nor did she eat breakfast that day.

It was Aaron. Aaron, the voice she had been waiting to hear for months, saying at last—now too late—the very words that she had dreamed all that time he would call up and say.

It was an Aaron without wit, without turn of phrase, without humor. Giving in completely to each of the points she had asked for all those months ago. It was an Aaron asking simply that she come home. Come home today. Come home this hour. Come home if she chose, one week or one month from now. Come home to stay, come home to try again. Or come home for a single meeting, a single hour.

But come home. Please.

There was no need for her to ask for anything. He knew what she wanted, and he recited every one of her conditions, verbatim, before she had the slightest chance even to mention them.

Yes, he would go to any psychiatrist, any analyst, of her choice—as soon as he could make the appointment. He was in deep trouble, he knew that; he wanted to begin to fight his way out of it, today. He was drowning in the past, and she, and treatment, were his last hopes for survival.

The agency's billings had doubled since she had left, he said. Once the new ads had reached the press, the phone had not stopped wringing. Therefore, there was no new crisis, no new fight, no new sacrifice necessary. There would never be another Albee dinner, nor another Mr. Eastman. Not even if he were about to starve.

He had been insane, he admitted. The confusion was still there, if he did not keep his mind taut, if he started to drink, or grew tired, or ran into a business crisis. He was aware of this. That was why he was going to seek help from a psychiatrist—whether or not she chose to come home and help him. Whether or not she chose to forgive his insanity.

And one last admission—the most painful to her of all—the one that tore her heart in two. Bring Lacey with you, he said. Give me back my daughter, now that I can see her and touch her, now that I can reach out and love her. Bring back the girl that I have crippled, and let me go down on my knees in front of her.

It all came out in a flood. She hardly said a word, but there was a fierce ache in her hand from the agony of holding the receiver. And when it was finished, when he had said everything he could say, she said, without drawing a breath, without conscious thought, without trusting anything more than her deepest instincts, "No."

"You won't help me?" he asked.

"I will help you," she said. "I will do anything in the world to help you. But not now."

There was silence on the other end of the line, and then she had the courage to go on. "Not until I know whether I have the tools to help you," she said.

"And you'll know that?"

"Three weeks from now," she said honestly. "Not before that."

"Why three weeks?" he asked.

She took a deep breath. "Because I'm going to California

with another man, Aaron, and I won't know about myself—or you—until then.''

''I understand,'' he said.

''You don't want to know anything more?'' she asked.

''No. You have every right, after what I've done to you. I need to know nothing more.''

''His name?''

''No,'' he said.

''Whether or not I love him?'' she asked.

''No.''

''Aaron,'' she said, ''I don't know whether we are still married.''

''I do,'' he answered.

''But I don't,'' she said. ''Not anymore. I'm going on this trip to find out. Do you understand?''

''Perfectly,'' he said. ''I understand perfectly.''

''If it had been a month ago—'' she said.

''But it's not,'' he said. ''I stayed insane too long. If you stay too long in a dream world, you lose the real world. I understand what you're saying. I hate every word of it, but I understand.'' He paused. ''When are you leaving?''

''Next Wednesday.''

''I'll be in treatment by then,'' he said. ''Starting tomorrow, if possible.''

''Whether I come back or not?'' she asked.

''Whether you come back or not. It doesn't matter. If I lose you, I still have myself to fight for. And when you return from California, I hope you're the most cruelly disappointed woman in the world. But I can't blame you. Good-bye.''

She put down the phone, and waded into the clouds of smoke to turn off the fire underneath the frying pan. Then she opened the front door, and all the windows in the apartment. She could hardly breath from coughing. She could hardly see from crying. But she sat on the couch in the middle of the smoke-filled living room, and stared straight ahead at the smoke-filled, tear-filled world that she had now created. And long after the smoke had cleared out of her apartment, there was no lessening at all in the tears.

40.

For the first twenty-four hours after they arrived in California, Melissa and Michael made love. They put everything aside—the beautiful seventeen-mile drive to Carmel included—and stayed in the single, light-flooded room at the Delmonte Lodge, and made love through all weathers, all lights, all times of day.

They had the first dinner, the first breakfast, the first lunch sent in. They made an athletic, explosive love, a completely sensuous love. There was no sense of time passing, no diminishment in the demands of either of their bodies. There was very little time to talk, to drink or eat. Very little time to do anything but come together in a flow of feeling on the massive king-sized bed. She gathered him inside her in a hundred different positions, and had him hold her in a hundred different positions, and had him turn her drunk . . . drunk . . . drunk . . . on sex—far more intoxicated on its mounting mysteries than she had ever been on mere alcohol alone.

The next day—their second day in California—they were up at four-thirty, dressed and out of the room by five, and at the marina at Monterey by five-thirty. Half an hour later they were in the open Pacific, in a small fishing boat, the hooks were baited and trailing out behind them, and he was going for a blue marlin he thought he'd spotted, and she was trying for some smaller fish that shone like opals when you pulled them into the boat.

An hour after they left the dock, his line began to tear itself out behind the boat at a pace so fast it looked as though it would pull the rod with it. She watched his face as the line spread out; he was first puzzled and then deeply disappointed. The line pulled out one hundred yards, then two hundred, then three hundred, then it reached the end of the reel, and strained against the chair, against the boat, against the man. And then it stopped.

Michael looked up at the captain and the mate.

"A shark," said the captain. "We'll cut the line."

"Wait," said Michael suddenly. "How big do you think he is?"

"What difference does it make?" the captain said.

"How big?" Michael asked again.

The captain thought a minute. "Anywhere over three-hundred pounds," he finally said.

"Then I'll pull him up," Michael said.

"Why?" asked the captain. "He won't give you a fight. He'll simply keep tugging at you till you wear him out. And what will you get when he does come up? Nothing but an ordinary shark. Average size. Average weight. Nothing but a killer and a scavenger."

"I want to see him," Michael said in a tone of voice Melissa didn't recognize. And then he turned to her. "The captain's right. It's a hell of a way to spend our morning. But I'd like to do it. Do you mind?"

There was something in Michael's voice that suggested to her both need and danger. The man wanted his shark—he wanted his shark on the surface of the water, with his hook in its mouth, with its energy drained from the fight to stay free from that hook. She knew no earthly reason why he wanted it, but she could feel the intensity of that need from every pore of his body. She nodded yes, and the deadly struggle began.

An hour passed. She caught six or eight smaller fish, had them put away for dinner, and then gave up. Two hours passed. Every five minutes or so, the reel would be drawn in another round. Michael's muscles were bulging during every minute of those two hours. Both the captain and the captain's mate had broken out some coffee, and were sitting on the deck, watching with absolute boredom. They saw no sport, no purpose in the game.

By the end of three hours, Melissa was beginning to feel slightly queasy from the gentle rocking of the boat on the calm sea. Suddenly, she looked over at Michael, and turned cold at the expression on his face. It was not sheer physical struggle that she saw in the contortion of that face now, not the pain from the blisters that were forming from the clench of his hands, but a far deeper, far more agonizing pain that must be scorching his entire body like a blowtorch. Immediately she recognized the source of that pain. He had been sitting there, strapped in that chair for over three hours, with his right foot raised against the rear deck of the fishing craft, and his right leg bracing his entire body against the three hundred pounds of the shark beneath them.

Somewhere after the second hour, his right hip—the wounded right hip, with its scarred map of pain—had begun to weaken under the strain of supporting his body against all that unremitting underwater pull. Now it was telling him, in its unmistakable voice of pain, that the strain he was putting it under might break it again. His face was covered with sweat. Every breath he took now was so labored that she could hear it pass in and out of his open mouth. And yet he sat there unmoving, his eyes riveted on the line disappearing under the blue sea, his hands pulling so hard that she thought his arms might soon be pulled from their sockets, as he turned the reel another six inches.

"Michael," she said instinctively, "are you all right?"

"Fine," he said, almost in a hoarse whisper.

"Should we—"

"Shut up," he barked at her. And then: "Please."

After three hours and forty-five minutes, the mate suddenly rose from his sitting position and walked to the back railing of the ship. He pointed to a blue shadow, almost twenty-five feet long, slowly rising out of the water to the rear of them.

"There the bastard is," the mate said. "You beat him."

Within three minutes, the shark broke the water's surface, the hook lodged in its jaw, the gray leather of its skin now shimmering and shining, completely exhausted.

She looked at the huge, manacled beast with obsession and horror. It was facing the four of them in the boat now—its dull, deadly eyes looking up into theirs, its huge mouth with its triple set of giant razorlike teeth opening and closing as it tried for the ten-thousandth time to cut the line that was holding it to the boat.

It was horrible. It was death incarnate. Twenty-five feet of gray death, of kill-anything, now trapped by its own lust and its own greed, and slowly being pulled in, inch by inch, to its own death.

"Wait," said the mate, "let me get the gaff so I can help you haul the bastard right out of the sea."

"No," said Michael. "No gaff."

"What do you mean?" the captain interrupted. "You can't pull up a shark that heavy by yourself."

"I'm not going to pull him up," said Michael. "I'm going

to look at him for one more minute, and then you'll cut him free.''

''Fuck, no,'' said the captain, and then looked apologetically at Melissa. ''We're not going to cut it free. That bastard eats human beings. He's the offal of the ocean. If you cut him loose now, he'll attack anything in the vicinity. If there was a swimmer out here—''

''There's no swimmer out here. You know it,'' Michael said.

''We're not going to cut him free,'' the captain said. ''You're out of your mind, mister. You spend almost four hours dragging that monster up, and then you want him to go free?''

''Yes, I want him to go free,'' Michael said, stopping the reel. ''Now.''

''No.'' The captain turned to the mate. ''Get the gaff.''

Michael never took his eyes away from the creature being towed behind them. The pain had passed out of his face now, and was replaced by some expression she could not even begin to decipher.

''How much do I owe you?'' he said to the captain quietly.

''Eighty dollars,'' he said, as the mate came running with the gaff.

''A hundred and eighty dollars,'' Michael said, ''if you cut the line. Now.''

''No, mister,'' said the captain. ''There's a law to the sea. You catch those monsters, you kill them.''

''Two hundred and eighty dollars,'' Michael said.

''You're crazy, mister,'' said the captain.

''Two hundred and eighty dollars,'' Michael repeated. ''Cash. When we hit the dock. If you cut the line now.''

The captain paused for a moment. Then he said, softly, ''One of those things a relative of yours, mister?''

''Yes,'' Michael said.

''Have it your own way, mister,'' said the captain. ''Three hundred dollars, in cash, the moment we hit the dock.''

''Cut the line,'' said Michael.

''Cut the fuckin' line,'' said the captain, this time not even apologizing to Melissa.

The mate took out a huge cork-handled knife, and reached down. The shark looked up at them for one last time, and, as the hand with the knife passed through the line inches away from his mouth, his jaws opened and tried to take the hand with it.

Then the line gave way, the shark fell down into the ocean, and was gone in an instant.

Michael slumped back against the chair, now holding the slack reel in his paralyzed hands. The captain had turned back to the wheel, and was setting his course for home. Melissa went over to Michael and kissed the cold wet forehead under the sun hat. Then she reached down, and carefully pried away his blistered hands from the reel. She held Michael's hands in her own, and kissed the raw flesh on them.

She could not kiss the hip. She could not ease the pain of the hip—shooting through his body like raw electricity. And then she looked up at Michael's face, which was not the face of the Michael she knew, but of a Michael of a different lifetime ago. And then somehow she thought of the dull, unthinking eyes of the shark, and the cut of the line that had freed the shark to kill again. Her stomach turned, and she had to leave him sitting helplessly in the chair, and go below-decks, and give way to her nausea.

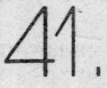

He had soaked in a hot tub for three-quarters of an hour. Now his hands were bandaged, he had been given five aspirin and half a bottle of Jack Daniels, and he was sitting in bed, ready to talk.

"All right," she said. "Why?"

"You won't like it," he said.

"Try me," she replied.

It was two o'clock on a wasted Pacific afternoon. The room was still as beautiful, the ocean was still as majestic, but she knew there would be no more love until they talked.

He said, simply, "He was me. The shark was me, twenty years ago. And I suddenly wanted to see what I looked like, those twenty years ago."

"A wounded shark?" she asked.

"A trapped, wounded shark," he said. "My cousin. My

blood brother. The perfect killing machine, that kills cleanly, instantly, without even a rational thought.'' He smiled. ''So deadly,'' he said. ''So very beautiful.''

Then he looked up at her, brown eyes penetrating blue eyes, and she could see the pain in his body diminish and almost vanish as his mind took over all feeling from it.

''Did you see him when he finally surfaced?'' he asked. ''Have you ever seen anything more grand? Not a single wasted ounce. Designed by nature over twenty million years ago to do one thing—kill.''

She shuddered at the worshipful look in his eyes, the look of one who has observed grandeur. He was Aaron looking at a Pollock, Albee looking at a Renoir, herself looking at— what? And then she smiled to herself—at his nude body, above her, poised and ready to descend into her.

''And you felt kinship with that—beast?'' she said. ''That monster? That killing machine? You, who hate death, who war constantly on death—you are cousin to that?''

''No,'' he said immediately. ''I *was* cousin to that. Over twenty years ago. I was lashed into my jet—I was part of that jet, the human brain of that jet. Trained for almost one and a half years to do nothing more than that shark—kill.''

''And you killed well?''

''Extremely well,'' he replied. ''Six MIG's shot down in five weeks. Three truck convoys destroyed. At least one hundred Korean corpses left lying on the road.'' He laughed. ''Oh, I killed well. I was as much a genius at killing as that gray monster out there.''

''And then?'' she asked.

''I too was hooked,'' he said. ''But the hook didn't enter my mouth.'' He drew down the blanket. ''It entered here,'' he said, pointing to the middle white scar on his hip. ''A piece of shrapnel three quarters of an inch thick, that entered here—but didn't leave for twenty-four days.

''I landed behind North Korean lines. But it was early in the war, do you understand? And they were in South Korean territory when I landed. I was picked up by two South Korean peasants, and carried by them a hundred and thirty-five miles over hilly country, on a rough stretcher, when every step the two men took would tear off the back of my brain.''

She turned her head away. ''Don't go on,'' she said involuntarily. ''I've heard this before,'' she said. ''I don't want to go through it again.''

"With Aaron?" he said immediately. "In his war?"

She looked up at his tormented, face. "Yes," she said.

"But you've got to hear it again," he replied. "Women of your age must hear the suffering of men my age. It molds our relationships. And right now, believe me, women half your age are sitting by the beds of men half my age, and hearing the same, terrible stories of Viet Nam. There's no way you can tune out of it. If you want to survive it, you have to absorb it, and convert it to understanding, and accommodation, and love."

"And if accommodation is impossible?" she asked.

"Then you've lost one more victim—who didn't die quickly then, but far more slowly years later."

"All right," she said. "Go on. At least I can listen to your war during the day."

"I don't understand."

"It doesn't matter," she said. "Go on."

"When the Americans got me again," he said, "they flew me back to the United States. By then, of course, the hip had become infected, splinters of the hip were spread over the entire area, and it took three years before I learned to walk like this again."

"Michael . . ."

"You would have loved me at age twenty-three to twenty-six," he said. "They would operate on me, they would try me out, and then they would operate on me again. Twelve operations in all. Two years of wheelchairs, of crutches, of operations, of failure—until—until" and his voice stopped.

"Until what?" she asked softly.

He laughed. With the face of Lucifer after the fall. Of heaven's most blessed angel turned into hell's blackest demon. Somewhere, deep inside her, she knew there was a laugh like that stored up in Aaron. But Aaron was too gentle to have released it yet, openly. The man she was sitting next to had released that rage almost twenty years ago. Now, Aaron might be releasing that same rage in some psychiatrist's office, and escaping at last his own inner hell.

"Until," Michael went on, "until no one, the doctors included, believed I'd ever walk again. Some of the doctors told me I'd have to get used to walking on crutches the rest of my life. Others talked amputation. Others—the optimistic ones—talked about the beauty of using a cane till you're eighty. And, after a while, some of you began to believe them."

"Some of you? Who is some of you?" she asked.

"Some of you are male—that was me—and some of you are female. The two of you have loved each other, so you said, since the first time you saw each other as sophomores in high school. The match made in heaven, both as beautiful as the sun, and both so pure in love that you didn't screw—not for the seven years you went together."

"So that's where . . ." she said, almost to herself.

"I get all my nongenital tricks," he said. "Because it took me three years after I learned how to walk—six years in full—before I could gain the physical movement to make love. Do you know what it means not to have the capacity to make love? Just to lie there and be jerked off? To satisfy that girl with your hands, or your mouth? But never know whether you are ever going to hear her moan beneath you, be inside her—inside her—at that moment of orgasm."

"She left you?" Melissa said. "After waiting two years?"

"Two years of jerking each other off. Of making love in hospital beds—"

A flush mounted Melissa's face. He didn't see it, and went on.

"After giving each other pathetic little solitary orgasms. Finally love wears away like that beach outside when the ocean pounds against it. It wears away imperceptibly, and then one day you look for it, and there's nothing there. Only the pounding. Only the pain. Only the aloneness. Only the note, the good-bye, the best wishes, the self-explanation, and the self-excuse."

"So that explains the fourteen girls in three years," she said.

"No," he replied. "There were twenty girls in three years. You dive girls like you dive airplanes. You push them to their limits. You try to make them moan loud enough, and often enough, so that you think that those moans equal—or are as good as—what you insanely call 'love.' "

"But you did love," she said.

"Yes," he admitted. "I did love."

"So you do know the meaning of love," she asked. "Love does exist in your world after all. Not merely the substitute for love."

''Yes,'' he said. ''Love does exist in my world. And it's the most hated word of them all.''

''Or the most misunderstood,'' she corrected.

''Nothing, even the six years of the hip,'' he said, ''hurt as much.''

''I agree,'' she said. ''I've never felt your pain. But I have my own pain to tell me that what you say is the absolute truth.''

''Then what did you do? What can any of us do?''

''You fight for the love,'' she answered immediately, ''just as you fought for the hip.'' Her face suddenly tightened, as new certainty swept over her. ''You tell the pessimistic doctors in your own mind that you won't end up a love cripple for the rest of your life. You take the old love, no matter how many operations it's had performed on it, and you drag it up out of the wheelchair, and onto crutches, and you limp on it again, until it moves by its own accord, or until you fall flat on your face. Then, by God,'' she said, ''if it still won't walk, you take it back to another operating room, and you try again. And then,'' and tears were now forming in her eyes, ''you try again. And then again. And again.''

''And wonder if it won't walk even then,'' he said quietly. ''Wonder if the man can't stop mixing the dreams up with reality,'' he continued, as her face snapped up to stare into his. ''Wonder if the man can't stop going out with other women, can't keep away from the proof that other women give him, that he's really recovered. Wonder if there are no men in this world who are strong enough to love you as deeply as you love them. Then what?''

''Then,'' she said, ''you take your love—because your love is still there, still strong, still healthy, still waiting only to find the right doctor—and you leave both of the men.'' And her eyes never blinked, and her face never changed expression. ''You pack your suitcase, and you put your love tenderly in it, and you go looking for another man,'' and her hand reached out and laid gently on top of his hip, ''whose scars have healed enough, at least inside, to give you back the love you need. And,'' she said, after some thought, ''deserve.''

41.

Three days later, at the air show, she was sitting in the grandstand, fifteen rows up, on an absolutely clear, windless, blisteringly hot day. Behind her were two older men who had evidently flown planes of this type in World War II, and who probably attended these shows regularly. As each new entry in the show flew past them, and did their routine of stunts, the men—neither of whom had flown a plane for at least thirty years—made crude and caustic comments about the pilot's handling of the plane.

Three-quarters of an hour into the show, five beers apiece later, one of the men behind Melissa said to the other, "Watch this one. This son-of-a-bitch is crazy. He'd pick his teeth with the whirling blade of a P-51 if he felt like it."

The plane came whizzing at them out of the empty, hot blue sky. Its body was silver. Its wings were painted in a black and white checkerboard pattern. It was a single-seated fighter, kept in perfect condition. It flew twenty feet off the ground at over four hundred miles an hour, sideways to the reviewing stand. She could barely see Michael's face below the helmet, heard the storm of applause as the plane turned straight up, rolled on its back, and flew again past the grandstand at over four hundred miles an hour, now resting directly on its upper wings.

Then there were the spin-outs, the dives, the Immelmanns, the tail-stands. Each one received polite applause, but she knew that everyone in the stand was waiting for the final stunt—when one of the mechanics ran out into the center of the green field in front of them, and placed a slightly larger than ordinary orange handkerchief on the ground, with its tip standing six inches above the green and deadly earth. The plane swung lazily around, and retreated away from the stand to gather speed—four hundred miles an hour, which, the man behind her told his friend, was the fastest speed at which a handkerchief that size had ever been picked up. Only one man had done it—Michael Black. Only one man, the beer-filled voice behind her said, had the craziness even to attempt it at that speed.

The plane began coming toward the stand, at an altitude of about fifty feet.

"Jesus Christ," the man behind her said, "a crosswind. Where the hell did that come from?"

Within seconds, the plane had dipped low, and turned itself over on its side, the top of the cockpit, the top of Michael's black hair, without the helmet on, showing through, as the plane made its first pass at the handkerchief. It was five inches too high. The wind from the plane as it passed over the orange handkerchief flattened it to the ground, and the plane roared angrily up into the air again, turned over on its back, and retreated away from the stands for another pass.

The crowd moaned in unison. The man in white ran out again, and propped up the handkerchief. The crosswind that had come up from nowhere was now growing so strong that he finally had to put the ordinary handkerchief away, and use a stiff plastic handkerchief, with weighted ends. It too was orange. It could still be picked up by the plane's wing, but it was far heavier, and the crosswind would have to be half-hurricane strength to knock it over.

The plane turned around again, and started to come at them.

"You're right," said the other man. "He is crazy. One sudden gust, and he'll be splattered all over this field."

"Uh huh," was his friend's only comment; he was mesmerized by the sight of the plane on its side as it speeded toward them. Melissa suddenly realized that the entire audience in the grandstand, aficionados of this sport, recognized the dangerous conditions. There wasn't a breath inhaled by the fifteen hundred people sitting in the grandstand. All were watching, no longer a stunt, but a rendezvous with death. None of them—she was sure of it—none of them wanted the stunt to succeed. All of them, every man, woman, and child in the grandstand, wanted the plane to lose control, wanted the wing to smash helplessly into the ground, wanted the motor to burst into flame, wanted the plane to tear itself into smithereens in front of them, wanted to see the pilot thrown out of the cockpit, and burn to a crisp before their eyes.

The plane roared in front of them; the wing edged lower as it approached the orange plastic handkerchief. It got down to about two inches above the handkerchief in the split second that it approached.

And then suddenly there was the slightest twitch of Michael's hand on the control stick. The plane edged up just above the handkerchief; it missed the top of the handkerchief by four inches. It hit a sudden gust of wind about forty feet away, and dropped that four inches, and then recovered and righted itself so that the winds were horizontal, and then turned away from the audience—the bewildered and infuriated audience—climbed straight up into the sky in a scream of triumph and pain, did a double Immelmann at the top of the climb, and simply flew away.

For a moment there wasn't the slightest sound from the gathering of fifteen hundred men and women. She could feel the anger building in the entire crowd. Had he come down four inches lower, he would have picked up the handkerchief. And then, forty feet later, he would have rammed that same wing, carrying that same handkerchief, into the ground, and it would have all been over.

The audience knew this. They felt cheated. A murmur, a soft deadly murmur spread through the audience like the hum of a hive of deadly bees. The man behind her said to his friend, "Sorry about that. The low-life bastard. He's getting old. Must be losing his nerve."

"Yeah," said the second man. "Kills the whole afternoon. Here, have another beer."

She heard him take three or four deep gulps of the beer.

"Funny," the first man said. "Wonder what the hell suddenly makes them grow old. Too bad. He was a damn good pilot before."

42.

Michael's plane never returned to the landing strip. She waited an hour, till the show was over, and the stands started to empty. Then she sat there and waited another hour, till even the help from the air show had gone, and there was nothing left but the empty stands, the parked planes of the other contestants, and herself. Then, finally, she left the empty stand, got into the rented car, and drove the forty-five empty miles back to San Francisco.

She took the elevator up to their room. He wasn't there. You could see the fog rolling in, a red-tinted fog, over the red towers of the bay bridge. She turned around one of the chairs at the table near the window, and watched the fog roll in for an hour and a half, till finally it had swallowed up the entire day. Then she just continued to sit there, and watch the gray, swirling mass outside her window.

Fog, she thought. She remembered the first time she had met Michael, and the fog—the fog of desire—that had enveloped her then. Now, one year later, fog was covering her life.

Five days with this man; she had expected to stay seven. Fourteen years with the last man; she had expected to stay forever. There are only a few such men in your lifetime—if you're lucky. Men who loom up in your life like mountains, and who disappear, from time to time, in the inevitable fogs of life.

Two oceans. Two fogs. Herself, lost, on both sides of the continent.

Lost here, for sure. But perhaps—just perhaps—not lost there.

She watched the fog, and waited. Finally she heard a key fumbling at the lock, and he walked in.

He had been drowning himself in bourbon. The smell of it overwhelmed her nostrils. His eyes were red. His face was by no means beautiful.

She said nothing. She waited for him to speak first.

"You make me old," he said finally.

"No," she replied quietly.

"You make me a hundred years old," he went on. "Aged. Ugly." And then he threw the worst insult at her. "Afraid."

"No," she said calmly, "just mature."

"Doddering," he said, and then turned around and circled the room easily. "Don't we have a bottle here? Wasn't there a bottle here from last night?"

"No," she said flatly.

He sat down on the edge of the double bed, near the table at the window. "I should have picked up that handkerchief," he said.

"You would have been smashed to smithereens the next second."

"It doesn't matter," he said. "I pulled up."

"It does matter," she said. "You saved your life by pulling up. You had no chance at all, if you dipped your wing a little further."

"I had no right to lift that wing," he said. "The crowd expected me to get that handkerchief. That's what they paid for."

Her eyes blazed. "The crowd expected you to kill yourself," she said. "That's what they really paid for. I was sitting among them, remember? They knew what was going on with the wind as well as you did. I could feel the thrill run through them when they realized what would happen when you made your second pass at the handkerchief. I could feel that thrill, Michael. It was a blood thrill. They wanted to see your plane in flames. They wanted to see your body burned to a crisp. They didn't want daring, they wanted death. There was no heroism connected with it, no human triumph. You bring them nothing but danger, and the possible taste of death in their mouths!"

"You make me old," he repeated.

"I make you real," she said. "You gave me a pinch of reality. It burned—but it worked for me. Now I'm trying to give some of that back to you." She got up from the chair, went over to the bed and sat next to him, and took one of his hands in hers. "For God's sake, Michael, take it. Use it. Build on it."

"Afraid," he said.

"Yes," she said, "Afraid. Afraid like every other human being. Not an invulnerable god with wings, but a flawed model like all the people in that stand, waiting for you to prove it to them."

Now both her hands encircled his hand. "Accept it, Michael. Welcome it. Give up the godhood. Become one of us. The war is over, Michael. The age of knighthood and heroism has passed. All we have is people like ourselves, doing people-things, not god-things, Come, please. Join us."

He pulled his hand out of hers, and went over to the mirror on the bathroom door. He looked carefully at his own face. It was tired, drunk, haggard, lined. "I'm old," he said.

"Yes," she replied. "You're forty-three years old."

He turned around and looked at her. "And what do you think," he said, "of this old man?"

She stopped cold. This was no dream-world question. They

were back now in the real world, of decision and consequence, of choice and loss.

"I think you are the most gorgeous, most intelligent, most sexually talented," and then her voice lowered, "adolescent I have ever met. As deeply mired in adolescence as I was when you first met me. Adolescence, Michael, is an escape, from childhood. And most people never make it all the way out. I hadn't when I met you—perhaps I never will. But all I can say to you is that you haven't made it now. And Michael, forty-three is time to start."

"Will you help?"

"Yes," she said, "as a friend. Not as anything else."

"Which means?" he asked.

"That the vacation is over," she said quietly.

"You're going back?"

"On the next plane. I only waited to talk to you. I wouldn't have left without doing that."

"There are only two more days left," he said.

"No, Michael," she said. "There are no days left. And no nights. I'm sorry, but it isn't our vacation that's ended, it's my vacation. My running away—I guess from myself. My vacation really ended ten days ago, in New York, just after you and I talked. The only problem was," and she felt herself leaning toward him, "you were so magnificent that I wouldn't let myself realize it then."

"I don't understand."

"No, you couldn't be expected to. When you asked me to come, and I accepted, I heard from Aaron less than five minutes later. I heard from Aaron," she said very slowly, "what I'd been waiting to hear for over a year. Nothing final. Nothing assured. But a promise. And that promise imposed an obligation on me that I didn't hear—that I couldn't hear—until today."

"Because we had one fight?" he asked. "Because I failed you once? Because I got drunk?"

"No. None of those. Rather, believe it or not, because I was alone in this room for an hour and a half. Because I had a chance to think about how miraculously beautiful you are, Michael. How divine you are in bed. How charming, and intelligent, and even full of nascent love you are. How much of you there is that is actually beyond the human, and into the dream. And how I should be in love with you by now. But I'm not."

"Because of a man who—"

"Yes, who would have sold me, just as he was trained to sell everything else he loved—probably including, eventually, his own life. Because of a man who has flaws far more profound than yours, who has whirlpools in his soul far deeper than yours. But, God help me, whom I love."

She walked past him to the phone, and dialed the operator.

"It won't work," he said.

"Probably not," she replied. Then she asked the operator to get the airline for her.

A recorded voice on the other end of the phone said, "This is American Airlines. All our operators are busy now. Please hold on."

She looked down at the gaunt, lost man sitting beside her on the bed. "It doesn't matter," she said again. "I love him, and it doesn't matter if I lose, gambling on that love."

And then a real voice said on the other end of the line, "This is Miss White. Can I help you?" Melissa put her hand over the phone, looked down at Michael, and said, "I hope that someday you have the joy of knowing a hopeless love like that."

43.

They met, the tall man and the blond woman, at an Indian restaurant on East 58th Street that they both loved. He was waiting at the table when she arrived. He rose and took her hand, stared at her face for a moment, and slowly bent and kissed her gently on the cheek. She sat on the other side of the table, and he just looked at her until the captain came over and took their orders for drinks.

"I hear you've seen a great deal of Lacy," she finally said.

"Every day," he said. "We act together. I play the male roles. She plays the female. She has—" and then he stopped.

"Go on," she said.

"My memory," he said. "If she reads a passage twice— only twice—she has it, forever."

"And you?" she asked.

"I find myself memorizing along with her. Soon we can do entire scenes together, without the book. I know my part; she lives hers. She is," and his eyes narrowed in reflective wonder, "so many women in that one tiny body."

"And when the acting is over?" she asked.

"Then we talk a little. Mostly about the script, and the author's intention in that scene. Nothing yet about ourselves or the past. Certainly nothing yet about the future." He picked up his fork, turned it over, and traced parallel lines across the white tablecloth. "But we talk. And we feel. Other people's feelings now. Perhaps our own feelings tomorrow."

She raised her glass of wine. "To feeling our own feelings," she said.

"To feeling our own feelings," he repeated, and they both drank.

"I would like to come back," she said. "Experimentally."

"On your terms?" he said.

"No terms," she said. "No more terms. I gave you terms; you met them. Now all that's left is—" and she searched for the right word.

"Hope?" he volunteered.

"Hope," she repeated.

"And effort. And risk," he said.

"And—" she said, and again stopped.

"And love," he said. "I think, unquestionably love."

"You know where I've been?" she asked.

"I know where you've been. And, far more important, I know where you are right now. The rest is trivial."

She looked at the gray-haired man, who was not gorgeous, but who was all-consuming. She put her hand on the white tablecloth. "Here," she said.

His hand moved across the tablecloth, and embraced hers. "Here," he said.

She looked at the hand on top of hers. And then she felt the power of that hand.

"Are you hungry?" she asked. "Shall we stay and have dinner?"

"No," he said. "I don't feel like dinner right now." His voice was deep and commanding.

"Neither do I," she said.

44.

Alice was away. So was Little John. He might have been sent, or gone knowingly—it didn't matter. She stood at the door to her own apartment, watching Aaron open the lock. She remembered the first night, so infinitely long ago, when she had stood at the same door, and watched the same man release the lock to her new future. It was a strange and fantastic apartment then. It was a strange and fantastic apartment now.

Nothing had changed visibly on the first floor. As she watched him hang up her coat in her closet, memories of the room rose up and embraced her. She was a stranger in her own home; a lost fourteen years were awaiting her; and she could feel the invisible barrier within her own body barring her—still barring her—from reaching out and taking them back in again.

He turned and touched her shoulders. They said nothing. He did not kiss her. Then he silently turned and walked up the carpeted stairs to the second floor. And she silently followed.

She walked into a strange bedroom, that had not changed by one stitch of fabric from the day she had left it. He closed the door behind them, and she welcomed the feeling of fright, of guilt, of terror that now blocked her body from feeling the immensity and masculinity of the strange man—her husband—standing beside her, and now reaching out his arms to recapture her.

His arms touched her, his lips touched her, his body touched her. They were standing in the bedroom, still with their clothes on, and she felt, for the first time in fourteen months, all of him touching her.

The first time we did this, she thought, I was naked and pure. Now, she thought, I am soiled. Inside my body, she thought, courses the pill. Inside my vagina is the indelible memory of another man's penis, that I took again and again, of my own free will. I am soiled, she said silently to his hands, his lips, his body. Take me. Possess me. Erase me. Purify me. Sanctify me, if you can.

And then her lips opened, and a new man's tongue—her own husband's tongue—came into her mouth again. Her own tongue came up and tasted this new but familiar tongue, and she threw her arms around those towering shoulders so hard that her hands ached, and her tongue made slow electric circles around his, till his tongue had left its imprint on every atom of her tongue and mouth, till it had cleansed every nerve-ending, till it had made her tongue and her mouth and her feelings and her needs and her desires and her memory and her soul and her body—all of them—all of them—merely an extension of his tongue and his feelings and his soul and his body.

She pulled back her head, and looked at this great familiar face. She turned her head, and looked at this lovely familiar room. She moved her shoulders slightly backward, and felt them encased, protected, at home in those tender familiar arms.

Nothing—nothing of the slightest importance—had changed. Home was here, and she was home. Love was here, and she was in love. Her man was here, and she was—at last, at long last—with her man.

He bent to kiss her again. His hands lowered to carry her to bed. She felt herself lifted, lightened, soaring.

How simple it was, she thought, the rite of purification. How true it was, she thought, the myth of Sleeping Beauty. You wait, you suffer, you struggle in whatever darkness the fates ordain for you—until one kiss, from the right man, awakens you from whatever ugly or beautiful dream you were trapped in, and brings you back to the real world . . . of love . . . again.

They made love, this time, not in the dark, but in the light. When they had finished he was lying on his back, and she was leaning above him on one elbow, looking down at the familiar face, on the familiar pillow, in the familiar bed.

One man, she thought. For this female body, one man. No question of skill or talent. No question of looks or experience. No question of adventure or orgasms. Love is the great aphrodisiac. Love makes it more than body. Forget faces, forget hands, forget penises. Without passion, without commitment, without love, they might just as well be made of rubber.

She looked down at the man who had given her so much love and much suffering. His eyes were riveted on her face, but he said nothing. It was her turn to speak, her turn to lead.

Suddenly she reached over his body and turned off the table lamp. Once again, the bedroom was plunged into darkness. Now they were lost to each other's eyes. Now they were reduced to voices, feelings, memories.

"Aaron," she said softly, "Give me your hand."

He did. She guided it to her hair, stroked that huge hand through the softness of her hair.

"Aaron," she said, "what color is this hair?"

"Blond," he said.

She kissed the hand. "And what color was her hair?"

There was a moment's silence from the dark shape beneath her. And then he said, "Raven. As black as night, when all the stars have been buried together in its shine."

"And my hair is what color?" she asked.

"Blond," he said again.

"And my name is what?"

"Melissa."

"And her name was?"

"Liebchen. Her name, to me, was Liebchen. The name her parents gave her didn't matter."

"And you loved her?"

"Yes," the answer came proudly. "Without limit."

"So you have loved twice."

"Yes. Twice."

"And I am here?"

"Yes, you are here," he said. "But more than you is here—"

"In what way?" she said, startled.

"You are here," he went on, "but Little John is also here—brought by you. And the little one, the second raven-haired one, my Lacy, is also here. And also brought by you."

"Is Lacy like her?" she asked.

"Like her," he answered, "in her hair, and in the love I can release for her—fight to release for her. Now that I can see she is Lacy, and not her."

And now she dared all. "And the boy?" she asked. "The infant in the cellar?"

Now the blackness had no voice. And she continued to lean

above him, listening to his breath, and for words to replace the blackness.

"He was the son that you gave me back in Little John. The son I mourned. And now, the son I have again, in your son."

She was leaning over him, shielded by the blackness, and crying. There was no sound to her crying. The tears simply came from her eyes and dropped from her face into the unspeakable years lost in the blackness.

She felt his hand leave her hair, and touch, almost imperceptibly, her wet eyelids.

"That was a lifetime ago," he said. "They're both gone now. There were millions of others like them. All of them gone now, resting. But we are somehow here. Alive, in this bed. Torches—yes, torches of love that light their night. Going forward where they failed. Celebrating them, affirming them by making new love, by bringing new children into this treacherous world—to give meaning to their lives, and their deaths."

The light flashed on, lit by his hand. He was sitting up now, reaching out his man's arms and putting them around her shoulders to shield her from the past and the blackness.

"They're gone," he said again. "I've admitted their loss. I lost a son, you gave me back a son. I lost a raven-haired little girl I loved beyond limit. You gave me back a raven-haired little girl that I shall love again beyond limit. The circle is closed. The past is over. We have only—now—ourselves, and the future."

"A new beginning?" she asked.

"A new beginning," he repeated, as they lay down on the bed in each other's arms. "If God permits, a new beginning."

45.

There were silver clouds under a black sky as he flew the P-51 back into Teaneck. As he brought the plane in for the landing, the cloud cover started to break, and he could see the magic towers of Manhattan glimmering off to his right.

A four-day flight from San Francisco. He'd had almost no sleep. Lots of booze, yes, lots of booze, and the memories of long golden hair running down her back to touch his stomach.

He pulled into the all-night terminal, and had the tank filled again. While the gas was being pumped in, he went inside to the bar, and sat there, playing the juke box, swirling down Jack Daniels, thinking about the second handkerchief that he should have dipped down and caught, even if it meant his wing hitting the ground.

When you fly, and when you've flown in a war, you can feel the dawn break before the first rays of light streak the sky. He kept thinking about that second handkerchief, and the blond woman who was out there in that city across the river, and he decided to go out and pick up that handkerchief now.

The silver plane was still on the runway, now with a full tank of gas. He walked over to it and climbed in. In three minutes he was taking off into the black dawn, and pointing the silver nose of the plane toward the now-cloudless city.

He flew up the Hudson, over the George Washington Bridge, and parallel to the West Side Highway. He reached over and snapped off the radio. He wanted no voice, no static to interfere with his thoughts. He was looking for a second handkerchief—a second handkerchief big enough to attract her attention—a second handkerchief that he could scoop up, and use to wave good-bye.

The sun broke through the sky to the left of the World Trade Center. Suddenly, the twin towers were aflame with the orange glow of their thousands of windows. They stood above everything else in the New York skyline, they stood the highest. He flew slowly down the Hudson, directly at them. Not one huge orange handkerchief, he thought, but two. How appropriate, he thought. How perfect.

A few clouds at ten, maybe fifteen thousand feet. Otherwise, a baby blue sky being born out of the dawn. He flew past the twin towers once, on the Hudson River side, over the water, toward the Statue of Liberty. He saw a police helicopter. He turned the P-51 directly toward it, flew one hundred feet over it at three hundred miles an hour, made sure that he had caught its attention, and then circled lazily back toward the steel and glass twin giants.

He had no idea what the wind would be like between the two towers. Could be calm, could be turbulent. Could shift direction in a fraction of a second. Could blow you from side to side, or it could suck you down into the ground, like a dead weight, like a golf ball dropping, into a hole.

Only one way to find out, he thought. He turned the nose of the plane toward the twin towers, gunned the engine till it was pulling him forward at close to four hundred miles an hour, and watched the police helicopter turn and stare in his direction. Then he saw the great white towers loom up directly in front of him, went between them at about the level of the fortieth floor, and was in and out in a blink of an eyelash. He pulled the plane up before it hit the building behind them, turned it over on its back, and made a slow series of circles with the wings as he gained altitude again.

It felt good, he thought. He flew out over the ocean again, past the Statue of Liberty, past the police helicopter with its crew screaming frantically into their radio, and a man waving him down with his right arm.

To the west of him, one new helicopter, then two, then three appeared. Two of them belonged to the police. The third had the letters, NBC, painted on its side. Good, he thought. They'd come in less than five minutes.

He gunned the motor again to four hundred miles an hour, especially for NBC. Again, he flashed through the center of the two towers, this time with his wings vertical to the ground, this time passing through the two towers around the twentieth floor. When he straightened the plane out, and looked down at the streets below, he could see traffic halted, people looking up, windows in the apartment house to the right opening, and heads sticking out.

He turned over the Hudson River again. By now the Air Force should have been alerted. He wondered if they'd send up fighters. Probably not.

More helicopters were hovering over the bay now. He saw the one marked CBS. Where in hell was ABC? He wanted all three networks for his final signature. Then he looked south, and saw the telltale streams of jets coming up from New Jersey. So they were going to butt in after all. He turned the plane around, heading toward the two towers again. He would have to settle for two networks.

This time he pushed the throttle as far forward as it would go. A little over four hundred miles an hour. Only ten stories from the ground. He knew that television cameras were recording him. When he reached the edge of the towers, he flipped the plane into a turn and went through them, spinning, wing over wing, to make as good a picture as possible for the folks back home.

His second orange handkerchief, and he still hadn't smashed into the ground. The jets—three of them—were now coasting overhead, directly above him, going so slow that he wondered if the pilots weren't afraid they would flame out. Soon they would come down, and see if they could crowd him over the bay or over the river. He didn't think he wanted to go over the water again. And now ABC had arrived. Time for the signature.

He moved up to three thousand feet, forcing the three jets above him to climb or crash. Then, when he reached three thousand feet, and when he was sure that the television cameras were directly on him, he pulled back the stick, turned the plane's nose up till it climbed to four thousand feet, and began to write his message in the sky.

It took thirty seconds. He wrote it only once. He hoped somebody had the sense to be able to read it. And then rather tired, he turned the P-51 around, and slowly led the three trailing jets back, behind him, over the green of Central Park, over the gray of the George Washington Bridge, to the black and white runway of Teaneck airport.

46.

Later that morning, first on the "Today" show, and then on "Good Morning America," she saw it all. A madman—a gorgeous madman—flying a World War II fighter plane, had zipped three times through the gap between the two World Trade Center towers. She saw the flights through the towers, saw how close his wing had come to one building when he made the turn in between them. Saw him land at Teaneck and be immediately surrounded by police and reporters—saying nothing, not even identifying himself, and then being led away into the waiting police car. And then she saw the replays of the flights through the towers, and then the strange twists and turns his plane had made afterward in the open air.

"What do they mean?" asked one of the "Today" show hosts.

"They're writing," answered the others. "Skywriting without smoke. Let's slow down the film of the plane now, and trace out the letters it's making with an animated line."

Melissa watched spellbound as the film flashed back to the first rise of the P-51's nose into the air, but now in slow motion. She watched as the animated white line followed the tail of the plane as if by magic.

"See," said the man on the screen. "There's the first letter, in perfect Spencerian script."

"It's 'G,' " said the other.

"And the second letter is 'O.' And then another 'O,' " the host went on.

And Melissa watched the close-up of the rising and dipping plane as it spelled out its first word—"Goodbye."

Then the plane spun around three times. The animated white line recognized this spinning as a gap between words and did not follow the tail of the plane while it turned. And then the plane rose up again, and another capital "G" appeared. When the second word was finished the commentator looked at the other man on the screen and said, " 'Goodbye Goddess.' But what does that mean?"

"Simple," was his reply. "Probably his way of saying farewell to someone on the street below who was watching."

No, Melissa thought, not watching then. But watching now. As he knew she'd watch.

And as he knew she'd answer.

She reached for the phone and called his office. He was not in. Nor was he in the next day, Thursday or Friday. But, he reached her at her office, late that Friday afternoon.

"Thank you for calling," he said.

"Are you all right?" she asked.

"Perfect," he said. "Better than I've been in years."

"The police—" she began.

"Will probably fine me an impossible amount of money. Or tuck me away where I belong, for a few months. Nothing more."

"It was insane," she said. "But it was beautiful."

"I wanted to get your attention," he said.

"Oh, you certainly did," she said. "Mine and the entire city of New York's."

"I didn't think a bouquet of flowers would quite do it," he

went on. "I had a little more to say than I could put on a card."

"Or in the sky?"

"Well, I didn't really have that much time," he answered. "And the rest of the message was private."

There was a lilt in his tone, almost an underlying laughter, that she hadn't heard since before the fishing trip. He was, she realized, enormously seductive when he abandoned honesty for charm.

"And that message?" she asked.

"Is multifold. Do you have a moment?"

"Of course."

"Then let me list the ways I leave thee. First, I thank you for the trip. For its incomparable pleasures, as well as its painful, but liberating insights."

"And I thank you for it immeasurably."

"Secondly," he went on, "I take it you're back together again, and happy."

"Very," she said. "A good new start."

"Then I'm going to give you my proposal for the rules of our relationship from now on. I intend to be your steadfast friend."

"Agreed."

"Your coworker."

"Agreed."

"Your adviser, when you ask for advice, and want the unbiased, and not the male chauvinist variety."

She laughed. "Agreed again. With thanks."

"I shall adore working with you," he said. "And being with you. But I promise you that I will never probe your marriage for weaknesses, or welcome any temporary signs of stress in it, or attempt to beguile you, or confuse you in your relationship with Aaron."

Involuntarily she stiffened. No, she thought, there was only one real world. A world that inevitably takes when it gives. That makes you pay for each positive decision—no matter how right that decision may be.

And then she realized that she'd said nothing for almost thirty seconds, and that this silence was far more of a message to him than any words she could possibly have uttered. So she laughed—laughed at herself, laughed at Michael, laughed at the real world—and then asked, "Never?"

The laughter was returned—the pre-California laughter. "Well," he said, "almost never."

"What a lovely word," she replied. "Almost."

They both laughed.

"It won't happen, Michael," she said.

"I know," he said.

"But I thank you for taking away the never," she said.

"And I thank you for erasing it from my vocabulary," he added. "Forever."

And again they laughed. Strange, she thought, that a phone, using nothing but their voices, could be as strong a bond now as only a bed had been before.

"And I'm sending you a special present for your renewed marriage." His tone had not changed at all. "It's a letter from some people you should really be more closely aquainted with—at Revlon."

Wintry fingers ran down the back of her spine. It was the real world, she suddenly thought. "Why would they write you?" she asked.

"Because they finally found out what I knew all along—that there's not one axe-virus that can break down those big face-proteins . . . there're five."

Her throat was tightening. Let me list the ways I leave you, he had said. And now he was completing his list. "And they wrote you?" she asked, forcing her voice to remain calm.

"Because I'd patented all five," he said with a very small laugh. "Not the viruses themselves, but the way they interact with the proteins. You have one in your cream. The other four work just as well, I guess. And they'd rather buy them than fight me in court for ten years."

"And the price?" she asked.

"One million dollars per patent," he said. "Plus a continuing five percent royalty."

"Would you like to play a game of backgammon?" she said suddenly, involuntarily.

"I beg your pardon," he replied.

"It doesn't matter," she said. "You'll be very rich."

"I am very rich," he said, and her heart disappeared from her chest. And then he went on: "I have a silver fighter plane, I have some damn good work to do, I have incredibly beautiful memories of an incredibly beautiful woman, and I have a whole new definition of 'hopeless love' to build on." Again the laugh, this time so strong that you could erect the

Empire State Building on it. "I don't need four million dollars to be rich. There's a second letter attached to the first—my letter to them. It's one paragraph. It says I sold all five patents some months ago—for a far higher price than they could ever offer."

She said nothing for a long time. She looked helplessly across the room at Pam. And then she said what she had to say. "Michael Black, I'll never be able to marry you, I'll never be able to make love to you again, but I want you to know I was wrong in San Francisco. I do love you. Very much."

"As I said, a much higher price than they could ever offer." His voice contained nothing now but friendship. "In three years they'll catch up with us, darling. But by then, we'll be three years ahead. In any case, I've got some striking new ideas about the hand cream. And I may be able to show them to you, in the office, by Monday."

"That would be marvelous," she said.

And there was no sound of his hanging up as his voice melted into silence. She put down the phone, and looked across the otherwise empty office at Pam. The two women stared at each other for a long moment. And then Pam nodded, and said, "I think you burned that bridge behind you."

"I think I did."

"I wouldn't have had the nerve to do it," Pam said.

"I wouldn't have had the nerve not to," Melissa replied.

47.

The next day was their first new Saturday together. That night, they would be taking the children to the Four Seasons, to sit by the sparkling pool and eat New York's best food. But this afternoon they were alone, talking incessantly, bringing each other up to date on the state of their business lives.

"So," Aaron said, "I have ten, possibly eleven new accounts. Plus invitations to bid on three more, even bigger.

But there are still problems. The new management that Albee's son put in—that may cost at least two of the six million. Plus, money is tight now. Plus . . . . God only knows in this insane business.''

She laughed, and thought of Albee, and his crying-wall descriptions of his business—terrible disasters that never came true. She shifted into the mock Jewish accent that Albee used at such moments, and said, ''You think you've got problems. Listen to these catastrophes.''

He smiled in return, and said, ''My back is strong. Begin.''

''Well, first of all,'' she began, ''the stores like the cream, the customers like the cream, but, in the volume we're producing now, we're not maintaining the original quality. We may have to change suppliers, and God help us if we do.''

His face grew serious for a moment. Then his eyes searched her face. And the tautness around his eyes relaxed, and he said, matter-of-factly, ''But Michael will supervise the new factory, won't he?''

''I imagine he will,'' she said.

''Good,'' he replied instantly, ''then I think you'll work that out.''

She felt a tension flow out of her body. It was the first time they had mentioned Michael since she had come back. And Aaron had said more in those two simple sentences than he might have in an entire hour's speech of forgiveness. The issue was closed.

''That's just the beginning,'' she said. ''Sally—'' she began.

''Oh, yes,'' he interrupted.

''What?''

''Never mind,'' he went on. ''Go ahead.''

''Sally got a huge new job. Almost immediately. And I understand, through the grapevine, that she's convinced this new company to make a product which she calls 'Mother's Milk for Your Skin.' So the giants are coming in.''

''Absolutely logical,'' Aaron said. ''I'm surprised it took them that long. But we're going to make sure they stay one fatal step behind.''

She looked at him for a moment, and she wrestled violently within herself. And then she decided. ''Aaron,'' she said. ''I love you and value you. But I really don't want you to write my copy. Or even to give me suggestions for that copy— unless I first specifically ask you for them.''

He stared at her for a second. "Perfect," he said. "It removes my last lingering suspicion."

"Which was?" she asked.

"That you might have come back to me for—"

"No," she interrupted. "It was one of the last barriers that held me away from you."

He got up from the couch, came over to the armchair where she was sitting, sat next to her on one of the arms, and took her hands in his.

"I want this to be your business," he said. "Your idea. Your accomplishment. And your triumph. Yours alone. I never want you to have to look back, someday in the future, and say 'Aaron did it for me.' "

He went on. "I wanted to call you a hundred times when I saw the first ads. But any suggestions—even compliments— would have clouded your thinking with my own. Do you understand?"

She remembered the freezing walk to the hospital, and then back to the tiny magazine stand at 80th Street and Broadway, and she said, simply, "Yes. I understand."

"If you want comment, then ask me for it, and I'll give you as little or as much as you request. But it's your creation, and I love you far too much to allow myself to tamper with it."

"Thank God," she said.

"Ask Him first," he replied.

"I will," she smiled. "I have. Anyway—" she concluded, "you and I both have pretty big problems."

"No doubt," he said. "And you know what I think we should jointly do about them? I think we should forget them completely this afternoon, and go out and have some fun."

"Marvelous," she said.

"Zero-cost fun," he added.

"Agreed," she said. "With problems like ours, I think we should spend no money. Not even the cost of two movie tickets."

"Well, that's going a little far," he said. "Where in New York can you go without spending money? Even the museums have an admission fee."

"But the art galleries don't."

"That's true," he said. "The art galleries don't. We won't even buy a catalog," he added.

And they both laughed, and left the house hand in hand.

48.

It was the sixth gallery they had visited that day. Posh, deeply carpeted, almost churchlike, with its usual collection of too-pretty or too-original paintings lined up on its exhibition walls. And then, after they had made their required courtesy round of those walls, they happened to pass the inner office of the owner—and there they saw it.

She was walking slightly ahead of him, and she stopped, stock still. He stared at her first, and then silently came alongside her, and looked into the office himself and took her hand.

They stood staring at it for perhaps three or four minutes. Behind the desk next to it was a man, probably in his seventies, making entries in a notebook. For the first minute or so he didn't notice them. Then the intensity of their stares reached him, and he looked up, saw the expression on both their faces, and then said, "Whey don't you come in for a little while?"

She went first, with Aaron behind her. She had glanced at the man to acknowledge his invitation, but then her eyes flowed back to the massive sculpture. She walked across the carpeted floor till she was standing beside it, until she could reach out her arms, and softly, slowly, tenderly, fold them around it.

Aaron turned to the older man, and asked, "Do you mind if she touches it for a moment?"

"Not at all," the owner said. "I believe that sculpture should be touched. Especially when it's loved as much as she obviously loves it."

"I'm Aaron Carpenter, and this is my wife, Melissa. For many years, we owned a *Walking Man* by Giacometti, slightly smaller, but with almost exactly the same feeling as this."

"Of course," the owner said. "You sold it about a year and a half ago."

"That's right."

"This one is slightly better, but yours was exquisite too."

Melissa had now stood away from the larger-than-life sculpture, and was letting her hand run over every inch of its rough, metallic surface.

"Is it for sale?" Aaron asked.

"Only to a museum, I'm afraid," the owner replied.

"That's fortunate," she said—the first words she had spoken.

"Do you mind if we spend a few minutes with it?" Aaron asked.

"As long as you like," the owner replied.

Aaron moved across the office to a couch, and sat down, watching Melissa. For the first time since she had left him, since he had gained back his sanity, he felt the power of a masterpiece of art envelop him. All of life, he thought, in a single work of art. The war, he thought, the war that killed—God, how many of those he loved. But did not kill him and did not kill Giacometti. The war that was now over, everywhere but in their memories. And, thank God, in the art that those memories inspired. They had taken that war—the horror of that war—and had transformed it into art.

And he had done—what? Transformed it only into dream and near-madness. Now the dream was gone, the madness was slowly diminishing, and the woman beside him, who had not known that war, had left him and returned. But, in the leaving, had gone beyond him, and returned with the art of beauty as her discovered gift.

And what of him? What gift did he have to give her, upon her return? No art. Just a slight semblance of sanity. A new start toward success. A great deal of both old and new love.

He had spent his life writing honest advertisements for honest products. That craft had served him well during a period of convalescence. Now, however, the convalescence was over. Melissa had asked him, for years, to face those memories directly, on paper and not in dreams. And he knew now, in this chance moment of encounter with love, with art, and with obligation, that his free time—all his free time—would now be spent writing words of a different level, with a different aim and effect. That he would begin, tomorrow.

And she, Melissa Carpenter, with her hands touching the metallic aliveness of that huge work of art, knew that she truly had come home again. Not to the home of her birth, not to the home of her first, or even second marriage, but to the home of herself. She thought of the struggle Giacometti endured to find himself, before he could create universal men such as these. Symbols of the struggle we all must face—men and women alike—to become ourselves. To create ourselves. To maintain ourselves, against the winds and storms of the real world. And we come out—compressed, wounded, and yet, with that compression, and those wounds, somehow far more beautiful than we were before we dared to step out into that real world.

He, this statue, is me. He is my inside now. I am his outside now. He has borne the fire of the furnace and creation. I have borne the fire of love and creation. He is human. I am human. He is my symbol. I am his living projection.

She turned and looked at Aaron. And then she turned back to the Giacometti, this time with her eyes, and not her hands. And then she said to the owner, "Are you sure he isn't for sale?"

"I've only seen one other person touch that sculpture in this particular way," the owner said.

"Who?" Melissa asked.

"The man who gave birth to him—Giacometti," was the answer.

"There's no way to buy him?" she asked again.

"For a museum," the owner replied. And then he glanced at the look on Aaron's face, and studied again the look on hers. "Or," the owner replied. "to someone who loves him so much that a museum can wait another lifetime to end up with him."

Aaron stood up. Melissa looked at him again, got his approval, and said, "Then?"

The owner smiled, and said, "Three hundred thousand dollars."

Both of them took in their breath involuntarily. The owner's smile never wavered, and then he added, "Minus the usual ten percent courtesy discount, of course."

Melissa looked at Aaron. "I think I can rob one hundred and thirty-five thousand dollars from my company. Especially since Pam got that new bank line of credit while I was away."

Aaron equaled her smile with his own. "And I can steal one hundred and thirty-five thousand dollars from my company, though I might give up my salary for the next six months to do it."

"It's crazy," she said.

"It is completely crazy," Aaron repeated. Then he turned to the owner and asked, "When can you have it delivered?"

"Would next Tuesday be soon enough?" the owner replied.

"No," Aaron said. "But we'll take it. And we'll have certified checks waiting for your men then."

"The certification won't be necessary, Mr. Carpenter."
The owner shook Aaron's hand. "Congratulations," he said.
Then he turned to Melissa. "You've purchased a masterpiece."
And then, for the first time, he joined in their smiles. "And,
incidentally, I think all three of us are crazy."

"Exactly," Aaron said.

"Exactly," Melissa repeated. "Thank you." And she threw
her arms around the man, four inches smaller than she, and
kissed him.

They floated down the elevator to the street. By the time
they were ten steps away from the gallery, their arms were
wrapped around each other, and they were pushing each other
from one side of the sidewalk to the other.

"A zero-cost afternoon," she said.

"Not even the price of two movie tickets," he replied.

"Even the museums have an admission fee," she laughed.

"Thank God," he said, "the art galleries don't."

They laughed. They kissed in the middle of the street.
Passersby stopped for a moment and looked at them, and then
smiled and went on.

"Do you know what we need now?" Aaron asked.

"No," she said. "What?"

"A bottle of Dom Perignon," he replied.

"Where shall we go to get it?"

"Here," he said. And he reached his left hand over to a
traffic sign on the edge of the sidewalk, and the fingers of
that hand curled around an imaginary bottle of champagne, and
he lifted it out of its imaginary ice, and patted it gently in its
imaginary towel, and put out his right hand and slowly and carefully unwound the imaginary wire around its imaginary cork.

"Oh," she said, "it's a good year."

"A vintage year," he replied. "The best year possible."

Then he began to slowly unscrew the cork from the top of
the bottle. In a few seconds, in the middle of 57th Street and
Fifth Avenue, she heard that cork pop, and she heard her husband say, "Quick, grab a glass, before we lose the first foam."

"I've got it," she said. "And yours too." She held out
both her hands.

He poured the imaginary wine into the imaginary glasses
with great delicacy. Then he slid the bottle, that only the two
of them could see, back into its silver bucket. And then he
took one of the glasses from her, raised his glass to hers, and
they heard the clink as the two glasses met.

"To love," he said.

"To love," she said. "And to risk."

"To risk," he agreed. "And to trust."

"Always," she said. "Above everything else, equal only to love."

And at exactly the same instant, they raised their glasses to their lips and drained them in a single draft. Then they looked at each other and laughed, and both, spontaneously, with the same gesture, flung the glasses over their shoulders, and heard them crash with a tinkle against the pavement of 57th Street and Fifth Avenue.

They kissed again. Then they threw their arms around one another, and turned onto Fifth Avenue, and began to weave their way through the crowd toward home.

Twenty feet away, a sixty-year-old woman had watched the entire scene. Her eyes had not strayed from the distinguished-looking man, and the beautiful blond woman, who were so evidently in love, so incredibly happy, so completely wrapped up in each other that the street, to them, was empty except for themselves. She saw the bottle being opened. She saw the liquid being poured. She heard the toasts. And then she saw the kiss, and the arms encircling each other, and the two of them walk away from her, without ever noticing that she was watching them at all.

How beautiful they were, she thought. How naive. She's so happy now, isn't she, the woman thought. All life is a fantasy for her now. Isn't it nice to be that young, and that beautiful, and that gifted with love, the woman thought as she moved to the limousine waiting for her, and as the chauffeur opened the door.

She paused a moment and looked into the swirling crowd again, to see if she could get a last glimpse of the two of them. She could not. The day was again dull and grim.

She got into the leather-lined back seat of the limousine, and heard the chauffeur close the door that quietly entrapped her in the car.

Just wait till she turns thirty, the woman thought. Then she'll find out what life is really like.